THE
DESIRED WOMAN

WILL N. HARBEN

1st WORLD
LIBRARY
Literary Society

The Desired Woman

Will N. Harben

© 1st World Library, 2006
PO Box 2211
Fairfield, IA 52556
www.1stworldlibrary.com
First Edition

LCCN: 2007901846

Softcover ISBN: 978-1-4218-4317-9
Hardcover ISBN: 978-1-4218-4219-6
eBook ISBN: 978-1-4218-4415-2

Purchase *"The Desired Woman"*
as a traditional bound book at:
www.1stWorldLibrary.com/purchase.asp?ISBN=978-1-4218-4317-9

1st World Library is a literary, educational organization
dedicated to:

- Creating a free internet library of downloadable ebooks

- Hosting writing competitions and offering book
  publishing scholarships.

Interested in more 1st World Library books?
contact: literacy@1stworldlibrary.com
Check us out at: www.1stworldlibrary.com

1ˢᵗ World Library Literary Society

Giving Back to the World

"If you want to work on the core problem, it's early school literacy."

-James Barksdale, former CEO of Netscape

"No skill is more crucial to the future of a child, or to a democratic and prosperous society, than literacy."

-Los Angeles Times

Literacy... means far more than learning how to read and write... The aim is to transmit... knowledge and promote social participation."

-UNESCO

"Literacy is not a luxury, it is a right and a responsibility. If our world is to meet the challenges of the twenty-first century we must harness the energy and creativity of all our citizens."

-President Bill Clinton

"Parents should be encouraged to read to their children, and teachers should be equipped with all available techniques for teaching literacy, so the varying needs and capacities of individual kids can be taken into account."

-Hugh Mackay

TO

VELLA AND BILLY

PART I

CHAPTER I

Inside the bank that June morning the clerks and accountants on their high stools were bent over their ponderous ledgers, although it was several minutes before the opening hour. The gray-stone building was in Atlanta's most central part on a narrow street paved with asphalt which sloped down from one of the main thoroughfares to the section occupied by the old passenger depot, the railway warehouses, and hotels of various grades. Considerable noise, despite the closed windows and doors, came in from the outside. Locomotive bells slowly swung and clanged; steam was escaping; cabs, drays, and trucks rumbled and creaked along; there was a whir of a street-sweeping machine turning a corner and the shrill cries of newsboys selling the morning papers.

Jarvis Saunders, member of the firm of Mostyn, Saunders & Co., bankers and brokers, came in; and, hanging his straw hat up, he seated himself at his desk, which the negro porter had put in order.

"I say, Wright"—he addressed the bald, stocky, middle-aged man who, at the paying-teller's window, was sponging his fat fingers and counting and labeling packages of currency— "what is this about Mostyn feeling badly?"

"So that's got out already?" Wright replied in surprise, as he approached and leaned on the rolling top of the desk. "He cautioned us all not to mention it. You know what a queer, sensitive sort of man he is where his health or business is concerned."

"Oh, it is not public," Saunders replied. "I happened to meet Dr. Loyd on the corner. He had just started to explain more fully when a patient stopped to speak to him, and so I didn't wait, as he said Mostyn was here."

"Yes, he's in his office now." Wright nodded toward the frosted glass door in the rear. "He was lying on the lounge when I left him just now. It is really nothing serious. The doctor says it is only due to loss of sleep and excessive mental strain, and that a few weeks' rest in some quiet place will straighten him out."

"Well, I'm glad it is not serious," Saunders said. "I have seen him break down before. He is too intense, too strenuous; whatever he does he does with every nerve in his body drawn as taut as a fiddle-string."

"It is his *outside* operations, his *private* deals," the teller went on, in a more confidential tone. "Why, it makes me nervous even to watch him. He's been keyed high for the last week. You know, I'm an early riser, and I come down before any one else to get my work up. I found him here this morning at half past seven. He was as nervous as a man about to be hanged. He couldn't sit or stand still a minute. He was waiting for a telegram from Augusta concerning Warner & Co. I remember how you advised him against that deal. Well, I guess if it had gone against him it would have ruined him."

The banker nodded. "Yes, that was foolhardy, and he seemed to me to be going into it blindfolded. He realized the danger afterward. He admitted it to me last night at the club. He said that he was sorry he had not taken my advice. He was afraid, too, that Delbridge would get on to it and laugh at him."

"Delbridge is too shrewd to tackle a risk like that," Wright returned. He glanced about the room cautiously, and then added: "I don't know as I have any right to be talking about Mostyn's affairs even to you, but I am pretty sure that he got good news. He didn't show me the telegram when it came, but I watched his face as he read it. I saw his eyes flash; he smiled at me, walked toward his office with a light step, as he always does when he's lucky, and then he swayed sideways and keeled over in a dead faint. The porter and I picked him up, carried him to his lounge, and sprinkled water in his face. Then we sent for the doctor. He gave him a dose of something or other and told him not to do a lick of work for a month."

"Well, I'll step in and see him." Saunders rose. "I guess he won't mind. He's too big a plunger for a town of this size. He lets things get on his nerves too much. He has no philosophy of life. I wouldn't go his pace for all the money in the U. S. Treasury."

"Right you are," the teller returned, as he went back to his work.

Opening the door of his partner's office, Saunders found him seated on the lounge smoking a cigar. He was about thirty-five years of age, tall, broad-shouldered, with blue eyes, yellow mustache, and was good-looking and well built. Glancing up, he smiled significantly and nodded. There were dark rings round his eyes, and the hand holding his cigar quivered nervously.

"I suppose you heard of that silly duck fit of mine?" he smiled, the corners of his rather sensuous mouth twitching.

Saunders nodded as he sat down in the revolving-chair at the desk and slowly swung it round till he faced his partner.

"It's a wonder to me that you are able to talk about it," he said, sharply. "You've been through enough in the last ten days to kill a dozen ordinary men. You've taken too many stimulants, smoked like the woods afire, and on top of it all instead of getting natural sleep you've amused yourself at all hours of the night. You've bolted your food, and fussed and fumed over Delbridge's affairs, which, heaven knows, have nothing at all to do with your own."

"I suppose I *do* keep track of the fellow," Mostyn smiled. "People compare us constantly. We started about the same time, and it rankles to hear of his making a lucky strike just when I've had a tumble. This matter of my backing Warner when I went to Augusta they told me they had met with more bad luck, and if I didn't advance fresh funds they would have to go under. It was the biggest risk I ever took, but I took it. I raised the money on my street-railway bonds. For a day or so afterward I was hopeful, but they quit writing and wouldn't answer my wires. My lawyer in Augusta wrote me that they were all three on the verge of suicide, and if they could not close a certain deal in Boston they would go under. That's what I've been waiting on for the last week, and that's why I've been crazy. But it is all right now—all right. I'm safe, and I made money, too—money that Delbridge would like to have."

"There are no two ways about it." Saunders reached for a cigar in a tray on the desk and cut off the tip with a paper-knife. "You've got to take a rest and get your mind off of business."

"Nobody knows that better than I do," Mostyn said, a sickly smile playing over his wan face, "and I'm in the mood for it. I feel as a man feels who has just escaped the gallows. I'm going to the mountains, and I don't intend to open a business letter or think once of this hot hole in a wall for a month. I'm going to fish and hunt and lie in the shade and swap yarns with mossback moonshiners. I've just been thinking of it, and it's like a soothing dream of peace and quiet. You know old Tom Drake's place near your farm? I boarded there two weeks three years ago and loved every cat and dog about. Tom told me to come any time I felt like it."

"No better place anywhere," Saunders said. "I shall run up home now and then, and can see you and report, but you needn't bother about us; we'll keep this thing afloat. I'm wondering how you are going to get away from your social duties. They usually claim you at this time of the year. Old Mitchell and his daughter will certainly miss you."

Mostyn stared at his friend steadily. "They are off for Atlantic City Monday. They hinted at my joining them, but I declined. I was worried at the time over this deal, but I need something quieter than that sort of trip. You are always coupling my name with Miss Irene's. I'm not the favorite in that quarter that you make me out."

"I have eyes and ears and *some* experience in human nature." Saunders puffed at his cigar. He felt that his friend was expecting what he was saying. "Mitchell is getting in his dotage, and he talks very freely to me at times."

"Surely not about—about me and Irene?" Mostyn said, a ripple of interest in his tone.

"Oh yes, he quite lets himself go now and then. He thinks the sun rises and sets in you. He is constantly talking about your rapid rise and keen business judgment."

"You can't mean that he's ever gone so—so far as actually to speak of me in—in connection with his daughter?" Mostyn said, tentatively.

"I may as well tell you that he has." Saunders felt that the subject was a delicate one. "At least, he has expressed the hope that you and she would care for each other. He knew your father and liked him, and he has been afraid that Miss Irene might fancy some young fellow with no sort of chance in the world. He speaks quite freely of her as his sole heiress, often showing me the actual figures of what he expects to leave her."

A touch of red appeared in Mostyn's cheeks. "He is getting old and garrulous," he said. "I really have been of some help to him. It happens that I've never advised him wrongly in any venture he has made, and I suppose he overrates my ability; but, really, I give you my word that I have not thought seriously of marrying *any one.* I suppose some men would call me a fool—a cold-blooded fellow like Delbridge would, I am sure, but I've always had a dream of running across my ideal somewhere and of marrying solely for the sake of old-fashioned love itself."

"What man hasn't?" Saunders responded, thoughtfully. "After all, very few men, at least here in the South, marry for convenience or financial advancement. There is Stillman; he married a typewriter in his office, a beautiful character, and they are as happy as a pair of doves. Then you remember Ab Thornton and Sam Thorpe. Both of them could have tied up to money, I suppose, but somehow they didn't. After all, it is the best test of a man."

"Yes, that certainly is true," Mostyn said, "the ideal is the thing. I really believe I have two distinct sides to me—the romantic and the practical. So you needn't count on—on what you were speaking of just now. I think the young lady is somewhat like myself. At times she seems to have dreams, and I am not the Prince Charming that rides through them."

At his own desk a few minutes later Saunders sat wrapped in thought. "He doesn't really love her," he mused, "and she doesn't love him, but they will marry. His eyes kindled when I mentioned her money. He may think he can stand out against it, but he can't. In his better moments he leans toward the higher thing, but the current of greed has caught him and will sweep him along."

At this juncture Saunders's attention was drawn to the paying-teller's window.

"I tell you you can't see him this morning." Wright was speaking firmly to an elderly man who stood clinging desperately to the wire grating. "He's not well and is lying down."

Will N. Harben

"So he's lying down, is he?" was the snarling response. "He's lying down while I have to walk the streets without a cent through his rascality. You tell him I'm going to see him if I have to wait here all day."

"Who is it?" Saunders asked, being unable to recognize the speaker from his position.

Wright turned to him. "It's old Jeff Henderson," he said, "still harping on the same old string. He's blocking up the window. A thing like that ought not to be allowed. If I was the president of this bank, and a man like that dared to—"

"Let him in at the side door, and send him to me," Saunders ordered, in a gentle tone. "I'll see him."

A moment later the man entered, and shuffled in a slipshod way up to Saunders's desk. He was about seventy years of age, wore a threadbare frock coat, baggy trousers, disreputable shoes, and a battered silk hat of ancient, bell-shaped pattern. He was smooth-shaven, quite pale, and had scant gray hair which in greasy, rope-like strands touched his shoulders. He was nervously chewing a cheap, unlighted cigar, and flakes of damp tobacco clung to his shirt-front.

"You were inquiring for Mostyn," Saunders said, quietly. "He is not at work this morning, Mr. Henderson. Is there anything I can do for you?"

"I don't know whether you can or not," the old man said, as he sank into a chair and leaned forward on his walking-cane. "I don't know whether *anybody* can or not. I don't believe there is any law or justice anywhere. You and him are partners, but I don't believe you know him clean to the bottom as well as I do. You wouldn't be in business with him if you did, for you are a straight man—a body can tell that by your eye and voice—and I've never heard of any shady, wildcat scheme that you ever dabbled in."

"We are getting away from the other matter," Saunders reminded him, softly. "You came to see Mostyn."

"I came to give him a piece of my mind, young man—that's what I'm here for. He dodges me. Say, do you know how he got his start—the money he put in this bank? Well, *I* can tell you, and I'll bet he never did. He started the Holly Creek Cotton Mills. It was his idea. I thought he was honest and straight. He was going round trying to interest capital. I never had a head for business. The war left me flat on my back with all the family niggers free, but a chunk of money came to my children—fifty thousand dollars. It stood in their name, but I got their legal consent to handle it. Mostyn knew I had it and was constantly ding-donging at me about his mill idea. Well, I went in—I risked the whole amount. He was made president although he didn't hold ten thousand dollars' worth of stock. Then I reckon you know what happened. He run the thing plumb in the ground, claimed to be losing money—said labor was too high; claimed that the wrong sort of machinery had been put in. It went from bad to worse for twelve months, then it shut down. The operatives moved away, and it was sold under the hammer. Who bought it in—my God, who do you reckon bid it in for twenty-five cents on the dollar? Why, the same smooth young duck that is taking a nap in his fine private quarters back there now. Then what did he do? Why, all at once he found that the machinery *was* all right and labor *could* be had. Out of his own pocket with money he had made in some underhand deal or other he added on a wing, filled it with spindles and looms, built more cottages, and three years later the stock had hopped up to two for one, and little to be had at that. He next started this bank, and here I sit in it"— the old man swept the interior with a slow glance—"without a dollar to my name and my daughters hiring out for barely enough to keep rags on their bodies. Say, what do you think—"

"I am afraid the courts are the only place to settle a matter upon which two parties disagree," Saunders said, diplomatically, though a frown of sympathy lay on his handsome dark face.

"The courts be damned!" the old man growled, pounding the floor with his stick. "I *did* take it to law. I spent the twelve thousand and odd dollars that I rescued from the ruin in suing him, only to discover that the law itself favors the shyster who has money and is sharp enough to circumvent it."

"I am sorry, but there is absolutely nothing I can do to help you, Mr. Henderson," Saunders said, lamely. "Of course, I mean in regard to this particular matter. If you are in want, however, and any reasonable amount would be of service to you—why, on my own account I am willing—"

"I don't mean that," the old man broke in, tremulously. "You are very kind. I know you would help me, you show it in your face; but I don't want that sort of thing. It is—is my rights I'm after. I—I can't face my children after the way I acted. I simply trusted Mostyn with my all—my life's blood—don't you see? I remember when I was hesitating, and a neighbor had hinted that Mostyn was too high a flyer—going with fast women and the like—to be quite safe—I remember, I say, that the commandment 'Judge not that ye be not judged' came in my head, and I refused to listen to a word against him. But you see how it ended."

"I wish I could help you," Saunders said again, "but I don't see what I can do."

"I don't either." The old man sighed heavily as he got up. "Everybody tells me I am a fool to cry over spilt milk when even the law won't back me; but I'm getting close to the end, and somehow I can't put my mind on anything else." He laid his disengaged hand on Saunders's shoulder almost with the touch of a parent. "I'll say one thing more, and then I'm gone. You've done me good this morning—that is, *some*. I don't feel quite so—so hurt inside. It's because you offered to—to trust me. I won't forget that soon, Saunders, and I'm not going to come in here any more. If I have to see him I will meet him somewhere else. Good-by."

Saunders watched the bent form shamble between the counters and desks and disappear.

"Poor old chap!" he said. "The shame of his lack of judgment is killing him."

Just then the door of Mostyn's office opened, and Mostyn himself came out. He paused over an electric adding-machine which was being manipulated by a clerk, gave it an idle glance, and then came on to his partner.

"Albert says old Henderson was here talking to you," he said, coldly. "I suppose it's the old complaint?"

"Yes," Saunders nodded, as he looked up. "I did what I could to pacify him; he is getting into a bad mental shape."

"He seems to be growing worse and worse." Mostyn went on, irritably. "I heard he had actually threatened my life. I don't want to take steps to restrain him, but I'll have to if he keeps it up. I can't afford to have him slandering me on every street-corner as he is doing. Every business man knows I was not to blame in that deal. The courts settled that for good and all."

Saunders made no comment. He fumbled a glass paper-weight with one hand and tugged at his brown mustache with the fingers of the other. Mostyn stared into his calm eyes impatiently.

"What do you think I ought to do?" he finally asked.

"I am in no position to say," Saunders answered, awkwardly. "It is a matter for you to decide. His condition is really pitiful. His family seem to be in actual need. Girls brought up as his daughters were brought up don't seem to know exactly how to make a living."

"Well, I can't pay money back to him," Mostyn said, angrily. "I'd make an ass of myself, and admit my indebtedness to many others who happened to lose in that mill. His suit against me cost me several thousand dollars, and he has injured me in all sorts of ways with his slanderous tongue. He'll have to let up. I won't stand it any longer."

Therewith Mostyn turned and went back to his office. Closing the door behind him, he started to throw himself on the lounge, but instead sat down at his desk, took up a pen and drew some paper to him. "I'll write Tom Drake and ask him if he has room for me," he said. "Up there in the mountains I'll throw the whole thing off and take a good rest."

CHAPTER II

J. Cuyler Mitchell got out of his landau in the *porte cochere* of his stately residence on Peachtree Street, and, aided by his gold-headed ebony cane, ascended the steps of the wide veranda, where he stood fanning his face with his Panama hat. Larkin, the negro driver, glanced over his shoulder after him.

"Anything mo', Marse John?" he inquired.

"No, I'm through with the horses for to-day," the old man returned. "Put them up, and rub them down well."

As the landau moved along the curving drive to the stables in the rear Mitchell sauntered around to the shaded part of the veranda and went in at the front door. He was tall, seventy-five years of age, slender and erect, had iron-gray hair and a mustache and pointed goatee of the same shade. He was hanging his hat on the carved mahogany rack in the hall when Jincy, a young colored maid, came from the main drawing-room on the right. She had a feather duster in her hand and wore a turban-like head-cloth, a neat black dress, and a clean white apron.

"Where is Irene?" he inquired.

The maid was about to answer when a response came from above.

"Here I am, father," cried Miss Mitchell. "Can't you come up here? I've been washing my hair; I've left it loose to dry. There is more breeze up here."

"If you want to see me you'll trot down here," the old gentleman said, crustily. "I put myself out to make that trip down-town for you, and I'll be hanged if I climb those steps again till bed-time."

"Well, I'll be down in a minute," his daughter replied. "I know you have no *very* bad news, or you would have been more excited. You see, I know you."

Mitchell grunted, dropped his stick into an umbrella-holder, and turned into the library, where he again encountered the maid, now vigorously dusting a bookcase.

"Leave it, leave it!" he grumbled. "I don't want to be breathing that stuff into my lungs on a day like this. There is enough dust in the streets without having actually to eat it at home."

With a sly look and a low impulsive titter of amusement the yellow girl restored a vase to its place and turned into the study adjoining.

"Get out of there, too!" Mitchell ordered. "I want to read my paper, and you make me nervous with your swishing and knocking about."

"I can slide the doors to," Jincy suggested, as she stood hesitatingly in the wide opening.

"And cut off all the air!" was the tart response. "From now on I want you to pick times for this sort of work when I'm out of the house. My life is one eternal jumping about to accommodate you. I want comfort, and I'm going to have it."

Shrugging her shoulders, the maid left the room. Mitchell had seated himself near an open window and taken up his paper when his daughter came down the steps and entered. She was above medium height, had abundant chestnut hair, blue eyes, a good figure, and regular features, the best of which was a sweet, thin-lipped, sensitive mouth. She had on a blue kimono and dainty slippers, and moved with luxurious ease and grace.

"You ought to have more patience with the servants, father," she said, testily. "Jincy is slow enough, heaven knows, without you giving her excuses for being behind with her work. Now she will go to the kitchen and hinder the cook. If you only knew how much trouble servants are to manage you'd be more tactful. Half a dozen women in this town want that girl, and she knows it. Mrs. Anderson wants to take her to New York to nurse her baby, and she would propose it if she wasn't afraid I'd be angry."

Mitchell shook out his paper impatiently and scanned the head-lines over his nose-glasses. "You don't seem very much interested in my trip downtown, I must say."

"Well, perhaps I would be," she smiled, "but, you see, I know from your actions that he isn't much sick. If he had been you'd have mounted those steps three at a time. Do you know everybody is laughing over your interest in Dick Mostyn? Why, you are getting childish about him. I'm not so sure that he is really so wonderful as you make him out. Many persons think Alan Delbridge is a better business man, and as for his being a saint—oh my!"

"I don't care what they think," Mitchell retorted. "They don't know him as well as I do. He wouldn't be under the weather to-day if he hadn't overworked, but he is all right now. The doctor says he only needs rest, and Dick is going to the mountains for a month. As for that, I can't for the life of me see why—"

"Why, Atlantic City with us wouldn't do every bit as well," Irene laughed out impulsively. "Oh, you *are* funny!"

"Well, I don't see why," the old man said. "If you two really *do* care for each other I can't see why you really would want to be apart the best month in the year."

Irene gave her damp, fragrant hair a shake on one side and laughed as she glanced at him mischievously. "You must really not meddle with us," she said. "Three people can't run an affair like that."

Mitchell folded his paper, eyed her suspiciously for a moment, and then asked: "Is Andrew Buckton going to Atlantic City? If he is, you may as well tell me. I simply am not going to put up with that fellow's impudence. People think you care for him—do you hear me?—some people say you like him as well as he does you, and if he wasn't as poor as Job's turkey that you'd marry him."

Miss Mitchell avoided her father's eyes. She shook out her hair again, and ran her white, ringed fingers through its brown depths. "Haven't I promised you not to think of Andy in—in any serious way?" she faltered. "His mother and sister are nice, and I don't want to offend them. You needn't keep bringing his name up." Her fine lips were twitching. "I'd not be a natural woman if I didn't appreciate his—his honest admiration."

"Honest nothing!" Mitchell blurted out. "He thinks you are going to have money, and he believes you'll be silly enough to be influenced by his puppy love to make a fool of yourself. Besides, he's in the way. He took you to a dance not long ago when Mostyn wanted to go with you. Dick told me at the bank that he was going to invite you, and then that young blockhead called for you."

Miss Mitchell had the air of one subduing interest. She forced a faint smile into the general gravity of her face. "Andy had asked me a month before," she said, "or, rather, his mother asked me for him the day the cards were sent out."

"I knew *she* had a hand in it," Mitchell retorted, in a tone of conviction. "That old woman is the most cold-blooded matchmaker in the State, and she's playing with you like a cat with a mouse. They want my money, I tell you—that's what they are after. I know how the old thing talks to you—she's always telling you her darling boy is dying of grief, and all that foolishness."

Irene avoided her father's eyes. She wound a thick wisp of her hair around her head and began to fasten it with a hairpin. He heard her sigh. Then she looked straight at him.

"You are bothering entirely too much," she half faltered, in a tone that was all but wistful. "Now, I'll make *you* a promise if—if you'll make *me* one. You are afraid Dick Mostyn and I will never come to—to an understanding, but it is all right. I know I must be sensible, and I intend to be. I'm more practical than I look. Now, here is what I am going to propose. Andy Buckton *may* be at Atlantic City with his mother, and I want you to treat them decently. If you will be nice to them I will assure you that when Dick gets back from the mountains he will propose and I will accept him."

"You talk as if you knew positively that he—"

"I understand him," the young lady said. "I know him even better than you do, with all your business dealings together. Now, that will have to satisfy you, and you've got to let me see Andy up there. You simply must."

"Well, I don't care," the old man said, with a breath of relief. "This is the first time you ever have talked any sort of sense on the subject."

"I know nothing else will suit you," Irene said, with a look of abstraction in her eyes, "and I have made up my mind to let you have your way."

There was a tremulous movement to her breast, a quaver in her voice, of which she seemed slightly ashamed, for she turned suddenly and left the room.

CHAPTER III

At the gate in front of his farmhouse in the mountains Tom Drake received a letter from the rural mail-carrier, who was passing in a one-horse buggy.

"That's all this morning, Tom," the carrier said, cheerfully. "You've got good corn and cotton in the bottom below here."

"Purty good, I reckon, if the drouth don't kill 'em," the farmer answered. The carrier drove on, and Tom slowly opened his letter and turned toward the house. He was a typical Georgia mountaineer, strong, tall, broad-shouldered, middle-aged. He wore no beard, had mild brown eyes, heavy chestnut hair upon which rested a shapeless wool hat full of holes. His arms and legs were long, his gait slouching and deliberate. He was in his shirt-sleeves; his patched jean trousers were too large at the waist, and were supported by a single home-knitted suspender. He was chewing tobacco, and as he went along he moved his stained lips in the audible pronunciation of the words he was reading.

His wife, Lucy, a slender woman, in a drab print dress with no sort of adornment to it or to her scant, tightly knotted hair, stood on the porch impatiently waiting for him. Behind her, leaning in the doorway, was her brother, John Webb, a red-haired, red-faced bachelor, fifty years of age, who also had his eyes on the approaching reader.

"Another dun, I reckon," Mrs. Drake said, tentatively, when

her husband had paused at the bottom step and glanced up from the sheet in his hand.

"Not this time." Tom slowly spat on the ground, and looked first at his wife and then at his brother-in-law with a broadening smile. "You two are as good at guessin' as the general run, but if I gave you a hundred trials—yes, three hundred—and all day to do it in, you wouldn't then come in a mile o' what's in this letter."

"I don't intend to try," Mrs. Drake said, eagerly, "anyways not with all that ironin' to do that's piled up like a haystack on the dinin'-room table, to say nothin' of the beds and bed-clothes to be sunned. You can keep your big secret as far as I'm concerned."

"It's another Confederate Veteran excursion to some town whar whisky is sold," said the bachelor, with a dry cackle. "That's my guess. You fellows that was licked don't git no pensions from Uncle Sam, but you manage to have enough fun once a year to make up for it."

Tom Drake swept the near-by mountain slope with his slow glance of amusement, folded the sheet tantalizingly, and spat again.

"I don't know, Luce," he said to his wife, as he wiped his lips on his shirt-sleeve, "that it is a good time to tell you on top o' your complaint of over-work, but Dick Mostyn, your Atlanta boarder, writes that he's a little bit run down an' wants to come an' stay a solid month. Money seems to be no object to him, an' he says if he kin just git the room he had before an' a chance at your home cooking three times a day he will be in clover."

"Well, well, well!" Lucy cried, in a tone of delight, "so he wants to come ag'in, an' all this time I've been thinkin' he'd never think of us any more. There wasn't a thing for him to do that summer but lie around in the shade, except now an' then when he was off fishin' or huntin'."

"Well, I hope you will let 'im come," John Webb drawled out, in his slow fashion. "I can set an' study a town dude like him by the hour an' never git tired. I never kin somehow git at what sech fellers *think* about or *do* when they are at home. He makes money, but *how*? His hands are as soft an' white as a woman's. His socks are as thin an' flimsy as spider-webs. He had six pairs o' pants, if he had one, an' a pair o' galluses to each pair. I axed him one day when they was all spread out on his bed what on earth he had so many galluses for, an' Mostyn said—I give you my word I'm not jokin'—he said"—Webb laughed out impulsively—"he said it was to keep from botherin' to button 'em on ever' time he changed! He said"—the bachelor continued to laugh—"that he could just throw the galluses over his shoulders when he was in a hurry an' be done with the job. Do you know, folks, if I was as lazy as that I'd be afraid the Lord would cut me off in my prime. Why, a feller on a farm has to do more than that ever' time he pulls a blade o' fodder or plants a seed o' corn."

"Well, of course, I want 'im to come." Mrs. Drake had not heard a word of her brother's rambling comment, and there was a decidedly expectant intonation in her voice. "Nobody's usin' the company-room, an' the presidin' elder won't be here till fall. Mr. Mostyn never was a bit of trouble and seemed to love everything I set before him. But I reckon we needn't feel so flattered. He's coming here so he'll be near Mr. Saunders when he runs up to his place on Sundays."

John Webb, for such a slow individual, had suddenly taken on a new impetus. He left his sister and her husband and passed through the passage bisecting the lower part of the plain two-story house and went out at the rear door. In the back yard he found his nephew, George Drake, a boy of fifteen years, seated on the grass repairing a ragged, mud-stained fish-net.

"Who told you you could be out o' school, young feller?" John demanded, dryly. "I'll bet my life you are playin' hookey. You think because your sister's the teacher you can run wild like a mountain shote. My Lord, look at your clothes! I'll swear it would be hard to tell whether you've got on anything or not—that is, anything except mud an' slime. Have you been tryin' to pull that seine through the creek by yourself?"

The boy, who had a fine head and profile and was stoutly built and generally good-looking, was too busy with his strings and knots to look up. "Some fool left it in the creek, and it's laid there for the last month," he mumbled. "I had to go in after it, and it was all tangled up and clogged with mud. Dolly knew I wasn't going to school to-day."

"She knew it when you didn't turn up at roll-call, I bound you," Webb drawled. "Say, do you know a young gal like her ain't strong enough to lick scholars as sound as they ought to be licked, and thar is *some* talk about appointin' some able-bodied man that lives close about to step in an' sort o' clean up two or three times a week. I don't know but what I'd like the job. A feller that goes as nigh naked as you do would be a blame good thing to practise on."

"Huh!" the boy sniffed, as he tossed back his shaggy brown hair. "You talk mighty big. I'd like to see you try to whip me—I shore would."

"Well, I may give you the chance if Dolly calls on me to help 'er out," Webb laughed. "Say, I started to tell you a secret, but I won't."

"I already know what it is," George said, with a mischievous grin.

"You say you do?" Webb was caught in the wily fellow's snare.

"Yes, you are going to get married." The boy now burst into a roar of laughter and threw himself back on the grass. "You and Sue Tidwell are going to get spliced. The whole valley's talking about it, and hoping that it will be public like an election barbecue. You with your red head and freckled face and her with her stub nose and—"

"That will do—that will do!" Webb's frown seemed to deepen the flush which, fold upon fold, came into his face. "Jokin' is all right, but it ain't fair to bring in a lady's name."

"Oh no, of course not." The boy continued to laugh through the net which he had drawn over him. "The shoe is on the other foot now."

"Well, I'm not goin' to tell you the news," Webb declared, with a touch of propitiation in his voice; and, not a little discomfited, he turned away, employing a quicker step than usually characterized his movement.

"The young scamp!" he said. "He's gittin' entirely too forward—entirely, for a boy as young as he is, and me his uncle."

Crossing a strip of meadow land, then picking his way between the rows of a patch of corn, and skirting a cotton-field, he came out into a red-clay road. Along this he walked till he reached a little meeting-house snugly ensconced among big trees at the foot of the mountain. The white frame building, oblong in shape, had four windows with green outer blinds on each of its two sides, and a door at the end nearer the road. As Webb traversed the open space, where, on Sundays, horses were hitched to the trees and saplings, a drone as of countless bees fell on his ears. To a native this needed no explanation. During five of the week-days the building was used as a schoolhouse. The sound was made by the students studying aloud, and John's niece, Dolly Drake, had sole charge of them.

Reaching the door and holding his hat in his hand, Webb cautiously peered within, beholding row after row of boys and girls whose backs were turned to him. At a blackboard on the platform, a bit of chalk in her fingers, Dolly, a girl eighteen years of age, stood explaining an example in arithmetic to several burly boys taller than herself. Webb glanced up at the sun.

"They haven't had recess yet," he reckoned. "I swear I'm sorry for them boys. I'd rather take a dozen lickin's than to stay in on a day like this an' try to git lessons in my head. I don't blame George a bit, so I don't. I can't recall a thing in the Saviour's teachin's about havin' to study figures an' geography, nohow. Looks to me like the older the world gits the further it gits from common sense."

Patiently Webb held his ground till Dolly had dismissed the class; then, turning to a table on which stood a cumbersome brass bell, she said: "I'm going to let you have recess, but you've got to go out quietly."

She had not ceased speaking, and had scarcely touched the handle of the bell, when there was a deafening clatter of books and slates on the crude benches. Feet shod and feet bare pounded the floor. Merry yells rent the air. On the platform itself two of the arithmetic delinquents were boxing playfully, fiercely punching, thrusting, and dodging. At a window three boys were bodily ejecting a fourth, the legs and feet of whom, like a human letter V, were seen disappearing over the sill.

Smilingly Webb stood aside and let the clamoring drove hurtle past to the playground outside, and when the way was clear he entered the church and stalked up the single aisle toward his niece. Dolly had turned back to the blackboard, and was sponging off the chalk figures. She was quite pretty; her eyes were large, with fathomless hazel depths. Her brow, under a mass of uncontrollable reddish-brown hair, was high and indicative of decided intellectual power. She was of medium height, very shapely, and daintily graceful. She had a good nose and a sweet, sympathetic mouth. Her hands were slender and tapering, though suggestive of strength. She wore a simple white shirtwaist and a black skirt than which nothing could have been more becoming. Hearing her uncle's step, she turned and greeted his smile with a dubious one of her own.

"Why don't you go out and play with the balance an' limber yourself up?" he asked.

"Play? I say *play*!" she sighed. "You men don't know any more about what a woman teacher has to contend with than a day-old kitten. My head is in a constant whirl. Sometimes I forget my own name."

"What's wrong now?" Webb smiled eagerly.

"Oh, it's everything—everything!" she sighed. "Not a thing has happened right to-day. George flatly refused to come to school—even defied me before some other boys down the road. Then my own sister—"

"What's wrong with Ann? I remember now that I didn't see her in that drove just now, and she certainly ain't at home, because I'm just from thar."

"No, she isn't at home," Dolly frowned, and, for an obvious reason, raised her voice to a high pitch, "but I'll tell you where she is, and as her own blood uncle you can share my humiliation." Therewith Dolly grimly pointed at a closet door close by. "Open it," she said. "The truth is, I told her she would have to stay there twenty minutes, and I've been bothered all through the last recitation for fear she wouldn't get enough air. All at once she got still, though she kept up a terrible racket at first."

With a grin Webb mounted the platform and opened the door of the closet. He opened it quite widely, that Dolly might look into the receptacle from where she stood. And there against the wall, seated on the floor, was Dolly's sister Ann, a slim-legged, rather pretty girl about fourteen years of age, her eyes sullenly cast down. Around her were some dismantled, ill-smelling lamps, a step-ladder, an old stove, and a bench holding a stack of hymn-books.

"She ain't *quite* dead," John said, dryly. "She's still breathin' below the neck, an' she's got some red in the face."

"She ought to be red from head to foot," Dolly said, for the culprit's ears. "Ann, come here!"

There was no movement on the part of the prisoner save a desultory picking of the fingers at a fold of her gingham skirt.

"Didn't you hear what Dolly—what your teacher said?" Webb asked, in an effort at severity which was far from his mood.

"Of course she heard," Dolly said, sharply. "She thinks it will mend matters for her to pout awhile. Come here, Ann."

"I want to stay here," Ann muttered; "I like it. Shut the door, Uncle John. It is cool and nice in here."

"She wants to stay." Webb's eyes danced as he conveyed the message. "She says she likes it, an' I reckon she does. Scripture says them whose deeds is evil likes darkness better'n light. You certainly made a mistake when you clapped 'er in here—that is, if you meant to punish 'er. Ann's a reg'lar bat, if not a' owl."

"Pull her out!" Dolly cried. "I've got to talk to her, and recess is almost over."

"Come out, young lady," Webb laid hold of the girl's wrist and drew the reluctant creature to her feet, half pushing, half leading her to her sister.

"I'm glad you happened in, Uncle John," Dolly said. "I want you to take a look at that face. How she got the money I don't know, but she bought a dozen sticks of licorice at the store as she passed this morning and brought them to school in her pocket. She's been gorging herself with it all day. You can see it all over her face, under her chin, behind her neck, and even in her ears. Look here at her new geography." Dolly, in high disgust, exhibited several brown smudges on an otherwise clean page.

Webb took the book with all the gravity of a most righteous, if highly amused judge. "Looks like ham gravy, don't it?" he said. "An' as I understand it, the book has to be handed on to somebody else when she gits through with it. What a pity!"

"I know you are ashamed of her, Uncle John, for I am," Dolly continued. "You see, she's my own sister."

"And my own sister's child," Webb deplored. "Of course, she ain't *quite* as close to me as she is to you, but she's nigh enough to make me feel plumb ashamed. I've always tuck pride in both you gals; but lawsy me, if Ann is goin' to gaum 'erself from head to foot like a pig learnin' to root, why, I reckon I'll jest hang my head in shame."

"I've lost all patience," the teacher said. "Go home, Ann, and let mother look at you. Don't come back to-day. I don't want to see you again. I've lost heart completely. I want to be proud of you and George, but I'm afraid I never can be. She can't write, Uncle John; she can't spell the simplest words in three syllables; and as for using correct grammar and pronuncia-tion—" But Ann was stalking off without looking back.

Dolly sat down at the table and drew a sheet of paper toward her. "She's got me all upset," she sighed. "Mr. DeWitt, the new teacher, has been sending about a test example in arithmetic to see who can work it. He says he can do it, and one or two other *men*, but that he never has seen a woman teacher yet who could get the answer. I was within an inch of the solution when I caught sight of that girl's face, and it went from me in a flash. Uncle John, if fifteen men own in common three hundred and eighty-four bushels of wheat, and three men want to buy sixty-seven and three-fourths of—"

"Oh, Lord—thar you go!" Webb groaned. "Let me tell you some'n', Dolly. The fool feller that concocted that thing to idle time away with never hoed a row of corn or planted a potato. Do you know what that's meant for? It is for no other reason under the shinin' sun than to make the average parent think teachers know more'n the rest o' humanity. In the first place, the fifteen common men must be common shore enough if they couldn't own all told more than that amount o' wheat in this day and time when even a one-horse farmer can raise—"

"You don't understand," Dolly broke in, with an indulgent smile.

"And I don't want to, either," John declared. "It is hard enough work to sow and reap and thresh wheat in hot weather like this without sweatin' over fifteen able-bodied men that are jowerin' about a pile no bigger'n that."

Dolly glanced at the round rosewood clock on the plastered wall and reached for the bell-handle. "My time's up," she said. "I wish I could stop my ears with cotton. They always come in like a drove of iron-shod mules on a wooden bridge."

"Your pa's got a piece o' news this mornin'." Webb knew his words would stay the hand now resting on the bell.

"What is it?" Dolly inquired.

"He got a letter from Mr. Mostyn; he's comin' up to board at the house for a month."

The pretty hand dropped from the bell-handle. Dolly was staring at the speaker in surprise. She said nothing, though he was sure a flush was creeping into her cheeks.

"I sorter thought that 'ud stagger you," Webb said with a significant grin.

"Me? I don't see why." Dolly was fighting for perfect composure under trying circumstances, considering her uncle's mischievous stare.

"Well, I do, if you don't, Miss Dolly," he tittered. "You wasn't a bit older 'n Ann is when he was here last, but you was daffy about 'im the same as your ma an' all the rest o' the women. In fact, you was wuss than the balance."

"Me? I'm ashamed of you, Uncle John; I'm ashamed to hear you accuse me of—of—why, I never heard of such a thing."

"No matter, I wasn't plumb blind," Webb went on. "You kept puttin' fresh flowers in his room an' you eyed his plate like he was a pet cat to see if he was bein' fed right. La me, I'm no fool! I know a *little* about females, an' I never saw a mountain woman yet that wouldn't go stark crazy over a town man or a' unmarried preacher. I reckon it must be the clothes the fellers wear or the prissy stuff they chat about."

Dolly put her hand out toward the bell, but dropped it to the table. "When is he coming?" she asked, her eyes holding a tense, eager stare.

"Thursday," was the answer, accompanied by a widening grin. "I wouldn't give the children a holiday on the strength of it if I was you. Part o' these mountain folks is men an' moonshiners, an' they don't think any more about a feller that owns a bank in Atlanta 'an they do of a mossback clod-hopper with the right sort o' heart in 'im. Say, Mostyn ain't nothin' but human, an' if what *some* say is so he ain't the highest grade o' that. Over at Hilton's warehouse in Ridgeville t'other day I heard some cotton-buyers talkin' about men that had riz fast an' the underhanded tricks sech chaps use to hoodwink simple folks, an' they said Dick Mostyn capped the stack. Accordin' to them, he—"

"I don't believe a word of it!" Dolly stood up and angrily grasped the bell-handle. "It's not true. It's a meddlesome lie. They are jealous. People are always like that—it makes them furious to see another person prosper. They are mean, low back-biters."

"Oh, I don't say that Mostyn will actually be arrested before he gits up here," John said, dryly. "From all reports he generally has the law on his side, an'—"

But Dolly, still angry, was ringing the bell. She had turned her back to Webb; and, unable to make himself heard, he made his way down the aisle to the door.

"She's a regular spitfire when she gits 'er back up," he mused. "Now I *know* she likes 'im. It's been three years since she laid eyes on 'im, but she's as daffy now as she was then. It must 'a' been the feller's gallant way. I remember he used to say she was the purtiest an' brightest little trick he ever seed. Maybe he said somethin' o' the sort to her, young as she was. I remember I used to think Sis was a fool to let 'im walk about with Dolly so much, pickin' flowers an' the like. Well, if he thought she was purty an' smart then he'll be astonished now—he shore will."

CHAPTER IV

As Mostyn's train ascended the grade leading up to the hamlet of Ridgeville, within a mile of which lay the little farm to which he was going, he sat at an open window and viewed the scene with delight, drawing into his lungs with a sense of restful content the crisp, rarefied air. To the west, and marking the vicinity of Drake's farm, the mountain loomed up in its blended coat of gray and green, growing more and more indistinct as the range gradually extended into the bluish haze of distance.

"I'm going to like it," he said, almost aloud, with the habit he had of talking to himself when alone. "I feel as if I shall never want to look inside a bank again. This is life, real, sensible life. I have, after all, always had a yearning for genuine simplicity. It must have come to me from my pioneer, Puritan ancestry. That man over there plowing corn with his mule and ragged harness is happier than I ever was down there in that God-forsaken turmoil. The habit of wanting to beat other men in the expert turning over of capital is as dangerous, once it clutches you, as morphine. I must call a halt. That last narrow escape shall be a lesson. I am getting normal again, and I must stay so. What are Alan Delbridge's operations to me? He has no nerves nor imagination. He could have slept through that last tangle of mine which came within an inch of laying me out stiff and stark. I wonder how all the Drakes are, especially Dolly. She must be fully grown now. Saunders says she is beautiful and as wise as Socrates. I suppose there are a dozen mountain boys after her by this time. For a little girl she was astonishingly mature in manner and thought. I ought not to have talked to her as I did. I have never forgotten her face and voice as I saw and heard them that last night. I see the wonderful eyes and mouth, the like of which I have never run across since. I am ashamed to think that I acted as I did, and she only an inexperienced child; but I really couldn't help it. I seemed to be in a dream. It was really an unpardonable thing—and proves that I *do* lack character—for me to tell her that I would often think of her. But the worst of all, really the most cowardly, considering her unsuspecting innocence and exaggerated faith in me, was my kissing her as I did there in the moonlight. How exquisite was her vow that she'd never kiss any other man as long as she lived! Lord, I wonder what ails me. Surely I am not silly enough to be actually—"

Mostyn's meditations were interrupted by a shrill shriek from the locomotive. Leaning out of the window, he saw the little old-fashioned brick car-shed ahead and heard the grinding of the brakes on the smooth wheels beneath the car. Grasping his bag in his hand, he made his way out and descended to the ground.

He saw the long white three-story hotel close by with its green blinds, extensive veranda, and blue-railed balustrade, the row of stores and law-offices, forming three sides of a square of which the car-shed, depot, and railway made the fourth. In the open space stood some canvas-covered mountain-wagons containing produce for shipment to the larger markets, and the usual male loungers in straw hats, baggy trousers, easy shoes, and shirts without coats.

A burly negro porter hastened down the steps of the hotel and approached swinging his slouch hat in his hand, his eyes on the traveler's bag.

"All right, boss—Purcell House, fus'-class hotel, whar all de drummers put up. Good sample-rooms an' fine country cookin'."

Mostyn held on to his bag, which the swarthy hands were grasping. "No, I'm not going to stop," he explained. "I'm going out to Drake's farm."

"Oh, *is* you? Well, suh, Mr. John Webb is in de freight depot. I done hear 'im say he fetched de buggy ter tek somebody out."

At this juncture the florid and flushed face of Webb was seen as he emerged from the doorway of the depot. He was bent under a weighty bag of flour, and smiled and waved his hat by way of salutation as he advanced to a buggy at a public hitching-rack and deposited his burden in the receptacle behind the single seat. This done, he came forward, brushing the sleeve of his alpaca coat and grinning jovially.

"How are you?" He extended a fat, perspiring hand luckily powdered with flour. "I reckon you won't mind riding out with me. Tom said he'd bet you'd rather walk to limber up your legs, but Lucy made me fetch the buggy along, as some said you wasn't as well as common. But you look all right to me-that is, as well as *any* of you city fellers ever do. The last one of you look as white as convicts out o' jail. I reckon thar is so much smoke over your town that the sun don't strike it good and straight."

"Oh, I'm all right," Mostyn said, good-naturedly, "just a little run down from overwork, that's all."

"Run down?" Webb seemed quite concerned with getting at the exact meaning of the statement, and as he took Mostyn's bag and put it in with the flour he eyed the banker attentively. *"Run down?"* he repeated, with his characteristic emphasis. "I don't see how a man as big an' hearty as you look an' weighin' as much could git sick or even *tired* without havin' any more work to do than you have. I've always meant to ask you or Mr. Saunders what you fellers do, *anyway.* I reckon banks are the same in big towns as in little ones. They haven't got a regular bank here in Ridgeville, but I've been to the one in Darley. I went in with Tom when he wanted to draw the cash on a cotton check. Talk about hard work—I'll swear I couldn't see it. Me 'n' Tom had been up fully three hours knockin' about the streets tryin' to kill the best part o' the day before that shebang opened up for business, an' *then* somebody said they shet up at three o'clock an' went home to take a nap or whiz about in their automobiles. The whole thing's bothered me a sight, for I *do* like to understand things. How *could* a checker-playin' business like that tire anybody?"

"It's head-work," Mostyn obligingly explained, as he followed John into the buggy and sat beside him. *"Head-work,"* Webb echoed, the cloud still on his brow. He clucked to his horse and gently shook the reins. "To save me I don't see how head-work—if there is such a thing—could tire out a man's legs and arms and body."

"There is a good deal of worry attached to it," Mostyn felt impelled to say. "Nowadays they are saying that worry will kill a man quicker than any sort of physical ailment. You see, good sound sleep is necessary, and when a man is greatly bothered he simply can't sleep."

"Oh, I see, I see," Webb's blue eyes flashed. "Thar may be something in that, but it does seem like a man would have more gumption 'an to worry hisse'f to death about something that won't be of use to 'im after he dies. That's common sense, ain't it?"

Mostyn was compelled to admit the truth of the remark. They had driven out of the village square and were now in the open country.

"Thar is one more thing about town folks an' country folks that I've always wanted to know," John began again after a silence of several minutes, "and that is why town folks contend that country folks is green. As I look at it it is an even swap. Now, you are a town man, an' I'm a country feller. I could take you to the edge o' that cotton-field whar it joins on to the woods on that slope thar, an' point out a spot whar you couldn't make cotton grow more'n six inches high though it will reach four feet everywhar else in the field. Now, I'd be an impolite fool to lie down thar betwixt the rows an' split my sides laughin' at you for not knowin' what I jest got on to by years an' years o' farm life. The truth is that cotton won't take any sort o' root within twenty feet of a white-oak tree."

"I didn't know that," Mostyn said.

"I knowed you didn't, an' that's why I fetched it up," Webb went on, blandly, "an' me nor no other farmer would poke fun at you about it, but it is different in town. Jest let a spindle-legged counter-jumper at a store with his hair parted in the middle git a joke on a country feller, an' the whole town will take a hand in it. Oh, I know, for they've shore had *me* on the run."

"I'm surprised at that," Mostyn answered, smiling. "You seem too shrewd to be taken in by any one."

"Humph, I say!" Webb laughed reminiscently. "I supplied all the fun Darley had one hot summer day when all hands was lyin' round the stores and law-offices tryin' to git cool by fannin' and sprinklin' the sidewalks. Did you ever hear tell of the Tom Collins gag?"

"I think not," the banker answered.

"Well, I have—you bet I have," John said, dryly, "an' it is one thing that makes me afraid sometimes that a country feller railly hain't actually overloaded with brains. Take my advice; if anybody ever tells you that a feller by the name o' Tom Collins is lookin' for you an' anxious to see you about something important, just skin your eye at 'im, tell 'im right out that you don't give a dang about Tom Collins. La me, what a fool—what a fool I was! A feller workin' at the cotton-compress told me that a man by the name o' Tom Collins wanted to see me right off, an' that he was up at the wholesale grocery. Fool that

I was, I hitched my hosses an' struck out lickity-split for the grocery. I axed one of the storekeepers standin' in front if Tom Collins was anywhars about, and, as I remember now, he slid his hand over his mouth an' sorter turned his face to one side and yelled back in the store:

"'Say, boys, is Tom Collins back thar?' An' right then, Mr. Mostyn, if I had had the sense of a three-year-old baby I'd have smelt a mouse, for fully six clerks, drummers, and all the firm hurried to whar I was at an' stood lookin' at me, their eyes dancin'. 'He *was* here, but he's just left,' a clerk said. 'He went to the hotel to git his grip. He was awfully put out. He's been all over town lookin' for you.' Well, as I made a break for the hotel, wonderin' if somebody had died an' left me a hunk o' money, the gang at the grocery stood clean out on the sidewalk watchin' me. When I inquired at the hotel, the clerk an' two nigger waiters said Tom was askin' about me an' had just run over to the court-house, whar I'd be shore to find him."

"I see the point," Mostyn laughed.

"I'm glad you do so quick, for I had to have it beat into me with a sledge-hammer," Webb said, dryly. "I was so mad I could have chawed nails, but I blamed myself more'n anybody else, for they was just havin' their fun an' meant no harm."

"I suppose not," Mostyn said.

"Well, I can't complain; they have their sport with one another. Dolph Wartrace, you know, that keeps the cross-roads store nigh us, clerked in Darley before he went in on his own hook out here, an' I've heard 'im tell of a lot o' pranks that they had over thar. He said thar was an old bachelor that, kept a dry-goods store who never had had much to do with women. He was bashful-like, but thar was *one* young woman that he had his eye on, an' now an' then he'd spruce up an' go to see 'er or take 'er out to meetin', but Jeff said he was too weak-kneed to pop the question, an' the gal went off on a visit to Alabama and got married. Now, the old bach' had a gang o' friends that was always in for fun, an' with long, sad faces they went about askin' everybody they met if they had heard that Bob Hadley—that was the feller's name—if they had heard that he was. dead. Bob knowed what they was sayin' an' tried to put a pleasant face on it, but it must have been hard work, considerin' all that happened.

"Well, one thing added to another till a gang of Bob's friends met the next night in a grocery store after he had gone to bed and still with sad, solemn faces declared that, considerin' his untimely end, it was their bounden duty to bury 'im in a respectable way. So they went to the furniture store close by an' borrowed a coffin an' picked out pall-bearers. A feller that slept with Bob in the little room cut off at the end o' his store was in the game, an' he had a key an' unlocked the door, an' the solemn procession marched in singin' some sad hymn or other with every man-jack of 'em wipin' his eyes an' snufflin'. Now, that was all well an' good as far as it went, but thar was a traitor in the camp. Somebody had let the dead man in on the job, an' when the gang got to the door of the little room he jumped out o' bed with a surprised sort o' grunt an' let into firin' blank-cartridges straight at 'em. Folks say that thar was some o' the tallest runnin' an' jumpin' an' hidin' under counters an' bustin' show-cases that ever tuck place out of a circus. After that night Jeff said the whole town was meetin' the gang an' tellin' 'em that thar must 'a' been some mistake about the report of Bob Hadley's death anyway."

Mostyn laughed heartily. Indeed, he was conscious of a growing sense of deep content and restfulness. The turmoil of business and city life seemed almost dreamlike in its remoteness from his present more rational existence. With the handle of his whip Webb pointed to the roof of the farmhouse, the fuzzy gray shingles of which were barely showing above the trees by which it was shaded.

"You haven't told me how the family are," Mostyn said, "I suppose the children are much larger now. Dolly, at least, must be a young lady, from what Saunders tells me of her school-work."

Webb's blue eyes swept the face of the banker with a steady scrutiny. There was a faint twinkle in their mystic depths as he replied.

"Yes, she's full grown. She's kin folks o' mine, an' it ain't for me to say, but I'd be unnatural if I wasn't proud of 'er. She's the head of that shebang, me included. What she says goes with young or old. She ain't more'n eighteen, if she's that, an' yet she furnishes brains for us an' mighty nigh all the neighborhood. You wait till you see 'er an' hear 'er talk, an' you will know what I mean."

CHAPTER V

The next morning the new boarder waked at sunrise, and stood at a window of his room on the upper floor of the farmhouse and looked out across the fields and meadows to the rugged, mist-draped mountain. The beautiful valley was flooded with the soft golden light. An indescribable luster seemed to breathe from every dew-laden stalk of cotton or corn, plant, vine, blade of grass and patch of succulent clover. Cobwebs, woven in the night and bejeweled with dewdrops, festooned the boughs of the trees in the orchard and on the lawn. From the barn-yard back of the farmhouse a chorus of sounds was rising. Pigs were grunting and squealing, cows were mooing, a donkey was braying, ducks were quacking, hens were clucking, roosters were crowing.

"Saunders is right," Mostyn declared, enthusiastically. "I don't blame the fellow for spending so much time on his plantation. This is the only genuine life. The other is insanity, crazy, competitive madness, for which there is no cure this side of the grave. I must have two natures. At this moment I feel as if I'd rather die than sweat and stew over investments and speculations in a bank as I have been doing, and yet I may be sure that the thing will clutch me again. One word of Delbridge's lucky manipulations or old Mitchell's praise, and the fever would burn to my bones. But I mustn't think of them if I am to benefit by this. I must fill myself with this primitive simplicity and dream once more the glorious fancies of boyhood."

Finishing dressing, he descended the stairs to the hall below and passed through the open door to the veranda. No one was in sight, but from the kitchen in the rear he heard the clatter of utensils and dishes, and smelt the aroma of boiling coffee and frying ham. Already his appetite was sharpened as if by the mountain air. He decided on taking a walk, and, stepping down to the grass, he turned round the house, coming face to face upon Dolly, whom he had not yet seen, as she came from a side door.

"Oh!" she exclaimed, flushing prettily. "I did not think you would rise so early—at least, not on your first morning."

He eyed her almost in bewilderment as he took the hand she was cordially extending. Could this full-blown rose of young womanhood, this startling beauty, be the slip of a timid girl he had so lightly treated three years ago? What hair, what eyes, what palpitating, sinuous grace! She was fast recovering calmness. There was a womanly dignity about her which seemed incongruous in one so young.

"I am rather surprised at myself for waking so early," he answered. "I slept like a log. It is the first real rest I have had since—since I was here before. Why, Dolly"—he caught himself up—"I suppose I must say Miss Drake now—"

"No, I am not that to any one in all this valley, and don't want to be!" she cried, the corners of her mouth curving bewitchingly. "Even the little children call me 'Dolly,' and I like it."

"I mustn't stop you if you are going somewhere," he said, still in the grasp of her wondrous beauty.

"I'm going down to Tobe Barnett's cabin in the edge of our field." She showed a small vial half filled with medicine in the pocket of her white apron. "His baby, little Robby, was taken sick a few days ago. I sat up there part of last night. They have no paragoric and I am taking some over."

Will N. Harben

"So that's where you were; I wondered when I didn't see you at supper," Mostyn said, turning with her toward the gate. "I'll go with you if you don't mind."

"Oh yes, come on," Dolly answered. "We'll have plenty of time before the breakfast-bell rings. It is not far. I am awfully sorry for Tobe and his wife; they are both young and inexperienced."

"And you are a regular grandmother in wisdom," Mostyn jested. "Only eighteen, with the world on your shoulders."

"Well, I *do* seem to know a few things, a few *ordinary* things," Dolly said, seriously, "but they are not matters to boast about. For instance, Tobe and Annie—that's his wife—were so scared and excited when I got there last night that they were actually harming the poor little baby, and I set about to calm them the very first thing. I can't begin to tell you how they went on. Think of it, they had actually given up and were crying—both of them—and there lay the little mite fairly gasping for breath. I made Tobe go after some wood for the fire, and put Annie at work helping me. Then I forced them to be still until the baby got quiet and fell asleep."

"You'd make a capital nurse." Mostyn was regarding her admiringly. "It would be a pleasure to be sick in your hands."

Dolly ignored his compliment. She was thinking of something alien to his mood and deeper. "Do you know," she said, after she had passed through the gate which he had held open, "the world is all out of joint."

"Do you think so?" he asked, as he walked beside her, suiting his step to hers.

"Yes, for if it were right," she sighed, her brows meeting thoughtfully, "such well-meaning persons as the Barnetts would not have to live as they do and bring helpless children into the world."

"Things do seem rather uneven," Mostyn admitted, lamely, "but you know really that we ought to have a law that would keep such couples from marrying."

"Poof!" She blew his argument away with a fine sniff of denial, and her eyes shot forth fresh gleams of conviction. "How absurd to talk about a human law to keep persons from doing God's infinite will. God intends for persons to love each other. Love is the one divine thing that we can be absolutely sure of. Annie and Tobe can't help themselves. They are out in a storm. It is beating them on all sides—pounding, driving, dragging, and grinding them. They love each other with a love that is celestial, a love that is of the spirit rather than of their poor ill-fed, ill-clothed bodies."

Mostyn's wonder over the girl's depth and facility of expression clutched him so firmly that he found himself unable to formulate a fitting reply.

"Oh yes, their love is absolutely genuine," Dolly ran on, loyally. "Tobe could have married the daughter of a well-to-do farmer over the mountain whom he had visited several times before he met his wife. The farmer was willing, I have heard, to give them land to live on, and it might have been a match, but Tobe accidentally met Annie. She was a poor girl working in the Ridgeville cotton factory at two or three dollars a week, which she was giving to her people. She had only two dresses, the tattered bag of a thing she worked in and another which she kept for Sundays. Tobe met her and talked to her one day while he was hauling cotton to the factory, and something in her poor wretched face attracted him, or maybe it was her sweet voice, for it is as mellow as music. She wasn't well—had a cough at the time—and he had read something in a paper about the lint of a factory causing consumption, and it worried him; people say he couldn't keep from talking about it. She was on his mind constantly. He was still going to see the other girl, but he acted so oddly that she became angry with him and, to spite him, began to go with another young man. But Tobe didn't seem to care. He kept going to the factory

Will N. Harben

and—well, the upshot of it was that he married Annie."

"And then the *real* trouble began," Mostyn said, smiling lightly.

"And actually through no fault of their own," Dolly declared. "He rented land, bought some supplies on credit, and went to work to make a crop. You ask father or Uncle John; they will tell you that Tobe Barnett was the hardest worker in this valley. But ill luck clung to him like a leach. The drouth killed his first crop, and the winter caught him in debt. Then Annie got sick—she had exposed herself to the bad weather milking a cow for a neighbor to earn a little money. Then no sooner was she up when a wagon ran over Tobe and hurt his foot so that he could hardly get about. Then the baby came, and their load of trouble was heavier than ever."

"A case of true love, without doubt," Mostyn said.

"And the prettiest thing on earth," Dolly declared. "Sometimes it seems to make their poor shack of a place fairly glow with heavenly light."

"You are a marvel to me, Dolly—you really are!" Mostyn paused, and she turned to him, a groping look of surprise on her face.

"What do you mean?" she asked.

"Why, you have such an original way of speaking," he said, somewhat abashed by her sudden demand. "I mean—that—that what you say sounds different from what one would naturally expect. Not ordinary, not commonplace; I hardly know how to express it. Really, you are quite poetic."

He saw her face fall. "I am sorry about that," she faltered. "I have been told the same thing before, and I don't like to be that way. I am afraid I read too much poetry. It fairly sings in my head when I feel deeply, as I do about Tobe and Annie, for instance, or when I have to make a speech."

"Make a speech? You?" Mostyn stared.

"Oh yes, these people expect all that sort of thing from a teacher, and it was very hard for me to do at first, but I don't mind it now. One is obliged to open school with prayer, too, and it mustn't be worded the same way each time or the mischievous children will learn it by heart and quote it. The most of my speeches are made in our debating society."

"Oh, I see; you have a debating society!" Mostyn exclaimed.

"Yes, and as it happens I am the only woman member," Dolly proceeded to enlighten him. "The men teachers in the valley got it up to meet at my school twice a month, and the patrons took a big interest in it and began to make insinuations that my school ought to be represented. They talked so much about it that I was afraid some man would get my job, so one day when Warren Wilks, the teacher in Ridgeville, asked me to join I did."

"How strange!" Mostyn said, admiringly, "and you really do take part."

Dolly laughed softly. "You'd think so if you ever attended one of our public harangues. I've heard persons say I was the whole show. Of course, I'm joking now, but the women all take up for me and applaud everything I say, whether it has a point to it or not. *'Whole show!'* I oughtn't to have said that. When I try to keep from using bookish expressions I drop plumb into slang; there is no middle ground for me."

"What sort of subjects does your society take up?" Mostyn inquired, highly amused.

"Anything the human mind can think up," Dolly answered. "Warren Wilks reads all the philosophical and scientific magazines, and he fairly floors us—there I go again; when I talk I either grab the stars or stick my nose in the mire. I mean that Warren's subjects are generally abstruse and profound."

"For instance?" Mostyn suggested, still smiling.

"Well, the last one was—and there was a crowd, I tell you, for the presiding elder had just closed a revival in our church and a good many stayed over for the debate. We all tried to show off because he was present, and it was a religious subject. It was this: Is it possible for human beings in the present day to obey the commandment of Jesus to love your neighbor as yourself?"

"And which side were you on?" the banker asked.

"I was affirmative, and almost by myself, too," Dolly answered. I oughtn't to say that either; it sounds like bragging, for there were two men on my side, but I saw at the start that I couldn't depend on them. They were weak-kneed—afraid of our premise. They didn't believe Jesus meant it, anyway. I did the best I could. I not only think He meant it, but I am sure the day will come when the whole world will live up to the rule. Christ wouldn't be for all time, as He is, if His best ideas were acceptable to such a grossly material age as ours. Neither side won in that debate—the judges couldn't agree. I wish you had been here last month. We had up a subject that you could have helped me on. The question was: Which is the better place to rear a man, the city or the country? Or, in other words, can the mind of man develop in a busy, crowded place as well as in a quiet spot in the country? I was on the side of the rural districts that night, and we won. We had no trouble showing that the majority of great characters in all lines of endeavor had come from rural spots. I think it is the same to-day. I know I wouldn't live in a big town. City people are occupied with automobiles, golf, dances, card parties, and gossip—of course, I don't mean anything personal, you understand, but it is a fact that they are that way. And it is a fact, too, that here our crowd, at least, will get a good book and actually wear it to tatters passing it around. That is the sort of education that sticks when it once gets hold of a person."

"I am sure you are right," Mostyn admitted, and he felt the blood rise to his face as he thought of the emptiness of his own life in Atlanta, which now, somehow, seemed like a vanishing dream. The morning sun was blazing over the verdant landscape, filling the dewdrops on the grass with red, blue, and yellow light. An indescribable aura seemed to encircle the exquisite face of his young companion. There was a restful poise about her, a sure grasp of utterance, that soothed and thrilled him. Something new and vivifying sprang to life in his breast. The thought flashed into his consciousness that here with this embodiment of intellectual purity he could master the cloying vices of his life. He could put them behind him— turn over a new leaf, be a new man in body and spirit. Perhaps he could kill the temptation to gain by sordid business methods; perhaps he could subdue the reluctant intention to marry for ulterior motives regardless of the magnitude of the temptation. It really was not too late. He couldn't remember having said anything to Mitchell or his daughter which would bind him in any absolute sense. Yes, the ideal was the thing. Providence had rescued him from his recent financial danger, and meant this encounter as a chance for redemption. He could make some sort of compromise with old Jefferson Henderson—a reasonable sum of money to one so hard pressed for funds would not only silence the too active tongue, but win his gratitude and the approval of all business men. Then there was the other thing—the thing he scarcely dared think of in the presence of this pure young girl—the disagreeable case of Marie—but there was no use reflecting over what could not be helped. A man ought to be pardoned for mistakes due to uncontrollable natural passion. The woman is generally as much to blame as her companion in indiscretion, especially one of the sort to whom his mind now reverted. She had shown her lack of character, if not her prime motive, by accepting and using the money he had offered her. She had been troublesome, and more so of late than before, but she might be persuaded to let him alone. His conscience was clear, for he had made no promises to her. He remembered distinctly that he had made no effort actually to win her affections. How different was this pure mountain flower from

Will N. Harben

such a soiled and degraded creature!

"There," Dolly was speaking again, and the soft cadences of her voice put his shameful memories to flight as she pointed to an opening between the trees of the wood on the right, "you can see your partner's house from here. He has had it repainted. It is a beautiful old place, isn't it?"

He nodded as he surveyed the stately mansion in the distance, the white porch columns of which shone like snow in the slanting rays of the sun. "It is Saunders's pride," he said. "Atlanta is becoming more and more distasteful to him. He is never really happy anywhere but up here. He yawns his head off at every party, dance, or dinner down there. They all laugh at him and call him 'Farmer.'"

"Well, he is that," Dolly declared. "He works in the fields like a day-laborer when he is up here on a holiday."

They walked on a few paces in silence; then Dolly said: "Mr. Saunders has been very kind to our club; he gave us a lot of good books; he comes to our debates sometimes and seems very much interested. We all like him. The boys declare they could elect him to the legislature from this county if only he would let them, but he doesn't care a fig for it."

"He is something of a dreamer, I think," Mostyn remarked, "and still he's practical. He has a long head on him—never gets excited and seldom makes a wrong move in a deal."

They were now nearing the cabin occupied by Tobe Barnett. It was a most dilapidated shack. It was made of pine logs, the bark of which had become worm-eaten and was falling away. The spaces between the logs were filled with dried clay. It had a mud-and-stick chimney, from the cracks of which the smoke oozed. It contained only one room, was roofed with crudely split boards of oak, and was without a window of any sort. Outside against the wall on the right of the shutterless door was a shelf holding a battered tin water pail and a gourd.

Within, as the visitors approached nearer, was heard the grinding of feet on the rough planks of the floor and the faint, tremulous cry of a child. A lank young man appeared at the door. He wore a ragged, earth-stained shirt and patched pants. His yellowish hair was tousled, a scant tuft of beard was on his sharp chin, and whiskers of a week's standing mottled his hollow cheeks. His blue eyes peered out despondently from their shadowy sockets.

"How is Robby now, Tobe?" Dolly asked.

The man stepped down to the ground, and in his tattered, gaping shoes slowly shambled forward.

"I can't see no change, Miss Dolly," he gulped. "He seems to me as sick as ever. If anything, he don't git his breath as free as he did. Annie's mighty nigh distracted. I don't know which way to turn or what to do when she gives up."

"I know it—poor thing!" Dolly answered. She turned to Mostyn. "Wait here. I'll be out before long."

Followed by the anxious father, she went into the cabin. Mostyn sat down at the root of a big beech tree and glanced over the peaceful landscape. How wonderful the scene! he thought. The top of the mountain was lost in the lifting mist along its base and sides. The level growing fields stretched away to the north in a blaze of warming yellow. A boy was leading a harnessed horse along the road; behind him lagged a dog to which the boy was cheerfully whistling and calling. A covey of quails rose from a patch of blackberry vines and fluttered away toward the nearest hillside.

Yes, he was going to turn over a new leaf. Mostyn was quite sure of this. He would take Saunders for his model instead of that crack-brained Delbridge who had the hide of an ox and no refinement of feeling. Yes, yes, and forget—above all, he would forget; that was the thing.

At this moment he saw Dolly crossing the room with the child in her arms. It was only for an instant, and yet he noted the unspeakable tenderness which pervaded her attitude and movement. He was reminded of a picture of a Madonna he had seen in a gallery in New York. The crying of the child had ceased; there was scarcely any sound in the cabin, for Dolly's tread was as light as falling snow.

From the doorway came Tobe Barnett. He approached Mostyn in a most dejected mien.

"This is Mr. Mostyn, ain't it?" he asked. "I heard Tom Drake say they was expectin' you up."

The banker nodded. "How do you think the baby is now?" he asked, considerately.

"Only the Lord could answer that, sir," the man sighed. "I believe it would have died in the night if Miss Dolly hadn't got out o' bed an' come over."

"I was half awake," Mostyn said. "I thought I heard some one calling out at the gate." It was about two o'clock, I think." "That was the fust time, sir. "The second time was just before daybreak. I didn't go for her that time. She come of her own accord—said she jest couldn't git back to sleep. She loves children, Mr. Mostyn, an' she seems to think as much o' Robby as if he was her own. I ketched 'er cryin' last night when she was settin' waitin' in the dark for 'im to git to sleep. La, la, folks brag powerful on Miss Dolly, but they don't know half o' the good she does on the quiet. She tries to keep 'em from findin' out what she does. I know I'm grateful to 'er. If the Lord don't give me a chance to repay 'er for her kindness to me an' mine I'll never be satisfied." The speaker's voice had grown husky, and he now choked up. Silence fell. It was broken by a sweet voice in the cabin humming an old plantation lullaby. There was a thumping of a rockerless chair on the floor. Presently the mother of the child came out. She blinked from the staring blue eyes which she timidly raised to

Mostyn's face. Her dress was a poor drab rag of a thing which hung limply over her thin form. Her hair was tawny and drawn into a tight, unbecoming knot at the back of her head. No collar of any sort hid her sun-browned, bony neck.

"Miss Dolly said please not wait for her," she faltered. "Breakfast at the house will be over. She's done give the child the medicine an' wants to put it to sleep. It will sleep for her, but won't for me or Tobe. We have sent for a doctor, but we don't know whether he will come or not. Doctors can't afford to bother with real pore folks as much out o' the way as this is."

"He won't be likely to come," Barnett sighed. "They are all out for cases whar they kin git ready cash an' plenty of it."

Mostyn turned away. What a wonderful girl Dolly was, he said to himself, as he strode along, his heart beating with strange new elation. He was sure she still liked him. She showed it in her eyes, in her tone of voice. She had not forgotten his last talk with her; she was so young, so impressionable, and, withal, so genuine!

At the front gate he saw John Webb waiting for him. "You'd better hurry," Webb smiled, as he swung the gate open. "The bell's done rung. I seed you an' Dolly walkin' off, an' I was afeared you'd git cold grub. As for her, she don't care when she eats or what is set before her."

CHAPTER VI

It was the following Tuesday. Dolly, with a bundle of books and written exercises under her arm, was returning from school. Close behind her walked George and Ann.

"I'm ashamed of you both," Dolly said, with a frown. "We've got company, and you are both as black as the pot. If I were you I'd certainly stop at the branch and wash the dirt off before getting home."

"That's a good idea," George laughed. "Come on, Sis!" He caught the struggling Ann by the arm and began to drag her toward the stream. "I'll give you a good ducking. Dol' said I could."

Leaving them quarreling, and even exchanging mild blows, Dolly walked on. "They are beyond me—beyond *anybody* except an army of soldiers with guns pointed," she said. "I don't know what Mr. Mostyn thinks of us, I'm sure. People don't live that way in Atlanta—that is, *nice* people don't; but he really doesn't seem to care much. He doesn't seem to notice the mistakes father and mother make, and he lets Uncle John talk by the hour about any trivial thing. I wonder if he really, *really* likes me—as—as much as he seems to. It has been three years since he first hinted at it, and, oh, my! I must have been as gawky and silly as Ann. Still, you never can tell; the heart must have a lot to do with it. I wasn't thinking of looks, or clothes, or the rich man they all said he was, and I guess he wasn't thinking of anything but—" She checked herself; the blood had mounted to her face, and she felt it wildly throbbing in the veins. "Anyway, he seems to like to be with me now even more than he did then. He listens to all I say—doesn't miss a word, and looks at me as if—as if—" Again she checked herself; her plump breast rose high, and a tremulous sigh escaped her lips. "Well," she finished, as she opened the gate and saw her mother in the doorway, "people may say what they like, but I don't believe anybody can love but once in life, either man or woman. God means it that way just as He doesn't let the same sweet flower bloom twice on the same stem."

Mrs. Drake had advanced to the edge of the porch. "Hurry up," she said, eagerly. "Miss Stella Munson is in my room waiting for you. She come at two o'clock and has been here ever since."

"What does she want?" Dolly asked, putting her books down on the upper step of the porch.

"I don't want to tell you till you see it," Mrs. Drake said, smiling mysteriously; "it is by all odds the prettiest thing you ever laid eyes on, an' she says she is willin' to let it go for the bare cost of the material. She is in a sort o' tight for cash."

"A hat?" Dolly inquired, eagerly.

"Something you need worse than a hat," the mother smiled. "It is a dress—an organdie, a regular beauty. She made it for Mary Cobb, and you know Mary always orders the best, but, the poor girl's mother bein' dead, the dress come back on Miss Stella's hands. She could force Mary to stick to her agreement, but she hates to do it when the girl has to put on black and is in so much trouble. Even as it is, you wouldn't have had the chance at it, but you and Mary are exactly of a size, an' there'll be no alterations to make."

"Oh, I want to see it!" Dolly sprang lightly up the steps and hurried into her mother's room on the right of the hall, where a tall, angular, middle-aged spinster sat with her stained and needle-pricked fingers linked in her lap.

"How are you, Miss Stella?" she cried, kissing the thin cheek cordially. "I've already heard about that dress. Winnie Mayfield helped Mary pick out the cloth and trimmings, and she said you would make it the sweetest thing in the valley. Pink is my color. Where is—oh!" She had descried it as it lay on the bed, and with hands clasped in delight, she sprang toward it. "Oh, it is a dream—a dream, Miss Stella! You are an artist."

She picked the flimsy garment up and held it at arm's length. Then she hung it on one of the tall bed-posts and stood back to admire it, uttering little ejaculations of delight. "I know it will fit. I wore one of Mary's dresses to a party one night, and it was exactly right in every way. Oh, oh, what a beauty! You are a wonder. You could get rich in a city." "I think Miss Stella is trying to advertise her work," Mrs. Drake jested. "She knows Mr. Mostyn will see it, and he'd have to talk about it. Town men are close observers of what girls put on—more so, by a long shot, than country men. I wouldn't be surprised if some rich person wrote to you to come down to Atlanta, Miss Stella."

Dolly was dancing about the room like a happy child, now placing herself in one position, then another, in order to view the dress from every possible point of vantage. She even went out into the hall and sauntered back as if to surprise herself by a sudden sight of the treasure.

"Stop your silliness!" her mother laughingly chided her. "You are a regular circus clown or monkey in a cage when you try yourself."

"I just want you to put it on, Dolly," the seamstress said, with elation. "All the time I was at work on it I kept thinking how nice it would look on you. Mary is plain; I reckon there is no harm in saying that, even if her mother *is* dead."

"She will look better in black," said Mrs. Drake, "or pure white. Colors as full of life as this dress has would die dead on a dingy complexion like Mary's, or any of the Cobb women, for that matter. They look for the world as if they lived on coffee and couldn't git it out of their systems. Dolly, shuck off your dress and try it on."

Dolly needed no urging. In her excitement she forgot to correct her mother's speech, which she would have done on any other occasion, and began at once to divest her slender form of her waist and skirt, dropping the latter at her feet and springing lightly out of the circular heap. The seamstress took up the dress carefully and held it in readiness.

"You will be a regular butterfly in it," she said, laughingly. "You are light on your feet as a grasshopper anyway."

While the two women were buttoning and hooking the garment on her Dolly kept up a running fire of amusing comments, arching her beautiful bare neck as she eyed herself in the mirror on the bureau.

"It will come in handy for meeting on the First Sunday," Mrs. Drake remarked. "Folks will have on their best if the weather is fine, an' I don't see no sign o' rain. It will make Ann awful jealous; she is just at the age to think she is as big as anybody, an' don't seem to remember that Dolly makes 'er own money. But Dolly's to blame for that; she spoils Ann constantly by letting her wear things she ought to keep for herself."

"Growing girls are all that way about things to put on," mumbled Miss Munson, the corner of her mouth full of pins. "I know *I* had all sorts o' high an' mighty ideas. I fell in love with a widower old enough to be my grandfather. And I was— stand a little to the right, please. There, that is all right. Quit wiggling. I was such a fool about him, and showed it so plain that it turned the old scamp's head. He actually called to see me one night. Oh, it was exciting! Father took down his shotgun from the rack over the fireplace and ordered him off the place. Then he spanked me—father spanked me good and sound and made me go to bed. You may say what you please, but that sort o' medicine will certainly cure a certain brand o' love. It did more to convince me that I was not grown than anything else had ever done. From that day on I hated the sight of that man. All at once he looked to me as old as Santa Claus. I had a sort of smarting feeling every time I thought of him, and he did look ridiculous that night as he broke an' run across the yard with two of our dogs after him."

"Oh, *isn't* it lovely?" Dolly was now before the looking-glass, bending right and left, stepping back and then forward, fluffing out her rich hair, her cheeks flushed, her eyes gleaming with delight.

"I wish you could just stand off and take a good look at yourself, Dolly," Mrs. Drake cried, enthusiastically. "I simply don't know what to compare you to. Where you got your good looks I can't imagine. But mother used to say that *her* mother in Virginia come of a long line of noted beauties. Our folks away back, Miss Stella, as maybe you know, had fine blood in 'em."

"It certainly crops out in Dolly," Miss Munson declared. "I've heard folks say they took their little ones to school just to get a chance to set and look at her while she was teaching. I know that I, myself, have always—"

"Oh, you both make me sick—you make me talk slang, too," Dolly said, impatiently. "I'm not good-looking—that is, nothing to brag about—but, Miss Stella, this dress would make a scarecrow look like an angel, and it *does* fit. Poor Mary! I hope she won't see it on me. It is hard enough to lose a mother without—"

"Go out on the grass and walk about," Mrs. Drake urged her. "An' let us look at you from the window. I want to see how you look at a distance."

"Do you think I'm crazy?" Dolly demanded, but as merrily as a child playing a game, she lifted the skirt from the floor and lightly tripped away. The watchers saw her go down the porch steps with the majestic grace of a young queen and move along the graveled walk toward the gate. At this point an unexpected thing happened. John Webb and Mostyn had been fishing and were returning in a buggy. The banker got out and came in at the gate just as Dolly, seeing him, was turning to retreat into the house.

"Hold on, do, please!" Mostyn cried out.

Dolly hesitated for a moment, and then, drawing herself erect, she stood and waited for him quite as if there was nothing unusual in what was taking place.

"What have you been doing to yourself?" he cried, his glance bearing down admiringly on her.

"Oh, just trying on a frock," she answered, her face charmingly pink in its warmth, her long lashes betraying a tendency to droop, and her rich round voice quivering. "Those two women in there made me come out here so they could see me. I ought to have had more sense."

"I'm certainly glad they did, since it has given me a chance to see you this way. Why, Dolly, do you know that dress is simply marvelous. I have always thought you were—" Mostyn half hesitated—"beautiful, but this dress makes you—well, it makes you—indescribable."

Avoiding his burning eyes, Dolly frankly explained the situation. "You see it is a sort of windfall," she added. "I've got enough saved up to pay for it as it is, but if it were not a bargain I could never dream of it. Mary's father is well off, and she is the special pet of a rich uncle."

Glancing down the road, she saw the bowed figure of a man approaching, and at once her face became grave. "It is Tobe

Barnett," she said. "I want to ask him about Robby."

Leaving Mostyn, she hastened to the fence, meeting the uplifted and woeful glance of Barnett as he neared her. "Why, Tobe, what is the matter? You look troubled. Robby isn't worse, is he?"

"I declare, I hardly know, Miss Dolly," the gaunt man faltered. "I'm no judge, nor Annie ain't neither. She's plumb lost heart, an' I'm not any better. The doctor come this morning. He said it was a very serious case. He—but I don't want to bother you, Miss Dolly; the Lord above knows you have done too much already."

"Tobe Barnett, listen to me!" Dolly cried. "What are you beating about the bush for? Haven't I got a right to know about that child? I love it. If anything was to happen to that baby it would kill me. Did the doctor say there was no—no hope?"

"It ain't that, exactly, Miss Dolly." Barnett avoided her eyes and gulped, his half-bare, hairy breast quivering with suppressed emotion.

"Well, what is it, then?" Dolly demanded, impatiently.

"Why, if you will know my full shame it is this, Miss Dolly," he blurted out, despondently; he started to cover his face with his gaunt hand, but refrained. "I'm a scab on the face of the world. I've lost the respect and confidence of all men. The doctor left a prescription for several kinds of medicine and a rubber hot-water bag and syringe. I went to the drug store in Darley and the one here in Ridgeville but they wouldn't credit me—they said they couldn't run business on that plan. And I can't blame 'em. I owe 'em too much already."

"Look here, Tobe!" Dolly was leaning over the fence, regardless of the fact that the sleeves of the new dress were against the palings. "How much do those things cost?"

Barnett turned and stared hesitatingly at her. "More than I'd let *you* pay for," he blurted out, doggedly. "Six dollars. When I git so low as to put my yoke on your sweet young neck I—I will kill myself—that's what I'll do. I tell you I've had enough, an' Annie has, too; but we ain't goin' to let you do no more. We had a talk about it last night. We are fairly blistered with shame. You've already give us things that you couldn't afford to give."

Dolly's sweet face grew rigid, the lips of her pretty mouth twitched. "Look here, Tobe," she said, huskily. "You've hurt my feelings. I love you and Annie and Robby, and it is wrong for you to talk this way when I'm so worried about the baby. You are not a cold-blooded murderer, are you? Well, you will make yourself out one if you let silly false pride stand between you and that sweet young life. Why, I would never get over it. It would haunt me night and day. Turn right around and go to the Ridgeville drug store and tell them to charge the things to me. I will pay for them to-morrow. They are anxious for my trade. They are eternally ding-donging at—bothering me, I mean, about not buying from them."

"Miss Dolly, I can't. I just *can't.*"

"If you don't, then *I'll* have to go myself, as soon as I can get out of this fool contraption," she answered, with determination. "You don't want to make me dress and go, I know, but I will if you don't, and I won't lose a minute, either."

"Why, Miss Dolly—"

"Hush, Tobe, don't be a fool!" Dolly was growing angry. She had thrust her hand over her shoulder to the topmost hook of the dress at the neck, that no time should be lost in changing her clothes. "Hurry up, and I'll go straight to Annie. I'll have the hot water ready. I know what the doctor wants. It is the same treatment I helped him give Pete Wilson's baby."

"Lord have mercy!" Tobe Barnett groaned.

"Well, I'll go, Miss Dolly. I'll go. God bless you! I'll go."

She watched him for a moment as he trudged away, and then, still trying in vain to unfasten the hook at the back of her neck and jerking at it impatiently, she turned toward the house.

Mostyn was waiting for her at the porch steps, having put down his game-bag and fishing-rod.

"I declare you are simply stunning in that thing," he said, admiration showing itself in every part of him. "It is a dream!"

She frowned, arching her brows reflectively. She bit her lip.

"Oh, I don't know!" she said. "I was just trying it on to please mother and Miss Stella. Look at the silly things gaping like goggle-eyed perch at the window. One would think that the revolutions of the earth on its axis and the movement of all the planets depended on this scrap of cloth and the vain thing that has it on."

"Take my advice and buy it," Mostyn urged. "It fairly transforms you—makes you look like a creature from another world."

She shrugged her shoulders. She cast a slow glance after the figure trudging along the dusty road. She looked down at her breast and daintily flicked at the pink ribbons which were fluttering in the gentle breeze.

"It is a flimsy thing," he heard her say, as if in self-argument. "It wouldn't stand many wearings before it would look a sight. It wouldn't wash—man as you are, Mr. Mostyn, you know it wouldn't wash. I'm going to take it off and try to have some sense. I'm in no position to try to make a show. School-teachers here in the backwoods have no right to excite comment by the gaudy finery they wear. I'm paid by people's taxes. Did you know that? I might find myself out of a job—out of employment, I mean. Some of these crusty old fellows that believe it is wrong to have an organ in church had just as soon as not enter a complaint against me as being too frivolous to hold a position of trust like mine."

"Oh, I think you are very wrong to allow such an idea as that to influence you," Mostyn argued, warmly. He was about to add more, but Tom Drake sauntered round the corner, chewing tobacco and smiling broadly. He scarcely deigned to notice Dolly's altered appearance.

"John says you didn't git a nibble," he laughed. "I hardly 'lowed you would. The water is too low and clear. I've ketched 'em with my hand under the rocks in such weather as this."

Leaving them together, Dolly went into the house, where she was met by the two eager women.

"I'll bet Mr. Mostyn thought it was nice," Mrs. Drake was saying.

"Well, I certainly hope so," Miss Munson answered. "They say Atlanta men in his set are powerful good judges of women's wear."

Dolly had advanced straight to the mirror and stood looking at her reflection, a quizzical expression on her face.

"Hurry, unhook me!" she ordered, sharply. "Quick! I've got to run over to Barnett's cabin. Robby isn't any better. In fact, he is dangerous and Annie needs me."

The two women, eying each other inquiringly, edged up close to her, one on either side. "Dolly, what is the matter? I knew something was wrong the minute you come in the door."

"It is all right," Dolly said, in a low tone. "It is very sweet and pretty, Miss Stella, but I have decided not to—not to take it." "Not take it!" The words came from two pairs of lips simultaneously. "Not take it!" The miracle happened again, in tones of double bewilderment.

"Well, I can't say I really expected you to," Miss Munson retorted, in frigid tones. "I only stopped by. To tell you the truth, I am on the way over to Peterkins'. Sally is the right size and will jump at it."

Dolly's lips were tight. Her eyes held a light, half of anger, half of an odd sort of doggedness.

"Please unhook me!" she said, coldly. "There is no time to lose. Annie is out of her head with trouble."

"Well, well, well!" Mrs. Drake sank into a chair and folded her slender hands with a vigorous slap of the palms. "Nobody under high heavens can ever tell what you will do or what you won't do," she wailed. "I never wanted anything for myself as much as for you to have that dress, and—" Her voice ended in a sigh of impatience.

With rapid, angry fingers the seamstress was disrobing the slender form roughly, jerking hooks, ribbons, and bits of lace. "Huh, huh!" she kept sniffing, as she filled her mouth with pins. "I might as well not have stopped, but it don't matter; it don't make a bit o' difference. You couldn't have it now if you offered me double the cost."

Dolly seemed oblivious of what was passing. Getting out of the garment, she quickly put on her skirt and waist, noting as she did so that her father was seated behind her on the window-sill, nursing his knee and chewing and spitting vigorously on the porch floor.

"What a bunch o' rowin' she-cats!" she heard him chuckling. "An' about nothin' more important than a flimsy rag that looks like a hollyhock bush with arms an' legs."

Without noticing him Dolly hurriedly finished buttoning her waist, and, throwing on her sun-bonnet, she dashed out of the room.

"I don't blame you for losin' patience, Miss Stella," Mrs. Drake sighed, "but I've thought it out. It is as plain as the nose on your face. You know an' I know she was tickled to death with it till she met Mr. Mostyn in the yard just now. Mark my words, he said something to her about the style of it. Maybe it's not exactly the latest wrinkle accordin' to town notions."

"Yes, that's it." Miss Munson paused in her flurried efforts to restore the dress to its wrapper. The twine hung from her teeth as she stood glaring. "Yes, *he's* at the bottom of it. As if a man of *his* stripe an' character would be a judge. I have heard a few items about him if you all haven't. Folks talk about 'im scand'lous in Atlanta. They say he leads a fast life down there. You'd better keep Dolly away from 'im. He won't do. He has robbed good men an' women of their money in his shady deals, an' folks tell all sorts o' tales about 'im."

"Thar you go ag'in," Tom Drake broke in, with a hearty laugh. "First one thing an' then another. You would swear a man's life away one minute an' hug it back into 'im the next. Now, I kin prove what I say, an' you both ought to be ashamed. Mostyn not only told Dolly that dress was the purtiest thing he ever seed, but he told me to come in here an' make 'er take it."

The twine fell from the spinster's mouth. She eyed Mrs. Drake steadily. Mrs. Drake rose slowly to her feet. She went to the dressmaker and touched her tragically on the arm. She said something in too low a voice for her husband to catch it.

"Do you think that's it?" Miss Munson asked, a womanly blaze in her eyes.

"Yes, I saw her talkin' to Tobe at the fence," Mrs. Drake said, tremulously. "He turned square around and went back to town. Then you remember Dolly wanted to hurry over there. Miss Stella, she is my own daughter, an' maybe I oughtn't to say it, bein' 'er mother, but she's got the biggest, tenderest heart in her little body that ever the Lord planted in human form." Miss Munson stood with filling eyes for a silent moment, then she tossed the dress, paper, and twine on the bed.

"I'm goin' to leave it here," she faltered. "She can pay me for it if she wants to, in one year, two years, or ten—it don't make no odds to me. She needn't pay for it at all if she doesn't want to. I never want to see it on anybody else. She is a good girl—a regular angel of light."

Therewith the two women fell into each other's arms and began to cry.

A sniff of amusement came from Tom Drake. "Fust it was tittle-tattle, then a bar-room knock-down-and-drag-out fight, an' now it is a weepin' camp-meetin'. I wonder what will happen when the wind changes next."

CHAPTER VII

It was a warm, sultry evening in the middle of the week. They had just finished supper at the farmhouse. Dolly, with a book, a manuscript, and a pencil, stood in a thoughtful attitude under a tree on the lawn. She was joined by her uncle, his freckled face beaming with a desire to tease her.

"What time do you all begin your meetin' to-night?" he inquired, introductively.

"Eight o'clock," she said, absently, her gaze bent anxiously on the figures of two men leaning over the barn-yard fence in the thickening shadows. "Who is that father is talking to, Uncle John?" she asked, with a frown.

"It's Gid Sebastian," Webb said. "I saw 'im back on the mountain road lookin' for your pa as I come home."

"That's who it is," Dolly said, dejectedly, a soft sigh escaping her lips. The man had changed his position, and even in the twilight the broad-brimmed hat, sinister features, and dark sweeping mustache were observable. "Uncle John, you know Gid is a moonshiner, don't you?" "Folks says he is," Webb smiled. "An' fellers that like good corn mountain-dew ought to know who makes it. I reckon Gid is about the only moonshiner that has escaped jail up to date. Somehow he knows how to cover his tracks an' let his men git caught an' take the punishment."

Dolly held her pencil to her lips, and, still frowning, looked at the blank manuscript paper. "Uncle John," she faltered, "I want you to—to tell me what he comes to see father so often about?"

Webb's face waxed a trifle more serious. "I don't know—never give it much thought," he said. "I don't know but what your pa once in a while sells Gid some corn to help out his still in a pinch when the authorities are watchin' his movements too close for comfort. I've seed the pile in our crib sink powerful in a single night. You remember the time your ma thought some niggers had broke in an' stole a lot that was shelled? Well, I noticed that your pa kicked powerful agin sendin' for the sheriff an' his dogs, an' you know in reason that he would if he had laid it to the darkies."

Dolly exhaled a deep breath. "Uncle John, I'm awful afraid—I never was so worried in my life. I'm afraid father is actually mixed up with Sebastian's gang, or is about to be."

"Do you think so?" Webb stared seriously. "That would be bad, wouldn't it—that is, if the officers ketched 'im an' had enough proof agin 'im to put 'im in limbo."

Dolly's eyes flashed, her breast rose high and fell tremblingly; she grasped her pencil tightly and held it poised like a dagger.

"Uncle John, I've been through a lot; I've stood, a great deal, kept patience and hope; but if my own father were actually arrested and put in prison I'd give up—I'd quit, I tell you. I'd never try to raise my head again. Here I am trying to put high manly ideas into George's head, but if the boy's father is a lawbreaker all I do will be thrown away. I want to see Ann grow up and marry well, but what decent man would care to tie himself to a family of jail birds? Hush! There comes Mr. Mostyn. You are always joking, but for goodness' sake don't mention this. If it is true we must keep our shame to ourselves."

"I've got *some* sense left," Webb said, quite earnestly. "It ain't a thing to joke about, I'm here to state. Men, as a rule, say it ain't no lastin' disgrace to be jerked up for distillin' here amongst the pore folks the Union army trampled under heel and robbed of their all, but it ain't no fun to stand up before that United States judge an' git a sentence. I was a witness in Atlanta once, an' I know what moonshiners go through. Your pa ain't to say actually loaded down with caution, an' he's just the easy-goin' reckless sort that Sebastian makes cats'-paws of."

"'Sh!" said Dolly, for Mostyn was quite near He was smoking an after-supper cigar.

"Got the mate to that?" Webb asked easily. "I don't like to see fine tobacco-smoke floatin' about in hot weather unless I'm helpin' to make it."

Mostyn gave him a cigar. "What is this I hear Of your club-meeting to-night?" he asked, smiling at Dolly.

"It is an impromptu affair," she answered, almost reluctantly. Then she began to smile, and her color rose. "The truth is, the whole thing started as a joke on me. I could have backed down if I had wished, but I didn't, and now it is too late."

"You'll think it's too late"—Webb was drawing at his cigar, which he held against the fire of Mostyn's—"when them fellers git through arguin', an' you the only one on your side!"

"How is that?" Mostyn asked, wonderingly.

Dolly averted her eyes. "Why," she explained, "for a long time the club has threatened to select some subject to be discussed only between Warren Wilks and myself. I didn't think much about it at the time and said it would suit me, thinking, of course, that it would only be heard by a few club-members, but now what do you think they have done?"

"I can't imagine," Mostyn answered, heartily enjoying her

gravity of tone and manner.

"Why, they are not only holding me to my agreement, but they have selected a topic for discussion which of all subjects under the sun is completely beyond me. They are doing it for a joke, and they expect me to acknowledge defeat. I've been at the point all day of ignoring the whole business, and yet somehow it nearly kills me to give in. I laugh when I think about it, for the joke is on me, sure enough."

"But the subject," Mostyn urged her, "what is it?"

"Have women the right to vote?'" dropped from the girl's smiling lips.

"Oh, great! great!" the banker laughed. "I hope you are not going to let a few silly men back you down."

"I don't really see how I am going to escape going through with it," Dolly said. "They have sent notices all up and down the valley, and the house will be full. Look! there goes a wagon-load now. Two things are bothering me. I came out here to try to write down a few points, but not one idea has come in my head. That's the first stumbling-block, and the other is even more serious. You see, up to this time my side has generally won because when it was left to the audience the women all stood up and voted for me. I've seen them so anxious to help me out that they would force their children to stand on the benches so their heads would be counted."

"But aren't the women going to-night?" Mostyn inquired.

"More than ever got inside *that* house," Dolly said, despondently, "but, as much as they like me and think I know what I'm talking about as a general rule, they won't be on my side of *this* argument. They think woman's suffrage originated in the bad place. They will think I'm plumb crazy, but I can't help it. I understand that a lawyer doesn't have actually to believe in his side of a question—he simply makes as big a display of the evidence as he can muster up. Warren Wilks and the other men are tickled to death over the fun they are going to have with me to-night."

"I wouldn't miss it for any amount of money," Mostyn said, winking at the contented smoker on his right.

"I wouldn't, nuther," Webb chuckled. "Warren Wilks is a funny duck on the platform, an' he don't let a chance slip to git a joke on Dolly. She has downed him several times, but I reckon he'll swat 'er good an' heavy to-night."

"Well, I'll certainly have nothing to say if I stand here listening to you two," Dolly said, with a smile. "I'm going to my room to try to think up something. I'm awfully tired, anyway. I was at Barnett's till twelve o'clock last night."

"How is Robby?" Mostyn asked.

"He is out of danger," Dolly answered, as she turned away. "The doctor told me to-day that the child had had a narrow escape. A week ago he gave him up, and was surprised when he saw him doing so well yesterday."

Will N. Harben

CHAPTER VIII

Half an hour later the little cast-iron bell in the steeple of the meeting-house rang. Tom Drake and his wife and John Webb left the farmhouse, and, joining some people from the village, sauntered down the road. Tom was in his shirt-sleeves, for the evening was warm, but Mrs. Drake wore her best black dress with a bright piece of ribbon at the neck, a scarf over her head. Webb carried his coat on his arm and was cooling himself with a palm-leaf fan.

Mostyn was on the lawn watching for Dolly to appear, and was glad that the trio had left her to his care. They were out of sight when Dolly came out of the house, a piece of writing-paper in her hand. Mostyn met her at the gate and opened it for her.

"Well, what luck have you had with your speech?" he asked, as they passed out.

"'What luck,' I say!" She shrugged her shoulders and smiled despondently. "The harder I thought, the fewer ideas seemed to come my way. I give you my word, Mr. Mostyn, I haven't a ghost of an argument. I don't want to vote myself, you see, and I don't see how I am going to make other women want to. Just at present I have so many matters to bother about that I can't throw myself into an imaginary position. I'd break down and cry—I feel exactly like it—if I hadn't been this way before and managed to pull through by the skin of my teeth. You see, standing up before a crowd makes you feel so desperate and hemmed-in-like that you have to fight, and somehow you manage to say something with more or less point to it. If I don't think of something between here and the meeting-house—don't talk, please! I'm awfully nervous. I feel for the world as if I'm going to laugh and cry myself into hysterics. If Warren Wilks were to see me now he'd have the biggest argument for his side he could rake up. If I was running for office and the returns went against me I suppose I'd lie flat down in the road and kick like a spoilt child."

At this moment a buggy containing two women and a man passed. One of the women, a fat motherly creature, glanced back. "Is that you, Dolly?" she asked.

"Yes; how are you, Mrs. Timmons?"

"I'm as well as common, thanky, Dolly. Drive slower, Joe. What's the use o' hurryin'? They can't do a thing till *she* gits thar; besides, I want to git at the straight o' this business. Say, Dolly, it ain't true, is it, that you intend to stand up for women goin' to the polls?"

Dolly swept Mostyn's expectant face with a startled look and then fixed her eyes on the speaker.

"It is this way, Mrs. Timmons," she began, falteringly. "Warren Wilks suggested the subject, and—"

"That ain't what I axed you," the woman retorted, sharply. "Pull in that hoss, Joe, or I'll git out an' walk the balance o' the way afoot. That ain't what I axed you, Dolly Drake. I want to know now an' here if you are goin' to teach my gals an' other folks' gals a lot o' stuff that was got up by bold-faced Yankee women with no more housework to do, or children to raise, than they have up thar these days. I want to know, I say, for if you are I'll keep my young uns at home. I've always had the highest respect for you, an' I've cheered an' stomped my feet every time you made a speech at the schoolhouse, but if speechmakin' is goin' to make you put on pants an'—"

"Git up!" The driver was whipping his horse. "Don't pay no attention to 'er, Miss Dolly," he called back over his shoulder. "She's been jowerin' ever since she stepped out o' bed this mornin'. If she had a chance to vote she'd stuff the ballot-box with rotten eggs if the 'lection didn't go her way."

"You see that?" Dolly sighed, as the buggy vanished in the gloom. "This fool thing may cost me my job. Warren Wilks ought to be ashamed to get up a joke like this."

"Why don't you throw it over and be done with it?" Mostyn asked, sympathetically.

"Because I'm like the woman you just heard talking," Dolly returned. "I'd rather drop dead in my tracks here in this sand than to have those devilish boys beat me. For the Lord's sake, tell me something to say."

"I'm not daft about voting *myself*," Mostyn laughed, "and to save my life I can't be enthusiastic about *women* doing it."

"I wish we could walk through the woods the rest of the way," the girl said. "We'll meet another spitfire in a minute, and then I *will* lose patience."

They were soon in sight of the four lighted windows of the schoolhouse. "Packed like sardines," Dolly muttered. "Who knows? They may mob me. I don't care—those men pushed this thing on me against my will, and I'm going to fight. Do you know when I'm bothered like this I can actually feel the roots of my hair wiggling as if it were trying to stand up, like the bristles on a pig. The women in this neighborhood have been my best friends till now, and if I can't think of some way to stir up their sympathy I shall be down and out."

Mostyn looked at her admiringly. She was so beautiful, so appealing in her youth and brave helplessness. Being what she already was, what would not opportunity, travel, higher environment bring to her? She was a diamond in the rough.

His heart beat wildly. Lucky chance had thrown her in his way. He might win her love, if she did not already care for him. As his wife he could gratify her every desire, and yet—and yet—The situation had its disagreeable side. How could he think of becoming the son-in-law of a man like Tom Drake? What would old Mitchell say? What would his fashionable sister and his entire social set think? Yes, Dolly was all that could be desired, but she was not alone in the world, and she was absolutely true to her family. Mostyn here felt a touch of shame, and shame was a thing he had scarcely been conscious of in his questionable career. That was one of the advantages which had come of his contact with this mountain paragon of womanhood. In his unbounded respect for her he was losing respect for himself. In the presence of her courage he saw himself more and more as the coward that he was. He was beginning to long for her as he had really never longed for any other woman. He wanted to clasp her in his arms and then and there declare his fidelity to her forever.

"Hurry up, we are late!" Dolly warned him, and she quickened her step. They were now among the horses and various kinds of vehicles in front of the meeting-house. A fire of pine-knots near the doorway cast a weird reddish glow over the scene.

"Come right on up to the front with me," Dolly said. "There will be a vacant seat or two near the platform. Say, if you laugh at me while I am speaking—that is, if I *do* speak—I'll never forgive you—never!"

There was no chance for a reply. She was already leading him into the crowded room. Every bench was full, and men and boys sat even on the sills of the open windows. Seeing Dolly entering, somebody started applause and hands were clapped, whistling and cat-calls rang through the room, no part of which disturbed the girl in the least as she calmly walked ahead of her escort finding seats for them on the front bench.

Eight young men, all neatly dressed, sat in chairs on the platform, and they smiled and bowed to Dolly.

"That's Warren Wilks at my desk," she whispered to Mostyn. "He is grinning clear down the back of his neck. Oh, I'd give anything to get even with him."

Mostyn took the man in with a sweeping glance. He was nice-looking, about twenty-five years of age, tall and slender, and had a clean-shaven intellectual face which was now full of suppressed merriment. He rose with considerable ease and dignity and called the house to order by rapping sharply on Dolly's desk with the brass top of an inkstand. He announced the subject which was to be debated with great gravity, adding with a smile that, of course, it was only through special favor to the only lady member of the club that such a topic had been selected. But—and he smiled down on his amused colleagues—that lady member had lately shown such strong tendencies toward the new-woman movement that, one and all, the members hoped that she might be convinced of the fallacy of her really deplorable position.

"Scamp!" Mostyn heard Dolly exclaim, and, glancing at her profile, he saw a half-smiling expression on her flushed face. "That is the way he always talks," she whispered in the banker's ear. "His great forte is making fun."

Wilks's speech consumed half an hour, during the whole of which Mostyn noticed that Dolly sat as if in restless thought, now and then hastily penciling a few words on a scrap of paper in her hand. At the conclusion of Wilks's speech there was great applause, during which Dolly looked about the room, seeing the hands of all the women as active as the wings of humming-birds hovering over flowers.

"Just look at the silly things!" she sniffed, as she caught Mostyn's eye. "They are voting against me already. They are as changeable as March winds. Look at Mrs. Timmons; she is actually shaking her fist at me. When I speak I always keep my eye on somebody in the crowd. I'll watch that woman to-night, and if I can win her over I may influence some of the rest."

CHAPTER IX

Therewith Dolly rose and went to the platform. Silence fell on the room as she made a pretty, hesitating bow. To Mostyn she was a marvel of beauty, animation, and reserved force as she stood lightly brushing back her flowing hair.

"I'm going to tell you all the plain truth," she began. "You don't know the facts in this case. The able-bodied men behind me, all rigged out in their best togs for this occasion, simply got tired of having the side I was on win so many times, and they put their heads together to change it. They decided, in their sneaking, menlike way, that I won because the women usually voted on my side, so they asked me one day if I'd let them pick a theme; and, being too busy doing my work to suspect trickery, I consented; and then what did they do? Why, they promptly threw the defense of this—I started to say silly question on my shoulders, but I won't call it silly, because, do you know, as I sat there listening to Warren Wilks reel off all that harangue it occurred to me that he was employing exactly the same threadbare method of browbeating women that has been the style with *men* ever since the world began to roll. Now, listen—you women that blistered your hands clapping just now—how are you ever going to get at the straight of this thing if you hug and kiss the men every time they tell you that you are narrow between the eyes and haven't a thimbleful of brains? Do you know what is at the bottom of it all? Why, nothing but old-fashioned, green-eyed jealousy, as rank as stagnant water in a swamp. The men don't *want* you to get up-to-date. Up-to-date women don't hop out of bed on a cold, frosty morning and make a blazing fire for their lords and masters to dress by. Up-to-date women are not willing to stand shoe-mouth deep in mud in a cow-lot milching a cow and holding off a calf while their husbands are swapping tales at the cross-roads store."

A laugh started and swept over the room. There was considerable applause, both from the men and the women.

"Well, that's one thing I wouldn't do for narry man that ever wore shoe-leather!" came from Mrs. Timmons, who seemed to think that Dolly's fixed glance in her direction called for an open opinion.

Dolly smiled and nodded. "That is the right spirit, Mrs. Timmons," she said. "So many robust men wouldn't have skinny-looking, consumptive wives if they would draw the line at the cow-lot." Then she resumed her speech:

"The masculine opinion that women haven't got much sense originated away back in the history of the world. *We* get it from the savages. I'll tell you a tale. Among the Indians in the early days there was a certain big chief. They called him Frog-in-the-face because his nose looked like a toad upside down trying to crawl between his thick lips. He and the other braves loafed about the wigwams in disagreeable weather, and on fine days went hunting. Now, Frog-in-the-face, savage as he was, was a quite up-to-date man. He would please the women in this audience mightily, and the men would elect him to office. He didn't believe squaws had enough sense to shoot straight or catch fish on the bank of a river, so he made his wife cook the grub, clean up the wigwam, and with a wiggling papoose strapped to her back hoe corn in the hot sun. This was the regular red-man custom, but one day a meddlesome squaw began to think for herself. She called some other squaws together while Frog-in-the-face and his braves were off hunting, and she had the boldness to tell them that she believed they could shoot as well as the men. She said she could, because she had tried it on the sly. With that they got out some old worn-out bows and arrows and went into the woods to try their luck. Well, do you know, those squaws killed so many bears and deer and ducks and turkeys that, loaded down with a baby each, they had hard work getting the meat home, but somehow they did. Well, as luck would have it, Frog-in-the-face and his sharp-shooters had got hold of some fire-water and smoking-tobacco, and they didn't do any hunting that day at all, but came back hungry and tired out over a big pow-wow they had had about another tribe infringing on their rights away off somewhere. Then the women brought out the roast meat, owned up like nice little squaws, and expected to get some petting and praise, for they had done well and knew it. But, bless you! what happened? The more the braves gorged themselves on the turkey and duck, the madder they got, and after supper they all met out in the open and began to fret and fume. They sat down in a ring and passed a pipe from one to another, and Frog-in-the-face laid down the law. Squaws were having too much liberty. If they were allowed to go hunting it wouldn't be long before they would want to take part in the councils of war, and then what would become of the papooses? Who would grind the corn and till the soil and do all the rest of the dirty work? So they passed a new law. The first squaw that ever touched a bow and arrow in the future would be severely punished."

As Dolly paused at this point there was great laughter among both men and women. Even Mrs. Timmons was clapping her hands.

"Warren Wilks," Dolly resumed, with a pleased smile, "drew a funny picture just now of an election under the new idea. You all laughed heartily when he spoke of there being so many fine hats and waving plumes and women with low-necked dresses and open-work stockings about the polls that bashful men would be afraid to vote. But, mind you, Warren Wilks was making all *that* up. Listen to me, and I'll tell you what one of your elections really looks like. I've seen one, and that was enough for me. At the precinct of Ridgeville, where only two hundred votes have ever been polled, there were at the last county election fully a hundred drunk from morning to night, including the candidates. They had ten fights that day; three men were cut and two shot. The price of a vote was a drink of whisky, but a voter seldom closed a trade till he had ten in him, and then the candidate who was sober enough to carry him to the box on his back got the vote." [Laughter, long and loud.]

"Go it, Miss Dolly! You've got 'em on the run!" Farmer Timmons cried. "Swat 'em good an' hard! They started it!"

"That's the way men conduct their elections," Dolly went on, smilingly. "But the women of the present day wouldn't stand it. They would change it right away. They wouldn't continue giving the men an excuse two or three times a year to engage in all that carnage and debauchery for no rational reason. Do you know the sort of election the women will hold, Warren, if they ever get a chance?"

"I'm afraid I don't," Wilks answered, dryly. "It would be hard to imagine."

"Well, I'll tell you," Dolly said to the audience. "They will do away with all that foolishness I've been talking about. That day at Ridgeville a dozen carriages were hired at a big expense to bring voters to the polls. Hundreds of dollars were spent on whisky, doctors' bills, lawyers' fees, and fines at court. But sensible women will wipe all that out. On election day in the future a trustworthy man will ride from house to house on a horse or mule with the ballot-box in his lap. It will be brought to the farmhouse door. The busy wife will leave her churning, or sweeping, or sewing for a minute. She will scribble her name on a ticket and drop it in the slit while she asks the man how his family is. She may offer him a cup of hot coffee or a snack to eat. She will go to the back door and call her husband or sons in from the field to do their voting, and then the polls of that election will be closed as far as she is concerned."

"Good, good, fine, fine!" Timmons shouted. "That's

the racket!"

"But," Dolly went on, sweeping the faces of the masculine row beside her and turning to the audience, "this stalwart bunch of Nature's noblemen here on the platform will tell you that women haven't got sense enough to vote. That's it, Mrs. Timmons, they think at the bottom of their hearts that women have skulls as thick as a pine board. They don't know this: they don't know that some of the most advanced thinkers in the world are now claiming that intuition is the greatest faculty given to the human race and that woman has the biggest share of it. Oh no, women oughtn't to be allowed to take part in any important public issue! Away back in France, some centuries ago, a simple, uneducated country-girl, seventeen years of age —Joan of Arc—noticed that the men of the period were not properly managing the military affairs of her country, and she took the matter under consideration. She stepped in among great generals and diplomats and convinced them that she knew more about what to do than all the men in the realm. The King listened to her, gave her power to act, and she rode at the head of thousands of soldiers to victory first and a fiery death later. Now, Warren Wilks will tell you that a woman of that sort ought never be allowed to do a thing but rock a cradle, scrub a floor, or look pretty, according to her husband's disposition or pocket-book.

"Then, after all, did you all know—while you are talking so much about the harm of a woman voting—that if it hadn't been for a woman there wouldn't have been a single vote cast in all these United States? In fact, you wouldn't be sitting here now but for that woman. Away back (as I was teaching my history class the other day) Columbus tramped all over the then civilized land trying to get aid to make his trial voyage, and nobody would listen to him. He was taunted and jeered at everywhere he went. Men every bit as sensible as we have to-day said he was plumb crazy. He was out of heart and ready to give up as he rode away from the court of Spain on a mule, when Isabella called him back and furnished the money out of her own pocket to buy and man his ships. Folks, that is the

Will N. Harben

kind of brain Warren Wilks and his crowd will tell you ought to be kept at the cook-stove and the wash-tub. Oh, women will be given the vote in time, don't you bother!" Dolly said, with renewed conviction. "We can't have progress without change. I never thought about it myself before, but it is as plain as the nose on your face. It has to come because it is simple justice. A law which is unfair to one single person is not a perfect law, and many a woman has found herself in a position where only her vote would save her from disaster. Women are purer by nature than men, and they will purify politics. That's all I'm going to say to-night. Now, I'm not managing this debate, but it is getting late and I want everybody that feels like it to vote on my side. Stand up now. All in favor, rise to your feet. That's right, Mrs. Timmons—I knew you would wake up. Now, everybody! That's the way!" Dolly was waving her hands like an earnest evangelist, while Wilks, with a look of astonishment, was struggling to his feet to offer some sort of protest.

"Don't pay attention to him!" Dolly cried. "Vote now and be done with it!"

The house was in a turmoil of amused excitement. Timmons stood by his wife's side waving his hat and slapping his thigh.

"Stand up, boys—every man-jack of you!" he yelled. "Them fellers got this thing up agin that gal. Give it to 'em good an' sound."

The entire audience was on its feet laughing and applauding. Dolly stood waving her hands with the delight of a happy child. She turned to the teachers behind her, and one by one she gradually enticed them to their feet.

"That makes it unanimous," she said, and, flushed and panting, she tripped down the steps to the floor.

Mostyn edged his way through the chattering throng toward her. He was beside himself with enthusiasm. A lump of tense emotion filled his throat; he would have shouted but for the desire not to appear conspicuous.

"Wonderful, wonderful!" he said, when he finally reached her, and caught her hand and shook it.

"Do you think so?" she said, absent-mindedly; and he noticed that she was staring anxiously toward the door.

"Why, you beat them to a finish!" he cried. "You fairly wiped up the ground with them."

"Oh, I don't know!" she said, excitedly. "Come on, please. I want to—to get out."

Wondering what could be in her mind, he followed her as well as he could through the jostling throng. Women and men extended their hands eagerly; but she hurried on, scarcely hearing their congratulations and good-natured jests. At the door she reached back, caught Mostyn's hand, and drew him out into the open. A few paces away stood a couple under a tree. And toward them Dolly hastened, now holding to the arm of her companion. Then he recognized Ann and saw that she was with a tall, ungainly young man of eighteen or twenty. The two stood quite close together.

"Ann," Dolly said, sharply, pausing a few feet from the pair, "come here, I want to see you."

Doffing his straw hat, the young man moved away, and Ann slowly and doggedly approached her sister.

"What do you want, Dolly?"

"I want you to walk straight home!" Dolly retorted. "I'll talk to you there, not here."

"I wasn't doing anything," Ann began; but Dolly raised her hand.

"Go on home, I tell you. I'm ashamed of you—actually ashamed to call you sister."

Without a word Ann turned and walked homeward.

"You certainly got the best of those fellows," Mostyn chuckled, still under the heat of her triumph. "I never was so surprised in my life. It was funny to watch their faces."

"I couldn't do myself justice," Dolly answered. "I don't know how it sounded, I'm sure. I know I never can do my best when I have anything on my mind to bother me. I'll tell you about it. You saw that fellow with Ann just now? Well, it was Abe Westbrook, one of the worst young daredevils in the valley. He belongs to a low family, and he hasn't a speck of honor. For the last two months he has been trying to turn Ann's head. I stopped him from coming to our house, but as soon as I stepped on the platform to-night I saw him and her on the back seat. He was whispering to her all the time, bending over her in the most familiar way. Once I saw him actually brush her hair back from her shoulder and pinch her ear. Oh, I was crazy! If I said anything to the point in my speech it is a wonder, for I could hardly think of anything but Ann's disgraceful conduct."

They were now entering a shaded part of the road. Ann was almost out of sight and walking rapidly homeward. There was no one close behind Mostyn and Dolly. A full moon shone overhead, and its beams filtered through the foliage of the trees. He felt the light and yet trusting touch of her hand on his arm. A warm, triumphant sense of ownership filled him. How beautiful, how pure, how brave and brilliant she was! What man of his acquaintance could claim such a bride as she would make? A few months in his social set and she would easily lead them all. She was simply a genius, and a beautiful one at that. He had a temptation to clasp her hand, draw her to him, and kiss her as he had kissed her three years before. Yet he refrained. He told himself that, soiled by conventional vice as he was soiled, he would force himself to respect in the highest this wonderful charge upon his awakened sense of honor. He found something new and assuring in checking the passion that filled him like a flood at its height. Yes, she should be his wife; no other living man should have her. Fate had rescued him in the nick of time from the temptation to wed for ulterior motives. Another month in Atlanta and he would have lost his chance at ideal happiness. Yes, this was different! Irene Mitchell, spoiled pet of society that she was, could never love him as this strong child of Nature would, and without love life would indeed be a failure. He walked slowly. She seemed in no hurry to reach home. Once she raised her glorious eyes to his, and he felt her hand quiver as she shrank from his ardent gaze. Another moment, and he would have declared himself, but, glancing ahead, he saw that her father and mother and John Webb had paused and were looking toward them.

"I can wait," Mostyn said to himself, with fervor. "She is mine—she is mine."

CHAPTER X

The next morning after breakfast John Webb met Mostyn as he stood smoking on the front porch.

"If you haven't got nothin' better to do," he said, "you might walk down with me to Dolph Wartrace's store, at the cross-roads. Thar will be a crowd thar to-day."

"Anything special going on?" Mostyn asked.

"If the feller keeps his appointment we'll have a sermon," John smiled. "For the last seven or eight years a queer tramp of a chap—John Leach, he calls hisself—has been comin' along an' preachin' at the store. Nobody knows whar he is from. Folks say he makes his rounds all through the mountains of Tennessee, Georgia, an' North Carolina. He won't take a cent o' pay, never passes the hat around, an' has been knowed to stop along the road an' work for poor farmers for a week on a stretch for nothin' but his bed an' board. Some say he's crazy, an' some say he's got more real Simon-pure religion than any regular ordained minister. I love to listen to 'im. He tells a lot o' tales an' makes a body laugh an' feel sad at the same time."

"I certainly would like to hear him," the banker declared, and with Webb he turned toward the gate.

"Are you a member of any church?" he inquired, when they were in the road.

"No, I never jined one," Webb drawled out. "I'm the only feller I know of in this country that don't affiliate with *some* denomination or other."

"That is rather odd," Mostyn remarked, tentatively. "How did you manage to stay out of the fold among so many religious people?"

"I don't exactly know." Webb's freckled face held a reflective look. "I kept puttin' it off from year to year, thinkin' I would jine, especially as everybody was constantly naggin me about it. Seems to me that I was the chief subject at every revival they held. It bothered me considerable, I tell you. The old folks talked so much about my case that little boys an' gals would sluff away from me in the public road. But I wasn't to blame. The truth is, Mr. Mostyn, I wanted to give 'em all— Methodists, Baptists, and Presbyterians—a fair show. You see, each denomination declared that it had the only real correct plan, an' I'll swear I liked one as well as t'other. When I'd make up my mind to tie to the Methodists, some Baptist or Presbyterian would ax me what I had agin *his* religion, an' in all the stew an' muddle they got me so balled up that I begun to be afeard I wasn't worth savin' nohow. About that time this same tramp preacher come along, an' I heard 'im talk. I listened close, but I couldn't make out whether he stood for sprinklin', pourin', or sousin' clean under. So after he finished I went up an' axed 'im about it. I never shall forget how the feller grinned—I reckon I remember it because it made me feel better. He ketched hold o' my hand, he did, an' while he was rubbin' it good an' kind-like, he said: 'Brother, don't let that bother you. I'm floatin' on top myself. In fact, my aim is to stay out o' the jangle so I kin jine all factions together in brotherly bonds.' As he put it, the light o' God was shinin' on every earthly path that had any sort o' upward slope to it."

At this moment there was a vigorous blowing of the horn of an automobile in the road behind them, and in a cloud of dust a gleaming new car bore down toward them. To the banker's surprise, Webb paused in the center of the road and made no effort to move.

"Look out!" Mostyn cried, warningly. "Here, quick!"

"Humph!" Webb grunted, still refusing to move, his eyes flashing sullenly. "I'm goin' to pick up a rock some o' these days an' knock one o' them fellers off his perch."

Still immovable he stood while the honking car, with brakes on, slid to a stop a few feet away.

"What the hell's the matter with you?" the man at the wheel, in a jaunty cap and goggles, cried out, angrily. "You heard me blowin', didn't you?"

"I ain't deef," John flashed at him. "I wanted to see what *the hell'*—to use your words—you'd do about it. You think because you are in a rig o' that sort, Pete Allen, you can make men an' women break the'r necks to git out o' your way. If you had touched me with that thing I'd have stomped the life out o' you. I know you. You used to split rails an' hoe an' plow, barefooted over in Dogwood. 'White trash,' the niggers called your folks. You've been in town just long enough to make you think you can trample folks down like so many tumble-bugs."

"Well, you have no right to block the road up," the driver said, quite taken aback, his color mounting to his cheeks. "There is a law—"

"I don't care a dang about your law!" Webb broke in. "I'm law-abidin', but when a law is passed givin' an upstart like you the right to make a decent man jump out of your way, like a frost-bitten grasshopper, I'll break it. The minute a skunk like you buys a machine on credit an' starts out he thinks he owns the earth."

Still flushed, the man grumbled out something inarticulately and started on his way.

"I hit 'im purty hard," John said, as Mostyn rejoined him, "but if thar is anything on earth that makes me rippin' mad it is the way fellers like that look an' act."

They found thirty or forty men, women, and children at the store awaiting the coming of the preacher. The building was a long, one-story frame structure made of undressed planks whitewashed. It had a porch in front which was filled with barrels, chicken-coops, and heavy agricultural implements. The people were seated in the shade of the trees, some on the grass and others in their own road-wagons.

Wartrace, the storekeeper, in his shirt-sleeves, stood in the front door. He was about thirty years of age and had only one arm. "Come up, come up, Mr. Mostyn," he called out, cheerily. "The preacher is headed this way. A feller passed 'im on the mountain road ten minutes ago. If you hain't heard John Leach talk you've missed a treat."

Mostyn accepted the chair Wartrace drew from within the store, and Webb took a seat near by on an inverted nail-keg. Wartrace was called within, and the banker began to watch the crowd with interest. Back in the store men were lounging on the long counters, chewing tobacco, smoking and talking of their crops or local politics.

"I see 'im!" a woman cried, from the end of the porch, as she stood eagerly pointing up the mountain-road. Mostyn saw a tall man of middle age, smooth-shaven, with long yellow hair falling on his broad shoulders, easily striding down the incline. He had blue eyes and delicate, rather effeminate features. He wore a broad-brimmed felt hat, dark trousers, and a black frock-coat without a vest. Reaching the store, he took off his hat, brushed back his hair from a high pink forehead, and with bows and smiles to the people on all sides, he cried out cheerily:

"How are you, everybody? God bless your bones. I hope the Lord has been with you since I saw you last fall. Hello, Brother

Wartrace! You see, old chap, I *do* remember your name," he called out, as the storekeeper appeared in the doorway. "Say, I wish you would have some of those roustabouts inside roll out a dry-goods box for me to stand on."

"All right, Brother Leach," Wartrace answered. "I've got the same box you spoke on before. I intend to keep it for good luck."

"All right, all right, roll it out, gentlemen. I'd help you, but I've had a pretty stiff walk down the mountain to get here on time, and want to sorter get my wind."

He stood fanning his perspiring face with his hat while two obliging farmers brought the box out. "There under that tree," he ordered. "Show me a cheaper pulpit than that, and I'll buy it for kindling-wood. By the way, friends, two preachers over the mountain told me last night that I was doing more harm than good, talking without pay on the public highway as I am doing. I'd like to please every living soul, including them, if I could. It makes them mad to see you all gather to hear a jumping-jack like me. They say it's making salvation too cheap, and quote Scripture as to 'the laborer being worthy of the hire.' That would be all right if this was labor to me, but it isn't; it is nothing but fun, an' fun full of the glory of God, at that."

The box was now in the required spot; and, mounting upon it, Leach stamped on the boards vigorously to test their strength. "I'm gaining flesh," he laughed. "Free grub is fattening. I'll have to gird up my loins with a rope before long."

Then he was silent. The look of merriment passed from his face. Mostyn thought he had never seen a more impressive figure as the man stood, a ray of sunlight on his brow, looking wistfully over the heads of his little audience toward the rugged mountains. Then slowly and reverently he raised his hands and began to pray aloud. It was a conventional prayer, such as the average rural preacher used in opening a meeting; and when it was over he took a worn hymn-book from his coat pocket, and after reading a hymn he began to sing in a deep, sonorous voice. Some of the women, with timid, piping notes and the men in bass tones joined in. This over, Leach cleared his throat, stroked his lips with a tapering, sun-browned hand, and began to talk.

"Somebody over the mountain yesterday wanted to know, brethren, how I happened to take up this roving life, and I told them. They seemed impressed by it, and I'm going to tell you. To begin with, the best temperance talker is the man who has led a life of drunkenness and through the grace of the Lord got out of it to give living testimony as to its evil. Now, I'm pretty sure, for the same reason, that a man who has been through the mire of hell on earth is competent to testify about that. I'm that sort of a man. I was once up in the world, as you might say. My folks had means. After I got out of school I went into business on my own hook in my home town. You will be interested in this, Brother Wartrace; so make them fellers come out of the store and be quiet."

Order was restored. The mountaineers who were talking within slouched out on the porch and stood respectfully listening.

"I went into the grain business," Leach continued. "I was young then, and I thought I owned the market. My old daddy cautioned me to go slow, but I paid no attention to him. Folks called me a hustler, and I was proud of it. I got into fast ways. I played poker; I had a pair of fast horses, and I was guilty of other habits that I sometimes mention at my 'men-only' meetings. After awhile I slid into the hole that is at the foot of every ungodly slope on earth. I was facing ruin. I had only one chance to save myself, and that was to gamble big on wheat. To do it I actually stole some money out of a bank run by a friend of mine. It's awful to think about, but I did it. I was found out. I was accused and arrested. I was tried and found guilty. Lord, Lord, I shall never forget that day! My mother and father were in the courtroom. She fainted dead away, and an eternal blight fell on his white head.

"I was sent to prison. My hair was clipped, and I was put in stripes and steel shackles. All hell was packed in me. Instead of being conquered, as most convicts are, I kept swearing that I was innocent. I'd lie awake at night in my cell concocting lie after lie to bolster up my case and stir up sympathy. I wrote letters to my home papers. While I was clanking along by my fellow-prisoners who were taking their medicine like men I was hating the whole of creation and studying devilish ways to fight.

"I got to writing to the Governor of the State. I had heard he was kind-hearted, and I thought I might make him believe I was innocent, so I wrote letter after letter to him. I used every pretext I could think of. Once I told him that I hoped God would strike me dead in my tracks and damn me eternally if I had not been falsely imprisoned. Now and then he would answer, in a kind sort of way, and that made me think I might convince him if I kept up my letters.

"I was that sort of a fiend for a year. Then a strange thing happened. A little, mild-mannered man was put in for murder. He had the cell adjoining mine. He wasn't like any other prisoner I'd ever seen. He had a sad, patient face, and didn't look at all strong. I took to him because he used to pass his tobacco through to me—said he had quit using it. Well, what do you think? One night as I lay with my ear close to the partition I heard him praying. And the strangest part of it was that he wasn't praying like a guilty man. He was begging the Lord to be good to the other prisoners, and open their eyes to the spiritual light, which he declared was even then shining in his cell.

"Well, do you know, I listened to him night after night, and got so I could sleep better after I'd heard him pray. And in the daytime I loved to find myself by his side in any work we had to do. I never shall forget the thing I'm going to tell you. We were carrying brick to repair a wall where an attempt was made by some fellows to get out. It was out in the sunlight, and I hadn't seen the sun many times for a year past. I don't know how it come up, but somehow he happened to remark that he was innocent of the charge against him. Circumstantial evidence had landed him where he was. He wasn't the one that did the killing at all. I remember as I looked at him that I was convinced he was telling the truth. He was innocent and I was guilty. I had an odd feeling after that that I had no right to be near him.

"He used to talk to me in the sweetest, gentlest way I ever heard. He told me that if a convict would only turn to God the most wretched prison ever built would be full of joy. He said, and I believed him, that he didn't care much whether he was out or in jail, that God was there by his side and that he was happy. Lord, Lord, how he did plead with me! His eyes would fill chock full and his voice would shake as he begged and begged me to pray to God for help. I remember I *did* try, but, having lied to the Governor and everybody else, somehow I couldn't do it right. Then what do you reckon? I heard him in his cell every night begging God to help Number Eighty-four—that was all he knew me by—Eighty-four. He was Number Seventy-two. Every night for a month I would stick my ear to the partition and listen and listen for that strange, strange mention of me. I got so that when we would meet in the daytime I'd feel like grabbing hold of him and telling him that I loved him.

"Now, on the first of every month I was in the habit of writing a letter to the Governor, and the time had come round again. I got the paper and pen and ink from the warden, and started to go over again my old lying tale, but somehow I couldn't put the old fire in it. I kept thinking of Seventy-two and his prayers. I remember I cried that night, and felt as limp as a rag. I had changed. Then, I don't know how it happened, but it was as though some voice had spoken inside of me and told me not to write to the Governor about *myself,* but about Seventy-two, who really was innocent. So I started out, and with the tears pouring down my face and blotting the paper I told the

Governor about the prayers of Seventy-two, and how good he was, and begged him to give him a pardon, as I knew positively that he was innocent. Then a queer thing took place. I couldn't begin to explain it, but in trying to think of some way to convince the Governor of the fellow's innocence I came out with this: I said, 'Governor, I am the man that has been writing to you all this time swearing he is innocent. I have written you a thousand lies. I am guilty, but I'm telling you the truth this time, as God is my judge. I don't ask release for myself, but I want justice done to Seventy-two. No purer or better man ever lived.'"

"I sent the letter off; and, friends, I'm here to tell you that I never felt so happy in all my life. The very prison walls that night seemed to melt away in space. My poor cot was as soft as floating clouds. I didn't feel the shackles on my ankle and arm, and the low singing of Seventy-two in his cell was as sweet as far-off celestial music. I remember he called out to me just before bed-time, 'Brother, how goes it?' and for the first time I answered, with a sob in my throat: 'I'm all right, Seventy-two—I'm all right!' And I heard him say, 'Thank the Lord, blessed be His holy name!'"

"Now comes the best part, friends—I'm glad to see you've been so quiet and attentive. Lo and behold! One morning the warden sent for me to come to his private sitting-room, and there sat a dignified, kind-faced man. It was the Governor. He wanted to talk to me, he said, about Seventy-two. I don't know how it was, but I give you my word that somehow I didn't have a single thought beyond trying to get Seventy-two pardoned. Once the Governor broke in and said, 'But how about *your own* case?' And I told him I was guilty and had no hope as far as I was concerned. He put a lot of questions to me about Seventy-two, about his habits and talk to me and other prisoners; and I heard him say to the warden, 'This is an interesting case; I must look further into it.'"

"Then I was sent back, and Seventy-two was ordered out. He was with the Governor for about an hour, and then he came back to his cell, and I heard him praying and sobbing. Once I heard him say, 'Lord, Lord, Thou hast answered my call. Justice is to be done.'"

"The next day it went around that Seventy-two was pardoned. He put on his old clothes, packed up his things, and come to shake hands with us. When he come to me he pulled me to one side and clung to my hand and began to cry. 'It was all through you,' he said. 'The Governor wouldn't have believed it in any other way.' Then he told me not to feel bad, that— well"—Leach's voice clogged up here, and he wiped his twitching lips with his slender hand—"well, Seventy-two said that a look had come in my face which showed that peace was mine at last. He said he was going to keep on praying for me, and advised me to try to do good among the prisoners.

"He went away, and I *did* try to follow his advice. I read my Bible every spare chance I got and told the convicts that I believed in a merciful God who was ready and willing to forgive all sins and lighten punishment. I got so I loved to talk to them, and sometimes when the chaplain was sick or away he let me take his place on Sundays, and it was there that I learned to preach. I served my time out. A sharp blow met me on the day of my release. I was thinking of going back home to make a new start when a letter from my father told me that my mother had been dead a month. A young sister of mine was to be married to a fellow high up in society, and father wrote me that he wished me well, but thought that perhaps I ought not to come home branded for life as I was.

"Friends, that was a lick that only God's omnipotent hand could soften. I was without home or blood-kin. There was nothing I could do to make a living, for an ex-convict is never encouraged by the world at large. That's how I came to take up this work. It seems to me at times that I was made for it—that all my trouble was laid on me for a divine purpose."

The speaker paused to take a drink of water from a dipper Wartrace was holding up to him, and Mostyn slipped back into the store. Going out at a door in the rear, he went into the adjoining wood and strode along in the cooling shade toward the mountain. The sonorous voice of the speaker rang through the forest, and came back in an echo from a beetling cliff behind him.

Mostyn shuddered. The speaker's experiences had vividly brought to mind many of his own questionable exploits in finance. He recalled his narrow escape from bankruptcy when, by an adroit lie, he had secured the backing of Mitchell and other money-lenders. Old Jefferson Henderson's ashen face and accusing eyes were before him. He had broken no law in that case, but only he and Henderson knew of the false statements which had ensnared the credulous man's whole fortune.

The preacher's warning had come in time. Pate had intended it as a check to a perilous pace. He would speculate no more. He would follow Saunders's example and lead a rational life. He would live more simply. He would—his heart sank into an ooze of delight—he would marry the sweetest, most beautiful, and bravest girl in the world. He would win Dolly's whole heart, and in the future devote himself solely to her happiness. What more admirable course could a penitent man pursue? He quickened his step. He was thrilled from head to foot. He had reached the turning-point, and what a turning-point it was! In fancy, he saw himself taking the pretty child-woman in his arms and pledging his brain and brawn to her forever. It was really a most noble thing to do, for it meant the uplifting, as far as lay in his power, of her family. It would materially alter their sordid lives. He could give employment to Dolly's brother; he might be the means of educating and finding a suitable husband for Ann. Perhaps Saunders might sell him his plantation; Tom Drake could manage it for him, and the Colonial mansion would make a delightful summer home. Ah, things were coming about as they should! Dolly, Dolly, beautiful, exquisite Dolly was to be his wife, actually his wife!

He sat down on a moss-covered stone aflame with a passion,

which was of both blood and spirit. How beautiful the world seemed! How gloriously the sun shone on the pines of the mountain! How blue was the sky! How white the floating clouds!

The preacher was singing a hymn.

Will N. Harben

CHAPTER XI

One cloudy night a few days later Mostyn was walking home from the river where he had spent the day fishing. Thinking that he might shorten the way by so doing, he essayed a direct cut through the dense wood intervening between the river and Drake's. It was a mistake, for he had gone only a short way when he discovered that he had lost his bearings. He wandered here and there for several hours, and it was only when the moon, which had been under a cloud since sundown, came out, that he finally found a path which led him in the right direction.

He was nearing the house when in the vague light, due to the moon's being veiled again, he saw a man stealthily climb over the fence, stand as if watching the house for a moment, and then creep through the rose bushes and other shrubbery to the side of the house beneath the window of Dolly's room.

Wondering, and suspecting he knew not what, Mostyn crept to the fence, and, half-hidden behind an apple tree, he stood watching. The figure of the man was quite distinct against the white wall of the building, and yet it was impossible to make out who he was. Then a surprising thing happened. Mostyn saw the figure raise its hands to its lips, and a low whistle was emitted. There was a pause. Then the window of Dolly's room was cautiously raised, and her head appeared as she leaned over the sill.

"Is your father at home?" a muffled masculine voice was

heard inquiring.

"No, he's been gone all day." It was plainly Dolly who was speaking.

The stares of the two seemed to meet. There was a pause. It was as if the girl's head had furtively turned to look back into the room.

"Then come down. Meet me at the front gate. I'll keep hid."

"Very well—in a minute."

She was gone. Mostyn saw the man glide along the side of the house, treading the grass softly and making his way round to the front gate. Filled with suspicion and hot fury, Mostyn kept his place, afraid that any movement on his part might too soon betray his presence to the man he now saw near the gate.

"My God," he cried, "she's like all the rest! I've been a fool—*me*, of all men! Here I've been thinking she was to be for me and me alone. This has been going on for God only knows how long. She has been fooling me with her drooping lashes and flushed cheeks. I was ready to marry her—fool, fool that I was. She might, for reasons of her own, have married me. There is no knowing what a woman will do. Bah! What a mollycoddle I have been! She, and he too, perhaps, have been laughing at me for the blind idiot I am—*me*, the man who thought he knew all there was to know about women."

Mostyn heard the front door open softly. It was just as softly closed, and then the girl crossed the porch and advanced to the gate. She and the man stood whispering for a moment, and then they passed out at the gate and, side by side, went into the wood beyond the main road.

Filled with chagrin, to which an odd sort of despair clung like a moist garment, Mostyn advanced along the fence to the gate and entered the yard. Putting his rod and game-bag down, he seated himself on the step of the porch. His blood seemed cold and clogged in his veins. He could not adjust himself to the situation. He could not have met a greater disappointment. The discovery had completely wrecked his already strained faith in the purity of woman. He sat watching the moon as the clouds shifted, now thinly, now thickly, before it. He heard a step in the wood. Some one was coming. He started to rise and flee the spot, but a dogged sort of resentment filled him. Why should he let the matter disturb him? Why should he conceal from any one the knowledge of her shame? He remained where he was. The step was louder, firmer. It was Dolly, and she was now at the gate. He saw her, as with head hung low, she put her hand on the latch. She opened the gate, entered, and paused, her face toward the wood. There she stood, not aware of the silent, all but crouching spectator behind her. Mostyn heard something like a sigh escape her lips. Then a furious impulse to denounce her, to let her know that he now knew her as she was, flashed through him. He rose and went to her. He expected her to start and shrink from him as he approached, but she simply looked at him in mild surprise.

"Have you just got home?" she inquired. "Mother and I were worried about you, but George and Uncle John said you were all right."

He stared straight at her. She would have noted the sinister glare in his eyes but for the half darkness.

"I was lost for a while," he said. "I got back just in time to see a man climb over the fence and whistle to you."

"Oh, you saw that!" She exhaled a deep breath. "I'm sorry you did, but it can't be helped. I suppose you know everything now."

"I can guess enough," he answered, with a bitterness she failed to catch. "I don't know who he was, but that is no affair of mine."

"I ought to have told you all along." She was avoiding his eyes. "I felt that I could trust you fully, but I was ashamed to have you know. I was anxious for you to take away as good an opinion of us all as was possible. You have been so kind to us. I'm sure no such degradation has ever come into your family."

"Nothing like *this*, at any rate," he answered. "As far as I know the—women of my family have—"

"Have what? What are you talking about? Do you think—do you imagine—is it possible that you—who do you think that man was?"

"I have said I did not know," he retorted, frigidly.

She stepped closer to him. She put her little hand on his arm appealingly. She raised her fathomless eyes to his. "Oh, you mustn't think it was any young man—any—Why—it was—I see I must tell you everything. That was Tobe Barnett. He has wanted to help me for a long time, and he got the chance to-night. He knows the one great sorrow of my life. Mr. Mostyn, my father is a moonshiner. I don't mean that he is a regular member of a gang, but he helps a certain set of them, and to-day Tobe accidentally heard of a plan of the Government officers to surround the still where my father happens to be to-night. He heard it through a cousin of his who is employed in the revenue detective service. Tobe is law-abiding; he didn't want to have anything to do with such things, but he knew how it would break my heart to have my father arrested, so he came to me late this afternoon to see if father had returned. He was going to tell him, you see, and warn him not to be with the men to-night. But father was still away. Tobe went home; he said he would come later to see if father was back. I sat up waiting for him all alone in my room in the dark. I did not want George or Ann or my mother to know about it. So just now when Tobe came to my window and found that father had not returned, he determined to go to the still and warn him. He may get there in time, and he may not, though it is not far. I promised to wait here at the gate till he returns. I could not possibly close my eyes in sleep with a thing like that hanging over me."

Her voice shook; she turned her head aside. The cold mass of foul suspicion in Mostyn's breast gave way to a higher impulse. A sense of vast relief was on him. He would have taken her into his arms, confessed his error, and humbly begged her forgiveness, but for an unlooked-for interruption. There was a sound in the distance. It was the steady beat of horses' hoofs on the hard clay road in the direction of Ridgeville.

"It is the revenue men!" Dolly gasped. "Quick, we must hide!" And, catching his hand as impulsively as a startled child, she drew him behind a hedge of boxwood. "Crouch down low!" she cried. "We must not let them see us. They would think—"

She failed to finish. Seated on the dewy grass, side by side, they strained their ears for further sounds of the approaching horsemen. Mostyn marveled over her undaunted calmness. She still held his hand as if unconscious of what she was doing, and he noted that there was only a slight tremor in it. The horses were now quite near. A gruff voice in command was distinctly heard.

"We'll dismount at the creek," it said, "creep up on the scamps, and bag the whole bunch. If they resist, boys, don't hesitate to fire. This gang has bothered us long enough. I'm tired of their bold devilment."

"All right, Cap!" a voice returned. "We'll make it all right this time. I know the spot."

A dozen horsemen, armed with rifles, came into view and passed on, leaving a hovering cloud of dust in their wake. Moving swiftly, and paler and graver, Dolly stood up, her steady gaze on the departing men.

"Did you hear that?" she said, dejectedly. "He ordered his men to—to fire. Who knows? Perhaps before daybreak I shall have no—" She checked herself, her small hand at her throat. "I shall have no father, and with all his faults I love him dearly. He doesn't think moonshining is wrong. Some of the most respectable persons—even ministers—wink at it, if they don't actually take part. My father, like many others, has an idea that the Government robbed the Southern people of all they had, and they look on the law against whisky-making as an infringement on their rights. I wish my father would obey the law, but he doesn't, and now this has come. He may be killed or put in prison."

"You must try not to give way," Mostyn said, full of sympathy. "Don't forget that Barnett has had time, perhaps, to warn them, and they may escape."

"Oh, I hope so—I do—I do!" Still holding his hand, she led him back to the gate, and stood resting her arms on its top, now almost oblivious of his presence. Half an hour dragged by, during which no remark of his could induce her to speak. Presently a low whistle came from the wood across the road.

"That's Tobe now!" she cried. "Oh, I wonder if he was in time!" Then, as she reached for the gate-latch he heard her praying: "God have mercy—oh, Lord pity me—pity me!"

She opened the gate and passed out. He hung back, feeling that she might not desire his presence at the meeting with Barnett, but again she grasped his hand.

"Come on," she said. "Tobe will understand."

Crossing the road and walking along the edge of the wood for about a hundred yards, they were presently checked by another whistle, and the gaunt mountaineer emerged from the dense underbrush. Seeing Mostyn, he paused as if startled, saying nothing, his eyes shifting helplessly.

"It's Mr. Mostyn—he knows everything, Tobe," Dolly threw in quickly. "He's on our side—he's a friend. Now, tell me, what did you do?"

"Got to the still just in the nick o' time," Tobe said, panting, for he had been running. "The gang started to handle me purty rough at first—thought I was a spy—but your pa stepped in an' made 'em have sense. They couldn't move any of their things on such short notice, but the last one escaped just as the officers was ready for the rush."

"But my father?" Dolly inquired, anxiously.

"He's all right—he said he'd be home before morning. He has no idea that you know about it."

"I'm glad of that. Oh, Tobe, you have been good to me tonight!" Dolly took the humble fellow's hands and shook them affectionately.

"Well, if you hain't been good to me an' mine nobody ever was to a soul on *this* earth," Barnett half sobbed. "Mr. Mostyn, maybe you don't know what Miss Dolly has—"

"Yes, I do, Barnett," Mostyn declared. "I know."

"Now, go back to Annie and Robby, Tobe," Dolly advised. "Poor girl! She will be uneasy about you."

"No, she won't bother," Barnett answered, firmly. "She'd be willing to have me go to jail to help you, Miss Dolly. She is that grateful she'd cut off her hands to oblige you, an' she will be powerful happy when she knows this went through all right. Good night, Miss Dolly; good night, Mr. Mostyn."

Dolly and her companion turned back toward the house as Barnett trudged off down the road.

"Well, I'm glad it came out all right," Mostyn said, lamely; but Dolly, still listless, made no reply. Silently she walked by his side, her pretty head down. An impulse of the heart impelled him to take her hand. He was drawing her yielding form to him when she looked straight into his eyes.

"I was wondering—" she began, but checked herself.

"What were you wondering, Dolly?" The fire of his whole being was roused; it throbbed in his lips, thickened his tongue, and blazed in his eyes. It filled his voice like a stream from a bursting dam.

"Why, I was wondering"—her sweet face glowed in the moonlight as from the reflection of his own—"I was wondering how you happened to think that Tobe was some young man that—that I cared enough for to—"

"I was insanely jealous." Mostyn put his arm about her, drew her breast against his, and pressed his lips to hers. "I was mad and crazy. I couldn't think—I couldn't reason. Dolly, I *love* you. I love you with all my heart."

"Yes, I know." She seemed not greatly surprised at the avowal. She put her hand on the side of his face and gently stroked it. Then, of her own accord, she kissed him lightly on the lips. "There," she said, "that will do for to-night. I ought not to be here like this—you know that—but I am happy, and—"

"You have not said"—he held her closer to him, now by gentle force, and kissed her again—"you have not said that you love me."

"What is the use?" she sighed, contentedly. "You have known it all these years. I have never cared for any one else, or thought of any one else since you were here before. I was only a child, but I was old enough to know my heart. You are the only man who ever held me this way. There is no use saying it—you know I love you. You know I couldn't help it. I'd be a queer girl if I didn't."

He tried to detain her at the steps, but she would not stay. She entered the house, leaving the door open so that he might go up to his room.

CHAPTER XII

The next day was Sunday. Mostyn did not see Dolly at breakfast. Drake sat at the head of the table as unconcerned as if nothing unusual had happened to him in the night. He spoke to John Webb and Mrs. Drake about the meeting to be held that day at the church and praised the preacher's powers and sincerity. It was the philosophical Webb who had something to say more in harmony with Mostyn's reflections.

"I understand the revenue men made another haul last night," he said, a watchful eye on his brother-in-law.

"You don't say?" Drake calmly extended his cup and saucer to Ann, to be handed to George, and from him to Mrs. Drake, for a filling. "Whose place was it?"

"Don't know whose still it was," Webb answered, "but they landed the whole shootin'-match—sour mash, kegs, barrels, jugs, demijohns, copper b'ilers, worms, a wagon or two, and some horses."

"Who did they ketch?" Drake asked. "I reckon it happened when I was t'other side the mountain."

"Nobody, it seems," Webb answered. "The gang was too slick for 'em. They must have had sentinels posted around the whole shebang."

Drake apparently found no further interest in the subject, for

Will N. Harben

he began to talk of other matters. He had heard that Saunders was expected to spend the day at his farm, and added to Mostyn: "I reckon you will see 'im an' get news of business."

"I almost hope he won't mention it," the banker smiled. "I have scarcely thought once of the bank. I never allow my mind to rest on it when I am off for a change like this."

"Fine idea," Drake said, "but I don't see how you can help it, 'specially if you are concerned in the rise and fall of market-prices. But I reckon you've got that down to a fine point."

Mostyn made some inconsequential response, but Drake's remark had really turned his thoughts into other channels. After all, he reflected, with a sudden chill of fear, how could he know but that some of his investments were not so prosperous as when he had left Atlanta? He became oblivious of the conversation going on around him. He failed to hear the cautious dispute over some trifle between George and Ann.

A little later, Mostyn was walking to and fro on the lawn in front of the house when Dolly came down-stairs. She had on the pretty pink dress he had admired so much the day she had tried it on for the first time. He threw down his cigar and went to the steps to meet her, his troubled thoughts taking wing at the sight of her animated face.

"Why have you not worn it before?" he said, sweeping her slender figure from head to foot in open admiration.

"For the best reason in the world," she laughed. "I only got the cash to pay for it yesterday, and I would not wear it till it was mine. I collected some money a man owed me for giving private lessons to his children and sent it right away to the dressmaker."

"It is simply wonderful," he said, glad that no one else was present. "I'm proud of you, little girl. You are the most beautiful creature that ever lived."

"Oh, I don't know!" She shook her head wistfully. "I wish I could think so, but I can't. There are so many other things that count for more in the world than good looks. Do you know I didn't sleep more than an hour last night?"

"I'm sorry," he said. "What was the matter?"

She glanced through the open door into the house as if to see if any one was within hearing. Then she came nearer to him, looking down on him from the higher step on which she stood, her pretty brow under a frown. "I was bothered after I went to bed," she said, frankly. "I don't think I ought to—to have kissed you as I did there at the gate. I would have scolded Ann for the same thing, even if she were as old as I am. I trust you—I can't help it—and last night I was so happy over Tobe's message that—Tell me honestly. Do you think that a man loses respect for a girl who will act as—as boldly as I did? Tell me; tell me truly."

"Not if he loves her as I do you, Dolly," he said, under his breath, "and knows that she feels the same way. Don't let a little thing like that trouble you. It is really your wonderful purity that makes you even think of it."

She seemed partially satisfied, for she gave him her glance more confidingly. "It is queer that I should have let it worry me so much," she said. "It was as it some inner voice were reproving me. All sorts of fears and queer ideas flocked about me. I—I am just a simple mountain girl, and you now know what my—my people are like. Why, if my father were now in prison I could not refuse to—to stick to him as a daughter should, and for a man in your position to—to—" She broke off, her eyes now on the ground.

"You mustn't think any more about it," he managed to say, and rather tardily. "You can't help what he does." Mostyn's passionate gaze was fixed on her again. "How pretty, how very pretty that dress is!" he flared out. "Are you going to church this morning?"

Will N. Harben

"Oh yes," she replied, half smiling down into his eyes. "I must set a good example to Ann and George."

Burning under the memory of her kiss of the night before, Mostyn told himself that he must by all means see her alone that day. He must hold the delicious creature in his arms again, feel the warmth of her lips, and capture the assurance of a love the like of which was a novelty even to him.

"What are you thinking about?" she suddenly demanded.

"I am thinking, Dolly, that you have the most maddening mouth that ever woman had, and your eyes—"

"Don't, don't!" she said, with a shudder. "I can't explain it, but, somehow, when you look and speak that way—"

"I can't help it," he blurted out, warmly. "You make my very brain whirl. I can hardly look at you. It is all I can do to keep from snatching you to my arms again, even here where any one could see us. Say, darling, do me a favor. Don't go to church to-day. Make some excuse. Stay at home with me and let the others go. I have a thousand things to tell you."

The slight, shifting frown on her face steadied itself. She gave him a swift glance, then avoided his amorous eyes.

"Oh, I couldn't do that, *even for you*," she faltered. "They have asked me to sing in a quartette. That is why I put on this dress. The other girls are going to fix up a little."

"Then you won't oblige me?"

"I can't. I simply can't. It would be deceitful, and I am not a bit like that. I'm just what I am, open and aboveboard in everything. And that is why I know—*feel* that I did not act right last night."

"There you go again," he cried, lightly, forcing a laugh. "When will you ever drop that? You say you love me, and I *know* I love you, so why should you *not* let me kiss you? I'll tell you what I'll do. I'll order a horse and buggy sent out from Ridgeville this afternoon, and we will take a nice drive over the mountain."

"To-day?—not to-day," Dolly said, firmly. "There is to be an afternoon service at the church. I'd be a pretty thing driving about the country with a handsome city man while all the other girls were—oh, it never would do! I'm sorry, but I couldn't think of it. People talk about a school-teacher more than any one else, and this valley is full of malicious gossips."

He was wondering if a little pretense of offense on his part— which, to his shame, he remembered using in former affairs of the heart—might make her relent, when he noticed that she was watching something on the road leading to the village. It was a horse and buggy. Her sight was keener than his, for she said, in a sudden tone of gratification:

"It is Mr. Saunders. He is on his way out home."

"So it is," Mostyn said, impatiently. "I'll go down to the gate and speak to him. Will you come?"

With her eyes on the vehicle, and saying nothing, Dolly tripped down the steps. How gracefully she moved, he thought. They reached the gate just as Saunders drew rein.

"Hello!" he cried, cheerily. "How are you, Dolly?" And, doffing his hat, he sprang down and shook hands with them both. "I'm lucky to catch you," he added to the girl. "I have something for you."

"Oh, I'm so glad!" Dolly cried. "You are always so kind and thoughtful."

"It is only a couple of books." Saunders had flushed slightly, and he turned back to the buggy, taking from beneath the seat a parcel wrapped in brown paper. "Mostyn, they have a most wonderful reading-circle here in the mountains. I have quit trying to keep pace with them." He held the parcel toward Dolly. "I heard you say all of you wanted to know something of Balzac's philosophy. I find that he has expressed it in his novels *Louis Lambert* and *Seraphita*. The introductions in both these volumes are very complete and well written."

"Oh, they are *exactly* what we want." Dolly was very happy over the gift, and she thanked the blushing Saunders warmly. Mostyn stood by, vaguely antagonistic. He had not read the books in question, and he had a feeling that his partner was receiving a sort of gratitude which he himself could never have won. Then another thought possessed him. How well the two seemed mated! Why, Saunders—plain, steady, ever-loyal Saunders, with his love of books and Nature, and his growing aversion to gay social life—was exactly the type of man to make a girl like Dolly a good husband.

Dolly was trying to break the twine on the parcel. "Let me!" Saunders, still blushing, was first to offer assistance. He took out his pocket-knife, cut the twine, unwrapped the books, and handed them back to her.

"Oh, they are so pretty—you always get such costly bindings!" Dolly added, almost reproachfully, as she fairly caressed the rich red leather with her hands. "You—you intend to lend them to the club, of course, and we must be very careful not to soil them. I shall have some covers made to—"

"Oh no!" Mostyn had never noticed before that his partner was such a weakling in the presence of women, and he wondered over the man's stumbling awkwardness. "Oh no," Saunders stammered. "I have inscribed them to—to you, as a little personal gift, if—if you don't mind."

"Oh, how sweet, how lovely of you!" Dolly cried. "Now, I sha'n't even want the others to handle them. I'm awfully selfish with what is *really* my own. Oh, you are *too* good!" Her richly mellow voice was full of genuine feeling, and a grateful moisture glistened in her shadowy eyes. Saunders heard, saw, and averted his throbbing glance to the mountain.

"Well, well," he said, awkwardly, "I must be going. It is Sunday, but I must talk to my overseer about his work. He was down in Atlanta the other day, and I did not like his showing as well as I could have done. I shall throw up banking, Mostyn, one of these days and settle down here. I see that now."

He was returning to the buggy, Dolly having gone to the house eager to exhibit her gift, when Mostyn stopped him. "Shall I see you again before you go back?" he inquired.

Saunders reflected. "I hardly think so, unless—Say, why couldn't you get in and go over home with me? My cook, Aunt Maria, will give us a good dinner, and we can lounge about all day."

"I don't think I could stay to dinner"—Mostyn was thinking that it might prevent a possible chat with Dolly in the parlor or a stroll to the spring—"but I'll ride over with you and walk back. I need the exercise."

"All right, hop in!" There was a ring of elation in Saunders's voice which was not often heard from him during business hours.

"These outings seem to do you a lot of good," Mostyn remarked. "You are as lively as a cricket this morning."

"I love the mountains," was the answer. "I love these good, old-fashioned people. Back at the station as I left the train I saw some revenue officers with the wreck of a mountain still piled up in the street. I know the moonshiners are breaking the law, but they don't realize it. Many a poor mountain family will suffer from that raid. Do you know, I was glad to hear that no arrests were made. Imprisonment is the hardest part of ft."

Mostyn was discreetly non-communicative, and as they drove along the conversation drifted to other topics. Suddenly Saunders broke into a laugh. "You know, Mostyn, you are doing your very best to force me to talk about business. You have edged up to it several times."

Mostyn frowned. "I have succeeded in keeping my mind off of it fairly well so far," he declared; "but still, if anything of importance has taken place down there I'd like to know it."

"Of course, you would," Saunders answered; "and from now on you'd fairly itch to get back to your desk. Oh, I know you!"

"Not if everything was all right." There was a touch of rising doubt in Mostyn's voice.

Saunders hesitated for a moment, then he said: "I have something for you from—from Marie Winship." He rested the reins in his lap, took a letter from his pocket, and gave it to his companion. It was a small, pale blue envelope addressed in a woman's handwriting. In the lower left-hand corner was written "Personal and important."

Mostyn started and his face hardened as he took it. He thrust it clumsily into his pocket. "How did you happen to—to get it?" he asked, almost angrily. "I see it was not mailed."

Saunders kept his eyes on the back of the plodding horse.

"The truth is, she came to the bank twice to see you—once last week and again yesterday. I managed to see her both times alone in your office. The clerks, I think, failed to notice her. She was greatly upset, and I did what I could to calm her. I'm not good at such things, as you may know. She demanded your address, and, of course, I had to refuse it, and that seemed to make her angry. She is—inclined, Mostyn, to try to make trouble again."

Mostyn had paled; his lower lip twitched nervously. "She had better let me alone!" he said, coldly. "I've stood it as long as I intend to."

"I don't know anything about it," Saunders returned. "I could not pacify her any other way, and so I promised to deliver her letter. She would have made a scene if I had not. She has heard some way that you are to marry Miss Mitchell, and it was on that line that her threats were made."

"Marry? I have never said that I intended to marry—*any one,*" Mostyn snarled, a dull, hunted look in his eyes.

"I know," Saunders said, still unperturbed, "but you know that the people at large are generally familiar with all that society talks about, and they have had a lot to say about you and that particular young lady. If you wish to read your letter, don't mind me—I—"

"I don't want to read it!" Mostyn answered. "I can imagine what's in it. I'll attend to it later. But you have seen her, Saunders, since I have, and you would know whether the situation really is such that—"

"To be frank"—Saunders had never spoken more pointedly— "I don't feel, Mostyn, that I ought to become your confidant in exactly such a thing. But through no intention of mine I have been drawn into it—drawn into it, Mostyn, to protect the dignity and credit of the bank. She was about to make a disturbance, and I *had* to speak to her."

"I know—of course, I understand that"—Mostyn's fury robed him from head to foot like a visible garment—"but that is not answering my question."

"Well, if you want my opinion," Saunders said, firmly, "I think if the woman is not appeased in some way that you and I, the directors, and all concerned—friendly depositors and everybody-will regret it. Scandal of this sort has a bad effect on business confidence. Mitchell came in just as she was leaving.

Of course, he is not a great stickler on such matters, but—"

"I didn't know he was in town," Mostyn said, in surprise.

"Yes, they returned rather suddenly the day before yesterday. By the way, he is impatient to see you. He wouldn't mind my telling you, for that is what he wants to do. He has had a great streak of luck. You remember the big investments you advised him to make in wild timberlands in Alabama and North Georgia a few years ago? Well, your judgment was good— capital. His agent has closed out his entire holdings for a big cash sum. I don't know the exact figure, but he banked a round one hundred thousand with us yesterday, and said more was coming."

Mostyn stared excitedly. "I thought it would be a good thing, but I didn't expect him to find a buyer so soon."

Saunders smiled. "I know you thought so," he chuckled. "He is as happy as a school-boy. He is crazy to tell you about it. He thinks a lot of you. He swears by your judgment. In fact, he said plainly that he expected you to handle this money for him. He says he has some ideas he wants you to join him in. He sticks to it that you are the greatest financier in the South."

Mostyn drew his lips tight. "He is getting childish," he said, irritably. "I have no better judgment than any one else— Delbridge, for instance, is ahead of me."

"Delbridge *is* lucky," Saunders smiled. "They say he has made another good deal in cotton."

"How was that?" Mostyn shrugged his shoulders and stared, his brows lifted.

"Futures. I don't know how much he is in, but I judge that it is considerable. You can always tell by his looks when things are going his way, and I have never seen him in higher feather."

Mostyn suppressed a sullen groan. "That is what *they* are doing while I am lying around here like this," he reflected. "Mitchell thinks I am a financial wonder, does he? Well, he doesn't know me; Irene doesn't know me. Dolly doesn't dream—my God, I don't know *myself!* A few minutes ago I was sure that I would give up the world for her, and yet already I am a different man—changed—full of hell itself. I am a slave to my imagination. I don't know what I want."

Then he thought of the unopened letter in his pocket. Light as it was, he could all but feel its weight against his side. They were now at the gate of Saunders's house. No one was in sight. The tall white pillars of the Colonial porch gleamed like shafts of snow in the sunlight. It was a spacious building in fine condition; even the grass of the lawn and beds of flowers were well cared for.

"You'd better decide to stop," Saunders said, cordially. "I will soon get over my talk with the overseer, and then I'll take you around and show you some of the richest land in the South— black as your hat in some places. I wouldn't give this piece of property for all you and Delbridge and Mitchell ever can pile up. Both my grandfather and father died in the room up-stairs on the left of the hall. It seems sacred to me."

Mostyn nodded absently. "No, thanks, I'll walk home," he said, getting out of the buggy. He was turning away, but paused and looked back.

"Would you advise—" he began, hesitatingly, "would you advise me to return to Atlanta to-morrow—on—on account of this silly thing?"

Saunders hesitated. "I hardly know what to say," he answered, frankly. "Perhaps you can tell better when you have read her letter. The situation is decidedly awkward. In her present nervous condition the woman is likely to give trouble. Somehow I feel that it is nothing but your duty to all of us to do everything possible to prevent publicity. She seems to me to have a dangerous disposition. She even spoke of—of using force. In fact, she said she was armed—spoke of killing you in cold blood. You might restrain her by law, but you wouldn't want to do that."

A desperate shadow hovered over Mostyn's face. "I'll go back in the morning," he said, doggedly. "Mitchell, you say, wants to see me. I'm not afraid of the woman. If I had been there she wouldn't have made such a fool of herself."

CHAPTER XIII

When Mostyn got back to the farmhouse he found no one at home, the entire family being at church. He strolled about the lawn, smoked many cigars, and tried to read a Sunday paper on the porch. His old nervous feeling had him in its grasp. Try as he would to banish them, the things Saunders had told him swept like hot streams through his veins. Mitchell had doubled his fortune; Irene was now a richer heiress than ever; Delbridge was in great luck; and a shallow-pated woman, whom Mostyn both feared and despised, was threatening him with exposure. Mitchell, and other men of the old regime, laughed at the follies of youth, it was true, but a public scandal which would cripple business was a different matter in any man's eyes. Besides, the old man must be told of his intention to marry Dolly, and that surely would be the last straw, for all of Mitchell's intimate friends knew that the garrulous old man was counting on quite another alliance.

Mostyn heard the voices of the Drakes down the road, and to avoid them he went up to his room, and from a window saw them enter the gate. How wonderfully beautiful Dolly seemed as she walked by her mother! The girl was happy, too, as her smile showed. The others came into the house, but Dolly turned aside to a bed of flowers to gather some roses for the dinner-table. Bitterly he reproached himself. He had won her heart—there was no doubt of it; she was his—soul and body she was his, and with his last breath he would stand to her. From that day forth, in justice to her, he would cleanse his life of past impurities and be a new man. Delbridge, Mitchell,

　　　　Will N. Harben

Henderson, Marie Winship—all of them—would be wiped out of consideration. He would get rid of Marie first of all. He would force her to be reasonable. He had made her no actual promises. She had known all along what to expect from him, and her present method was unfair in every way. He had paid her for her favors, and for aught he knew other men had done the same. However, that did not lessen the woman's power. She might even make trouble before he got back to Atlanta—there was no counting on what a woman of her class would do. He would send her a telegram at once, stating that he would be down in the morning. But, no, that would only add to the tangible evidence against him. He would wait and see her as soon as possible after his arrival. Yes, yes, that would have to do, and in the mean time—the mean time—

Mostyn paced the floor as restlessly as a caged tiger. There were mental pictures of himself as already a discredited, ruined man. Mitchell had turned from him in scorn; Saunders was placidly appealing to him to withdraw from a tottering firm, and old Jeff Henderson was going from office to office, bank to bank, whining, "I told you so!" At any rate—Mostyn tried to grasp it as a solace worth holding—there was Dolly, and here was open sunlight and a new and different life. But she would hear of the scandal, and that surely would alter the gentle child's view of him. Irene Mitchell would overlook such an offense if she gave it a second thought, but Dolly—Dolly was different. It would simply stun her.

Dinner was over. Tom Drake and John Webb were chatting under the apple trees in the orchard, where Webb had placed a cider-press of a new design which was to be tried the next day. Mrs. Drake had retired to her room for a nap. Ann had gone to see a girl friend in the neighborhood, and Dolly was in the parlor reading the books Saunders had given her. Mostyn hesitated about joining her, but the temptation was too great to be withstood. She looked up from her book as he entered and smiled impulsively, then the smile died away and she fixed him with a steady stare of inquiry.

"Why, what has happened?" she faltered.

"Nothing particular," he said, as he took a seat near her and clasped his cold, nervous hands over his knee.

She shook her head slowly, her eyes still on him. "I know better," she half sighed. "I can see it all over you. At dinner I watched you. You look—look as you did the day you came. You have no idea how you improved, but you are getting back. Oh, I think I know!" she sighed again, and her pretty mouth drooped. "You are in trouble. Mr. Saunders has brought you bad news of business."

He saw a loophole of escape from an embarrassing situation, and in desperation he used it. "Things are always going crooked in a bank like ours," he said, avoiding her despondent stare. "Men in my business take risks, you know. Things run smoothly at times, and then —then they may not do so well."

"Oh, I'm so sorry," she faltered; "you were getting on beautifully. You—you seemed perfectly happy, too, and I hoped that—" Her voice trailed away in the still room, and he saw her breast under its thin covering rise and fall suddenly.

"Don't let it worry you," he said.

"How can I help it?" She put the books on the window-sill and raised her hand to her brow. "I know how to fight my *own* troubles, but yours are too big, too intricate, too far away. What—what are you going to do?"

He felt the need of further pretense. He looked down as he answered:

"I shall have to take the first train in the morning, and—and—"

"Oh!" The simple ejaculation was so full of pain that it checked his tardy subterfuge. He rose to take her in his arms to soothe her, to pledge himself to her forever, but he only stood leaning against the window-frame, the puppet of a thousand warring forces. No, he would not touch her, he told himself; she was to be his wife—she was the sweetest, purest human flower that ever bloomed, and until he was freer from the grime of his past he would not insult her by further intimacy. So far he had not spoken to her of marriage, and he would not do so till he had a better right.

"So you really are going?" She had turned pale, and her voice shook as she stared up at him, helplessly.

"Yes, but I am coming back just as soon as I possibly can," he said. "Besides, I shall write you, if—if you will let me?"

"Why should you say *if* I will let you? Don't you know—can't you see? Oh, *can't* you see?"

Again the yearning to clasp her in his arms rose to the surface of his inner depths, and he might have given way to it but for the panorama of accusing pictures which was blazing in his brain.

"I wish you would try—try to understand *one* thing, Dolly," he said, pitying himself as much as her. "I have meant everything I have said to you. The little that is good in me loves you with all its force, but I do not want you to—to even trust me—to even count on me—till I have straightened out my affairs in Atlanta. Then—then if all goes well I shall come back, and—and talk to you as I want to talk to you now—but can't."

Her brows met in a troubled frown. Her pale lips were drawn tight as if she were suffering physical pain.

"I see, and I shall not ask questions, either," she said, calmly. "I realize, too, that you are speaking to me in confidence. I shall tell no one, but I am going to pray for you. I believe it helps. It seems to have helped me many, many times."

"No, no, you must not do that," he said, quickly, almost in alarm. "I am not good enough for that."

"But I can't help it. Some philosopher has said that every desire is a prayer, and in that case I shall be praying constantly till your trouble is over."

It was as if she understood, and appreciated the momentary check he had put upon his passion. They were quite alone. His face was close to hers; it was full of shadowy yearning, and yet he made no effort to repeat the blissful caresses of the night before.

Presently he heard her sigh again.

"What is it?" he asked, uneasily.

She was silent for a moment, then she asked: "Do you believe in premonitions?"

"I don't think I do," he said, wondering what was forthcoming. "Why do you ask?"

"Because I do to some extent," she said, slowly, a reminiscent expression in her eyes, "and something seems to tell me that you and I are in danger of being parted. I have felt forewarnings often. Once I actually knew my father was in trouble when he was several miles from me, and there was no hint of the matter from any external source."

"Strange," he said. "Was it something serious?"

"His life was in danger," Dolly said, "and he was on the point of committing a crime which would have ruined us all. It was this way. A rough mountaineer had become angry with me for keeping his disobedient child in after school was out. He was drinking, and he made a disrespectful remark at the store about me which reached my father's ears. My father has an awful temper which simply cannot be controlled, and, taking his revolver, he went to find the man. None of us at home knew what he intended to do, but exactly at the hour in which he met the man, fought with him, and shot him almost fatally, I felt that something was wrong, I was in the schoolroom trying to get my mind on my work, but I could not do it. I could think of nothing but my father and some crisis which he seemed to be going through. So I was not surprised later to learn of his trouble."

"I did not know your father had such a hot temper," Mostyn said. "He looks like a man who is not easily upset."

"It is all beneath the surface," Dolly answered. "You have no idea how careful I have to be. He seldom is willing for the young men about here to visit me at all. That is his worst fault."

Dolly rose. She put her hand lightly on Mostyn's. "I must go to my room now," she said. "I shall see you before you leave. I am going to do my best to subdue the premonition about you and me. It is so strong that it depresses me—fairly takes my breath away. It is exactly as if we are not going to meet again, or something just as sad."

Mostyn stood still, looking at her steadily. "Am I to understand, Dolly, that your father might not—not quite like for us to be together even like this, and is that why you are leaving me now?"

Dolly's long lashes flickered. She seemed to reflect as she kept her glance on the doorway. "I think I may as well tell you something, so that if anything comes up you may be somewhat prepared for it. Last night when Tobe Barnett called me to the window and I went out, as you know, to meet him, Ann, whose room is next to mine, was awake. She heard Tobe whistle and saw me leave. She couldn't see who it was, but later, when you and I were at the gate, she saw us quite clearly."

"Oh, I see," Mostyn said, anxiously, "and she thought that I called you out."

"I could not explain it any other way," Dolly answered. "I don't want her to know, you see, about father and the moonshiners. She began teasing me about you this morning, and I was afraid father would hear it, so I simply had to admit that I was with you. I even confessed—confessed"—Dolly's color rose—"that I care a great deal for you, for, you see, she actually saw—saw—"

"I understand." Mostyn tried to smile lightly. "You mean that she saw me kiss you?"

Dolly's flushed silence was her answer. "Ann is so young and romantic that it has made a great impression on her," Dolly added, lamely, as she moved toward the door, her eyes downcast. "You see how I am placed, and I hope you won't blame me. There was no other way out of it. I think I can keep her from mentioning it. I shall try, anyway. After all," she sighed, deeply, "it is only *one* of our troubles—yours and mine."

"Only *one* of them," he repeated, with a sudden guilty start—"what do you mean?"

She swept his face with a flash of her eyes, seemed to hesitate, then she said, resignedly: "I am quite sure that your Atlanta set, especially your relatives, would not approve of me—that is, if I were thrown with them as an equal."

"How absurd!" he began, awkwardly; but she fixed him with a firmness that checked him.

"Your sister, Mrs. Moore, would scarcely wipe her feet on me. You see, I met her once."

"When? how?" he asked, wonderingly.

"She was at the house-party Mr. Saunders gave last summer, and he introduced us on the road one day," Dolly explained, with an indignant toss of the head. "Oh, I could never—never like her. She treated me exactly as if I had been a hireling. She is your sister, but Lord deliver me from such a woman. Well, what's the use denying it—she is part of my premonition. You may settle your business troubles satisfactorily, but if—if you should tell her about me, she will move heaven and earth to convince you that I am unworthy of your notice."

"Nonsense!" he began; but with a sad little shake of the head she hurried away.

Left alone, Mostyn's heart sank into the lowest ebb of despair. Back and forth he strode, trying to shake off his despondency, but it lay on him like the weight of a mountain. What would the morrow bring forth? To him his sister's objections would be the very least. The real disaster lay in the matter Dolly's pure mind could not have grasped. He took out the letter Saunders had brought and read it again.

"She is simply desperate—the little cat!" he cried. "I might have known she would turn on me. For the last three months she has been 'a woman scorned,' and she is not going to be easily put aside. Fool, fool that I was, and always have been, I deserve it! It may ruin me—men have been ruined by smaller things than this. Can this be the beginning of my end?" He sank into the chair Dolly had vacated and rocked back and forth. Suddenly he had a sort of inspiration.

"I might take the midnight train," he reflected. "Why, yes, I could do that, and have my trunk sent on to-morrow. In that case I'd avoid riding back with Saunders and be there early in the morning. Surely she will be quiet that long."

CHAPTER XIV

Mostyn reached the city at five o'clock in the morning. The sun was just rising over the chimneys and dun roofs of the buildings. He lived in the house of his widowed sister, Mrs. John Perkins Moore, in a quiet but fashionable street, and thither he went in one of the numbered cabs which, in charge of slouching negro drivers, meet all trains at the big station.

At his sister's house no one was stirring; even the servants were still abed. He was vaguely glad of this, for he was in no mood for conversation of any sort. Having a latchkey to the front door, he admitted himself and went up to his room at the top of the stairs. Should he lie down and try to snatch a little sleep? he reflected, for his journey and mental state had quite deprived him of rest. Throwing off his coat and vest and removing his collar, necktie, and shoes, he sank on his bed and closed his eyes. But to no effect. His brain was throbbing; his every nerve was as taut as the strings of a violin; cold streams of despair coursed through his veins. For the thousandth time he saw before him the revengeful face of a woman—a face now full of fury—a face which he had once thought rarely pretty, rarely coy, gentle, and submissive. What could be done? Oh! what could be done?

He heard the iceman stop at the door, curiously noted his slow, contented tread as he trudged round to the kitchen to leave the block of ice. He saw the first reddish-yellow shafts of sunlight as they shot through the slats of the window-blinds, fell on his bureau, lighting up the silver toilet articles and the

Will N. Harben

leaning gilt frame holding a large photograph of Irene Mitchell. He sat on the edge of the bed, thrust his feet into his slippers, and stared at the picture. Was it possible that he had really thought seriously of marrying her? It seemed like a vague dream, his entire association with her. For months he had been her chief escort; he had called on her at least twice a week. He had made no denial when his and her friends spoke of the alliance as a coming certainty, and yet a simple little mountain girl had come into his life, and all the rest was over. But why think of that when the other thing hung like a sinister pall above him?

There was a step in the corridor close to the door, then a rap.

"Come!" he cried, thinking it was a servant. The door opened partially, and the reddish face of his sister, under a mass of yellowish crinkly hair, peeped in, smiling.

"I heard you on the stairs," she said. "I'm not dressed, and so I'll not kiss you. I've told the cook to get your breakfast at once, for I know you are hungry."

"Thanks, I am," he answered. "I have been up all night."

She was ten years older than he, short, and firmly built. Her blue, calculating eyes had a sleepy look.

"You must have been up late last night, yourself," he said, nothing more vital occurring to his troubled mind.

"Oh yes, Alan Delbridge gave a big reception and dance in his rooms. Supper was served at the club at one o'clock. Champagne and all the rest. I was the blindest chaperon you ever saw. Good-by—if I don't get down to breakfast it will be because I'm sound asleep. I knew you would cut your outing short."

"You say you did?" he cried, his heart sinking. "What made you think so?"

"The Mitchells are back." She laughed significantly, and was gone.

He had his breakfast alone in the pretty dining-room below, and at once started to town. His first thought was that he would go to the bank, but he decided otherwise. He shrank from the formality of greeting the employees in his present frame of mind. No, he would simply see Marie at once and face the inevitable. The earliness of the hour—it was only nine o'clock—would make no difference with her. In fact, by seeking her at once he might prevent her from looking for him. It would be dangerous, he was well aware of that, but the danger would not be any the greater under the roof of her cottage than at the bank, or even in the streets. He decided not to call a cab. The distance was less than a mile, and the walk would perhaps calm him and might furnish some inspiration as to his dealings with her.

Marie Winship lived in a quiet part of the city, near Decatur Street, and after a brisk walk he found himself at her door ringing the bell. He was kept waiting several minutes, and this was awkward, for he was afraid that some one in passing might recognize him and remark upon his presence there so early in the day. However, no one passed, and he was admitted by a yellow-skinned maid.

"Miss Marie just now got up," she said, as she left him to go into the little parlor off the hall.

"Tell her, Mary, that I want to see her, but not to hurry, for I have plenty of time," Mostyn said, "I have just got back."

"Yes, sir; I heard her say she was 'spectin' you to-day."

He had an impulse to make inquiries of the girl regarding her mistress's disposition, but a certain evasive, almost satirical expression in her eyes prevented it. He was sure the maid was trying to avoid any sort of conference with him.

He sat down at one of the two windows of the room and looked at the cheap, gaudy furniture—the green-plush-covered chairs of imitation mahogany; the flaming rugs; the little upright piano; the square center-table, on which were scattered a deck of playing-cards; some thin whisky glasses; a brass tray of cigarettes. Four straight-backed chairs at the table told a story, as did the burnt matches and cigar-stubs on the hearth. Marie was not without associates, both male and female.

He heard voices in the rear of the cottage. He recognized Marie's raised angrily. Then it died away, to be succeeded by the low mumbling of the maid's. Suddenly Mostyn noticed a thing which fixed his gaze as perhaps no other inanimate object could have done. Partly hidden beneath the blue satin scarf on the piano was a good-sized revolver. Rising quickly, he took it up and examined it. It was completely loaded.

"She really is desperate!" He suddenly chilled through and through. "She got this for me."

He heard a step in the rear, and, quickly dropping the revolver into his coat pocket, he stood expectantly waiting. She was coming. Her tread alone betrayed excitement. The next instant she stood before him. She was a girl under twenty-two, a pretty brunette, with Italian cast of features, and a pair of bright, dark eyes, now ablaze with fury.

"So you are here at last?" she panted, pushing the door to and leaning against it.

"Yes, Saunders gave me your letter yesterday," he answered.

"I thought it would bring you." Her pretty lips were parted, the lower hung quivering. "If you hadn't come right away you would have regretted it to the last day of your life—huh! and that might not have been very far off, either."

"I did not like the—the tone of your letter, Marie." He was trying to be firm. "You see, you—"

"Didn't like it? Pooh!" she broke in. "Do you think I care a snap what you like or don't like? You've got to settle with me, and quick, too, for something you did—"

"I *did?*" he gasped, in slow surprise. "Why, what have I—"

"I'll tell you what you did," the woman blazed out, standing so close to him now that he felt her fierce breath on his face. "Shortly before you left you were taken sick at the bank, or fainted, or something like it, and didn't even tell me about it. I read it in the paper. I was beneath your high-and-mighty notice—dirt under your feet. But the next day you went driving with Irene Mitchell. You passed within ten feet of me at the crossing of Whitehall Street and Marietta. You saw me as plainly as you see me now, and yet you turned your head away. You thought"—here an actual oath escaped the girl's lips—"you were afraid of what that stuck-up fool of a woman would think. She knows about us—she's heard; she recognized me. I saw it in her eyes. She deliberately sneered at me, and you—*you contemptible puppy!*—you didn't even raise your hat to me after all your sickening, gushing protestations. I want to tell you right now, Dick Mostyn, that you can't walk over me. I'm ready for you, and I'm tired of this whole business."

He was wisely silent. She was pale and quivering all over. He wondered how he could ever have thought her attractive or pretty. Her face was as repulsive as death could have made it. Aimlessly she picked up a cigarette only to crush it in her fingers as she went on.

"Answer me, Dick Mostyn, why did you treat me that way?"

"My fainting at the bank was nothing," he faltered. "I didn't think it was of enough importance to mention, and as for my not speaking to you on the street, you know that you and I have positively agreed that our relations were to be unknown. People have talked about us so much, anyway, that I did not want to make it worse than it already is. Besides—now, you must be reasonable. The last time I paid you a thousand dollars in a lump you agreed that you would not bother me any more. You were to do as you wished, and I was free to do the same, and yet, already—"

"Bother you! bother you! Is that the way to talk to me? Am I the scum of creation all at once? Didn't you make me what I am? Haven't you sworn that you care more for me than any one else? I was pretty, according to you. I was lovely. I was bright—brighter and better-read than any of your dirty, stuck-up set. You said you'd rather be with me than with any one else, but since then you've begun to think of marrying that creature for her money. Oh, I know that's it—you couldn't love a cold, haughty stick like she is. You are not made that way, but you *do* love money; you want what she's got, and if you are let alone you will marry her."

"I have no such idea, Marie," he said, falteringly.

"You are a liar, a deliberate, sneaking liar. Money is your god, and always will be."

He made no further denial. They faced each other in perturbed silence for a moment. Presently, to his relief, he saw her face softening, and he took advantage of it. "Marie," he said, "you are not treating me right. My conscience is clear in regard to you. I made you no promises. I paid your expenses, and you were satisfied. You are the one who has broken faith. Above all it was understood between us that I was not to be bound to you in any way. I have been indulging you, and you are growing more and more exacting. You are not fair—not fair. You went openly to my place of business. You made threatening remarks about me to my partner. You are trying to ruin me."

"Ruin you?" she smiled. "There are things worse than ruin. If I could have gotten your address I'd have followed you and shot you like a dog!"

"I am not surprised," he said, calmly. "By accident I found the thing you intended to do it with."

Her startled eyes crawled from his face to the piano. She strode to it, threw back the scarf, and stood facing him.

"You have it?" she said.

He touched his bulging pocket. "Yes, I may use it on myself," he retorted, grimly. "You say you've had enough; well, so have I. I have sown my wild oats, Marie, but they have grown to a jungle around me. During my vacation I made up my mind to turn over a new leaf, but I suppose I have gone too far for that sort of thing. I couldn't marry you—"

"You'd rather die than do it, hadn't you?" The woman's voice broke. "Well, I can't blame you. I really can't." Her breast rose and shook. "The devil is in me, Dick. It has been in me ever since—ever since—but it won't do any good to talk about that. I am down and out."

"What do you mean?" He sank into one of the chairs heavily, his despondent stare fixed on her softened face. "You may as well tell me. I am ready for anything now."

"Oh, it is a family matter." She evaded his eyes. "There is no use going over it, but it has thoroughly undone me."

"Tell me about it," he urged. "Why not?"

Eyes downcast, she hesitated a moment. Then: "You've heard me speak of my brother Hal, who is in business in Texas. You know he and I are the only ones of my family left. He is still a boy to me, and I have always loved him. He is in trouble. He has been speculating and taking money that did not belong to him. Through him his house has lost ten thousand dollars. I've had six appealing letters from his wife—she is desperate."

"Oh, I see," Mostyn said. "That is bad. Is—is he in prison?"

"No—not yet." Marie choked up. "The firm has an idea that his friends may help him restore the money, and they won't prosecute if he can make the loss good. He has been hoping to get help out there among his wife's people, but has failed. The time is nearly up—only two days left, and I—My God, do you think I can live after that boy is put in jail? It has made a fiend of me, for if I hadn't taken up with you I would have gone to Texas with him and it might not have happened. There is a streak of bad blood in our family. My father was none too good. He was like you, able to dodge the law, that's all. But poor Hal didn't cover his tracks."

"Stop, Marie!" Mostyn demanded, in rising anger. "What do you mean by mentioning *me* in that sort of connection?"

"Humph! What do I mean? Well, I mean that men say—oh, I've heard them talk! I don't have to tell you who said it, but I have heard them say if you hadn't broken old Mr. Henderson all to pieces several years ago you'd never have been where you are to-day."

"You don't understand that, Marie," Mostyn answered, impatiently. "Henderson took it to court, and the decision was—"

"Oh, I know!" She tossed her head. "Your lawyers pulled you through for a rake-off, and the Henderson girls went to work. They live in a shabby little four-room house not far from here. I often see them at the wash-tub in the back yard. The old man hates you like a snake, and so do the girls. I can't blame them. When you get down in the very dregs through dealing with a person you learn how to hate. The thing stays in the mind night and day till it festers like a boil and you want to even up some way."

"Marie, listen to me," Mostyn began, desperately deliberate. "Why can't we come to an agreement? You want to help your brother out of his trouble, I am sure. Now, that is a big amount of money, as you know, and even a banker can't always get up ready funds in such quantities as that, but suppose I give it to you?"

"You—you give it to me?" she stammered, incredulously, her lips falling apart, her white teeth showing. "Why, you said, not a month ago, that you were too hard pushed for money even to—"

"This is different," he broke in. "Through your conduct you are actually driving me to the wall and I am desperate. I am ready to make this proposition to you. I will get up that money. I'll send you a draft for it to-day provided—provided, Marie, that you solemnly agree not to disturb me at all in the future."

"Do you really mean it?" She leaned forward, eagerly. "Because—because if you *don't* you ought not to mention it. I'd cut off my hands and feet to save that dear boy."

"I mean it," he answered, firmly. "But this time you must keep your promise, and, no matter what I do in the future, you must not molest me."

"I am willing, Dick. I agree. I love you—I really do, but from now on you may go your way and I'll go mine. I swear it. May I—may I telegraph Hal that—"

"Yes, telegraph him that the money is on the way to him," Mostyn said.

Marie sank into a chair opposite him and rested her tousled head on her crossed arms. A trembling sob escaped her, and she looked up. He saw tears filling her eyes. "After all, I may not be so very, very bad," she said, "for this will be a merciful act, and it comes through my knowing you."

"But it must be the end, Marie," he urged, firmly. "It is costing me more than you can know, but I must positively be free."

"I know it," she answered. "I will let you alone, Dick. You may marry —you may do as you like from now on."

"Then it is positively settled," he said, a new light flaring in his eyes. "For good and all, we understand each other."

"Yes, for good and all," she repeated, her glance on the floor.

A moment later he was in the street. The sun had never shown more brightly, the sky had never seemed so fathomless and blue. He inhaled a deep breath. He felt as if he were swimming through the air.

"Free, free!" he chuckled, "free at last!"

Reaching the bank, he was about to enter when he met, coming out, a dark, straight-haired, beardless young man who promptly grasped his hand. It was Alan Delbridge.

"Hello!" Delbridge said, with a laugh. "Glad to see you back. You look better. The wild woods have put new life in you. I knew you'd come as soon as the Mitchells got home."

"It wasn't that," Mostyn said, lamely.

"Oh, of course not," Delbridge laughed. "You were not at all curious to learn the particulars of the old chap's big deal—oh no, you are not that sort! A hundred or two thousand to the credit of a fellow's fiancee doesn't amount to anything with a plunger like you."

Mostyn laid a hesitating hand on the shoulder of the other.

"Say, Delbridge," he faltered, "this sort of thing has gone far enough. I am not engaged to the young lady in question, and—"

"Oh, come off!" Delbridge's laugh was even more persistent. "Tell that to some one else. You see, I *know*. The old man confides in me—not in just so many words, you know, but he lets me understand. He says you and he are going to put some whopping big deals through, presumably after you take up your quarters under his vine and fig tree."

Mostyn started to protest further, but with another laugh the financier was off.

"Ten thousand dollars!" he thought, as he moved on. "He speaks of my business head; what would he think of the investment I have just made? He would call me a weakling. That is what I am. I have always been one. The woman doesn't live who could worry him for a minute. But it is ended now. I have had my lesson, and I sha'n't forget it."

At his desk in his closed office a few minutes later he took a blank check, and, dipping his pen, he carefully filled it in. Mechanically he waved it back and forth in the warm air. Suddenly he started; a sort of shock went through him. How odd that he had not once, in all his excitement, thought of Dolly Drake! Was it possible that his imagination had tricked him into believing that he loved the girl and could make actual sacrifices for her? Why, already she was like a figment in some evanescent dream. What had wrought the change? Was it the sight of Delbridge and his mention of Mostyn's financial prowess? Was it the fellow's confident allusion to Mitchell and his daughter? Had the buzz and hum of business, the fever of conquest, already captured and killed the impulses which in the mountains had seemed so real, so permanent, so redemptive?

"Dolly, dear, beautiful Dolly!" he said, but the whispered words dropped lifeless from his lips. "I have broken promises, but I shall keep those made to you. You are my turning-point. You are to be my wife. I have fancied myself in love often before and been mistaken, but the man does not live who could be untrue to a girl like you. You have made a man of me. I will be true—I will be honest with you. I swear it! I swear it!"

Will N. Harben

CHAPTER XV

A little later he and his sister were at luncheon in her dining-room.

"I am losing patience with you, Dick," she said, as she poured his tea.

"Is that anything new?" he ventured to jest, while wondering what might lay in the little woman's mind.

"You are too strenuous," she smiled, as she dropped two lumps of sugar into his cup. "Entirely too much so. I saw from your face this morning that you are already undoing the effects of your vacation. The old glare is back in your eyes; your hands shake. I really must warn you. You know our father died from softening of the brain, which was brought on by financial worry. You are killing yourself, and for no reason in the world. Look at Alan Delbridge. He is the ideal man of affairs. Nothing disturbs him."

"It is always Delbridge, Delbridge!" Mostyn said, testily. "Even *you* can't keep from hurling him in my teeth. He is as cold-blooded as a fish. Why should I want to be like him?"

"Well, take Jarvis Saunders, then," she returned. "What more success could a man want than he gets? I like to talk to him. He has a helpful philosophy of life. When he leaves his desk he is as happy and free as a boy out of school. I saw him pitching and catching ball in a vacant lot with one of your clerks the other day. Is it any wonder that so many mothers of unmarried daughters consider him a safe catch for their girls? I am not punning; he really is wonderful."

"Oh, I know it," Mostyn answered, drinking his tea, impatiently. "I was not made like him. I am not to blame."

Mrs. Moore eyed him silently for a moment, then a serious expression settled on her florid face. "Well," she ejaculated, "when are you going to make a real clean breast of it?"

A shudder passed through him. She knew what had brought him home. Marie's hysterical protest had leaked out. The girl had talked to others besides Saunders.

"What do you mean?" He asked the question quite aimlessly. He avoided her eyes.

"I want to know about your latest love affair," she laughed, softly. "Just one line in your last letter meant more to me than all the rest of it put together. As soon as I heard you were staying at Drake's I began to expect it. So I was not surprised. You see, I saw her a year ago. Jarvis introduced us one day. He put himself out to do it. According to him, she was wonderful, a genius, and what not."

"You mean Dolly?" Mostyn's tongue felt thick and inactive.

"Yes, I mean *Dolly*." Mrs. Moore continued to laugh. "When I saw her she was young enough to play with a doll, though I believe she was reading some serious book. Well, she *is* pretty—I can't dispute it—and Jarvis declares she is more than that. To do her full justice, she looked like a girl of strong character. I remember how the young thing stared through her long lashes at me that day. Yes, I knew she would turn your head. Dick, you are a man summer flirt. You are even more; you enjoy the distinction of actually believing, temporarily, at least, in every flirtation you indulge in. You have imagination, and it plays you terrible pranks. You wouldn't have been home so soon—you would even have been in your usual hot water over the girl—but for your obligation to Irene Mitchell."

Mostyn tried to be resolute. He was conscious of his frailty of purpose, of his lack of sincerity when he spoke.

"I am not obligated to Irene, and, what is more, Bess, I have positively made up my mind to marry the little girl you are speaking of."

The woman's eyes flickered, her lips became more rigid. It was as if a certain pallor lay beneath her transparent skin and was forcing itself out. He heard her exhale a long breath.

"To think that you could actually sit here and say as ridiculous a thing as that to me in a serious tone," she said, in an attempt at lightness. "Why, Dick, whatever your faults are, you are *not* a fool."

"I hope not," he said, weakly defiant. "I really care very much for the girl. You see, I knew her three years ago. You needn't oppose me, Bess; I have made up my mind."

"You have done no such thing!" Mrs. Moore blurted out. "That is the pity of it—the absurdity of it. You haven't made up your mind—that is just exactly what you haven't done. You thought you had, I don't doubt, when you said good-by to her, but already you are full of doubt, and in a frightful stew. You show it in your face. You know and I know that you cannot carry that thing through. You are not that type of man. Jarvis Saunders could. If he ever marries, he will marry like that. It wouldn't surprise me to see him walk off any day with some stenographer, with nothing but a shirt-waist for a trousseau, but you—*you*—Oh, Lord! You are quite a different proposition."

"You think you know me, Bess, but—" "I am the only person who *does* know you," she broke in. "I have watched you since you were in the cradle. When you were ten you fell in love with a little girl and cried when she fell and bruised her nose. You have imagined yourself in love dozens of times, and have learned nothing from it. But we are losing time. Tell me one thing, and let's be done with it. Have you engaged yourself to this *new* one?"

"No, but—"

"Thank God for the 'but,' and let it go at that," she laughed, more freely. "I understand why you didn't better than you do. You doubted your own feelings. You thought you would for once in your life think it over."

"It was not that which held me back."

"I know; it was Irene Mitchell, her fine prospects, and your natural good horse sense. Dick, you couldn't carry that silly dream through to save your life. You are not made that way. Suppose you really married that little country thing. What would you do with her? Well, I'll tell you. You would break her heart—that's what you'd do. You couldn't fit her into your life if you were deity itself and she were an archangel. She seemed perfect up there in her Maud Muller surroundings, but here in this mad town she would be afraid of you, and you would—ask her to keep her finger out of her mouth. Why, you would be the joke of every soul in Atlanta. Mr. Mitchell would despise you. You would lose his influence. In fact, my dear boy, you have gone too far with Irene Mitchell to turn back now. You may not be actually engaged to her, but she and everybody else consider it settled. For you to marry any one else now—to turn a woman like Irene down, after the way you have acted—would ruin you socially. The men would kick you out of your club. You'd never hold your head up afterward. Oh, I'm glad I got at you this morning. It would be a crime against that mountain child to bring her here on account of your—Dick, I have to speak plainly, more plainly than I ever did before. But it is for your good. Dick, passion is the greatest evil on earth. It has wrought more harm than anything else. Passion often fools the wisest of men. To be plain, you think, or thought, that you loved that pretty girl, but you do not and did not. It was simply passion in a new and more subtle dress. Up there, with plenty of time on your hands, you looked back on your life and became sick of it (for you have been wild and thoughtless—not worse than many others perhaps, but bad enough). You were disgusted and decided to make a fresh start. But what sort of start appealed to you? It wasn't to build a hospital with the better part of your capital. It wasn't really to undo any of the little things more or less wrong in your past. Oh no, it was something much more to your fancy. You decided to marry the youngest, most physically perfect girl you had ever found. You may have told yourself that you would lift her a bit socially, that you would aid her people, make her happy, and what not. But passion was at the bottom of it. Real love does not feed on ideal forms and perfect complexions. The man who marries beneath himself for only a pair of bright eyes is the prime fool of the universe—the whole world loves to sneer at him and watch his prize fade on his hands. Real love is above doubt and suspicion, but you would doubt that girl's honesty at the slightest provocation. Let another man be alone with her for a moment, and you—"

The remainder fell on closed ears. He was thinking of the night he stood watching Dolly's window in the moonlight. How true were the words just uttered! Had he not suspected Dolly, even when she had been most courageous and self-sacrificing? How well his sister understood him!

Just then the telephone bell rang. A maid-servant went to it and spoke in a low tone. Presently she came to the door and called her mistress. Mostyn sat limp, cold, undecided, miserable.

"She is right," he whispered, finding himself alone. "She is right. My God, she is right! I am a fool, and yet—and yet—what *am* I to do?"

Mrs. Moore came in at the door, a significant smile playing between her eyes and lips. He was too despondent to be curious as to its cause.

"Guess who had me on the 'phone?" she asked, sitting down in her chair.

"How could I know?" he answered, too gloomy to fight his gloom.

"Nobody but the most rational, well-rounded, stylish woman in Atlanta. It was my future sister-in-law, Irene Mitchell. She has had her little dream, too, and survived it. She thought she cared a lot for Andrew Buckton—or, rather, she liked to think that he was crazy about her, but he is penniless—has no more energy than a pet kitten, and, sensible girl that she is, she took her father's advice and sent him adrift. Everybody knows that affair is dead. He followed her away this summer, but came back with a long face, completely beaten. Dick, you are lucky."

"What was she telephoning you about?" Mostyn asked, listlessly.

"You."

"Me?"

"Yes; she asked for you."

"And you didn't call me?" He was studying the designing face apathetically.

"No, I fibbed out and out. I told her you were not here yet, but that I expected you to lunch every minute. Then, as sweetly as you please, I offered to deliver the message. It was as I thought, an invitation to dinner to-night. I knew you were in no shape to talk into a 'phone—the service is so bad lately—so I accepted for you, like the good sister I am."

He found himself unable to reply. Suddenly she rose, bent over him, and kissed him on the brow.

"Silly, silly boy!" she said, and left the room.

CHAPTER XVI

That evening at dusk, when Mostyn reached Mitchell's house, he found the old gentleman smoking on the veranda.

"I looked for you earlier," he said, turning his cigar between his lips and smiling cordially as he extended his hand. "You used to be more prompt than this. We won't stand formality from you, young man."

"I had a lot of work to do," Mostyn said. "Saunders let it pile up on me while I was away." "I see." Mitchell stroked his gray beard. "He is getting to be a great lover of nature, isn't he? I went in to see him about something the other day, and I could hardly get his attention. He has just bought a new microscope and wanted to show me how it worked. He had put a drop of stagnant water on a glass slide and declared he could see all sorts of sharks, whales, and sea-serpents in it. I tried, but I couldn't see anything. There are plenty of *big* affairs for fellows like you and me to choke and throttle without hunting for things too small for the naked eye."

A flash of light from behind fell upon them. A maid was lighting the gas in the drawing-room. Mostyn saw the cut-glass pendants of the crystal chandelier blaze in prismatic splendor. His mind was far from the lined countenance before him. He was heavy with indecision. His sister's confident derision clung to him like a menace from some infinite source.

"A man never marries his ideal." He remembered the words

Will N. Harben

spoken by a college-mate who was contemplating marriage. Mostyn shuddered even as he smiled. It was doubtlessly true, and yet he had gone too far with Dolly to desert her now. He couldn't bear to have her know him for the weakling that he was. The next moment even Dolly was snatched from his reflections, sharp irritation and anger taking her place, for Mitchell was speaking of Delbridge and his recent good fortune.

"You two are a wonderful pair to live in the same town," Mitchell chuckled. "I have been in his office several times since we got home. Not having you to loaf with, I turned to him for pastime. He certainly is a cool hand in a deal. He doesn't get excited in a crisis, as you do, and when he wins big stakes he hardly seems to notice it. Ten minutes after he got the wire on his good luck the other day he could talk of nothing better than a new golf-course he is planning."

"He is nothing more nor less than a gambler," Mostyn said, with irritation. "He is on top now, but he may drop like a load of bricks any minute. Who can tell?"

"Oh, *you* needn't be jealous of him," Mitchell began, blandly. "He can't crow over *you*."

"Jealous of him!" Mostyn smirked. "I am not jealous of any one, much less Delbridge."

"Of course not, of course not," and the old man laid a caressing hand on Mostyn's shoulder. "You don't play second fiddle to any man in Georgia in *my* opinion. I know your ability well enough. If I didn't I wouldn't trust you as I do. Lord, I've told you everything. We are going to work together, my boy; I have some big plans. Of course, Saunders told you of my land deal?"

"Yes, that was fine," Mostyn said. "A big thing."

"I owe it all to you, and wanted to ask your advice before

closing out"—Mitchell glowed with contentment—"but as you were not here, I went it alone. The parties seemed to be in a hurry, and I was afraid they might accidentally change their minds, so I took them up."

Throwing his cigar into the grass, Mitchell led the way into the drawing-room. His hand was now on Mostyn's arm. In the hall they met Jincy, the maid. "Tell my daughter to order dinner," he said, curtly, "and ask her to come down."

The two men stood near the big screened fireplace and plain white marble mantelpiece. There was a rustling sound on the stair in the hall, and Irene came in. She was beautifully attired in a gown Mostyn had not yet seen. It was most becoming. How strange! There seemed, somehow, to-night more about her to admire than on any former occasion. Was it due to his return to his proper social plane? Was the other life sheer delusion? What exquisite poise! What easy, erect grace! Her whole being was stamped with luxurious self-confidence. How soft was the feel of her delicate fingers as they touched his! Why had he clasped them so warmly? How charming the gentle and seductive glance of her eyes! He caught himself staring at her in a sort of reluctant pride of personal ownership. He thought of Dolly Drake, and a glaring contrast rose darkly before him. He fancied himself confessing his intentions to Irene and shuddering under her incredulous stare. How could he explain? And yet, of course, she must be told—her father must be told. All his friends must know. And talk—how they would chatter and—laugh!

"You certainly look improved," Irene cried, as she surveyed him admiringly. "You are quite tanned. Fishing or hunting every day, I suppose."

"Nearly," he answered.

"Cousin Kitty Langley is here to spend the night," Irene went on. "But I can't persuade her to come down to dinner. She is not hungry and is buried in a novel. She was at a tea this afternoon and ate too many sandwiches."

"Humph!" Mitchell sniffed, playfully. "You know that wasn't it. She asked Jincy to bring something up to her. She told me she simply would not break in on you two this first evening."

"Father is getting to be a great tease, Dick," Irene smiled. "The money he has made lately has fairly turned his head. Please don't notice him." The colored butler had come to the door, and stood waiting silently to catch her eye. Seeing him, she asked:

"Is everything ready, Jasper?"

He bowed. He looked the ideal servant in his dark-blue suit, high collar, and stiff white waistcoat. A wave of revulsion passed over Mostyn. He was thinking of the crude dining-room in the mountains; Drake, without his coat, his hair unkempt; Mrs. Drake in her soiled print dress and fire-flushed face, nervously waving the peacock fly-brush over the coarse dishes; Ann and George, as presentable as Dolly could make them, prodding and kicking each other beneath the table when they thought themselves unobserved; John Webb, with his splotched face in his plate; and Dolly—the sweetest, prettiest, bravest, most patient little woman Time had ever produced, and yet, what had that to do with the grim demands of social life? Was his sister right? Was his interest in the girl grounded only in a subtle form of restrained passion? Would he tire of her; would he be ashamed of her, here amid these surroundings? In fancy he saw Mitchell staring contemptuously at the little interloper. After all, had any man the right to inflict an ordeal of that sort upon an unsuspecting child? Plainly, no; and there would be no alternative but for him to renounce city life and live with her in the mountains. But could he possibly do such a thing? Had he the requisite moral strength for a procedure so foreign from his nature? Was his desire for reformation as strong as he had once thought it? Perhaps his release from Marie Winship's threatening toils had something to do with his present relapse from good intentions. He remembered how he had been stirred by the impassioned words of the mystic tramp preacher. How clear the way had seemed at that sunlit moment; how intricate and difficult now!

Mitchell led the way out to dinner, Irene's calm hand on the arm of the guest. What a superb figure she made at the head of the splendid table under the pink lights of the candle-shades! How gracefully she ordered this away, and that brought, even while she laughed and chatted so delightfully. And she—*she*—that superb woman of birth, manners, and position—could be had for the asking. Not only that, but the whole horrible indecision which lay on him like a nightmare could in that way be brushed aside. He felt the blood of shame rush to his face, but it ran back to its source in a moment. Dolly would soon forget him. She would marry some mountaineer, perhaps the teacher, Warren Wilks, and in that case the man would take her into his arms, and—No, Mostyn's blood boiled and beat in his brain with the sudden passionate fury of a primitive man; that would be unbearable. She had said she had kissed no other man and never would. Yes, she was his; her whole wonderful, warm, throbbing being was his; and yet—and yet how could it be?

"You seem preoccupied." Irene smiled on him. "Are you already worried over business?"

"I'm afraid I always have more or less to bother me," he answered, evasively. "Then, too, a hot, dusty bank is rather depressing after pure open mountain air."

"I had exactly that feeling when we returned," she smiled. "We certainly had a glorious time. We had quite an Atlanta group with us, you know, and we kept together. The others said we were clannish and stuck-up, but we didn't care. We played all sorts of pranks after father went to bed."

"You would have thought so if you had heard them, Dick," the old man said, dryly. "They stayed up till three one morning and raised such a row that the other guests of the hotel threatened to call in the police."

"It was the greatest lark I ever was in," Irene declared, with a hearty laugh. "That night Cousin Kitty put on a suit of Andy Buckton's clothes. In the dark we all took her for a boy. She was the most comical thing you ever saw. I laughed till I was sick."

Dinner over, they went out to the veranda. The lawn stretched green and luscious down to the white pavement under the swinging arc light over the street. Mitchell left them seated in a hammock and sauntered down to the side fence, where he stood talking to a neighbor who was sprinkling his lawn with a hose and nozzle.

At eleven o'clock Irene went up to her cousin, finding the young lady still reading her novel under the green shade of a drop-light. Miss Langley was a good-looking girl, slender, small of limb, active in movement, and a blonde.

"Well," she said, closing her book and looking up, sleepily, "I wanted to see what is coming to this pair of sweethearts, but they can wait. I am anxious to know what is going on in real life. I am tired of the poky way you and Dick Mostyn are courting. I want to be a swell bridesmaid, I do."

"Oh, you do?" Irene sat down in an easy-chair, and, locking her hands behind her head, she leaned back and sighed.

"Yes, I do. You were sure he would propose to-night. Well, did he—did he? That is what I want to know."

"Oh yes, it is settled." Irene transferred her linked hands to her knee, and leaned forward. "Kitty, I may be making a big mistake, but the die is cast. There was nothing else to do. You know how silly father is. You know, too, that poor Andy was out of the question."

"Yes, he was," Miss Langley agreed. "From every possible point of view. He adores you—he will no doubt suffer some, but you could not have married him."

"No, it wouldn't have done," Irene sighed, deeply. "I'm afraid I'll never feel right about it, but the poor boy understands. The way father bore with him and snubbed him on that trip was humiliating."

"So Dick declared himself?" Miss Langley smiled. "I wonder how he led up to it—he is a blooming mystery to me."

Irene tittered. "The truth is, I helped him out. Do you know, he is more sensitive than most persons think, and that side of him was uppermost to-night. I really felt sorry for him. He spoke frankly of having serious faults and being heartily ashamed of his past life. I think I know what he was hinting at. You know we have both heard certain reports."

"Not any more of him than any other man we know," Kitty said, with a shrug. "Andy Buckton, with his Presbyterian bringing-up, may be an exception, but he is about the only one in our crowd. They are all bad, I tell you, and a woman may as well make up her mind to it and hope marriage will cure the brute."

"I liked the way Dick talked to-night very, very much," Irene resumed, reflectively. "He declared he was unworthy of me. Do you know he is sensitive over a certain thing, and I admire it in him."

"What is that?" the other asked.

"Why, out on the steps to-night, after father had gone in, Dick seemed very much depressed. He was worried about something, and I determined to discover what it was. What do you think? The silly fellow was really upset by the money father has recently made; he never has liked the idea of marrying an heiress, and, you see, I am more of one now than I was a month ago."

"Somehow, I don't read him that way," Miss Langley mused, "but I may be wrong. So it is really settled?"

"Yes, it is settled. It was the common-sense thing to do. I am going to put Andy out of my mind. Poor boy! he is lovely, isn't he? What do you think he will do about it, Kitty?"

"Mope around like a sick cat for a month," the girl answered; "then he will marry some one else, and wonder what on earth he ever saw in you to be daft about."

"I don't believe it," Irene said, firmly. "Kitty, that boy will never marry; he will never love any other woman. If I thought he would—" Irene hesitated, a deepening stare in her eyes.

"You'd not marry Dick—Poof! Wouldn't you be a pretty idiot? If you read as many novels as I do you'd know that sentimental, puppy love is a delusion and a snare. Let it alone. You and Dick Mostyn are doing the only rational thing. You will be an ideal couple. Gosh, I wish I had some of the money you will have!"

CHAPTER XVII

One morning a few days later Mostyn entered the bank and went directly to his office. He had been seated at his desk only a moment when Wright, the cashier, came in smiling suavely. There was a conscious flush on his face which extended into his bald pate, and his eyes were gleaming.

"I want to congratulate you," he said. "We've all been reading the account in the paper this morning. Of course, we've suspected it for some time, but didn't want to talk about it till it was announced."

"I haven't seen the article," Mostyn answered, in a tone of curbed irritation. "It was written by some woman society reporter. Miss Langley told me to look out for it. I think she furnished the information."

"Very likely," Wright answered. "Women like nothing better than a wedding in high life."

"Has Saunders come down yet?" the banker inquired.

"Yes, he is at his desk. He just got back from his farm this morning."

"Please tell him"—Mostyn deliberated—"tell him when he is fully at liberty that I'd like to see him."

A moment later Saunders opened the door and came in. A

Will N. Harben

grave look was on his face, and he failed to respond to Mostyn's "Good morning." He paused, and stood leaning on the top of the desk, his glance averted.

"Wright says you wish to see me," he began.

"Yes, sit down; pull that chair up."

Saunders complied, his eyes on the floor.

"I suppose you've seen the morning paper?" Mostyn asked.

"You mean the—announcement of your—"

"Yes, of course."

"I saw the head-lines. I didn't read it through."

Silence crept between the two men. Mostyn touched a paper-weight with his slender, bloodless fingers, drew it toward him aimlessly, and then pushed it back.

"There is a matter," he began, awkwardly, "which I want to speak to you about. It is due you to know why I drew out that ten thousand dollars. It went to Marie Winship. If you are not satisfied with the collateral I can put up something else."

"It is all right." Saunders dropped the words frigidly. "I knew it was for her. The truth is, I supposed that little less would quiet her." "You, no doubt, consider me the champion idiot of the world." Mostyn essayed a smile, but it was a lifeless thing at best, and left his face more grimly masked than before. "However, it is all over now. She is satisfied, and agrees to quit hounding me from now on."

Saunders snapped his fingers impulsively, tossed his head, started to speak, but remained silent.

"Why did you—do that?" Mostyn demanded, yielding to

irritation against his will.

"Oh, there is no use going into it," Saunders said, sharply, "but if you think ten thousand dollars will stop a creature of that stamp, your long experience with such women has not taught you much. She will dog you to the end of her days."

"I don't think so, Jarvis." Mostyn seldom used Saunders's Christian name, and it came out now in a tone of all but insistent conciliation. "By giving her the money just now I rendered her a peculiar service. She wanted it to save her brother from arrest and disgrace."

"And you think that will silence her permanently? Well, it won't. You will hear from her again, if I am any sort of judge."

"You take a gloomy view of it," Mostyn protested. "In fact, I don't exactly know how to make you out to-day. You seem different. Surely you don't oppose my—my marriage?"

"Not in the slightest. I have scarcely thought of it."

"Well, then, what is the matter?"

The sudden set silence after such a demand showed plainly that the question was well-timed. Mostyn repeated it less urgently, but he repeated it.

"I have just got back from my plantation"—Saunders glanced at the closed door furtively—"and while I was there I heard some slight gossip about your attentions to my little friend Dolly Drake. You know mountain people, Mostyn, usually make as much as possible of such things. The truth is, some have gone so far as to say that you and *she* were likely to marry."

Mostyn's tanned skin faintly glowed. "They have no—no right to go so far as that," he stammered. "I was with her a good deal, for, as you know, she is very entertaining."

"No one knows it better," Saunders said, firmly. "She is the most courageous, beautiful, and brilliant creature I have ever met. More than that, she has long been the most wronged. She has her whole family, including her moonshining father, on her frail shoulders. It is because of these things that I am tempted to speak plainly about a certain—"

"Go on." Mostyn swallowed anxiously, for his partner had paused.

"I have no personal right to inquire into your conduct," Saunders continued, "but a certain thing has filled me with fear—fear for that poor child's happiness. I met her yesterday near her school, and the awful look in her face haunted me through the night. She had nothing to say, no questions to ask, but the dumb look of despair in her eyes could not be misread. I have known you a long time, Mostyn, and I can't remember your failing to make love to every pretty woman you have been thrown with. I hope I am mistaken this time—with all my soul, I do."

Mostyn turned in his revolving chair. He tried to meet the cold stare of his partner steadily. "Jarvis, I am in the deepest trouble that I ever faced."

"So it is true!" burst from Saunders's lips. "My God, it is true!"

"But don't misunderstand me." Mostyn laid an eager hand on the knee close to his own. "My reputation is so bad in your eyes that I must assure you that—that she is as pure as—"

"Stop!" Saunders shook the hand from his knee as if it were a coiled reptile. "You insult her even by mentioning such a thing. The man does not live who could tarnish her name. I have watched her since she was a little child. I know her as well as if she were my sister, and I respect her as much."

Mostyn was fiery red. "I will justify myself as far as possible," he blurted out, desperately. "You may not believe it, but as

God is my Judge, I intended, when I left her, to rid myself of Marie Winship and go back and ask her to be my wife."

"I can well believe it, even of you"—Saunders breathed hard— "and I know what happened. You were not proof against other influences."

"That is it," Mostyn fairly groaned. "I am as weak as water. I have wronged that noble girl, but it really was not intentional. Knowing her has been the one solely uplifting influence of my life. While I was there I was sure I could be—be worthy of her, but now I know that I am not."

"No, you are not!" Saunders cried. "You are not. The man does not live who is worthy of her. And you—*you*, with your past and that foul stench upon you, actually thought of mating with the purest—ugh! My God!"

Mostyn blinked; there was no trace of resentment in his manner, only cringing humiliation.

"What am I to do?" he faltered, helplessly.

"Do? Nothing! There is nothing you can do now. She will read the papers and know what to expect. It was not you she was in love with, anyway, Mostyn, but an ideal of her own in regard to you. I don't know her well enough to know how she will take it. She has had troubles all her life; this may crown them all; it may drag her down—break her fine spirit—*kill* her. Who knows? You've made a great many successful deals, Mostyn, but this one recently closed for money, as a main consideration, was deliberately advised by the fiends of hell. You have sold your birthright, and if you succeed in your investment it will be because there is no God in the universe. Mark my prediction, the marriage you are making cannot possibly result in happiness—it cannot, because you'll never be able to wipe this other thing from your soul."

Mostyn shrank into his chair. "I wouldn't take this from any one else, Jarvis," he said, almost in a piteous whine. "You have got me down. I'm in no shape for any sort of resentment."

"You got yourself where you are," Saunders ran on, fiercely. "If I am indignant, I can't help it. I would give my right arm to help that poor child, and this powerlessness to act when her suffering is so great drives me to absolute frankness."

"What is the use to talk more of it?" Mostyn said, desperately. "We are getting nowhere."

"There is something else, and I must speak of it," Saunders said, more calmly. "I happen to know the character of Dolly's father perhaps better than you do, and I must tell you, Mostyn, that he is the most dangerous man I ever met. It is my duty to put you on your guard. There is bound to be more or less talk up there, for there are a great many meddlers, and Tom Drake is more than apt to hear of this thing. If he does, Mostyn, an army couldn't stop him. When he is wrought up he is insane. He will come down here and try to kill you. I am going back up there to-day, and if I can possibly prevent trouble I shall do it."

Mostyn had turned deathly pale. "Surely he would not compromise his daughter by such a—a step as that," he stammered.

"Few other men would, but Tom Drake is not like other men. I have seen him fairly froth at the mouth in a fight with three men as big as he was."

Mostyn's lips moved, but no sound issued. Without another word Saunders turned and walked away.

"Great God!" Mostyn whispered in agony, "what *am* I?"

CHAPTER XVIII

That afternoon, Miss Sally-Lou Wartrace, sister of the keeper of the store at the cross-roads, was at her brother's counter eagerly reading an Atlanta paper while he stood looking over her shoulder. She had passed well into spinsterhood, as was shown by the inward sinking of her cheeks, the downward tendency of the lines about her mouth, the traces of gray in her brown hair, and a general thinness and stiffness of frame.

"Well, well, well!" she chuckled, her small, bead-like eyes flashing up into her brother's face. "So all this time their high and mighty boarder was engaged to be married. Did you ever in all your life hear of bigger fools? Mrs. Drake has been so stuck up lately she'd hardly nod to common folks in the road. She never come right out and said so, but she actually thought he was settin' up to Dolly. Old Tom did, too."

"Yes, I think Tom was countin' on it purty strong," Wartrace said, smiling. "I've heard him brag about Mostyn's money and big interests many a time. He knowed his gal was purty an' smart, an' he didn't see no reason why Mostyn shouldn't want her, especially as he was about with her so much."

"That is *it*," the old maid answered; "Mostyn never lost a chance to tag on to her. Dolph, mark my words, thar's goin' to be no end o' talk. Why, didn't Ann just as good as tell me t'other day, on her way home from school, that she was goin' to a fine finishin'-school in Atlanta? You know Tom couldn't send 'er. Besides, when I spoke—as I acknowledge I did—

about Dolly an' Mostyn, Ann grinned powerful knowin'-like an' never denied a thing. Even Ann's got a proud tilt to 'er, an' struts along like a young peacock. This here article will explode like a busted gun amongst 'em an' bring the whole bunch down a peg or two. Do you reckon they've got their paper yet?"

"Not yet," Wartrace answered. "The carrier has to go clean round by Spriggs's at the foot of the mountain 'fore he gits thar. He generally hits Tom's place about an hour by sun."

Miss Sally-Lou folded the paper and thrust it into the big pocket of her print skirt. "I am goin' over thar, Dolph," she said, with a rising smile. "I wouldn't miss it for a purty."

"You'd better keep out of it," the storekeeper mildly protested. "You know you have been mixed up in several fusses."

"I don't expect to have a thing to do with this un," was the eager reply. "But I would just like to see if they really are countin' on a man of that sort tyin' himself on to a lay-out of their stripe. Nobody in the valley believed Mr. Mostyn had any such intention. He was just killin' time an' amusin' hisse'f."

Leaving the store, Miss Sally-Lou strode briskly along the hot, dusty road toward Drake's. Every now and then a low giggle would escape her lips, and she would put her thin, gnarled fingers to her mouth as if to hide her smile from some observer. "John Webb wasn't tuck in by it, I'll bet," she mused. "He ain't nobody's fool. John's got a long, cool head on 'im, he has. He kin see through a mill-rock without lookin' in at the hole."

She found John near the front fence, lazily inspecting a row of beehives on a weather-beaten bench.

"Think they are goin' to swarm?" Miss Sally-Lou inquired, in her most seductive tone, as she unlatched the gate and entered.

"Wouldn't be a bit surprised," the bachelor returned, as he automatically touched his slouch hat. "It is time. We had fresh honey last year long 'fore this."

"Has Dolly got home from school?" was the next question.

"Yes'm," Webb answered. "She come in a minute ago. She may be lyin' down. She ain't as well as common; she looks sorter peaked; I told 'er she'd better take a tonic o' some sort. She's stickin' too close over them books; she needs exercise, an' plenty of it."

"I hate to bother her if she ain't up an' about"—Miss Wartrace had the air of a maiden lady who had as soon chat with a bachelor as feast upon any sort of gossip—"but I'm makin' me a new lawn waist, Mr. John, an' I want to ask Dolly if she'd put big or little buttons on. She has such good taste an' knows what the style is."

"By all means git the *right* sort, Miss Sally-Lou," Webb jested. "If they are as big as mule-shoes, or as little as gnats' eyes, stick 'em on."

"You are a great tease," the spinster smirked. "You always have some joke agin us poor women. You make a lot of fun, but you like to see us look our best, I'll bound you."

John's freckled face bore vague evidence of denial, but he said nothing. He moved toward the farthest hive and bent down as if to inspect the tiny entrance.

"Well, I'll run in a minute," she said. "Watch out an' don't git stung."

"If I do it will be by a *bee*," said the philosopher to himself, "an' not by no woman o' *that* stripe. Lord, folks advise me to set up to that critter! She'd talk a deef man to death. He'd kill hisse'f makin' signs to 'er to stop."

The visitor ascended the steps, crossed the porch, and, without rapping at the door, entered the sitting-room where she found Dolly, Ann, and her mother together. Mrs. Drake was patching a sheet at the window; Ann, sulky and obstinate, was trying to do an example on a slate; and Dolly stood over her, a dark, wearied expression on her face.

"Hello, folkses!" Miss Sally-Lou greeted them, playfully. "How do y-all come on?"

When she had taken a chair she mentioned the waist she was making, and as Dolly gave her opinion in regard to the buttons she eyed the girl studiously. She remarked the dark rings around the beautiful eyes, the nervous, almost quavering voice. "She hain't heard yet," the caller decided. "But she may suspicion something is wrong. Maybe he hain't writ to her since he went back—the scamp! He ought to be licked good an' strong."

"What are you fixing up so for, Miss Sally-Lou?" Ann wanted to know, a bubble of amusement in her young eyes and voice. "Are you going to get married?"

"Listen to her," Miss Wartrace tittered, quite unobservant of Ann's sarcasm. "The idea of a child of that age constantly thinking of marrying."

At this juncture John Webb came in and approached his sister. He had not removed his hat, but, catching Dolly's reproving glance, he snatched it off and stood whipping his thigh with it.

"You wanted to know about them bees," he said. "They don't intend to swarm to-day, so you needn't bother any longer about it."

"I was just laughin' at Ann, Mr. John." Miss Sally-Lou raised her voice tentatively, that she might rivet his attention. "Young as she is, I never see 'er without havin' 'er ax some question or other about me or somebody else marryin'."

"It's jest the woman croppin' out in 'er," Webb drawled, with unconscious humor. "Looks like marryin' is a woman's aim the same as keepin' out of it ought to be a man's."

"You needn't judge others by yourself," was the unoffended retort. "Plenty of men know the value of a good wife, if you don't."

Mrs. Drake seemed not to have heard these give-and-take platitudes. She raised her sheet to the level of her eyes and creased the hem of it with her needle-pricked fingers. "What sort o' cloth are you goin' to use in your waist?" she asked.

"White lawn," said Sally-Lou. "I got a rale good grade in a remnant in town yesterday at a bargain. It was a little dirty at the edges, but I'm goin' to trim them off."

"I'd make it plain, if I was you," Mrs. Drake advised. "At your age an' mine it doesn't look well to fix up fancy."

"Humph! I don't know as you an' me are so nigh the same—"

The final word was caught up by an impulsive snicker, which Webb muffled under his hat.

"Oh, I don't mean to say that I am not *some* older," Mrs. Drake floundered. "Bein' as you are unmarried, it wouldn't be polite for me with as old children as I got to—" "Oh, I'm not mad about it!" Miss Sally-Lou declared, hastily. "I know I'm not as young as Dolly an' her crowd o' girls."

The spinster now frowned resentfully. Nothing could have angered her more than such an allusion made in the presence of the amused bachelor. She nursed her fury in silence for a moment, only to become more set in the grim purpose of her present visit.

"Huh, wait till I git through with 'em!" she thought; then, as if merely to change a disagreeable subject for a happier one, she turned directly to Dolly.

"What do you hear from Mr. Mostyn?" she asked, in quite a tone of indifference.

There was marked hesitation on the part of Dolly, but Ann was more prompt. Her slate and pencil rattled as she dropped them in her lap. "He hasn't written a word," she said, staring eagerly, as if the visitor might help solve a problem which had absorbed her far more than the example on which she was now working.

"You don't say!" Miss Sally-Lou's eyes fired straight gleams at Dolly, as if Dolly herself had made the astounding revelation. "Why, I thought you an' him was powerful thick. Well, well, I reckon he told you all thar was to tell before he left. Young men usually are proud o' things like that, an' can't hold 'em in. Well, I hope he will be happy. I don't wish him no harm if he *is* high up in the world an' rich. I know I was awfully surprised when I read it in to-day's paper." She thrust a steady hand into her pocket, pushing her right foot well forward to give the rustling sheet better egress. There was silence in the room. Webb glanced at his sister and at Ann. No one, save the tormentor, noticed Dolly, who, pale as death, a groping in her eyes, and lips parted, stood behind her sister's chair.

"Is there something in the paper about him?" Ann cried, eagerly.

"Oh yes, nearly a column on the society page," was the studied reply. "The cat's out o' the bag. He's goin' to get married."

"Oh, Dolly!" Ann clapped her hands and leaned eagerly toward her ghastly sister. "Do you reckon he went and told it? I know; he just couldn't keep it—he is so much in love. Oh, Dolly, tell 'em about it. Here you are keeping it so close, while he is sticking it into a paper for everybody to read. I never could see any reason for you to be so awful secret, anyway. It has been all I could do to—"

"What's the child talkin' about?" The caller's eyes gleamed in guarded delight as she unfolded the paper and spread it out on her knee. "Accordin' to *this* account, he is marryin' the richest an' most popular woman in the State. I reckon everybody that reads society news has heard about Irene Mitchell."

"Irene Mitchell!" Ann gasped, rising in her chair, her slate and pencil sliding to the floor. "That isn't so. It isn't so, is it, Dolly? Why, what ails—" The half-scream was not finished. Dolly was reeling as if about to fall, her little hands pressed helplessly to her face. John Webb sprang quickly to her side. He threw his arm about her.

"Dry up all that!" he yelled, furiously. "Dry up, I say! She's sick."

Feeling his support, Dolly revived a little, and he led her out into the hall and saw her go slowly up the stairs to her room. As for Mrs. Drake and Ann, they had pounced on the paper and had it spread out before their wide-open eyes. Sally-Lou was now on her feet. She had gone to the door, seen Dolly's wilting form disappear at the head of the stairs, and was now breathlessly feasting on the bewildered chagrin of the stunned mother and daughter.

Ann finished reading sooner than her mother. Pale and indignant, she turned to the caller. She had opened her mouth when John Webb promptly covered it with his red paw. "Come out o' here!" he ordered, sharply. "You go up-stairs an' 'tend to Dolly. She ain't well. She's been ailin' off an' on for a week. You school-children have deviled the life out of the poor thing. What are you all talkin' about, anyway? Mostyn told me an' Dolly all about him an' that woman. We knowed all along that he was goin' to git married, but it was a sort o' secret betwixt us three."

Astounded, and warningly pinched on the arm, Ann, with a lingering backward look, left the room and reluctantly climbed the stairs.

"You'll have to excuse me, Miss Sally-Lou, here's your paper," Mrs. Drake was slowly recovering discretion. "I'll have to see about Dolly. John's right, she ain't well—she ain't—oh, my Lord, I don't know what to make of it!"

"I see she *is* sort o' upset," Miss Sally-Lou said, "an I don't wonder. I oughtn't to have sprung it so sudden-like. I'll tell you all good day. I'll have to run along. If thar's anything I kin do for Dolly just let me know. I'm a good hand about a sick-bed, an' I know how to give medicine. If Dolly gets worse, send word to me, an' I'll step right over. This may go hard with her. You know I think that idle scamp might 'a' had better to do than—"

But Mrs. Drake, obeying her brother's imperative nod, was moving toward the stairs. Sally-Lou and Webb were left together. Her glance fell before the fiercest glare she had ever seen shoot from a masculine eye, and yet Webb's freckled face was valiantly digging up a smile.

"I see what *you* thought," he laughed. "You went an' thought Dolly was in love with that town dude. Shucks, she seed through 'im from the fust throw out o' the box. She liked to chat with 'im now an' then, but la, me! if you women are so dead bent on splicin' folks why don't you keep your eyes open? Listen to me, an' see if I ain't right. You watch an' see if Dolly an' Warren Wilks—"

"Pshaw!" Miss Sally-Lou sniffed. "Dolly will never give Warren a second thought—not *now*, nohow. She's got 'er sights up, an' she'll never lower 'em ag'in."

Webb, almost outwitted, stood on the edge of the porch and watched the spinster trip down the walk. She glanced over her shoulder coquettishly. "You are losin' all your gal*lant* ways, Mr. John," she simpered. "You don't even open the gate for visitin' ladies here lately."

"I greased that latch t'other day," he answered, laconically. "It works as easy as the trigger of a mouse-trap. I don't know as I ever was a woman's jumpin'rjack. I ain't one o' the fellers that fan flies off'n 'em at meetin'. If they draw flies an' gnats that's the'r lookout, not mine."

CHAPTER XIX

Alone in her room, Dolly stood at a window, her distraught eyes on the placid fields lying between the house and the mountains. She was still pale. The tips of her fingers clung to the narrow mullions as if for support. She seemed scarcely to breathe. Her beautiful lips were drawn tight; her shapely chin had a piteous quiver.

"Oh, that was it!" she moaned. "I understand it now. He was engaged to her all the time, but wouldn't tell me. He got tired of us here and went back to her. I'll never see him again—never, never, never!"

The bed, with its snowy coverlet and great downy pillows, invited her. She was about to throw herself upon it, but her pride, pierced to the quick, rebelled. "I sha'n't cry!" she said. "He is marrying for her money. I sha'n't weep over it. He lied to me—to *me!* He said something was wrong with his business and when that was settled he would write. He was just trifling, passing time away this summer as he did three years ago, and I—I—silly little gump—actually kissed him. I trusted him as I trust—as I *trusted* God. I even confided father's secret to him. I loved him with my whole soul, and all the time he was comparing me to her."

Far across the sunlit meadows on the gradual slope of a rise she saw her father and George cutting and raking hay. How odd it seemed for them to be so calmly working toward the future feeding of mere horses and cattle when to her life itself seemed killed to its germ. There was a step on the stairs. The door was thrown open, and her sister rushed in.

"Oh, Dolly!" Ann cried, her begrimed fingers clutching at Dolly's arm, "what does it mean? Is it so? Do you think he really is going to—"

"Oh, go away, go away, *please* go away!" the older pleaded. "Don't talk to me now—not now!"

"But I want to know—I *must* know!" Ann ran on, hysterically, her young, piping voice rising higher and higher. "I can't stand it, Dolly. Ever since you told me about you and him I have thought about Atlanta and your beautiful home down there and the things I was going to do. Oh, I thought—I thought it was actually settled, but if—if the paper tells the truth—Why don't you talk? What has got into you all at once? Surely— surely he wouldn't—surely you wouldn't have gone out to meet him as late at night as you did and let him—you know, sister, I saw him holding you tight and—"

Dolly turned like an automaton suddenly animated. She laid her hands on her sister's shoulders and bore down fiercely. She shook her so violently from side to side that Ann's plaited hair swung like a rope in a storm.

"Don't tell that to a soul!" Dolly panted. "You must not— don't *dare* to! You promised you wouldn't. Sometime I will explain, but not now—not now. I'm losing my mind. Go away and leave me."

"I really believe you think the paper is telling the truth," Ann moaned. "You *must* think so, or you wouldn't look this way and beg me not to tell. Oh, I can't stand it!"

For a breathless moment Ann stood staring at her dumb-lipped sister, and then, tottering to the bed, she threw herself upon it, burying her face in a pillow. Sob after sob escaped her, but Dolly paid no heed. Her lifeless stare on the mountain view, she stood like a creature entranced.

The sun went down. Like a bleeding ball it hung over the mountain's crest, throwing red rays into the valley. A slow step was heard on the stair, the sliding of a dry hand on the balustrade. Mrs. Drake opened the door and advanced to Dolly.

"You mustn't take on this way," she began. "I want you to be sensible and strong. Thar is plenty of fish in the sea. I sort o' thought Mr. Mostyn was talking too much to you for it to be exactly right, but you always had such a level head—more level than I ever had—that I thought you could take care of yourself."

"Mother, please leave me alone for to-day, anyway," Dolly pleaded. "I —I'm not a fool. Take Ann down-stairs. I—I can't stand that noise. It makes me desperate. I hardly know what to do or say."

"I just asked her to tell me the truth." Ann sat up, holding her pillow in her lap as for comfort, her eyes red with rubbing. "But she won't say a word, when all this time I've been counting on—"

"Well, I'm going down and see about supper," Dolly said, desperately. "Father and George have stopped work and they will be hungry."

Her mother tried to detain her, but she went straight down the stairs. Mrs. Drake crept stealthily to the door, peered after her daughter, and then, heaving a sigh, she stood before the girl on the bed.

"Now," she said, grimly, "out with it! Tell me all you know about this thing—every single thing!"

"But, mother"—Ann's eyes fell—"I promised-"

"It don't make no difference what you promised," Mrs. Drake blurted out. "This ain't no time for secrets under this roof. I want the facts. If you don't tell me I'll get your pa to whip you."

Half an hour later, as Tom Drake trudged across the old wheat-field back of the barn, his scythe on his shoulder, he met his wife at the outer fence of the cow-lot. There she stood as still and silent as a detached post.

"Whar's your bucket?" he asked, thinking she had come to milk the cow, which was one of her evening duties.

"I'm goin' to let it go over to-night," she faltered. Then she laid a stiff hand on her husband's sweat-damp sleeve. "Tom Drake," she gulped, "I'm afraid me an' you are facin' the greatest trouble we've ever had."

"What's wrong now?" he asked, swift visions of moonshine stills, armed officers, and grim court officials flashing before him.

Haltingly she explained the situation. He bore it stolidly till, in a rasping whisper, she concluded with the information forced from Ann. She told him of the low whistle in the moonlight at their daughter's window, of Dolly's cautious exit from the house, of the tender embrace on the lawn. Drake turned his tortured face away. She expected a storm of fury, but no words came from his ghastly lips.

"Now, Tom," she half wailed, "you *must* be sensible. This is a family secret. For once in your life you've got to keep your temper till we can see our way clear. After all, goin' out that way to meet 'im don't actually prove that our girl is bad; you know it don't. Young folks these days—"

"Don't tell *me* what it meant!" He bent fiercely toward her. "I know. I've heard a lot about that whelp's sly conduct. No bigger blackguard ever laid a trap for a helpless girl. Oh no, I won't do nothin'. I wouldn't touch 'im. When I meet 'im I'll take off my hat an' bow low an' hope his lordship is well. I'm just a mountain dirt-eater, I am. Nobody ever heard of a Drake killin' snakes. A Drake will let one coil itse'f round his baby an' not take it off. We are jest scabs—*we* are!"

"Tom, for God's sake—"

"Look here, woman—you lay the weight of a hair in front o' me an' that devil—that rovin' mad dog—an' I'll kill you as I would a stingin' gnat! I won't bed with no woman with that sort o' pride. You've got to stand by me. I'll kill 'im if it takes twenty years. I'll keep my nose to his track like a bloodhound till I look in his eye, an' then, if he had a thousand lives, I'd take every one of 'em with a grin, an' foller 'im to hell for more."

Leaving her with her head on the top rail of the fence, stunned, wordless, he strode away in the dusk. Looking up presently, she saw him standing at the well, in the full light from the kitchen doorway. He seemed to be looking in at Dolly, who, with her back to him, was at work over the stove. The next instant he was gone.

CHAPTER XX

It was eight o'clock. Jarvis Saunders alighted from the train at Ridgeville, finding his horse hitched to a rack according to the instructions he had left with his overseer. Mounting, he started homeward in a brisk canter through the clear moonlight. He was soon in the main road, and exhilarated by the crisp mountain air, after a sweltering ride in the dusty train. He had reached the boundary fence of Drake's farm when he thought he heard some one crying out. He reined in and listened.

"Oh, father, please, please wait!" It was Dolly's voice, and it came from the more darkly shaded part of the road in front of her father's house. Urging his mount forward, Saunders was met by Drake on a plunging horse which he was violently whipping into action.

"What is the matter?" Saunders cried out; but with an oath of fury Drake flew past. He was hatless, coatless, and held something clutched in his hand other than the bridle-rein. Fairly astounded and not knowing what to do, Saunders remained in the road for a moment, then the sound of a low sob in the direction from whence Drake had come reminded him of Dolly's nearness, and he guided his horse forward. Suddenly in the corner of a rail fence, her face covered with her hands, he saw Dolly. Springing to the ground, he advanced to her.

"Dolly," he said, "what is it—what is wrong?"

She uncovered her face, stood staring at him helplessly. She raised her hand and pointed after her father, but, though she tried to speak, she seemed unable to utter a word.

"Is there anything I can do?" he asked. "For God's sake, tell me if there is. I want to help you."

"Yes, yes," she managed to articulate, "I know—and you are very kind, but—"

"You were trying to stop your father," he said. "Would you like for me—"

"You couldn't; he would kill you; he has his pistol; he doesn't know what he is doing."

"I think I know—I think I can guess—he is going to Atlanta."

Dolly nodded mechanically, her mouth open. "Oh, he is making an awful mistake, Mr. Saunders! He wouldn't let me explain. Ann told mother that I went out late one night to meet—meet Mr. Mostyn when he whistled. It was not Mr. Mostyn. It was Tobe Barnett, who came to warn me of father's danger of arrest by the officers. I can tell you—I can trust you, Mr. Saunders. Father is connected with some moonshiners, who—"

"I know it," Saunders broke in. "Now, listen to me, Dolly; this thing shall go no further if I can help it. He wants to catch the southbound train. I am going to stop him."

"No, no!" Dolly sprang forward, desperately clutching his arm. "He will shoot you."

"I *must* do it!" Saunders caught both her hands in his and pressed them. "You must let me—I have never been able to help you in any way, and I have always wanted to. I'd give my life to—to be of service to you to-night. I feel this thing, little friend. I must do something—I simply must!"

"I don't know what to say or do." Dolly clung to his hands desperately. She raised them spasmodically and unconsciously pressed them against her throbbing breast. "Oh, Mr. Saunders, it is so—so awful to be suspected of being bad when I—when I—"

"When you are the purest, sweetest child that ever breathed," he cried, fiercely. "They sha'n't start gossip about you." He dropped her hands and turned his horse round quickly. "I'll overtake him and stop him." He glanced at his watch. "I have no time to lose. I must go. Be brave, Dolly. It will come out right—it *must!*" He swung himself into his saddle; she clung to his foot which he was trying to put into the stirrup.

"He will kill you, too," she sobbed, "and I'll have *that* on my head also. Oh, Mr. Saunders—"

Gently he drew his foot from her clutch. There was a look in his eyes which she never forgot to the end of her life. "Excuse me, but I must hurry," he said. "He is on a fast horse, and the train may be on time. He must not get aboard. He mustn't, Dolly—good-by."

Away he dashed at full speed, bent to the mane of his mount like a chased Indian on the plains. Once he looked back, seeing the patient little figure standing like a mile-stone at the roadside. On he sped, tasting the dust pounded into the air by Drake's horse, and feeling the grit between his teeth. No one was in sight. The lights of the farmhouses on the road moved backward like ships in a fog. Suddenly, some distance ahead, he saw a rider dismounting. It was Drake, who now stooped down to pick up something he had dropped. As he did so he saw the pursuing horse, and, quickly springing into his saddle, was off again.

"Hold! Hold!" Saunders shouted.

"Hold—hell!" rippled back on the moonlight. "Bother me an' I'll put a ball in you. Back, I tell you!"

"Stop, Drake!" Saunders cried, without lessening his speed.

The only reply the pursued man made was the furious lashing of his horse. An ominous sound now fell on Saunders's ears. It was the whistle of a locomotive in the deep cut across the fields.

An oath of disappointment from Drake showed he had divined its full portent. It was now merely a question of speed. The race went on. The houses on the outer edge of the village flew past as if blown by a hurricane. Children in the yards looked up and cheered what they took for sport on the part of rollicking mountain riders. Saunders saw that he was gaining, and he urged his horse to even greater speed. He drew so close that the nose of his mount was lashed by the tail of Drake's horse.

"Stop a minute—just a minute!" Saunders pleaded. "I must see you."

Then, without lessening his gait, Drake turned half round in his saddle and pointed his revolver. Saunders heard the click of the hammer as it was cocked. Drake's demoniacal face in the white light had the greenish luster of a corpse—a corpse waking to life and grim purpose. "Fall back or I'll kill you!" he swore from frothing lips. "I know what you want; you want to take up for that dirty son of a—"

"No, no; you are mistaken. I don't. Wait—stop!"

They were now entering the open space between the station and the hotel. The train, with grinding brakes and escaping steam, was slowing up. Drake took aim over his shoulder. He fired. Saunders knew he was not hit. Frightened by the flash in his eyes, his horse reared up and almost threw him off behind. This delayed him for a moment, and Drake galloped on till he was close to the last car of the train. Saunders saw him throw the bridle-rein over the neck of his horse and spring down. The next instant Saunders was by his side and also on the ground. Again Drake raised his revolver, but Saunders was too quick for him. With a sudden blow he knocked the weapon from the other's grasp. It spun and flashed in the moonlight and fell in the weeds several yards away. Then Drake began to fumble in the pocket of his trousers for his knife. But again the younger man got the advantage. With the bound of a panther he had embraced and pinioned the arms of his antagonist to his sides. Back and forth they swung and pounded, Drake swearing, spitting, and trying even to bite. The locomotive whistled. It was off again. Seeing this, Drake swung himself free and made a break for the end car, but Saunders was at his heels; and, throwing out his hand, he grasped the runner's arm and violently threw him around. Again they were face to face. Again Saunders pinioned his arms. Drake was helpless. He struggled with all his strength, but it was unequal to that of his determined captor.

"You've *got* to listen to me, Drake!" Saunders said, fiercely. "You've got plenty of time to settle with that man if you insist on it, but you've got to hear me!"

"Well, let me loose then, damn you!" Drake panted. "Le' me loose!"

"All right, I'll let you loose." Saunders released him, and they stood facing each other, both out of breath. "I'm your friend, Tom Drake—and you know it," Saunders gasped. "I'm your daughter's friend, too. I'm sufficiently interested in her not to let you soil her good name as you are trying to do to-night. She is innocent, I tell you, and you are a coward to—"

"You say—you say—"

Several by-standers at the ticket-office and hotel, attracted by the combat, were approaching.

"Go back!" Saunders held up his hand warningly. "This is no affair of yours. I want to speak to him in private. Leave us alone."

The men halted, stared dubiously, and finally, seeing that the quarrel was over, they went back whence they had come. "Let's step over here," Saunders proposed; and he led the way to the railway blacksmith's shop, now closed and unlighted. In the shadow of its smoky wall they faced each other again.

"You said—" Drake began, "you said—"

"I said she was innocent of the foul charge you are making against her," Saunders said, sharply. "You are a crazy man, Drake. You tried to kill me back there, although I am bent on befriending you and your daughter. She is as sweet and pure as the angels in heaven."

"I—I know more than you do. Ann said—"

"Yes, I know what the child said," Saunders retorted. "And if you had been the right sort of a father you would not have acted on such slight evidence. Dolly is in this plight simply because she saved you—"

"Saved *me?* What the hell—"

"Yes, she saved you from arrest and imprisonment as a moonshiner. The whistle Ann heard was not a signal from Mostyn. It was Tobe Barnett, who had come to warn her of your danger. She did meet Mostyn that night, but it was by accident, and not appointment. Dolly could have explained it all to Ann, but she did not want the child to know of your connection with that gang. Now you've got the whole thing, Drake."

The mountaineer stared, his mouth open; the sinews of his face were drawn into distortion.

"You say—you tell me—you say—"

"That's the whole thing," Saunders said. "Now let's go home. Dolly deserves a humble apology from you—you ought to get down on your knees to her and beg her to forgive you. I know of no other woman like her in this world—none, none, anywhere. She has my admiration, my respect, my reverence."

"But—but"—Drake's dead face began to kindle—"Ann said she saw that dirty scamp actually holdin' her in his arms an' kissin' 'er. She said that Dolly made no denial of it, an' now, accordin' to the papers, he's goin' to marry a woman in Atlanta."

Saunders's glance sought the ground, his eyes went aimlessly to the two horses nibbling grass near by.

"Ah, ha, I see that floors you!" Drake flared out. "You admit that the low-lived scamp did take advantage of our confidence, an'—"

"You've got to face that part of it as I would do if she were my child," Saunders answered. "Listen to me, Drake. Mostyn is not a whit better or worse than many other men of his class. He has been fast and reckless, but when he met Dolly he met the first pure and elevating influence of his life. I am in his confidence. He told me the whole story. He determined that he would win her love and make her his wife. When he left here it was with the firm resolution of being wholly true to her. Now, I can only say that on his return home he found himself in a situation which would have taken more strength of character to get out of than he had. You cannot afford to attack him. Such a thing would reflect on your brave daughter, and you have no right to do it, no matter how you feel about it. From now on you've got to consider her feelings. If she cares for—for him, and—and—is depressed by the newspaper reports, that is all the more reason for your sympathy and support. Surely you can realize what she has escaped. As that man's wife her life would have been hell on earth. He is wholly unworthy of her. If she were my—sister, I'd rather see her dead than married to him."

Drake stood with hanging head. He stepped slowly to his

horse and grasped the rein. Saunders went a few feet to the right, searched on the ground a moment and picked up the revolver. Returning, he extended it to its owner.

Drake took it silently, and clumsily thrust it into his pocket. He hesitated; he gulped, swallowed, then said, huskily:

"You are my friend, Saunders. I've had some that I depended on in a pinch, but you've done me a big favor to-night. I'll never git forgiveness for tryin' to shoot you—never—never in this world."

"That is all right." Saunders extended his hand, and the other clasped it firmly.

A man with a polished club tied to his wrist was striding toward them. It was the village marshal, Alf Floyd. Drake eyed him helplessly.

"Let me talk to him," Saunders said, under his breath. "You ride on home. Leave him to me. This must not get out."

"What's the trouble here?" the officer asked, arriving just as Drake rode away.

Saunders laughed carelessly as he reached for the bridle of his grazing horse. "It means that I got the best of Tom Drake. He bet me a dollar he could catch that train and get aboard. He would have done it, too, if I hadn't caught him around the waist at the last minute and swung him back. He didn't like it much, but he is all right now."

"Somebody said they heard a pistol-shot," the officer said.

"An accident," Saunders replied. "Drake dropped it—horse jerked it from his hand. I suppose we may have violated an ordinance in racing in town, and if so I'm willing to pay the fine. I'm responsible."

"There *is* an ordinance," the marshal said, "but I won't make a case out o' this."

"All right, Alf; thanks. How goes it?"

"Oh, so-so. How is it in the city?"

"Hot and dusty." Saunders mounted deliberately. "Good night, Alf; I must get out home and eat something."

A few minutes later as Saunders was slowly riding past Drake's front gate he noticed a figure on the inside of the yard close to the fence. It was Dolly. She opened the gate and came out. He reined in and, hat in hand, sprang to the ground. Her head was covered with a thin white shawl held beneath her chin, and her pale face showed between the folds as pure and patient as a suffering nun's. He saw that she was trying to speak, but was unable to do so.

"What is it, Dolly?" he faltered. "I suppose your father got back?"

"Yes." It was a bare labial whisper. She nodded; she put her cold hand into his great, warm eager one, and he held it as tenderly as if it had been a dying sparrow.

"I am glad I happened to reach him," he said, in an effort to relieve her embarrassment. "We had it nip and tuck," he added, lightly. "My lungs are lined with dust."

He felt her fingers and palm faintly flutter.

"Oh, oh, Mr. Saunders!" she gulped. "I can never, never thank you enough. I met him down the road just now. He actually cried. I have never seen him give way before."

Saunders stared helplessly. He knew not what to say. In the moonlight he saw tears like drops of dew rise in her eyes and trickle down her cheeks.

"You must not cry," he managed to say. "Don't break down, Dolly; you have been so brave all along."

She released the shawl beneath her chin and began to fumble in her pocket for her handkerchief. Seeing she was unable to find it, he took out his own, and while he still held her hand with his left he tenderly dried her tears. Suddenly she clasped his hand with both of hers.

"I suppose you know everything—" she faltered. "How silly I have been to think—to imagine that Mr. Mostyn really meant—" A great sob struggled up within her and broke on her lips.

"I know *this*, Dolly." His face hardened to the appearance of stone in the white light from the sky. "I know that from this moment on you must never give him another thought."

"You don't understand a woman's feelings," she returned, in the saddest of intonations. "I know what you say is right and true, but—it is like this; he seems to have—died! I think of him only as dead, and a woman with a heart cannot at a moment's notice put her dead out of mind. I can't, somehow, blame him. You see, I think I understand him. He is not going to be happy, and I'm afraid I'll never be able to forget that fact. He was trying to get right. I saw his struggle. I did not fully know what it meant when we parted, but I see it all now. I thought I could help him, but it is too late—too late; and oh, that is the terrible part! I feel somewhat like a mother must feel who sees a son, hopelessly wrong, taken from her sight forever. Oh, I pity him, pity him, pity him!"

"Nevertheless, you must try to put him wholly out of your mind and heart," Saunders urged. "You deserve happiness, and this thing must not kill your chances for it. Time will help."

"Isn't it queer?" she sighed; "but in moments of deepest sorrow we don't want Time, God, or anything else to take our grief away. Really, I feel to-night like an invisible thing crushed out of its body and left intact to float forever in pitiless space."

He led her to the gate and opened it. "You must not indulge such weird thoughts," he said, his features set in a mask of tense inner pain. "You must go to bed and try to sleep."

"Sleep!" she laughed, harshly. "I'll have to wake. The happy chickens, ducks, turkeys, and twittering, chirping birds will rouse me at sun-up. I must teach to-morrow. I must answer questions about grammar, history, geography, and arithmetic. I must correct compositions, write on a blackboard with chalk, point to dots on maps, scold little ones, reprove big ones, talk to parents, and through it all *think, think, think!* I am Dolly Drake. Do you know, Mr. Saunders, the queerest thing to me in all the world is that I am Dolly Drake? Sometimes I pronounce the name in wonder, as if I had never heard it before. I seem to have been a thousand persons in former periods."

"Dolly, listen." Saunders bent till his face was close to hers. "I am your friend. I shall be true to you forever and ever. From now on nothing else on earth can be of so much importance to me as your welfare. To help you shall be my constant aim."

"I know it, dear, sweet friend." The words bubbled from a swelling sob. "And oh, it is sweet and comforting at a time like this! Don't—don't stop me." And therewith she raised his hand, pressed her lips upon it, and turned quickly away.

PART II

CHAPTER I

Five years passed. Again it was summer. Mostyn with his wife and his only child, Richard, Jr., lived in the Mitchell mansion, which, save for a new coat of paint, was unchanged. Mostyn himself was considerably altered in appearance. There were deeper lines in his face; he was thinner, more given to nervousness and loss of sleep; his hair was turning gray; he had been told by his doctor that he worried too much and that he must check the tendency.

Things had not gone in his married life as the financier had wished. One of the most objectionable was the unexpected change in his father-in-law, who had lapsed quite abruptly into troublesome dotage. From a shrewd business man old Mitchell had become a querulous child, subject to fits of suspicion and violent outbursts of anger. At the most embarrassing moments he would totter into the bank, approach his son-in-law, and insist on talking over matters which he was quite incapable of seeing in a rational light. Mostyn had tried to deal with him firmly, only to bring down a torrent of half-wild threats as to what the old man would do in regard to certain investments the two held in common. Indeed, it was plain to many that Mitchell had formed an intuitive dislike for his son-in-law, which, somehow, was not lessened by his great love for his grandson.

Saunders became a genial sort of escape-valve for the old man's endless chatter and complaint, doing all in his power to pacify him, though it required no little time and energy.

One warm day in the present June Mitchell came to the bank, and, frowning angrily, he went into Mostyn's office, where his son-in-law sat absorbed over some intricate calculations in percentage.

"Huh!" he sniffed. "Your nigger porter told me you were too busy to see me. If he hadn't dodged I'd have hit the whelp with this cane, sir. Busy! I say busy! If it hadn't been for me and my money I'd like to know where you'd be to-day. I guess you wouldn't run long."

Flushing with combined anger and sensitive shame, Mostyn put his papers aside and rose.

"Sit down, and rest," he said. "Albert meant no harm. I told him that I had some important work to do and that I did not want to be disturbed just now; but, of course, I had no reference to *you.*"

"Oh, I know you didn't!" Mitchell sneered, his chin and white beard quivering. "I know what your plan is. I'm no fool. You are handling my means, and you are afraid I'll want to know what you have done with them. I'll have a statement by law—that's what I'll do."

"You really *must* be reasonable," Mostyn said, helplessly. "Only last week I explained it all in detail in the presence of Saunders and Wright, and you were quite satisfied. You ought to know that we can't go over such matters every day. I assure you that everything is in good shape."

"Are you *sure?* That's what I want to know." The harsh expression in Mitchell's face was softening. "I—I get to worrying—I admit it. You and I used to get along all right, but you never consult me now as you used to do. I'm older than you are, but my judgment is sound. I'm not dead yet, and I won't be regarded that way."

"I know you are all right." Mostyn smiled pacifically. "Won't you take a seat?"

"No, I'm going back home. I don't like the way things are running there, either. Irene is never at home, it seems to me, and my grandson has nobody to look after him but that trifling nurse. Irene has gone to some fool reception to-day, and says she and Kitty are going to a dance at Buckton's country house to-night. You may call that right and proper, sir, but I don't. The way married couples live to-day is an outrage on common decency. If you had any backbone you'd make your wife behave herself. She is more of a belle, sir, right now than before you married her. She is crazy for excitement, and the whole poker-playing, wine-drinking set she goes with is on the road to perdition."

Laying his hand on the old man's arm gently, Mostyn led him toward the door. "Don't let it worry you," he said. "The boy is well and sound, and Irene means no harm. She has always loved society, and when we were married it was with the understanding that she should not be hampered."

"And that is right where you made the mistake of your life." Mitchell pulled back from the door. "The way you and she live is not natural. The Lord never intended it to be so. You know as well as I do that Irene used to have a silly sort of liking or fancy for Andy Buckton."

Mostyn nodded, his eyes averted. "Yes, yes, of course," he said, hesitatingly. "She told me all about it at the time, quite frankly."

"Well, you know, I presume, that his uncle left him a lot of money when he died the other day?"

"I heard something about it." Mostyn bit his lip in vexation, as he reached out for the doorknob and turned it cautiously.

"Well, it is true, and it has turned the fool's head; he is spending it like water. He is giving a big blow-out to-night, and it is all for your wife, sir—your wife."

Mostyn made no reply, though his face looked graver; the sharp-drawn lines about his mouth deepened.

"You heard what I said, didn't you?" Mitchell demanded.

"Yes, of course."

"Well, let me tell you one thing, and then you can do as you please about it. I am not going to take any hand in it. Irene has no respect for me or my opinion here lately. She gets mad the minute I say a word to her. Andy Buckton is as big a fool about her as he ever was. I got it straight, from a person who knows, that he makes no secret of it. And that isn't all, sir— that isn't all. Irene is just vain enough of her good looks to like it. Le'me tell you something, sir. This town is not Paris, and our country is not France, but that fast set Irene runs with is trying to think so. They read about the Four Hundred in New York, its scandals and divorces in high life, and think it is smart to imitate it. You seem to stay out of it, but what if you do? Are you going to sit like a knot on a log and have them say you made a loveless marriage for money, and—"

"Stop!" Mostyn flared out. "I won't stand it. You are going too far!"

"Ah, I see you can be touched," the old man laughed, putting his hand on Mostyn's arm in his most senile mood. "I just wanted to set you thinking, that's all."

When Mitchell was gone the banker sat down at his work again, but he could not put his mind on it. He fumbled the papers nervously. His brows met in a troubled frown. "I can't stand any more of this," he thought. "He is driving me insane—the man does not live who could put up with it day after day."

Will N. Harben

Going to the door, he asked one of the clerks to send Saunders to him if he was quite disengaged. A moment later his partner entered. The last five years had served him well. He had never looked better. His skin was clear, his eyes bright, his movement calm and alert.

"Did you want to see me?" he asked.

"If you are not busy," Mostyn replied.

"Nothing to do just now," Saunders said, sitting down near the desk.

Mostyn gave him a troubled look. "The old man has just left," he said.

"I thought I recognized his voice," Saunders answered. "He has a way of talking quite loud of late."

There was a pause, during which Mostyn continued to stare with fluttering lashes; then he said:

"He is giving me a great deal of trouble, Saunders—a great deal."

"I see he is; in fact, all of us have noticed it."

"It is getting more and more serious," Mostyn sighed, heavily. "You see, it is not only here that he talks. He goes to the other banks and to the offices of the brokers and chatters like a child about our confidential affairs. I am afraid he will do us absolute financial injury. He is insanely suspicious, and there is no telling what report he may set afloat."

"I think most persons understand his condition," Saunders returned. "Delbridge does, I know. He goes to see Delbridge often. I see your predicament and sympathize with you. The old man has lost all his discretion, and you really cannot afford to confer with him."

"The trouble is, he has his legal rights," Mostyn said, tentatively, "and the slightest thing may turn him against me. There are shyster lawyers here who would not hesitate to advise him wrongly. They would get their fee, and that is all they would want. As I look at it the situation is serious, and growing worse."

"It is awkward, to say the least," Saunders admitted, "and I confess that I do not know what to advise."

"Well, that is all," Mostyn concluded. "I wanted to speak to you about it. He upsets me every time he comes in, and he is quite as troublesome at home, I assure you. I envy you, old chap, with your care-free life, spent half in the country. How is your plantation?"

"Fine—never had better crops." Saunders's eyes kindled with latent enthusiasm. "The weather has been just right this season. Run up and spend next Sunday with me. It will do you good. You stay in town too much."

Mostyn shrugged his shoulders. He sighed and bowed his head over his papers. "Not this season," he said, as if his thoughts were far away. Suddenly he cast a wavering glance at his partner, hesitated, and said:

"I have always wanted to go back up there, Saunders. That was one period of my life that is constantly before me. I may as well speak of it and be done with it. You always seemed to shirk the subject, and I have hesitated to mention it, but there is no one else I could question. The last time I heard of Dolly Drake she was still unmarried. Is there any likelihood of her marrying?"

Mostyn's eyes were downcast, and he failed to see the half-angry flush which was creeping over Saunders's face.

"I really can't say," he returned, coldly. "She is still teaching school, and is in the best of health; but, Mostyn, you have no right to think—to fancy that she has remained single because—"

"Oh, I don't!" the other sighed. "I'm not such a fool. She knows me too well by this time for that."

There was an awkward pause. Saunders, with eyes on the door, was rising. With an appealing look of detention in his worn face Mostyn also stood up. "I'd give a great deal to see her. I'd be glad even to see a picture of her. I wonder what she looks like now. She was scarcely more than a child when she and I— when we parted. I don't think there can be any harm in my being frank in these days when the wives of men make a jest of matrimonial love, and I confess freely that I have never been able to forget—"

"Don't tell me about it!" Saunders interrupted. "You have no right, Mostyn, even to think of her after—after what took place. But you ought to have sense enough, at any rate, to know that she wouldn't continue to care for you all these years. I see her now and then and talk to her. I am helping her build a new schoolhouse up there on some land I donated, and have had to consult her several times of late about the building-plans. She is more beautiful and brilliant than ever, though she still has cares enough. Her father doesn't make much of a living, and her brother George is engaged to one of the girls in the neighborhood and so cannot be counted on for help. Ann is a young lady now, and Dolly dresses her nicely at her own expense."

"Of course, I know that she has forgotten me," Mostyn said, with feeling. "I made the one great mistake of my life when I—you know what I mean, Saunders?"

"Yes, I know," Saunders answered, quickly, "but that is past and gone, Mostyn. The main harm you did was, perhaps, to kill her faith in men in general. I don't really think she will ever give her heart to any one. She seems farther from that sort of thing than any woman I ever met. She has had, I think, many suitors."

"Then from what you say I gather that she doesn't mention me?" Mostyn said, heavily. "She has no curiosity at all to know how—how my marriage terminated?" "How *could* she have?" Saunders asked, frigidly. "We'd better not talk of it, Mostyn. I am sure she would not wholly approve of this conversation. But in justice to her I must insist that she is *not* broken-hearted by any means. She is as brave and cheerful as she ever was. Her character seems to have deepened and sweetened under the knowledge of the world which she acquired by her unfortunate experience with you."

When Saunders had left, Mostyn bowed his head on his desk.

"If I had been the sort of man Saunders is, Dolly would have been my wife," he thought. "My wife! my wife! actually my wife!"

CHAPTER II

That afternoon when the bank was closed Mostyn went home. He walked for the sake of the exercise and with the hope of distracting his mind from the many matters which bore more or less heavily on his tired brain. As he approached the gate the sight of his little son playing on the lawn with a miniature tennis racket and ball gave him a thrill of delight. The boy was certainly beautiful. He had great brown eyes, rich golden hair, was sturdy, well built, and active for a child of only four years.

The father opened the gate softly, and when within the yard he hid himself behind the trunk of an oak and cautiously peered out, watching the little fellow toss the ball and make ineffectual efforts to hit it with the racket. Then Mostyn whistled softly, saw the boy drop his racket and look all round, his sweet face alert with eagerness. Mostyn whistled again, and then the child espied him and, with hands outstretched, came running, laughing and shouting gleefully.

"I see you, Daddy!" he cried. Whereupon Mostyn slipped around the tree out of sight, letting the amused child follow him. Round after round was made, and then, suddenly stooping down, the father caught the boy in his arms and raised him up. Pressing him fondly to his breast, he kissed the warm, flushed cheeks.

Till dusk he played with the child on the grass, pitching the ball and teaching the little fellow to hit it. Then Hilda, the mulatto nurse, came for her charge, and little Dick, with many expostulations, was taken away.

Going into the house, Mostyn met his father-in-law in the hall. The old man stopped him abruptly at the foot of the stairs.

"Did any mail come for me on the noon train?" he demanded, querulously, a light of suspicion in his eyes.

"Not that I know of," Mostyn answered. "It was not put on my desk, I am sure."

"Well, some of it goes *somewhere*," Mitchell complained. "I know I don't see it all. I've written letters that would have been answered by this time, and it wouldn't surprise me if some-body down there was tampering with it."

Seeing the utter hopelessness of bringing his father-in-law to reason by explanation or argument, Mostyn went on up-stairs. Noticing that the door of his wife's chamber, adjoining his own, was ajar, he pushed it open and went in. The room was brightly illuminated with electric light, and standing before a tall pier-glass he found his wife. She wore a costly evening gown of rare old lace and was trying on a pretty diamond necklace.

"Oh!" she exclaimed, indifferently, as she caught sight of him over her bare powdered shoulder. "I thought it was Cousin Kitty. She promised to be here early. If she is late we'll have to go without her. She is awfully slow. I saw you playing with Dick on the grass. He makes too much noise, screaming out like that, and you only make him worse cutting up with him as you do. Between you and that boy and father, with his constant, babyish complaints, I am driven to desperation."

Mostyn shrugged his shoulders wearily, and sat down in a chair at her quaint mahogany dressing-table. Irene had not changed materially, though a close observer, had the light been that of day, might have remarked that she was thinner and more nervous. Her eyes held a shadowy, unsatisfied expression, and her voice was keyed unnaturally high.

Noticing his unwonted silence, she put down her hand-mirror and eyed him with a slow look of irritation. "Of course, you are not going to-night," she said.

"Hardly," he smiled, satirically, "being quite uninvited."

"Well, you needn't say it in *that* tone," she answered. "You have only yourself to blame. You never accept such invitations, so how could you expect people to run after you with them?"

"I don't expect them to," he answered, tartly. "If they asked me I'd decline. I simply don't enjoy that sort of thing at all."

"Of course you don't," she laughed. "The last time you went to a ball you looked like an insane man pacing up and down all by yourself. Kitty said you asked her to dance and forgot all about it. Dick, your day is over."

"I wonder if yours ever will be," he sniffed. "I see no prospect of it. You are on the go night and day. You are killing yourself. It is as bad as the morphine habit with you. You love admiration more than any woman I ever saw."

She arched her neck before the glass and turned to him wearily. "Do you know what you'll do in another minute? You'll talk yourself into another one of your disgusting rages over my own private affairs. You are a business man and would not violate an ordinary business agreement, but you are constantly ignoring the positive compact between us."

"I didn't expect at the time to have you going so constantly with a man that—"

"Oh, you didn't?" she laughed, tantalizingly. "You were to have all sorts of outside freedom, but I was not. Well, you were mistaken, that's all. I know whom you are hinting at. You mean Andy Buckton. I'm going with him to-night. Why shouldn't I? He's got up the party for me. Dick, don't tell me that you are actually jealous. It would be too delicious for anything."

"I can't ask you not to go with the fellow," Mostyn answered, "considering the well-known habits of your limited set to lay down new laws of conduct, but you nor no other woman can form the slightest idea of what it costs a man's pride to have people say that his wife is constantly seen with a man who always has been in love with her."

An almost imperceptible gleam of delight flashed into Irene's eyes, and a tinge of real color struggled beneath the powder on her face.

"You don't mean, Dick, that he really, really loves me?" she said, lingeringly.

"I think he does," Mostyn answered, bluntly. "He never got over your refusal to marry him. He shows it on every occasion. Everybody knows it, and that's what makes it so hard to—to put up with. I think I really have a right to ask the mother of my child to—"

"Don't begin that, Dick!" Irene commanded, sharply. "I have my rights, and you shall respect them. It is cowardly of you to always mention the boy in that way. I am not crazy about children, and I won't pretend to be. You know I did not want a child in the first place. I am not that sort. I want to have a good time. I like admiration. I like amusements. You men get the keenest sort of pleasure out of gambling in stocks and futures. All day long you are in a whirl of excitement. But you expect us women to stay at home and be as humdrum as hens in a chicken-house. You are to have your fun and come home and have us wives pet you and pamper you up for another day of delight. Dick, that may go all right with farmers' wives who haven't shoes to wear out to meeting, but it won't do for women with money of *their own* to spend."

"I knew *that* would come," he flashed at her. "It always does crop up sooner or later."

"You are out of temper to-night, Dick," she retorted. "And it is simply because I am going with Andy Buckton. You needn't deny it."

"I don't like the gossip that is going around." Mostyn frowned and bit his mustache as he said this. "The people of Atlanta, as a whole, are moral, conservative citizens, and the doings of your small set are abhorrent to them."

"*My* set!" Irene forced a harsh, mirthless laugh. "And for goodness' sake, what do they think of *your* set? You force me to say this, Dick. There is not a person in this city who has not heard of you and that unspeakable Winship woman."

Mostyn flinched beneath the gaze she bent on him. "That is a thing of the past, Irene, and you know it," he stammered, trying to keep his temper.

"I can consider it a thing of the past," she returned, coldly, "if I will take your word for it, just as you may or may not take my word for my conduct with Andy Buckton. Oh, I suppose it is nothing for a wife to see the knowing smiles that pass around when the gaudy creature shows up at the theater or ball-game accompanied by gamblers and bar-keepers. The brazen thing stares straight at me whenever I am near her."

Mostyn was now white with restrained fury. He stood up. "I will not go over all that again," he said. "The mistake I made was in ever owning up to the thing."

"You *had* to own up to it," Irene answered, bluntly. "I knew it when we were married, and I would not mention it now if you were not constantly nagging me about my actions. Dick, you will have to let me alone. I won't take advice from you."

He met her frank eyes with a shrinking stare. "I shall let you alone in the future," he faltered. "I see I have to. You are merciless. For the sake of the boy we must live in harmony. God knows we must!"

"All right," she laughed, coldly, "that is another agreement. Harmony is the word. Now, go away. Kitty is not coming. She may be going with some one else."

Mostyn went to his room across the hall. He bathed his bloodless face and hands and automatically brushed his hair before the glass, eying his features critically. "Can that actually be me?" he whispered to the grim reflection. "I look like a man of sixty. I'm as old and decrepit as—Jeff Henderson. Why did I think of him? Why am I constantly thinking of that old man, unless it is because he has predicted my ruin so confidently? He seems as sure of it as he is of the air he breathes. If evil thought bearing on a man can hurt him, as the mental scientists believe, Henderson's will eventually get me down. He would give his life to permanently injure me. So would Marie. She can't forgive me for ignoring her. She can't understand any more than I do *why* I ignore her."

There was a rap on the door. It was a servant to ask if he wanted his supper.

"Not now," he answered. "Keep it for me. I'll be in later."

CHAPTER III

He went down to the lawn, lighted a cigar, and began to smoke, striding nervously back and forth. A smart pair of horses hitched to a trap whirled into the carriage-drive and stopped in the porte-cochere. In the rays from the overhead lamp Mostyn saw Buckton alight and ascend the steps to the veranda. A half-smoked cigar cast into the shrubbery emitted a tiny shower of sparks. Mostyn saw the young man peering in at the window of the lighted drawing-room. He noted the spick-and-span appearance, the jaunty, satisfied air of expectancy, and his blood began to boil with rage.

"My God!" he groaned. "She may be falling in love with him—if she has not *always* loved him, and he now knows it. She may have told him so. And when they are alone together, as they will be in a few minutes on the road, what more natural than that he should caress her? I would have done it with any man's wife if I had felt an inclination. I am the joke of the town and must bear it. I must stand by and let my wife and another man—"

Buckton was at the door speaking to the maid who had answered his ring.

"No; tell her, please, that I'll wait out here on the lawn." Mostyn remarked the note of curbed elation in the voice, and saw Buckton turn down the steps.

A match flared in the handsome face as another cigar was

lighted. Fearing that he might have been seen from the drive, Mostyn was compelled to step forward and greet the man with the conventional unconcern he had been able to summon to his aid on former occasions.

"Hello," he heard himself saying, automatically, as he strode across the grass to the other smoker. "Fine evening for your shindig."

"Tiptop," Buckton said, with a sort of restraint Mostyn inwardly resented. "Couldn't have turned out better. Sorry you've cut out the giddy whirl, old man. As I passed your bank this morning I thought of asking you, but you have refused so many times that—"

"Oh no." Mostyn heartily despised the role he was playing. "I am no longer good at that sort of thing."

"Had your day, I see," Buckton laughed, significantly. "You certainly kept the pace, if all tales are true. The sort of thing we do these days must be tame by comparison."

"Oh, I don't know," Mostyn returned, with enforced care-lessness. "Men are the same the world over. I have not yet had a chance to congratulate you on your recent good fortune."

"Thanks, old man." Buckton puffed his smoke into the still moonlight. "It certainly was a lift to me. I was never cut out for business, and I was at the end of my row. I confess I am not complaining now. I am just at the age to know how to spend money."

The talk languished. Both men seemed suddenly burthened by obtrusive self-consciousness. Buckton twisted his mustache nervously and flicked at the ashless tip of his cigar, glancing toward the house. "Oh, I quite forgot to deliver Miss Kitty's message to Irene—to Mrs. Mostyn, I should say. She was to drive out with us, but at the last minute Dr. Regan found that he could get off and asked her to go in his car."

"Arranged between them," Mostyn thought, darkly. "I know the trick. Regan doesn't care a rap for Kitty. It is part of the game, and I am the tool."

"I understand you have a new car yourself," Mostyn said, aloud.

"Yes, and experts tell me that it is the best in town. I'll run around and take you out some day. But I really care more for horses. It may be due to my Virginia blood. I wouldn't swap this pair for all the cars in town. For a trip like this to-night horses come handy. There are some rough places between here and my home."

"It does away with the chauffeur," Mostyn said, inwardly, as his tongue lay dead in his mouth. He glanced toward the open doorway. "Irene may be ready," he remarked, moving toward the house.

"Yes, I see her coming down the stairs," answered Buckton, dropping his cigar, a look of boyish eagerness capturing his face. "I'll run on and help her with her wraps. So long, old man."

Mostyn made some inarticulate response of no import in particular, and dropped back, allowing Buckton to stride on to the veranda, his hat jauntily swinging at his side. Irene was now in the doorway, poised like a picture in a frame.

Slinking farther away beneath the trees and behind shrubbery, Mostyn heard the greetings between the two, and saw them shaking hands, standing face to face. Irene looked so young, so different from the calculating woman who had just asserted her financial and marital rights in her chamber. No wonder that her escort was fascinated when she had so long been withheld from him! Mostyn told himself that he well knew the "stolen-sweets" sensation. He peered above a clump of boxwood like a thief, upon grounds to which he was unaccustomed, and watched them as they got into the trap. Irene's rippling laugh, and Buckton's satisfied response as he tucked the robes about her, seemed things of Satanic design. They were off. The restive pair, with high-reined, arching necks, trotted down the drive to the street, and a moment later were out of sight.

Mostyn went into the house, back to the desolate dining-room, and sat down in his chair at the head of the table. The maid who came to receive his order and turn on a fuller light had a look in her eyes which indicated that she was aware of his mood. He would have resented it had he dared, but it was only one of many things which had of late grated on him but could not be prevented.

"Has Mr. Mitchell had his supper?" Mostyn asked, applying himself reluctantly to the simple repast before him.

"Yes, sir, and gone up to his room," the girl answered. "He is out of sorts to-day. I have never seen him so troublesome. He has threatened to discharge us all."

"Don't mind him." Mostyn's voice sounded to him as if uttered by some tongue other than his own. He half fancied that the maid, for reasons peculiar to her class, had a sort of contempt for him. She, as well as the other servants, no doubt thought of him as having married for money, Mitchell's fortune being so much larger than his own diminished and ever-lessening capital.

Supper over, he went back to the veranda. Should he go to the club, as he sometimes did to pass an evening? He had a feeling against it. He did not care for cards or drinking, and they were the chief amusements indulged in by the habitual loungers about the rooms. There might be some summer play on at one of the theaters, but as a rule they were very poor at that season of the year, and he knew he had a frame of mind which could not be diverted. At this juncture he became conscious of something of an almost startling nature. It was an undefinable, even maternal feeling that he ought to stay with his child. He shrugged his shoulders and smiled at the sheer absurdity of the idea, yet it clung to him persistently. He tried to analyze it; it eluded analysis. It had haunted him before, and the time had always been when Irene was away. Was it some strange psychic sympathy or bond of blood between his motherless offspring and himself? Was his guilty soul whispering to him that he was responsible for the deserted human bud, and that he, man though he was, should give it the care and love denied it?

Obeying an impulse he could not put down, he turned into the house and softly ascended the stairs. The door of the nursery was open. A low-turned light was burning in a night-lamp on the bureau. The nurse was below eating with the other servants. He was alone and unobserved. The child was asleep in its little white bed, and he crept forward and looked down upon it. The night being warm, little Richard was not covered, and, with his shapely legs and fair breast exposed, he lay asleep. There was a suggestion of a smile on the beautiful face, the pink lips were parted, the dainty fingers were clutched as if holding some dream-object tight in their clasp.

With a sigh that was almost audible the father turned away. At the door he glanced back, having noted the intense warmth of the room. The nurse, as many of her tropical race are apt to do, had forgotten to ventilate the chamber. The two windows were closed. Angrily he crept across the carpeted floor and noiselessly raised the sashes as high as they would go, feeling the fresh air stream in. With a parting glance at the sleeper he withdrew.

Descending the stairs, he went out on the lawn again. Even that scrap of Nature's realm had a tendency to soothe his snarled sensibilities. It might have been the dew which was rising and cooling his feet, or the pale, blinking stars, the sedative rays of which seemed to penetrate to his seething brain. He remembered John Leach's sermon that day in the mountains at the cross-roads store. The fellow had found something. He had found the way of the life spiritual, and it had come to him through sin, suffering, humiliation, and final self-immolation. Mostyn recalled the resolutions he had made under the influence of the man's compelling eloquence; he recalled the breaking of the resolutions. He thought of Dolly Drake, and groaned in actual pain of body and soul. He told himself that he had then deliberately trampled under foot his last spiritual opportunity. "Dolly Drake, Dolly Drake!" the words, unuttered though they were by lips which he felt were too profane for such use, seemed to float like notes of accusing music. Saunders had said she was more beautiful than ever. She might have been his but for his weakness. Perhaps she still thought of him now and then. If she could know of this unconquerable despair, she would pity him. How sweet such pity as hers would be! A sob struggled up within him and threatened to burst; he felt the sharp pain of suppression in his breast. It was as if his soul was urging his too-callous body to weep. Dolly was as unobtainable as the heaven of the tramp preacher's vision. For Mostyn only protracted evil was now available, and that was sickening to his very thought.

He wondered, seeing that it was now ten o'clock, if he could go to sleep. In deep sleep he would be able to forget. He decided to try. He went up to his room, and, aided only by the moonlight, which fell through the windows, he undressed and threw himself down on his bed. For an hour he was wakeful. He was just becoming drowsy when he heard voices in the nursery across the hall. He recognized the sharp, scolding voice of the nurse, and the timid reply of the child. Rising, Mostyn went to the open door of the nursery and looked in.

"What is it?" he asked.

"He is begging to go to your bed," the woman answered, peevishly. "You've spoiled him, Mr. Mostyn. He wants to do it every night. He is getting worse and worse."

A thrill of delight, yearning delight, passed over the father. He stood silent for a moment, ashamed to have even the black servant suspect what he so keenly desired.

"Daddy, Dick wants you," a voice soft, tremulous, and

unspeakably appealing came from the little bed.

"Hush, and go to sleep!" the nurse called out. "You are a bad boy, keeping us awake like this."

"No, let him come," Mostyn said, in a voice which was husky, and shook against his will. "Come, Dick!"

The little white-robed form slid eagerly from the bed and fairly ran to the arms which were hungrily outstretched. With the soft body against his breast, a confident arm about his neck, the father bore him to his room and put him down on the back side of the wide bed.

"Now you will sleep, won't you?" he said, his voice exultantly tender.

"Yes, Daddy." Dick stretched his pretty legs out straight. Silence filled the room; the mystic rays of moonlight falling in at the window seemed to bring with them the despondent murmur of the city outside. The deep, fragrant breathing of the child soon showed that he was asleep. Cautiously Mostyn propped himself up on his elbow and looked into the placid face. "He has my brow," he mused, bitterly; "my hands; my ears; my long ringers, with their curving nails; my slender ankles and high-instepped feet; and, my God! he has my telltale sensual lips. Here am I in the throes of a hell produced by infinite laws. What is to prevent him—the helpless replica of myself—from taking the way I took? The edge of the alluring abyss will crumble under his blind tread as it crumbled under mine, and this—this—this cloying horror which is on me to-night may be my gift to him—for whose sake I would die—yes, die!"

Silently Mostyn left the bed and took a seat on the broad sill of one of the windows overlooking the lawn.

"What will be the end?" he asked himself. "It can't go on like this. I am not man enough to stand it. If I were not afraid of death, I would —no, I wouldn't"—he glanced at the bed—"I am responsible for his being here. He is the flower of my corruption. God may desert him, but I won't. I will protect him, love him, pity him, care for him to the end."

A cold drop fell on his hand and trickled through his fingers. He was weeping.

CHAPTER IV

Saunders spent the end of that week on his plantation in the mountains. On Saturday morning he dropped in at Drake's to see Dolly. John Webb came to the door in response to his rap. He was quite unchanged. Even the clothes he was wearing had the same look as those he wore five years before.

"She ain't here," he said. "I seed 'er, with some books an' papers under 'er arm, headed for the schoolhouse just after breakfast. I reckon she's got some examples to work or compositions to write. They are fixin' for a' exhibition of some sort for the last Friday in this month. Dolly writes a big part o' the stuff the scholars read in public, an' you bet some of it is tiptop. When she is in a good humor she can compose a' article that will make a dog laugh. She is out o' sorts to-day."

"Oh, is that so?" Saunders was moving toward the gate. "Has anything gone wrong?"

"She is bothered about George," Webb answered. "It is first one thing and then another with her. George's crop is a failure this year and he is up to his neck in debt. On top o' that he wants to get married. You know him an' Ida Benson are crazy to get tied, and it was to come off in the fall, but George won't be able to buy a new shirt, to say nothin' of a whole outfit. The boy is awful downhearted, and so is his gal. Dolly busted out an' cried last night while George was a-talkin'. She says Ida will be the makin' of the boy, but they can't stir a peg as it is, for they hain't got a dollar betwixt 'em."

"Well, I'll walk by the schoolhouse and see if Dolly is there," Saunders remarked. "It is on my way home."

As he drew near the little building at the roadside he noticed that the front door was open, and, peering in, he saw Dolly at her desk. She was not at work; indeed, she seemed quite preoccupied with her thoughts, for she was staring fixedly at an open window, a troubled frown on her sweet face. She heard Saunders's step at the door, and, seeing him enter, she began to smile.

"You caught me," she laughed, impulsively. "I was having one of my silly fits of blues. I am glad you came in. You always make me ashamed of my despondency."

"You are freer from it than any human being I ever saw," he declared, as he shook hands with her. "I seldom have the blues; but if I did, one thought of your wonderful patience would knock them higher than a kite."

She laughed merrily, her eyes twinkling, the warm color flushing her face, as was always the case when she was animated. "I suppose it is generally due to one's point of view," she said. "When it concerns myself I can manage very well, but if it is any one else—"

"A dear brother, for instance," Saunders put in, sympathetically, "and his laudable desire to marry a worthy girl."

She looked at him steadily in mild surprise. "I see you know," she nodded. "I suppose half the county are sorry for that pair. George does try so hard, and yet everything the poor boy touches goes the wrong way. It is not his fault. He is young and inexperienced and so full of hope. He is so downhearted to-day that he wouldn't go to work. He got a letter from Cross & Mayhew last night. You know they advanced him his supplies for this season and took a mortgage on his crop as security. It seems that they sent a man out here the other day to see how he was getting on. The man reported the condition of George's crop, and they wrote him that they would not credit him for his supplies next season. That was the last straw. I found him actually crying down at the barn. He had gone into the stall where his horse was feeding and had his arms around the animal's neck. Mr. Saunders, you can't imagine my feelings. I love my brother with all my heart. I offered to help him with part of my wages, but he was too proud to accept a cent. That letter from Cross & Mayhew humiliated him beyond description. It bowed him down; young as he is, he is actually crushed. He is coming here this morning to talk to me. He wants to go West with the hope that he may get started there and come back for Ida. I can't bear to have him go—I simply can't stand it. I want him to stay here at home. It is the place for them both."

"I think so, too," Saunders said, sympathetically. "There is no better spot on earth for a young farmer."

"I am glad you agree with me"—Dolly brightened a little— "and if you should get a chance I wish you would advise him to stay. You have wonderful influence, with both him and my father."

"I didn't know that," Saunders said, modestly.

Dolly smiled, a far-off expression in her deep eyes. "They think you are the best and wisest man in the world. And as for Ann, do you know you did me a wonderful favor in regard to her?"

"You surprise me." Saunders flushed red. "I didn't know that I had ever—I don't remember-"

"No, I'm sure you don't, and I didn't mention it, but I'm going to tell you now, for I am very, very grateful. You know, perhaps, that Ann used to care a good deal for that reckless fellow Abe Westbrook?"

"Yes, I remember seeing them together frequently," Saunders answered.

"Well, he became more and more dissipated and so bold and ill-bred that he even came to see her when he was intoxicated. I was afraid to call father's attention to it for two reasons—first, father's temper, and then the fear I had that Ann might elope with the fellow. So I had to be very, very cautious. I tried talking to Ann, but it went in at one ear and out at the other. Nothing I said had the slightest effect on her. Then she got to meeting him at different places away from home, and I was almost crazy. Then you, as you always have done, came to my aid."

"I? Why, Dolly, I am sure that I have never—"

"You don't remember it"—Dolly's voice shook, and a delicate glow suffused her face—"but I'll remind you. You recall the picnic over the mountain last spring?"

"The day you didn't go," Saunders nodded. "I remember looking for you everywhere."

"Well, that day, when all the girls felt so highly honored by your presence, and you were so nice to them, you paid a good deal of attention to Ann, asking her to drive home with you."

"Of course I remember that," Saunders said; "I enjoyed the drive very much."

"It wasn't anything you said, exactly," Dolly went on, "but you may remember that Abe was drinking that day and misbehaved badly before every one, even when they were all eating lunch together. Ann told me all about it. She came to my bed away in the night and waked me. She told me she had made up her mind never to see Westbrook again. In contrasting him with you she saw what a failure he was. She said she had never before so plainly seen her danger. She saw the look of disgust in your face while Abe was acting so badly, and your failure to refer to the incident on the way home impressed her. That happening completely turned her round, opened her eyes, and already she has stopped thinking of him."

Saunders was modestly trying to formulate some protest when, looking toward the door, Dolly suddenly exclaimed: "Oh, there is George now! Don't leave," for Saunders was rising. "I can see him at home."

"I must be going, anyway," Saunders said, rather nervously, "but if you will let me I'd like to take you for a drive this afternoon. We could pass the new schoolhouse and see how it is coming on."

"I'll be glad to go," Dolly answered. "I understand the men are making fine progress."

Seeing Saunders coming out, George stepped aside just outside the door to let him pass, and they met face to face. The banker's sympathies were deeply touched by the dejected mien of the courageous young man, whom he had always liked.

"Hello, George," he greeted him, cordially. "Your sister tells me you are thinking of pulling up stakes and moving West."

"Yes, I think it is about the best thing for me, now, Mr. Saunders," George answered, gloomily. "I've given this thing a fair test. Perhaps out there among strangers I may have a change of luck. I can't make it go here. I'm a drawback to myself and everybody else. Even Dolly is upset by my troubles, and when she gives up things are bad, sure enough. You can't imagine how a fellow feels in my fix."

"I think I can, George." Glancing back, Saunders noted that Dolly was looking straight at them. He put his hand on the young man's shoulder and let it rest there gently while he went on: "Still, George, I would not advise you to leave home. You see, here you are surrounded by old friends and relatives. Among total strangers the fight for success would be even harder, and I am afraid you'd be homesick for these old mountains. I have met a good many who have come back after a trial at farming out there. They all say this country is as good as any."

"But I am actually at the end of my rope." George's voice shook afresh, and the shadow about his eyes deepened. "Has Dolly told you about Cross & Mayhew?"

"Yes, and I'm sorry you ever got in with them. George, they are nothing more nor less than licensed thieves. Have you ever calculated how much they make out of you?"

"Oh, I know their profit is big," George sighed, "but men of my stamp have to go to them when they need a stake to pull through on."

"I have figured on their method," Saunders said, "and I am quite sure that they get as their part fully half of the earnings of their customers. It may interest you to know, George, that our bank lends that firm money at only seven or eight per cent., which they turn over to you at no less than fifty."

"I see," George sighed; "the poor man has the bag to hold. Money makes money."

"I have a plan in my head, George"—Saunders was somewhat embarrassed, and looked away from the dejected face before him—"which, it seems to me, might help both you and me in a certain way."

"What is that?" George stared, wonderingly, his fine lips quivering.

"To begin with, George, I think that your bad crop this season is due largely to the poor land you rented. I noticed it early in the year and was afraid you'd not accomplish much."

"It was all I could get," George said. "I tried all around, but every other small farm either was to be worked by the owner or was rented already. It was root hog or die with me, Mr. Saunders."

"You have seen the Warner farm, haven't you?" the banker inquired.

"You bet I have!" George responded. "It is the prettiest small place in this valley."

"Well, I bought it the other day for two thousand dollars," Saunders said. "Warner owed me some money, and I had to take the farm to secure myself. Things like that often come up in a bank, you know."

"Well, you are safe in it, Mr. Saunders," George said. "You never could lose in a deal like that. It has a good house on it, and every foot of the land is rich. It has a fine strip of woodland, too."

"I really have no use for the place," Saunders went on, more awkwardly. "If it adjoined my plantation I would like it better, but it is too far away for my manager to see it often. I want to sell it, and it struck me that if you could be persuaded to give up this Western idea maybe you could take it off my hands at what it cost me."

"I? huh! That *is* a joke, Mr. Saunders," George laughed. "If farms were going at ten cents apiece I couldn't buy a pig-track in a free mud-hole."

"I wouldn't require the money down," Saunders went on, still clumsily. "In fact, I could give you all the time you wanted to pay for it. I know you are going to succeed—I know it as well as I know anything; and you ought to own your own place. I am willing to advance money for your supplies—and some to get married on, too. You and your sweetheart could be very snug in that little house."

George stared like a man waking from a perplexing dream. His toil-hardened, sun-browned hands were visibly quivering, his mouth was open, his lower lip twitching.

"You *can't* mean it—you *can't* be in earnest!" he gasped, leaning heavily against the door-jamb, actually pale with excitement.

"Yes, I mean it, George." Saunders put his hand on the broad shoulder again. "And I hope you will take me up. You will be doing me a favor, you see. I lend money every day to men I don't trust half as much as I do you."

At this juncture Dolly hurried down the aisle, a look of fresh anxiety on her face. "What is the matter, George?" she asked, eying her brother in surprise. "What has happened?"

Falteringly and with all but sobs of elation, George explained Saunders's proposition. "Did you ever in your life think of such a thing?" he cried. "Dolly, I'm going to take him up. If he is willing to risk me I'll take him up. I'll work my fingers to the bone rather than see him lose a cent. I'm going to take him up—I tell you, Sis, I'm going to take him up!"

Dolly said nothing. A glow of boundless delight suffused her face, rendering her unspeakably beautiful. Her eyes had a depth Saunders had never beheld before. He saw her round breast quiver and expand in tense agitation. She put her arm about her brother's neck and kissed him on the cheek. Then, without a word, her hand on her lips as if to suppress a rising sob, she turned back into the schoolhouse and, with head down, went to her desk, where she sat with her back to the door.

"She's gone off to cry," George chuckled. "She's that way. She never gives up in trouble, but when she is plumb happy like she is now she can't hold in. Look, I told you so—she's wiping her eyes, dear, dear old girl. Now, I'm going to run over and tell Ida. Lord, Lord, Mr. Saunders, she'll be tickled to death! Just this morning I told her I was going away. Good-by; God bless you!"

When George was gone Saunders stood at the door and

wistfully looked in at Dolly. An impulse that was almost overpowering drew him to her, but he put it aside.

"She wants to be alone," he reflected. "If I went now, feeling like this, I'd say something I ought not to say and be sorry I imposed on her at such a time. No, I will have to wait. I have waited all these years, and I can wait longer. To win I could wait to the end of time."

Turning, he strode into the wood. Deeper and deeper he plunged, headed toward the mountain, feeling the cooling shade of the mighty trees, whose branches met and interlaced overhead. Reaching a mossy bank near a limpid stream, he threw himself down and gave himself up to reveries.

CHAPTER V

Mostyn took long solitary walks. His habit of morbid intros-
pection had grown and become a fixed feature of his life. Even
while occupied with business his secret self stood invisible at
his elbow whispering, ever whispering things alien from
material holdings or profit—matters unrelated to speculative
skill or judgment.

He had wandered into the suburbs of the city one afternoon,
and, happening to pass an isolated cottage at the side of the
road, he was surprised to see Marie Winship coming out. She
smiled cordially, nodded, signaled with her sunshade, and
hurried through the little gate toward him. He paused, turned,
and stood waiting for her. He had not seen her, even at a
distance, for nearly a year, and her improved appearance struck
him forcibly. Her color was splendid, her eyes were sparkling
and vivacious. She was perfectly groomed and stylishly attired.

"Why, what are you doing away out here?" he asked, secretly
and recklessly soothed by the sight of her, for in her care-free
way she, at least, was a living lesson against the folly of taking
the rebuffs of life too seriously.

She smiled, holding out her gloved hand in quite the old way,
which had once so fascinated his grosser senses. "Mary Long,
my dressmaker, lives here." She glanced at him half chidingly
from beneath her thick lashes. "I come all the way out here to
save money. You think I am extravagant, Dick, but that is the
sort of thing I have to do to make ends meet. Mary is making

me a dream of a frock now for one-fourth of what your high and mighty *Frau* would pay for it in New York."

"Always hard up," Mostyn said. "You never get enough to satisfy you."

She smiled coquettishly. "I was born that way," she answered. "My brother sends me money often. He has never forgotten how you and I got him out of that awful hole. He has gone into the wholesale whisky business and is doing well. He paid me back long ago."

"And you blew it in, of course?" Mostyn said, lightly.

"Yes, that's how I got that last New York trip," she nodded, merrily. "Dick, that was one month when I really *lived*. Gee! if life could only be like that I'd ask nothing more of the powers that rule; I certainly wouldn't."

"But life can't possibly be like that," he returned, gloomily. "Even that would pall on you in time. I am older than you, Marie, and I know what I am talking about. We can go just so far and no farther."

"Poof! piffle!" It was her old irresponsible ejaculation. "Life is what you make it. 'Laugh, and the world laughs with you.' Eat, drink, and be merry—that is my motto. But, say, Dick"—she was eying his face with slow curiosity—"what is the matter? You look like a grandfather. You are thin and peaked and nervous-looking. But I needn't ask—I know."

"You know!" he repeated, sensitively. "I am working pretty hard for one thing, and—"

"Poof!" She snapped her fingers. "You used to get fat on work. It isn't that, Dick, and you needn't try to fool me. I know you from the soles of your feet to the end of the longest hair on your head."

He avoided her fixed stare. "I'm not making money as I did once. Many of my investments have turned out badly. I seem to have lost my old skill in business matters."

"I was sure you would when you married," the woman said, positively; and he flinched under the words as under a lash. "A man of your independent nature can't sell himself and ever do any good afterward. You lost your pride in that deal, Dick, and pride was your motive power. You may laugh at me and think I am silly, but I am speaking truth."

"You ought not to say those things," he said, resentfully.

"I will say exactly what I like," she retorted, cold gleams flashing from her eyes. "You never cared a straw for that vain, stuck-up woman. Dick, I hate her—from the bottom of my soul, I despise her, and she knows it. Whenever I pass her she takes pains to sneer at me. For one thing, I hate her for the way she is treating you and your child. Dick, that boy is the sweetest, prettiest creature I ever saw, and not a bit like her. One day I passed your house when he happened to be playing outside the gate. His nurse neglects him. Automobiles were passing, and I was afraid he might get run over. No one was in sight, and so I stopped and warned him. I fell in love with the little darling. Oh, he is so much like you; every motion, every look, every tone of voice is yours over and over! He took my hand and thanked me like a little gentleman. I stooped down and kissed him. I couldn't help it, Dick. I have always loved children. I went further—the very devil must have been in me that day. I asked him which he loved more, you or his mother. He looked at me as if surprised that any one should ask such a question, and do you know what he answered?"

"I can't imagine," Mostyn replied. "He is so young that—"

"Dick, he said: 'Why, Daddy, of course. Daddy is good to me.'"

A subtle force rising from within seized Mostyn and shook him sharply. He made an effort to meet the frank eyes bent upon him, but failed. He started to speak, but ended by saying nothing.

"Yes, I hate her," Marie went on. "I hate her for the way she is acting."

"The way she is acting?" The echo was a faint, undecided one, and Mostyn's eyes groped back to the wayward face at his side. "Yes, and it is town talk," Marie went on. "You know people in the lower and middle classes will gossip about you lucky high-flyers. They know every bit as much about what is going on in your set as you do. They can't have the fun you have, so they take pleasure in riddling your characters or talking about those already riddled. Dick, your wife's affair with Andy Buckton is mentioned oftener than the weather. People say he always loved her and, now that he is rich and rolling high, that he is winning out. Many sporting people that I know glory in his 'spunk,' as they call it. They are counting on a divorce as a sure thing."

"Can they actually believe that—" Mostyn's voice failed him; but the woman must have read his thought, for she said, quickly:

"Don't ask me what they think. I know what *I* think, and I'll bet I know her through and through. She is reckless to the point of doing anything on earth that will amuse her. She is so badly spoiled she is rotten. I know how you are fixed—oh, I know! You can't kill him; you don't love her enough for that; and besides, you know you can't prove anything serious against her. Her married women friends go about with men, and for you to object would only make you ridiculous. They sneer at women like me, I know; but Lord, they can't criticize me! I am myself, that's all. I can be a friend, and I can be an enemy. I want to be your friend, Dick."

"My friend?" he repeated, with an inaudible sigh drawn from the seething reservoir of his gloom.

"Yes, and not only that, but I want to give you some good, solid advice."

"Oh, you do?" He forced a smile of bland incredulity.

"I will tell you what is the matter with you, and how to get out of it. Dick, you have let this thing get on your nerves, and it is hurrying you to the grave or the mad-house. I know you well enough to know that it is on your mind day and night. Now, there is one royal road, and if you'll take it the whole dirty business will slip off of you like water off a duck's back."

"What is that road, Marie?" he asked, affecting a lighter mood than he felt.

"Why, it is simply to do as they are doing. Plunge in and have a good time. You made all the money you ever made when you were living the life of a red-blooded, natural man. Marrying that woman has given you cold feet, and she knows it. Forget it all. Sail in and be glad you are alive. Look at me. Things have happened to me that would have finished many a woman, but I took a cocktail, won a game of poker, and was as chipper as if nothing out of the way had happened."

"You don't understand, Marie," he said, with a bare touch of his old reckless elation. "That may be all right for you, but—"

"Piffle! Dick, you are the limit. I can turn you square about and make you see straight. Think things are bad, and they will be so. Your wife and her fellow are having a good time; why shouldn't you? People who used to admire you think you are a silly chump, but they will come back to you if you show them that you are in the game yourself. I like you, Dick—I always have, better than any other man I know. Come to see me to-night, and let's talk it over."

She saw him wavering, and laid her hand on his arm and smiled up at him in her old bewitching way. Some impulse surging up from the primitive depths of himself swayed him like a reed in a blast of wind. He touched the gloved hand with the tips of his fingers. The look beneath her sweeping lashes drew his own and held it in an invisible embrace. He pressed her hand.

"You are a good girl, Marie," he muttered, huskily. "I know you want to help me, but—"

"I am not going to take a refusal, Dick. I want to see you. I want you to take the bit in your teeth again. Come to see me to-night. I'll have one of our old spreads in my little dining-room. I'll sing and dance for you and tell you the funniest story you ever heard. I am going to expect you."

There was a genuine warmth of appeal in her face. In all his knowledge of her she had never appeared to such an advantage. After all, her argument was reasonable and rational. A titillating sensation suffused his being. In fancy he saw the little dining-room, which adjoined her boudoir; he saw her at the piano, her white fingers tripping, as in the old days, over the keyboard; he heard her singing one of her gay and reckless songs; he saw her dainty feet tripping through the dance he so much admired.

"You are coming, Dick," she said, confidently, withdrawing her hand and raising her sunshade. "I shall expect you by nine o'clock, sharp. I won't listen to a refusal or excuse. I shall have no other engagement."

He hesitated, but she laughed in his face, her red lips parted in an entrancing smile. He caught a whiff of her favorite perfume, and his hot brain absorbed it like a delicious intoxicant.

"I know you of old, Dick Mostyn. You used to say now and then that you had business that would keep you away, but you never failed to come when you knew *positively that I was waiting.* I am going to wait to-night, and if I don't make a new man of you I'll confess that I am a failure."

"I really can't promise." He was looking back toward the smoke-clouded city, at the gray dome of the State Capitol. "I may come, and I may not, Marie. I can't tell. If I shouldn't, you must forgive me. It is kind of you to want to help me, and I appreciate it."

"You are coming, Dick; that settles it." She smiled confidently. "Huh! as if I didn't know you! You are the same dear, old chap, ridden to death with silly fancies. Now, I'm going to run back and speak to Mary. I forgot something. She is all right. She won't talk even if she recognized you, which is doubtful, for she is a stranger here."

Turning, he walked back toward the city. Already he was in a different mood; his step was more active; all of his senses were alert; his blood surged through his veins as if propelled by a new force. He saw some vacant lots across the street advertised for sale by a real estate-agent, and found himself calculating on the city's prospective growth in that direction. It might be worth his while to inquire the price, for he had made money in transactions of that sort.

Returning to the bank, he found that the activity of the clerks and typewriters did not jar on him as it had been doing of late. He paused at Saunders's desk and made a cheerful and oddly self-confident inquiry as to the disposition of a certain customer's account, surprising his partner by his altered manner.

In his office, smoking a good cigar, he found a new interest in the letters and documents left there for his consideration. After all, life *was* a game. Even the early red men had their sport. Modern routine work without diversion was a treadmill, prisonlike existence. Delbridge was the happy medium. The jovial speculator had never heard of such a fine-spun thing as a conscience. What if Irene and Buckton were having their fun; could he not also enjoy himself? If the worst came, surely a man of the world, a stoical thoroughbred, who was willing to give and take a matrimonial joke would appear less ridiculous in the public eye than an overgrown crier over spilt milk. How queer that he had waited for Marie Winship to open his eyes to such a patent fact!

All the remainder of the day he was buoyed up by this impulse. A man came in to see him about buying a new automobile, and he made an appointment with him to test the machine the next morning. It was said to be better and higher-priced than Buckton's. He might buy it. He might openly ride out with Marie. That would be taking the bull by the horns in earnest. He smiled as he thought that many would think his relations with Marie had never been broken, but had only been adroitly concealed out of respect for a wife who no longer deserved such delicate consideration. The town would talk; let them— let them! Its tongue was already active on one side of the matter; it should be fed with a morsel or two from the other. Richard Mostyn was himself again.

CHAPTER VI

Mostyn remained in his office till eight o'clock that evening, writing letters about an investment in the West which had been threatening loss. Closing his desk and lowering the lights, he decided to walk home and dress for his visit to Marie. The exercise in the fresh air made him more determined in his new move. A society man he knew drove past in a glittering tally-ho filled with young ladies. One of the men recognized him in the arc light swinging over the street and blew a playful blast at him from one of the long horns. The gay party whisked around a corner and disappeared.

Reaching home and entering the gate, he saw his father-in-law striding back and forth on the veranda, and as he came up the walk the old man turned, pausing at the head of the steps.

"Do you know where Irene is?" he inquired, pettishly.

"I haven't the slightest idea." Mostyn's retort was full of almost genuine indifference. "I have quit keeping track of her ladyship."

His new note of defiance was lost on Mitchell, who seemed quite disturbed. "I haven't seen her since breakfast," he said, complainingly. "I thought she had gone to some morning affair, but when lunch came and passed and no sign of her I thought surely she would be home to supper; but that's over, and she isn't here. Have you happened to see Andy Buckton about town to-day?"

"No, I haven't," Mostyn answered, sharply. "I see your drift, sir, and your point is well taken. If you want to find your daughter, telephone around for Buckton. As for me, I don't care enough about it to bother."

"You needn't sniff and sneer," Mitchell threw back, sharply. "You are as much to blame for the way things are going as she is. The devil is in you both as big as a house. Old-fashioned Southern ways are not good enough for you; having a little money has driven you crazy. Irene was all right, no new toy to play with till Buckton ran into that fortune, and now nothing will hold her down. She used to fancy she cared for him, and, now that he has plenty of funds, she is sure of it. The society of this town, sir, is rotten to the core. It is trying to be French, trying to imitate foreign nobility and the New York Four Hundred. I am not pitying myself; I'm not sorry for you, for you are a cold-blooded proposition that nothing can touch; but I *am* pitying that helpless child of yours. I reckon you can turn in and sleep as sound as a log to-night, whether your wife comes home or not, but I can't."

A sudden fear that little Dick might hear the rising old voice came over Mostyn, and he restrained the angry retort that throbbed on his lips. Ascending the steps, he went into his room to prepare for his visit. How odd, but the vengeful force of his contemplated retaliation had lessened! As he stood at his bureau taking out some necessary articles from a drawer he felt his old morbidness roll back over him like a wave. Was it Mitchell's petulant complaints of his daughter's conduct, or was it what he had said about his grandchild? It was the latter; Mostyn was sure of it, for all at once he had the overpowering yearning for the boy which had so completely dominated him of late. He dropped the articles back into the drawer and stood listening. Dick must be asleep by this time. But no, that was a voice from the direction of the nursery. It was the low tones of Hilda the nurse.

"Now, go to sleep," she was saying. "You must stop rollin' an' tumblin' an' talkin'."

"I know it *is* my Daddy," the childish voice was heard saying. "He is in his room, and I want to sleep in his bed."

"You *can't* sleep in his bed," the nurse scolded. "You must be quiet and go to sleep."

Mostyn crept across the room to the door and stood listening, holding his breath and trying to still the audible throbbing of his heart. He heard Dick sobbing. Pushing the door open, Mostyn looked into the room, feeling the gas-heated air beat back into his face as he did so. In the light at a small table the nurse sat sewing, and she glanced up.

"What is Dick crying about?" he demanded.

"Because he's bad," was the reply. "He's been bad all day. In all my born days I've never seen such a bothersome child. He began cryin' to go to the bank just after you left this mornin'. He made such a fuss that his mother had to whip 'im, but it didn't do 'im a bit o' good. He has been watchin' the gate for you all day, threatenin' to tell you. He doesn't care for nobody in the world but you—not even his grandfather. I reckon you've spoiled 'im, sir, pettin' 'im up so much."

Mostyn crossed over to Dick's bed and looked down on the tear-marked face. The child's breast was spasmodically quivering with suppressed sobs. His lips were swollen; there was a red mark on the broad white brow, against which the locks lay like pliant gold.

"What caused this?" Mostyn demanded, pointing to the spot.

"It is where his mother slapped 'im this mornin'. She had to do it. He was cryin' an' kickin' an' wouldn't pay no 'tention to 'er. He kept up such a 'sturbance that she couldn't dress to go out. He said he was goin' to the bank to tell you, an' he got clean down the street 'fore I saw 'im."

The child was looking straight into Mostyn's eyes. To him the expression was fathomless.

"What is the matter, Dick?" he asked.

"I want my Daddy," the boy sobbed. "I don't like Hilda; I don't like mama; I don't like grandpa; I want to sleep in your room."

"Not to-night, Dick." Mostyn touched the angry spot on the brow lightly and bent down lower. "I have to go out this evening. I have an engagement."

The look of despair darkening the little flushed face went straight to the heart of the father, and yet he said: "You must go to sleep now. I must hurry. I have to dress. Good night."

Mostyn went back to his bureau. The reflection of his face in the tilted mirror caught and held his attention. Could that harsh semblance of a man be himself? Various periods of his life flashed in separate pictures before him. Glimpses of his college days; this and that gay prank of irresponsible youth. Then came incidents of his first business ventures; his dealings with Jefferson Henderson stood out sharply. The old man's first intuitive fears of coming loss rang in his ears, followed by curses of helpless, astounded despair. One after another these things piled thick and fast upon him. He saw his first meeting with Marie; then that crisis, the transcendent uplift in the mountains, when for the first time in his life he actually reached for something beyond and above himself through the mediumship of Dolly Drake, that wonderful embodiment of the, for him, unattainable. He had lost out there. He had slipped at the foot of the heights up which she was leading him.

He heard the gate-latch click, and old Mitchell's thumping tread on the veranda steps as he descended to meet some one. Going to a window and parting the curtains cautiously, Mostyn looked down on the walk. It was his wife. He saw her meet her father, but she did not slacken her brisk walk toward the house.

"Where have you been all day?" the old man demanded, following behind.

"I don't have to tell you," Irene answered. "You are driving me crazy with your eternal suspicions. If I keep on answering your questions you will never stop. Let me alone. You needn't watch me like a hawk. I am old enough to take care of myself."

An inarticulate reply came up from the old man, and the next moment Mostyn heard Irene ascending the stairs. The door of her room opened and shut. Mostyn distinctly heard the turning of the key. He looked at his watch. It was half past eight. He would have to hurry to catch a car. He went back to the bureau.

At this instant something happened. Hearing a low sound and looking in the glass, he saw a little white-robed figure creeping stealthily across the floor to his bed. He pretended not to see, and watched Dick as he softly crept between the sheets. Turning round, he caught the boy's sheepish stare, which suddenly became a look of grim, even defiant, determination.

"Why did you come, Dick?" he asked, and as he spoke he crept toward the bed like a man in a dream drawn to some ravishing delight. He sat down on the edge of the bed. He caught the child's little hand in his own. The nerves of his whole yearning soul seemed centered in his fingers.

"Daddy"—the boy hesitated; his words hung as if entangled in a fear of refusal—"let me stay in your bed till you come home. I am not afraid. I don't want to sleep in there with Hilda. I don't like her."

Till he came home! The words seemed to sink into and surge back from the core of his accumulated remorse. Till he came home, perhaps near dawn, reeking with the odor of licentiousness—the very licentiousness he was praying that his child might not be drawn into.

He put his hand on the little brow. He bent and kissed it. He felt his resistance falling away from him like the severed thongs of a prisoner. A force was entering him which mere flesh could not combat. He slid his hand under the child to raise him up, and felt the little body bound in surprised delight toward him. He pressed the soft form to his breast. He felt the keen pain of restrained emotion within him.

Taking the boy in his arms, he sat down in a rocking-chair, holding him as a mother might an adored infant. "Do you want Daddy to rock you to sleep?" he asked.

"Oh, will you, Daddy, will you?"

"Yes." Mostyn stroked the soft cool legs caressingly and pressed the child's brow against his cheek. The boy was quiet for a moment; then his father felt him stir uneasily.

"What is it now?" he inquired.

"When I get to sleep what are you going to do with me?"

Mostyn thought rapidly. "I'll put you in my bed," he said, slowly. Then he added, with firmness: "I'll go down to the library and read the papers, and then I'll come back and sleep with you. I shall not go away to-night."

The child said nothing. He simply put both his arms about his father's neck, kissed him on the cheek, and cuddled up in his arms.

CHAPTER VII

One morning, during the middle of that week, as Saunders was on his way to the bank, he was surprised to meet Dolly coming out of one of the big dry-goods shops. She wore a new hat and an attractive linen dress he had never seen her wear before. She smiled and flushed prettily as she extended her hand.

"You were not expecting to see this mountain greenhorn down here, were you?" she laughed. "As for me, I hardly know which end of me is up. I don't see how you can live in all this whizz, bustle, smoke, and dust."

"I am wondering what miracle brought you," he answered.

"Well, I'll tell you. It is simple enough when you know," Dolly smiled. "The rural schools of the State are holding a convention of teachers here. We meet at the Capitol at ten o'clock this morning. I'm a delegate, with all expenses paid. I represent our county. Isn't that nice? I feel like a big somebody. I was just wondering if the mayor will call on me. I think he ought to, but I really couldn't see him. My time is all occupied. They have asked me to make a talk. They've got me down for a few minutes' harangue, and I don't know more than a rat what I'll say. We are going to try for a State appropriation in our section, meet the members of the Legislature, and do some wire-pulling and lobby work."

"And where are you going at this minute?" Saunders

laughed, merrily.

"I was headed for the Capitol," she smiled, but I'm all turned around. I went in at the front of this store, but feel as if I had come out at the back."

"I will go with you if you will let me," Saunders ventured.

"But I'll be taking you from your business," she protested. "You must not feel called on to show me about. To be frank, that is the reason I didn't let you know I was coming. You can't afford to be nice to all your mountain friends. They would keep you busy jerking them from under cars and automobiles."

"I have absolutely nothing to do," Saunders declared. "This is the way to the Capitol. We pass right by our bank, and I can show you where we hold forth."

He saw a cloud fall over her face. "I'd rather not—not meet—" She did not finish what she started to say and bit her lip.

"I understand," he answered, quickly. "He is not in town. He is spending the day in Augusta."

"Oh!" she exclaimed, in a breath of relief. "You will think me silly, but I can't help it. I oughtn't to be so, but I dread it above all things. If I were to meet him face to face I wouldn't know what to say. It would be like seeing some one actually rise from the dead. I wouldn't think so much of my own feelings as—as his. Uncle John saw him in Rome not long ago. He says he has changed in looks—but let us not talk about him. It can't do a bit of good. He is unhappy—I know he is unhappy. I knew it would be so."

An awkward silence fell between them. They had to cross a crowded street, and Saunders took her arm to protect her. He felt it quivering, and his heart sank in grave misgivings. He told himself that she would never care for any other man than

Mostyn. She was the kind of woman who could love and trust but once in life, and was not changed by time or the weakness and faults of the beloved one.

Saunders indicated the bank among the buildings across the street, and he saw a wistful look steal into her grave face as she regarded it steadily.

"So that's the place where you men of affairs scheme, plan, and execute," she smiled. "It looks close and hot. Well, I couldn't stand it. I must have open air, sunshine, mountains, streams, and people—real, plain, honest, unpretending people."

"I have made up my mind to quit," he returned. "I have been staying in the country so much of late that I cannot do without it. I intend to sell my interests here, and settle down on my plantation."

"You will be wise," she said, philosophically. "Life is too short to live any other way than as close as possible to nature. All this"—she glanced up the busy street—"is madness—sheer madness. In the whole squirming human mass you could not show me one really contented person, while I can point to hundreds in the mountains. You are thinking about leaving it while my father is planning to come here. At his time of life, too. It is absurd, but he says it is the only thing open to him. I didn't tell you, but he came down with me. It is pitiful, for he is looking for work."

"Oh, really, is it possible?" Saunders exclaimed, in surprise. "Why, I thought he was one man who would always stay in the country."

Dolly sighed. "He has changed remarkably," she said, her face settling into almost pained gravity. "All at once he has become more ashamed of his condition than he ever was in his life. He is in debt to personal friends and has no way of paying them. He used to make money moonshining, but he has quit that, and doesn't seem able to make our poor farm pay at all. The storekeepers won't credit him, and he has become desperate. He is trying to get a job at carpenter work, but he will fail, for he can't do that sort of thing. Indirectly, George is the cause of his sudden determination."

"George? Why, I thought—"

"It is this way," Dolly went on, quickly. "You see, through your kindness George is so happy, is doing so well, and there is so much talk about his good luck that it has made my father realize his own shortcomings more keenly. Don't you bother; it is a good lesson for him; he has not been doing right, and he knows it. It is odd, isn't it, to see a man mortified by the success of his own son? In one way I am sorry for father, and in another I am not. Ann is trying to get a teacher's place in a school, and if she does, between us we may be able, for mother's sake, to keep father at home. Somehow, it makes me sad to think of his being in this hot town tramping about asking for work as a day-laborer, and yet I know it will be good for him. Mother cried pitifully when we left this morning, and he was the most wretched-looking man I ever saw. I don't care if he does suffer—*some*—but I don't like to see my mother sad. Do you know, that poor woman has had nothing but sorrow as her portion all her married life? First one thing and then another has come up to depress and dishearten her. At first it was father's drinking; then he quit that, and became a moonshiner in constant danger of arrest; and now he has left home to try his fortune among total strangers."

"It is sad; indeed, it is," Saunders said, sympathetically. "And the worst of it is that it troubles you, Dolly. You speak of your mother's hard lot. As I see it, you, yourself, have had enough trouble to kill a dozen girls of your age."

"Oh, I am all right! That is the Capitol, isn't it?" she added, as in turning a corner they came in sight of the vast stone building with its graceful, gray dome, standing on the grassy, low-walled grounds.

He nodded, and she ran on with a rippling laugh of self-depreciation. "Think of this silly country yap making a speech in that big building before the Governor, State senators, principals of schools, and no telling who else! Why, I'll want to sink through the floor into the basement. Do you know, when I was a little tiny thing playing with rag dolls and keeping house with broken bits of china for plates and stones for tables and chairs, I used to fancy myself growing up and being a great lady with servants and carriages; but that was crawling on the earth compared to this sky-sweeping stunt to-day. But if they call on me I'll go through with it in some shape or die."

"Is the meeting to be public?" Saunders asked. "Because if it is I should like to be present."

He saw her start suddenly. She looked down at the pavement for a moment; then she gave him a glance full of perturbation, laying her hand on his arm impulsively. "Jarvis—oh, I didn't mean to call you that!" The color ran in a flood to her face. "It was a slip of the tongue. I *do* call you that in my thoughts, for—for so many at home do, you know."

"I should like nothing better than to have you do it always," he heard himself saying; but the sight of her clouded face checked the words which packed upon his utterance.

"Oh, I could never be as bold as that," she put in quickly. "You said you would like to go to the meeting. It *is* public, but I am going to ask you a favor, and I never was so much in earnest in my life. Do you know, I think I could get through that speech better if not a soul was in the audience that I ever saw before. I would rather have you there than any one else, for I know you would be sympathetic, but I want to face it absolutely alone. I can't tell why I feel so, but it is a fact."

"I can understand it," Saunders answered. "I had to make a speech at a convention of bankers once, and the fact that I was a total stranger to them all made the task easier. But when are you going back home?"

"To-morrow at twelve," she said.

"And this evening?" he inquired.

"There is to be a reception given us at the Governor's mansion." Dolly shrugged her shoulders. "Somebody is to take us all from the hotel in a bunch. I have a new dress for it. That will be another experience, but, as it comes after my speech, I am not even thinking of it."

"Then I'll see you at the train in the morning," Saunders said. "I want to get the news of your speech. I am confident that you will acquit yourself beautifully. You can't fail. It isn't in you."

They had reached the steps of the Capitol. A number of women and men were entering, and Dolly turned to join them.

"That's some of my crowd," she smiled. "Can't you tell by the way they stare and blink, like scared rabbits? The men's clothes look as if they still had the price-tags on them—regular hand-me-downs. Good-by; I'll see you at the train."

CHAPTER VIII

That afternoon, in coming from a lawyer's office, Saunders saw Tom Drake standing in the crowd which was always gathered at the intersection of Whitehall and Marietta streets. Falling back unobserved into a tobacconist's shop on the corner, the young man looked out and watched the mountaineer. With hands in his pockets, Drake stood eying the jostling human current, a disconsolate droop to his lank form, a far-off stare in his weary eyes.

"He has tried and given up already," Saunders reflected. "Dolly knows him better than he knows himself. This is no place for a man like him. He is homesick, poor chap! He counts himself the most unfortunate man on earth, and yet he is the most blessed, for he is her father. How can he look at her, hear her voice, and not burn with triumphant pride? Her father! If I only dared, I'd treat him as I'd treat my own father, but she would resent it. It would hurt her feelings. I have to consider her. She didn't quite like what I did for George; but, no matter, I'm going to speak to him."

Therewith Saunders skirted the thickest part of the surging mass and suddenly came upon Drake, who, in order to be out of the way of pedestrians with more purpose than himself, had stepped back against the wall of the building. Their eyes met. Drake's wavered sheepishly, but he took the hand cordially extended, and made an effort to appear at ease.

"I saw Dolly this morning," Saunders began. "She told me you

Will N. Harben

came down with her."

"Yes, I thought—I thought I might as well." Drake's lips quivered. "I reckon she told you that I am sorter strikin' out on a new line?"

"She said something about it." Saunders felt that the topic was a delicate one. "I hope you are finding an—an opening to your liking."

Drake was chewing tobacco, and he spat awkwardly down at his side. There was a certain timidity in the man for one so bold as he had been in his own field of life among rough men of crude acts and habits.

"I've looked about some," he said, a flush creeping into his tanned cheeks. "I've been to the machine-shops and to two or three contractin' carpenters. They all said they was full up with hands—men waitin' on their lists for times to improve. Buildin' is slow right now, an' expert hands already on the spot get the pick of the jobs. Machinery is stealin' the bread out of the workin'-man's mouth. A machine takes the place of twenty men in many cases."

"I see, I see," Saunders said. "The country, after all, is the best place for a man brought up on a farm."

Drake, thrown off his guard, sighed openly. "I reckon you are right," he agreed. "To tell you the truth, Saunders, I don't think I'm goin' to land anything on this trip, and it makes a feller feel sorter sneakin' to go back empty-handed. I put my judgment up against all the rest. George, Dolly, and her mother, an' even John Webb, tried to get me to listen to their advice, but not me! Oh no, I was runnin' it! I reckon I'm bull-headed. Le'me tell you some'n'. I'd go back an' hire out to George as a day-laborer if I didn't have more pride than brains. He needs hands. He told me so. You are makin' a man out o' him, Saunders, an' I want to thank you."

"What have you got to do just now?" Saunders asked. "Couldn't you go to the bank with me?"

Drake hesitated. His color deepened. He avoided Saunders's tentative gaze. "I reckon I won't, to-day, anyway," he faltered. "I never was much of a hand to hang about big places o' business."

"Then suppose we step into the lobby of the Kimball House; it is close by," Saunders suggested. "There are some seats there, and we could sit down for a few minutes. The truth is, I want to ask your advice about my plantation. You are better posted up there than I can be, staying here as much as I do."

"Oh, that's different!"

A look of relief swept over the rugged face. "I only wish I could help you some, no matter how little. You did me the biggest favor once that ever one man did another. When you jerked me back from the train that night and forced me to behave myself you saved me from no end o' shame an' trouble. La, me! I've thought of that a thousand times."

"Don't mention it." Saunders was touched by the deep surge of gratitude in the despondent voice. "If I had not been a great friend of yours and of your family, I would not have dared to act as I did. But that is past and gone."

"Not with me—a thing like that never passes with me," Drake answered, as they crossed the street and entered at the side door of the hotel.

They found some unoccupied chairs in a quiet part of the big office. The clerks behind the counter were busy assigning rooms to a throng of passengers from an incoming train. A dozen negro porters and bell-boys were rushing to and fro. The elevators were busy. The tiled floor resounded with the scurrying of active feet. Saunders saw the mountaineer watching the scene with the lack-luster stare he had caught in his eyes a few minutes before.

"You said you wanted to ask me something about your place," Drake suddenly bethought himself to say.

"Yes, it is like this. You know my manager, Hobson, of course?"

"Yes, pretty well," Drake made reply, slowly. "That is, as well as any of us mountain men do. He never has been much of a chap to mix with other folks. To tell you the truth, most of us think he is stuck up. Well, I reckon he has a right to be. He gets darn good wages. Nobody knows exactly what he makes, but it is reported that you give 'im fifteen hundred a year. He has saved most of it, and has turned his pile over till there isn't any telling how much the feller is worth."

"Yes, I am paying him fifteen hundred," Saunders said, lowering his voice into one of confidential disclosure. "I want to talk to you about him, and I know you will help me if you can. He has, as you say, laid up money, and he has recently established a warehouse business at Ridgeville. For the last month he has scarcely been at my plantation half a dozen times."

"I noticed that," Drake said, "but he told me that he had it fixed so that he could be at both places often enough to keep things in shape. He is a good business man, and I reckon he will do what he contracts."

"But I am not at all satisfied as it is," Saunders answered. "I am thinking of disposing of my bank interest and settling down up there for good, and I'd like to have a manager with whom I can be in touch every day. I am interested in farming myself, and I don't want my manager to have too many irons in the fire. The trouble with Hobson is that he is now giving his best thought and energy to his own business."

"I see," Drake said. "Well, that's accordin' to human nature, I reckon. They say Hobson speculates in grain an' cotton, an' when a feller gets to playin' a game as excitin' as that it is hard for 'im to get down to humdrum matters."

Saunders linked his hands across his knee, and looked down at the floor for a moment in silence. He seemed to be trying to formulate something more difficult to express than what he had already touched upon.

"The truth is," he plunged, suddenly—"just between you and me, in confidence, I was compelled to speak to him about the matter the other day; and, to my surprise, he told me bluntly that as he was now placed he would not care to give full time to the management of my affairs. He has his sights pretty high. He is making money rapidly, and he feels independent."

"Good Lord! You don't mean that he would throw up the job?" Drake exclaimed, in astonishment. "He's a fool, a stark, starin' fool. Why, I never heard o' the like! It is by all odds the best berth in our county."

"He is to quit on the first of next month," Saunders said, "and that is what I want to see you about. The truth is that—well, I've had *you* in mind for some time, and I was rather disappointed when I heard you were thinking of getting work down here. You are the very man I want for the place, if you will do me the favor of accepting it."

The stare of astonishment in the eyes of the mountaineer became a fixed glare of almost childlike incredulity. So profound was his surprise that he was unable to utter a word. His hand, suddenly quivering as with palsy, went to his tobacco-stained lips and stayed there for a moment. Then his imprisoned voice broke loose.

"You can't mean that, Jarvis—you can't, surely you can't!"

"Yes, I do," Saunders responded, drawn into the other's emotional current. "I want a man who is popular with the people, and you have hundreds of friends. If—if you accept I'd like for you to remain here in Atlanta for a week at least, to help me buy some implements and supplies."

"*If* I accept—*if!*" Drake laughed at the sheer absurdity of the word. "Do I look like a fool? Just now I was ready to go back home, ashamed to look my family in the face because I couldn't find work at a dollar a day, and my board to pay out of it, and now—now—" The voice faltered and broke.

"Well, it is settled, then," Saunders said, in relief.

"As far as I am concerned, it is." Drake cleared his husky throat. "I know the sort of work you want done up there, and I can do it. I can get as much out of hands as anybody else, and you sha'n't lose by it; by God, you sha'n't!"

"Well, come to see me at the bank in the morning." Saunders rose. "You've taken a load off my shoulders. I was worried about it."

CHAPTER IX

The next morning, as Saunders sat at breakfast in the cafe of his club scanning the morning paper, his attention was fixed by the big-typed head-lines of a report of the school convention at the Capitol. The details and object of the meeting were given in only a few sentences, the main feature of the article being a sensational account of the brilliant speech of a young woman delegate in support of the bill before the Legislature favoring a much-needed appropriation for schools among the poor mountaineers.

The paper stated that the youthful beauty, vivacity, and eloquence of the speaker, the daughter of a Confederate veteran, had roused an enthusiasm seldom witnessed in the old State House. She was introduced by the Governor, who was chairman of the meeting, and fully three-fourths of the members of the Senate and the House were present. Miss Drake's speech was a rare combination of originality, humor, arid pathos. Her aptitude at anecdote, her gift for description and dialect had fairly astounded her audience. The applause was so constant and persistent that the brave young speaker had difficulty in pursuing her theme. And when it was over the members of the House and the Senate had pressed forward to congratulate her and pledge their support to the bill in question. Such a complete acceptance of any single measure had never been known before in the history of Georgia politics.

Following this account was the report of the reception to the convention of teachers at the Executive Mansion, which had been largely attended owing to the desire of many to see and meet the young heroine of the day. Saunders read and reread the article, in his excitement neglecting his breakfast and forgetting his morning cigar.

"God bless her!" he chuckled. "She is a brick. Put her anywhere on earth, against any odds, and she will win!"

When the hour approached for her train to leave he went down to the big station to see her off, finding her alone in the waiting-room looking quite as if nothing unusual had happened, though he thought he noticed a slight shade of uneasiness on her face.

"Anything gone wrong?" he inquired, anxious to help her if she needed assistance.

"I haven't seen my father," she answered. "You see, he went to a boarding-house. Rooms were in such demand that he didn't go with me and the other delegates to the hotel. Then, he had determined to economize as much as possible. I thought he would come around this morning, anyway. I don't want to go back home without seeing him; my mother would simply be wild with uneasiness."

"You have several minutes yet," Saunders answered. "He will be apt to turn up." Therewith Saunders began to smile. "Have you read the morning papers?"

"I haven't had time to read them carefully," Dolly declared. "Several of the men teachers sent copies up to my room before I came down for breakfast. The teachers had a lot to say about me and my talk. Really, I feel like a goose, and mean, too. It looks as if I thought I was the whole show. Why, there were women in the convention old enough to be the mothers of girls like me, and with a hundred times as much sense."

"But you turned the trick!" Saunders cried, enthusiastically.

"You did more with that speech than a dozen conventions of men and women could have done. You hit the nail square on the head. You won. The bill will pass like a flash. It is a foregone conclusion."

"Oh, I wish I could think so," Dolly cried, hopefully, her fine eyes beaming. Then she began to smile reminiscently. "That was the strangest experience I ever had in all my born days. Talk about the debates we used to have in our club; they were simply not in it! When they put me up there on that platform, side by side with the Governor of the State and three senators, and they were all so nice and polite, I was scared to death. My tongue was all in a knot, and I was as cold as if I had my feet in ice-water. Then when the Governor introduced me with all those compliments about my looks, and I had to stand up and begin, I give you my word, Jarvis, that big stone building, solid as it was, was rocking like a cradle. Every seat, from the front to the back, had a man or a woman in it, but I didn't see a single face. They were all melted together in one solid mass—and quiet! Why, it was so still that I heard my mouth click when I opened it to catch my breath. *It was simply awful.* I remember thinking I would pray for help if I had time, but I didn't have time for anything. It was lucky I thought about beginning with a funny tale, for when they all laughed and clapped I felt better. Then I forgot where I was. There were some young men reporters at a table right under my feet, and they kept laughing in such a friendly, good-natured way that I found myself talking to them more than any of the rest. The audience really made it easier for me, for while they were applauding I had a chance to think of something else to say. I found out the sort of thing they liked, and piled it on thick and heavy. And when I sat down and they all packed round me to shake hands, I was more surprised than I ever was in my life."

"It was the hit of the day," Saunders replied. "It was as great a success in its way as the speech of Henry W. Grady at the New England banquet. I am proud of you, Dolly. You will let me say that, won't you?"

"If you really mean it." She raised her eyes frankly to his, and a flush of gratification suffused her sweet face. "I would not like to be an utter failure on my first visit to your city. I didn't want you to hear my speech, but I do wish I had asked you to that reception. It was nice. I can see now what you all find in social things. It was like a dream to me—the music, the lights, the jewels, the dresses, the flowers, the brilliant talk, the courtesy of men, and—yes, the congratulations and compliments. I did like to have so many say they liked my speech—I really did. I almost cried over it."

"You shall have them all." Saunders restrained the words which throbbed on his lips. "Be my wife, little girl, and I'll gratify your every desire." She was looking into his eyes, and he glanced aside, fearing that she might read his thoughts.

"I wish I could have gone," was all he said. "I should have enjoyed your triumph immensely."

"It won't spoil me—don't think that." He heard her sigh and saw a slight cloud pass over her face. "I am young in years, but I have had my share of suffering. You are almost the only one who knows my great secret. It makes me feel very close to you, Jarvis. You made it easier for me to bear when you helped me hide it on the night you prevented my father from making my humiliation public. That was good of you—good and brave and thoughtful."

"My God, she still loves him!" Saunders thought, with a pang which permeated his whole being. "His very weakness has made him dearer. She never has a word to say against him."

Saunders was trying to make some sort of outward response when he saw Dolly start suddenly, her eyes on the doorway. "I see my father. Oh, I'm glad, for now I can find out what he intends to do. I see him looking for me. Wait; I'll run over to him."

Saunders watched her graceful figure as it glided through the crowd to Drake's side. He saw the mountaineer turn a face full of pride and contentment upon his daughter; and Saunders knew, from her rapt expression, that he was telling her of his good fortune. The watcher saw Dolly put her hand in a gesture of tender impulsiveness on her father's arm, and stand eagerly listening, and yet with a frown on her face. A moment later they came toward him. Dolly was regarding him with a steady, almost cold stare. Was it vague displeasure? Was it wounded pride? Surely his act was contrary to her wishes, for she made no immediate reference to it.

"Well," Drake said, "if you are goin' to put 'er on the train, I'll tell 'er good-by now. There's a feller waitin' for me at the front. Tell your mother, daughter, that I'll be up in a week or so. So long."

Drake was not a man given to embraces of any sort, and he was turning away when Dolly stopped him. "Kiss me, father," she said, raising her face to his; and, with a sheepish laugh, the mountaineer complied.

"She's like all the balance, Jarvis," he said, lightly. "They believe in things bein' done to the letter. You will be at the bank after a while, won't you?"

"Yes, as soon as the train leaves," Saunders, answered. Then he heard the porter announcing Dolly's train, and he took up her bag. She was silent as they walked along the pavement and down the iron stairs to the car, where he found a seat for her. Only a few minutes remained, and the feeling was growing on him that she was quite displeased with the arrangement he had made with her father. How could he part with her like that? The days of doubt and worry ahead of him as a consequence of what he had done seemed unbearable.

"Did your father mention the plan he and I—"

"Yes," she broke in, tremulously; "he told me all about it, Jarvis, and—and I want to ask you a question. I want you to be frank with me. I don't want the slightest evasion to—to save me from pain. I can't go up home without knowing the full truth. You are so—so kind and thoughtful, always wanting to—to do *me* some favor and aid *me* that—Oh, Jarvis, I want to know this: Do you think my father is capable of filling that place as it ought to be filled?"

Saunders was sitting on the arm of the seat in front of her. The car was almost empty, no one being near. He bent forward and laid his hand on her arm. "He is the very man I want," he declared. "The work is not difficult; he is so popular with the average run of men that he will make a far better manager than Hobson, or any one else I could get."

He heard her catch her breath. He saw a light of joy dawn in her eyes. "If only I could believe that, Jarvis," she said, "I would be the happiest girl in all the world. I would—I would—I would."

"Then you may be," he answered, huskily, his emotions all but depriving him of utterance. "He is doing *me* a favor, Dolly. Of all men he is the first I would select."

The bell of the locomotive was ringing. Saunders stood up, now clasping the hand she held out. He felt her timid fingers cling to his. Her blood and his throbbed in unison. Looking into her eyes, he saw that they were full of tears. He remembered how she had kissed his hand on the night he had prevented her father from going to Atlanta, and as he hurried from the slowly moving car he was like a man groping through a maze of doubt and bewildering fears. She could feel and show gratitude, he told himself, but a heart such as hers could never be won twice to actual love. It is said that suffering deepens character, and it was perhaps the fall of her ideal which had made her the heroic marvel she was. Mostyn still loved her in secret; of that Saunders had little doubt, for how could a man once embraced by such a creature ever forget it? And Dolly suspected the man's constancy and had no room for aught but secret responsiveness. But no matter, he would still be her watchful and attentive friend. He had helped her to-day in the midst of her triumph, and he would help her again and again. To serve her unrewarded would have to suffice.

CHAPTER X

One morning, a week or so later, Mostyn found a note from Marie Winship in his mail. It was brief and to the point. It ran:

DEAR DICK,-I am going to leave Atlanta for good and all, never to bother you again (believe me, this is the truth), but I want to see you to explain in full. I shall be at my dressmaker's in the morning after ten. Please walk out that way. I shall see you from the window, and you won't have to come in. Don't refuse this last request. This is not a "hold-up"; I don't intend to ask for money. I only want to say good-by and tell you something. My last effort to get you to come to see me proved to me how altered you are. MARIE.

Mostyn turned the matter over in his mind deliberately, and finally decided that he would comply with the request. It rang true, and there was comfort in the assurance that she was about to leave Atlanta, for her presence and instability of mood had long been a menace to his peace of mind.

At the hour mentioned he found himself somewhat nervously nearing the cottage in question. She was prompt; he saw her standing at a window, and a moment later she came out and joined him.

"Let's walk down toward the woods," she suggested, with a smile which lay strangely on her piquant features. "It will look better than standing like posts on the sidewalk."

He agreed, wondering now, more than ever, what she had to say. She had barely touched his hand in salutation, and bore herself in a sedate manner that was all but awkward. They soon reached a shaded spot quite out of sight of any of the scattered residences in the vicinity, and she sat down on the grass, leaving him the option of standing or seating himself by her.

"You are wondering what on earth I've got up my sleeve"—she forced a little laugh—"and well you may wonder, Dick, for I am as big a mystery to myself as I could possibly be to any one else."

"I was wondering if you really do intend to leave Atlanta," he answered, sitting down beside her. "You seemed very positive about it in your note."

"Yes, I am going, Dick; but that is not the *main* thing. Dick, I'm going to be married."

"Married!" he exclaimed. "Are you joking?"

"I suppose you do regard it as a joke," she said, listlessly, and with a little sigh. "Such a serious step would seem funny in me, wouldn't it? But I am not what I used to be, Dick. I have been quite upset for a long time—in fact, ever since you married. Then again, your life, your ways, your constant brooding has had a depressing effect on me. Dick, it seems to me that you have been trying to—well, to be good ever since you married."

He shrugged his shoulders. "What is the use of talking about that, Marie?" he asked, avoiding her probing stare.

"It affected me a lot," she returned, thoughtfully. "I tried to keep up the old pace and care for the old things, but your turn about was always before me. Dick, you have puzzled me all along. You do not care a snap for your wife; what is it that makes you look like a ghost of your old jolly self?"

He shrank from her sensitively. "I really don't like to talk

Will N. Harben

about such things," he faltered. "Tell me about your marriage."

"Not yet; one thing at a time." She dropped her sunshade at her feet and locked her white hands over her knee. "I shall never see you again after to-day, Dick, and I *do* want to understand you a little better, so that when I look back on our friendship you won't be such a tantalizing mystery. Dick, you never loved me; you never loved your wife; but you *have* loved some one."

He lowered his startled glance to the ground. She saw a quiver pass over him and a slow flush rise in his face.

"What are you driving at?" he suddenly demanded. "All this is leading nowhere."

She smiled in a kindly, even sympathetic way. "It can't do any harm, Dick, for, really, what I have found out has made me sorry for you for the first time in my life—genuinely and sincerely sorry."

"What you have found out?" he faltered, half fearfully.

"Yes, and it doesn't matter how I discovered it, but I did. I happened to stay for a week at a little hotel in Ridgeyille last month, and a slight thing I picked up about your stay up there five years ago gradually led me on to the whole thing. Dick, I saw Dolly Drake one day on one of my walks. One look at her and the whole thing became plain. You loved her. You came back here with the intention of marrying her and leading a different life. You would have done it, too, but for my threats and your partial engagement to your wife. You went against your true self when you married, and you have never gotten over it."

He was unable to combat her assertions, and simply sat in silence, an expression of keen inner pain showing itself in his drawn lips.

"See how well I have read you!" she sighed. "I always knew there was something unexplained. You would have been more congenial with your wife but for that experience. You are to blame for her dissatisfaction.

Not having love from you, she is leaning on the love of an old sweetheart. Dick, that pretty girl in the mountains would have made you happy. I read the article about her in the paper the other day. From all accounts, she is a remarkable woman, and genuine."

Mostyn nodded. "She *is* genuine," he admitted. "Well, now you know the truth. But all that is past and gone. You forget something else."

"No, I don't," she took him up, confidently. "You are thinking of your boy."

Again he nodded. "Love for a woman is one thing, Marie, but the love for one's own child passes beyond anything else on earth."

"Yes, when the child is loved as you love yours, and when you fancy that he is being neglected, and that you are partly responsible for it. Oh, Dick, you and I both are queer mixtures! I may as well be frank. Your struggles to make amends have had their effect on me. For a long time I have not been satisfied with myself. I used to be able to quiet my conscience by plunging into pleasure, but the old things no longer amuse. That is why I am turning over a new leaf. Dick, the man I am to marry knows my life from beginning to end. He is a good fellow—a stranger here, and well-to-do. My brother sent him to me with a letter of introduction. He has had trouble. He was suspected of serious defalcation, and the citizens of his native town turned against him. All his old ties are cut. He likes me, and I like him. I shall make him a true wife, and he knows it. I am going to my brother in Texas and will be married out there. Dick, I shall, perhaps, never see you again, but, frankly, I shall not care. I want to forget you as completely as you will forget me. I only wish I were leaving you in a happier frame of mind. You are miserable, Dick, and you are so constituted that you can't throw it off."

"No, I can't throw it off!" His voice was low and husky. "I won't mince words about it. Marie, I am in hell. I know how men feel who kill themselves. But I shall not do that."

"No, that would do no good, Dick. I have faced that proposition several times, and conquered it. The only thing to do is to hope—and, Dick, I sometimes think there is something—a *little* something, you know—in praying. I believe there is a God over us—a God of *some* sort, who loves even the wrongdoers He has created and listens to their cries for help now and then. But I don't know; half the time I doubt everything. There is one thing certain. The humdrum church-people, whom we used to laugh at for their long faces and childish faith, have the best of the game of life in the long run. They have—they really have."

He tried to blend his cold smile with hers, but failed. He stood up, and, extending his hand, he aided her to rise. "This is good-by, then, forever," he said. "Marie, I think *you* are going to be happy."

"I don't know, but I am going to try at least for contentment," she said, simply. "There is always hope, and you may see some way out of your troubles."

Quite in silence they walked back to the cottage gate, and there, with a hand-shake that was all but awkward, they parted. He tipped his hat formally as he turned away. Ahead of him lay the city, a dun stretch of roofs and walls, with here and there a splotch of green beneath a blue sky strewn with snowy clouds.

He had gone only a few paces when he heard the whirring sound of an automobile, which was approaching from the direction of the city. It was driven by a single occupant. It was

Andrew Buckton. Mostyn saw the expression of exultant surprise that he swept from him to Marie, and knew by Buckton's raised hat that he had seen them together. The car sped on and vanished amid the trees at the end of the road. Looking back, Mostyn saw that Marie was lingering at the gate. He knew from the regretful look in her face that she was deploring the incident; but, simply raising his hat again, he strode on.

All the remainder of the morning he worked at his desk. He tried to make himself feel that, now that Marie was leaving, his future would be less clouded; but with all the effort made, he could not shake off a certain clinging sense of approaching disaster. Was he afraid that Buckton would gossip about what he had just seen, and that the public would brand him afresh with the discarded habits of the past? He could not have answered the question. He was sure of nothing. He lunched at his club, smoked a dismal cigar with Delbridge and some other men, and heard them chatting about the rise and fall of stocks as if they and he were in a turbulent dream. They appeared as marvels to him in their unstumbling blindness under the overbrooding horrors of life, in their ignorance of the dark, psychic current against which he alone was battling.

All the afternoon he toiled at the bank, and at dusk he walked home. No one was about the front of the house, and he went up to his room. He had bathed his face and hands, changed his suit, and was about to descend the stairs when his father-in-law came tottering along the corridor and paused at the open door of the room.

"This is a pretty come-off," he scowled in at Mostyn. "Here you come like this as if nothing out of the way had happened, when your wife has packed up and gone off for another trip. She said she was going to write you—did you get a note?"

"No; where has she gone?" Mostyn inquired. "She didn't even mention it to me."

"One of her sudden notions. The Hardys at Knoxville are having a big house-party, and wrote her to come. I tried to get her to listen to reason, but she wouldn't hear a word. She is actually crazy for excitement—women all get that way if you give them plenty of rein, and Irene has been spoiled to death. I have never seen her act as strange as she did to-day. She cried when I talked to her, and almost went into hysterics. She gave the servants a lot of her clothes, and kept coming to me and throwing her arms around me and telling me to forgive her for this and that thing I forgot long ago. When she started for the train I wanted to go with her or telephone you, but she wouldn't let me do either—said I was too feeble, and she did not want to bother you. Say, do you know I'm to blame? I had no right to influence you and her to marry, nohow. You have never suited each other—you don't act like man and wife. You might as well be two strangers hitched together. Something is wrong, awfully wrong, but I can't tell what it is."

Mostyn made no reply. He heard little Dick's voice in the hall below, and had a sudden impulse to take him up. Leaving him, old Mitchell passed on to his own room, and Mostyn went down the stairs to the child, who was playing on the veranda.

"Poor child! Poor child!" he said to himself.

CHAPTER XI

The next morning at the bank a financial disappointment met him. A telegram informed him of the sudden slump in some stocks in which he was interested. The loss was considerable, and the tendency was still downward. He was wondering if he ought to confide this to Saunders, when his partner, of his own accord, came into his office and sat down by his desk.

"Busy just now?" Saunders inquired.

"No; what is it?" Mostyn returned. "Fire away."

Saunders seemed to hesitate. Through the partition came the clicking of a typewriter and an adding-machine, the swinging of the screened door in front. "It is a somewhat personal matter," Saunders began, awkwardly. "I have been wanting to mention it for a month, but hardly knew how to bring it up. You may know, Mostyn, that I have been thinking of giving up business here altogether. I have become more and more interested in my farming ventures, and my life in the country has taken such a grip on me that I want to quit Atlanta altogether."

"Oh, I see." Mostyn forced a smile. "I thought you would get to that before long. You are becoming a regular hayseed, Saunders. You are like a fish out of water here in town. Well, I suppose you want to put a man in your place so you will have freer rein in every way."

"Not that, exactly, Mostyn. The fact is, I want to realize on my bank stock. There are other things I'd like to invest in, and I need the money to do it with. I am planning a cotton-mill in my section to give employment to a worthy class of poor people."

Mostyn drew his lips tight. He stabbed a sheet of paper on the green felt before him, and there was a rebellious flash from his eyes.

"Come right out and be frank about it," he said, with a touch of anger. "Are you afraid your investment in this bank is not a safe one?"

Saunders looked steadily at him. "That certainly is not a businesslike question, Mostyn, and you know it."

"Perhaps it isn't, but what does it matter?" Mostyn retorted. "At any rate, that is a shrewd evasion of the point. Well, do you want to sell *me* your stock?"

"I would naturally give you the preference, and that is why I am mentioning it to you."

Mostyn sat frowning morbidly. There was a visible droop to his shoulders. "There is no use having hard feelings over it," he said, dejectedly. "You have a right to do as you please with your interests. But the truth is, I am not financially able to take over as big a block of stock as you hold."

Saunders hesitated for a moment, then began: "I was wondering if Mr. Mitchell—"

"Leave him out of consideration, for God's sake," Mostyn broke in. "He has grown horribly suspicious of me. He would have a regular spasm if you tried to sell to him. He would be sure we are on the brink of failure, and talk all over town. Don't mention it to him."

"And you say you are not in a position to—"

"No; many things have gone against me recently, but that needn't bother you. You can find a buyer."

"I have already found one, and the offer is satisfactory." Saunders glued his glance to the rug at his feet. "In fact, I have been approached more than once, Delbridge wants to buy me out."

"Delbridge!" Mostyn started. His lips parted and his teeth showed in a cold grimace. "Ah, I see his game!"

"I don't understand," Saunders said, wonderingly.

"Well, I do, if you don't. I suspected something was in the wind last month when he took over Cartwright's stock at such a good figure. Do you know if he gets your stock that he will hold a larger interest than mine?"

"I hadn't thought of it."

"I see his plan plainly. He wants to be the president of this bank, and he can elect himself if he buys you out. He has always wanted exactly this sort of thing to back up his various schemes. You must give me a little while to think it over, Saunders. I don't like to give in to him. He has always fought me, you know, and this would be a feather in his cap. Perhaps I can induce some one else to make the investment."

"Take all the time you want," Saunders answered. "I want you to be satisfied."

"Well, I'll let you know to-day, or to-morrow, at furthest," Mostyn said, wearily. "If I can't make some arrangement I'll have to give in, that's all. My affairs are getting pretty badly tangled, but I'll come out all right."

When Saunders had left him and the door had closed, Mostyn

leaned his head on his hand and tried to collect his wits, but to no avail. What was the intangible thing which had haunted him through the night, causing him to lie awake, reciting over and over old Mitchell's account of the scene with his daughter just before her departure? What was it that kept coupling this hurried trip of hers with Buckton? Was thought-transference a scientific fact, as many hold, and was the insistent impression due to the bearing of culpable minds upon his? He might telephone here and there and find out if Buckton was in town—but no, no, that would not do.

The porter opened the door and came in with a bundle of letters and papers which he put down before him and withdrew. A grim foreboding settled on him. Something seemed to whisper from the mute heap that here lay the revelation—here was the missing communication from Irene of which her father had spoken. A bare glance at the bundle was enough, for he recognized the pale-blue envelope belonging to Irene's favorite stationery. With bloodless fingers, breathlessly, he drew it out. It had been posted the night before. Surely, he told himself, there was meaning in this slower method of delivery, for what had prevented her from leaving it at home in his room or in her father's care? Or, for that matter, why had she not telephoned him? He laid the communication down, unopened. He was afraid of it. Had the skies been stone, their supports straws, his dread could not have been greater. He went to the door and softly turned the key. There should be no eye upon him. He came back. Taking a paper-knife, he slit the envelope and spread out the perfumed sheet. It read:

DEAR DICK,—There is no use keeping up this senseless farce any longer. I am sick to death with my very existence. I have been hungry for love all my life, and never had it. When I married I mistreated the only man I ever cared for, and I have resolved to do so no longer. Andy and I are leaving together. God only knows if we shall find the happiness we are seeking, but we are going to try. Father thinks I have gone to the Hardys'. Perhaps he may as well be kept in ignorance for a few days longer. The truth will leak out soon enough. Though you may do as you like about this. As for your following us and making things unpleasant, I have no fears, for, as you well know, I am entitled to my liberty in this matter. You have certainly not been molested by me in your own private life. I now know all about the cottage in the outskirts of town, but I am not blaming you in the least. I confess that I thought you had ceased your attentions in that quarter, but that was because I attributed a certain spiritual and remorseful quality to you which you do not possess. I am not blaming you at all—*at all*. In fact, somehow the discovery has had a soothing effect on me. It has confirmed the feeling that both you and I have been and are the mere playthings of Fate. As I see it, I am doing my duty. I led poor Andy on before my marriage. I kissed him—I've kissed him a thousand times, both before and since my marriage. He can't live without me, and I can't live without his love and future companionship. Life is too short to spend it in the sheer misery I have been in of late. He and I are going out into the great world to live, enjoy, and die together. People will talk, but we can't help that—the truth is, we don't care. You will blame me for leaving the child, for you do love him, but I can't help that. He was born out of love, and was always a reproach to me. You will take care of him; I know that, and better than if I were there.

Good-by.   IRENE.

Mostyn folded the sheet and thrust it into his pocket. Going to a window, he stood looking out on the dusty street. Drays and cabs were trundling by. Had his back been bared to the thonged scourge of the public whipping-post and the blows been falling under the strokes of a giant, he could not have cringed more. He saw himself the laughing-stock of the town, the fool provider for another man's passion. He saw his adored child, now worse than motherless, growing up into open-eyed consciousness of his hereditary shame. He saw his wreck of a father-in-law glaring at him in senile indignation. What was to be done—what *could* be done? Nothing—simply nothing. Men of honor in the past had been able to wipe out stains like those and keep their heads erect, but to assume that he was "a man of honor," as matters stood, would be the height of absurdity. He certainly would not announce the news to Mitchell. He would ward off the disclosure as long as possible, and then—well, there was no knowing what would happen.

Going to the door, he unlocked it and peered into the busy bank. His glance fell on Saunders's desk. Saunders was not there. He had decided to speak to him with finality in regard to the disposition of his stock. What mattered it now who held the office of president? In fact, the unsullied name of a man like Delbridge might rescue the institution from the actual ruin which was apt to follow such a scandal and the accompanying report of old Mitchell's financial estrangement from his son-in-law.

Mostyn approached Wright, the cashier, with the intention of inquiring where Saunders was when he heard Wright speaking to a man through the grating as he turned a check over in his hand. "I am sorry," he was saying, "but, while it is small, we could not cash it without identification."

"That's why I brought it to you," the man answered. "I know Mr. Saunders. I've seen him several times up in the mountains. He cashed a check for me up there once, and said if I ever happened to be down here to drop in to see him."

"He is out just now, but will be in very soon," Wright said. "Won't you come into the waiting-room and take a seat?"

Stooping down a little, Mostyn was enabled to see the face of the applicant. It was that of John Leach, the tramp preacher. Their eyes met. Mostyn bowed and smiled. Then he touched Wright on the arm just as he was about to shove the check back to its owner. "I know him," he said. "It is all right."

Mostyn noticed a look of astonishment struggling on the tanned features of the preacher, but he turned away just as Wright was counting out the money. He would go out and find Saunders, he decided, and get the detail pertaining to the sale of stock off his mind. Outside he looked up the street, seeing Saunders and Delbridge standing on the corner in conversation.

"Delbridge is crazy to make the deal," he said, bitterly. "That is what he is talking about now. Well, he may have it. I am down and out. I am in no shape to attend to business. Besides, I'll want to hide myself from the public eye. Yes, he will protect my interest, and I shall need all the funds I can rake together. Great God! how did this ever come about? Only the other day I had some hope, but now not a shred is left. Delbridge was my financial rival. Neck and neck we ran together, the talk of the town; but now—yes, he can wipe his feet on me. Look at him—he's grinning—he's laughing—he is telling one of his funny yarns to pretend to Saunders that he is indifferent about the stock. Huh! Well he may laugh. Who knows, perhaps *his* luck will turn? The man that counts on luck is God's fool."

Mostyn took out a cigar as he approached the two men. "Match?" he asked Delbridge. The financier gave him one, and Mostyn struck it on the canvas back of a small check-book and applied it to the end of his cigar. "Saunders says you have made him an offer for his block of bank stock," he puffed, slowly.

"Yes, I made him a proposition." Delbridge's face fell into sudden shrewd rigidity. "I have about that amount of money idle just now. Saunders says he feels that you are entitled to a preference of the stock, and that until you decide what you want to do my offer must hang in the air."

Mostyn flicked at the ashless tip of his cigar. "I have thought it over," he said, "and, on the whole, Delbridge, I am sure your name will help the bank's standing, and I hope you and Saunders will make the deal."

"Oh, that's all right, then," Delbridge beamed. "Well, Saunders, I'll consider it settled, then. I'll walk into the bank with you now. I may be too busy later in the day."

Mostyn moved on. He crossed the viaduct over the railway tracks and walked aimlessly for several squares, bowing to acquaintances on the way. Presently he turned and began to retrace his steps, without any plan of action other than keeping his legs in motion.

At the corner of the street he came face to face with Leach. The man smiled cordially and brushed his long hair back over his ear with his delicate hand. "I was just wondering where I've seen you before." He extended his hand. "You certainly surprised me in the bank just now when you stood for me like you did."

Mostyn explained that he had heard him preach at Wartrace's store five years before.

"Say, I remember now," Leach cried. "Wasn't you sitting on the porch of the store?"

Mostyn nodded. "Yes, and I enjoyed your talk very much. I have thought of it a good many times since."

"I remember you now powerful well—powerful well. I seldom forget a face, and if a man shows that he is listening close, as you did that day, it helps me along. Do you know, I put you down as about the best listener I ever had. I saw it in your face and eyes. You got up and left before I was through, or I'd have spoken to you. It seemed to me that you was bothered powerful over something. Being in prison as long as I was gave me what you might call second-sight. You may not believe it, but I can actually feel a stream of thought coming from folks now and then. I can detect trouble of any spiritual sort in the face or in the touch of a hand. It isn't any of my affair, but right now I have a feeling that you are bothered. I reckon you business men have a lot to trouble you in one way and another."

"Yes, it is constant worry," Mostyn answered, evasively.

"This ain't no time to preach," Leach went on, with his characteristic laugh; "but I feel like scolding every town man I meet. This place is no better suited to real happiness than a foundry is for roses to bloom in. If you want to breathe God's breath, smell the sweet perfume of His presence, and walk in the wonderful light of His glory, throw this dusty grind off and go out into nature. Get down on your all-fours and hug it. Stop making money. When you've got a pile of it as high as that sky-scraper there you haven't got as much actual wealth as a honey-bee carries in one single flight through the sunlight. I never saw Heaven's blaze in the eye of a money-maker, but I *have* seen it in the black face of a shouting nigger at a knock-down-and-drag-out revival. I intimated that I was happy when you heard me five years ago, I reckon. Well, since then I have become so much more so that that time seems like stumbling-ground, full of ruts and snags. Oh, I could tell you wonders, wonders, wonders! There never was an emperor I'd swap places with. If you ever get in trouble, come talk to me. Hundreds of men and women have opened their hearts to me and cried their troubles out like little children. I couldn't tell you how to get the best of a man in a speculation here in this hell-hole of iniquity, but I can show you how you can tie a thousand of God's spirit-cords to you and be drawn so high above all this that you won't know it is in existence. Going to the country this summer? I am. I'm headed for the mountains now. I just dropped in here to collect the little money that comes to me every quarter. I see you are in a hurry; well, so long. God be with you, friend. I'm going to pray for you. I don't know why, but I am. I'm going to pray for this whole rotten town, but I'll mention you special. Good-by."

"He may be right," Mostyn mused, as he strode on toward the bank. "He *is* right—he *is*!"

CHAPTER XII

Irene was on the train bound for Charleston. She was seated in one of the big easy-chairs in the parlor-car, idly scanning a magazine and looking out at the dingy and sordid outskirts of Atlanta through which the train was moving with increasing speed. The conductor passed, punched her ticket, and went on. He had glanced at her with masculine interest, for she showed by her sedate dignity, smallest detail of attire, and every visible possession, that she was a passenger of distinction.

Presently Buckton came in at the front door and approached her. An exultant smile swept his flushed face as he bent down over her.

"Thank God, we are off!" he chuckled. "I was simply crazy at the station—first with fear that you would not come, and next that we'd be noticed, but I don't believe a soul recognized us. I was seated behind a newspaper in the waiting-room watching for you like a hawk. I saw you get out of the cab and come in. God, darling, you don't know how proud I felt to know that you were actually coming to me! At last you are mine—all mine; after all these years of agony you are mine!"

She raised a pair of eyes to his in which a haunting dread seemed to lie like a shadow. "Oh, I feel so queer!" she sighed. "I realized that we had to hide and dodge, but I did not like the role. For the first time in my life I felt mean and sneaking. Already I am worried about father and the boy—father, in particular. He is getting old and feeble. Perhaps the shock to him may seriously harm him."

Buckton smiled, but less freely. He sat down in the chair in front of her and turned it till he faced her. "We have no time to bother about them, dear," he said, passionately. "We deserve to live in happiness, and we are going to do it. I am so happy I can hardly speak. Oh, we are going to have a glorious time! You should have been mine long ago. Nature intended it. We are simply getting our dues."

"I am doing it solely for your sake," she faltered. "Because you've suffered so on my account."

"And not for your *own* sake? Don't put it that way, sweetheart." He took her hand; but, casting a furtive glance at the backs of the few other passengers in the car, she withdrew it.

"Don't," she protested, smiling. "We must be careful." She dropped a penetrating gaze into his amorous eyes, and applied her handkerchief to her drooping lips. "I've been thinking, Andy, about a certain thing more seriously since the train started than I ever did before. Do you know, many persons believe that if a woman acts—acts—well, as I am doing now, the man to whom she gives in will, down at the bottom of his heart, cease to respect and love her—in time—in time, I mean?"

"Bosh and tommyrot!" Buckton fairly glowed. "Never, never, when the case is like ours. We are simply doing our duty to ourselves. Love you? Why, I adore you! You have saved my life, darling. I would have killed myself. I've been on the very brink of it more than once. I've suffered agonies ever since you married. The birth of your child fairly drove me insane. I groveled in blackest despair. It made me feel that—that you were, or had been, actually his. Oh, it was awful! Don't regret our step. Think of what is before us. We'll stop in Charleston, see the quaint old town, go on to Savannah, stop a day or so, and then sail for New York. The ships are good, and at this season the sea is as smooth as glass. When we get to New York we will simply paint the town red, and if you wish, then, we'll go on to Europe. What could be more glorious? Why, the whole world is ours."

She smiled, almost sadly, and then, as if to avoid his gaze, she glanced out of the window. He saw her breast heave. He heard her sigh. "You are a man and I am a woman," she muttered. "I suppose that makes a difference. In a case like ours a man never is blamed by society, but the woman is. They class her with the lowest. Oh, won't they talk at home? Nothing else will be thought of for months. Old-fashioned persons will say it was the life we led. Do you suppose it could possibly—in any way—injure Dick's business?"

"How could it?" Buckton said, with caustic impatience. "What has this to do with his affairs?"

"Oh, I don't know!" She exhaled the words, heavily. "I have heard my father say that depositors sometimes take fright at the slightest things concerning the private lives of bankers. Andy, I would not like for this to—cost Dick a cent. I couldn't bear that."

"Do you think you ought to entertain such fine-spun ideas in regard to him when—when he is living as he is?"

"That has bothered me, too," she said, quickly. "Somehow I can't believe that he ever really went back to that woman— that is, to live with her. I met her only a week ago on the street. She looked straight at me, and, somehow, I was sure that he and she were not as they used to be. Call it intuition if you like, but intuition is sometimes reliable. It may have been by accident that they were together when you saw them out there. He takes lonely walks in all sorts of directions. He is a strange combination. His love for little Dick, his constant worrying about him is remarkable. It used to make me mad, but in a way I respected him for it."

"Let's not talk about him," Buckton implored. "All this

rubbish is giving you the blues. They have called dinner. Let's go back to the dining-car. The service is fairly good on this line."

"I couldn't eat a bite," Irene answered.

"Well, let us go in, anyway. It will be a change," he said, "and will take your mind off this gloomy subject. Think of what is ahead of us, darling, not behind."

She rose, and, with a smile of resignation to his will, she followed him through the vestibule into the dining-car. As they went in they met a portly man who stood aside for them to pass.

"How are you, Mr. Buckton?" the man smiled, cordially.

"Oh, how are you?" Buckton answered, with a start and a rapid scrutiny of the passenger's face. Moving on, he secured seats at a table for two. As they sat down facing each other he noticed that the man, who had paid the cashier for his meal and was waiting for his change, was eying him and Irene with a curious, almost bold stare.

"Who is that man?" Irene questioned, rather coldly, as she spread out her napkin.

"His name is Hambright," Buckton answered, with assumed lightness. "He is a whisky salesman. Somebody brought him to the club the other night, and he told a lot of funny stories. He seems to have plenty of money; his house may give it to him for advertising purposes. He fairly throws it about to make acquaintances."

"I don't like his looks at all," Irene said, her lips curled in contempt. "Just then he stared at me in the most impertinent way. His hideous eyes actually twinkled. Do you suppose he could possibly know who I am?"

The compliment that every visitor to Atlanta would know her, at least by sight, rose to his lips, but he suppressed it as decidedly inappropriate to her mood.

"It isn't at all likely," Buckton answered, instead. "Besides, even if he *did*, what ground would he have for thinking that our being together on a train like this—you know what I mean."

"I know what you *want* to mean," Irene said, disconsolately. "I also know what such a creature as that would go out of his way to *think*."

"There, you are off again!" Buckton laughed in a mechanical tone, which betrayed his uneasiness. "You are going to keep me busy brushing away your fancies. I see that now. Pretty soon you will expect the engineer to shut off steam and come back to take a peep at us. Your imagination is getting the upper hand of you. Stop short now and smile like your true, sweet self. I am happy and care-free, and I want you to be so."

She said nothing, but gave him a faint, childlike smile. "You are a dear, good boy, Andy," she faltered. "I am going to try to be sensible. It isn't the first time persons have acted this way and come out all right, is it? I don't want anything but tea. Get a pot. I think it will do me good."

Half an hour later they returned to their seats in the other car. The tea seemed to have exhilarated her, for she smiled more freely. There was a touch of rising color in her cheeks, a faint, defiant sparkle in her eyes. In passing from one car to the other she had allowed him to take her hand, and he pressed it ardently. He was swinging back into his joyous and triumphant mood.

They had not been seated long when the train came to a sudden stop. There was no station near, and several of the passengers looked out of the windows, and one or two left the car to see what had happened.

"Wait, and I'll see what is the matter," Buckton said. "I hope we won't be delayed. It is my luck to be behind on every trip. I'm a regular Jonah."

The stop had been made evidently to take on passengers, for a wretchedly clad woman and a little barefooted girl in ragged clothing were courteously helped into the car by the conductor. Both the woman and the girl were weeping violently, their sobs and wailings being distinctly heard as they sat locked in each other's arms. The sight was indeed pitiful. The conductor bent over them, said something in a crude effort at comfort, and then left them alone. Buckton came back, a look of annoyance on his face.

"What is wrong?" Irene questioned him as he sat down by her.

"It seems that the woman's husband was a track-hand," Buckton explained. "He worked down the road a few miles from here, and was run over and killed about an hour ago. They nagged our train to take her and his daughter to him."

"Oh, how awful—how awful!" Irene cried, in dismay. "You can see she is broken-hearted."

"Yes, they both take it hard," Buckton said, frowning. "I wonder what we'll run up against next. I wouldn't care for myself, but such things upset you. Don't look at them. What is the use?"

"I can't help it," Irene answered. "She is the most wretched-looking woman I ever saw. I am going to—to speak to her."

He put out a detaining hand, but she rose, a firm look of kindly determination on her face. Going to the weeping woman, Irene sat down in a chair opposite her, and as she did so the woman raised her anguish-filled eyes.

"I am so sorry to hear of your trouble," Irene began. "Is there anything I can do to help you?"

The woman, who was thin, short, and of colorless complexion, wiped her eyes on a soiled apron. The scant knot of brown hair at the back of her head seemed a pathetic badge of feminine destitution. The eyes, peering from their red and swollen sockets, held an appeal that would have shaken sympathy from the heart of a brute.

"Thar is nothing you kin do, Miss." The voice was a wail which rose, swelled out, and cracked like floating ice against the shore of a mighty stream. "Thar ain't nothin' nobody kin do. My John is dead. Even God can't do nothin'. It's over, I tell you. Dead, dead! I can't believe it, but they say it is so. He wasn't well when he left the house this mornin', but he was afeard he'd lose his job if he didn't report for work. He was so sick he could hardly drag one foot after the other. But he just would go. We had no money. Thar was only a little dab o' meal in the box, and just a rind o' hog meat. Thar is two more littler children than this un, an' they was cryin' for some'n' to eat. I know how it was; John was jest too weak to git out o' the way o' the wheels. Oh, don't mind me, Miss! He's dead—he's dead—dead—dead! Oh, God, have mercy! Kill me—kill us all an' put us out o' pain."

Tears stood in Irene's eyes. Her breast shook and ached with sympathy. She was trying to think of something to say when the whistle of the locomotive sounded.

"Here's the place now!" the woman screamed. "Oh, God! oh, God! Where have they put 'im—where have they put 'im? Maybe he is mashed so bad I won't know 'im. Oh, God! oh, God—kill me!"

The conductor, his face set and pale with pity, had come to aid her to alight. Through the window Irene saw a stretch of wheat-fields, a red-clay embankment, a wrecking-car, a group of earth-stained laborers leaning on their picks and shovels, and something lying beneath a sheet on bare ground. Hastily opening her purse, Irene took out a roll of bills amounting to a hundred dollars and pressed it into the woman's hand.

"Keep it," she said, huskily.

"Thank you, Miss," the woman said, without looking at the money or seeming to realize that she had taken it. She dropped it to the floor as she rose to go, and the conductor picked it up and gave it back to her.

"Keep it," he said; "you will need it."

Irene watched the three pass out at the door of the car and then turned her face from the window. All was still outside for a moment, and then a loud scream, followed by a fainter one, rent the air. Irene covered her face with her hands and remained in darkness till the train moved on. Buckton came and sat beside her, a disturbed look on his face. He waited for several minutes. Then she dropped her hands and sighed.

"I'm sorry this has happened, darling," Buckton said, softly. "You are so sympathetic that such things unstring you."

She bent toward him. There was a haunted, groping expression in her eyes. "I'll never forget this as long as I live," she half sobbed. "It will cling to me till I die. The very pores of my soul seemed to open to that wretched woman's spirit. If she had been my sister I couldn't have felt—"

A welling sob checked her words. He stared at her blankly. He tried to formulate some helpful response, but failed. It was growing dark outside. The porter was lighting the overhead lamps, using a step-ladder to reach them and moving it from spot to spot between the chairs.

"I want to—to ask you something—something serious," Irene said, presently. "Do you believe in omens?"

He saw her drift and forced a smile. "Yes, in this way," he said, lightly. "Things go by opposites all through life. Something good or jolly always follows on the heels of gloom. We are going to be so happy that we won't have time to think of anything disagreeable."

She sighed audibly. That was all.

It was past midnight when they reached Charleston. He led her, still silent and abstracted, to a cab and helped her in. He then gave the name of their hotel to the driver and got in beside her. He took her gloved hand and held it tenderly as the cab rumbled over the cobble-stones through the deserted streets.

"It is too warm for gloves, dear," he said, his hot breath on her cheek; and with throbbing, eager hands he drew one off. He kissed the soft fingers and felt them, flutter like a captured bird. A moment later he put his arm about her and drew her head down to his shoulder. She resisted feebly, turning from him once or twice, and then allowed him to kiss her on the lips.

As they were nearing the hotel he suddenly bethought himself of something he had intended to say by way of precaution.

"You must understand that I sent separate telegrams for rooms," he said. "I took the precaution for absolute safety. I ordered yours in your name and mine in my name."

"I understand," she replied. His arm was still about her, but she shook it off. "Was it—was it wise for us to arrive like this—in the same cab?"

"Oh, that is all right," he answered, confidently. "I am a friend of your family, you know, and I have often traveled with ladies. It will not excite comment. Besides, we know no one here."

Leaving her at the ladies' entrance to go alone up to the parlor, he went into the office. A sleepy-eyed clerk bowed, turned the register around, and, dipping a pen, handed it to him.

"Lady with you, sir?" he inquired.

"In my care, yes." Buckton wrote the two names rather unsteadily. "She and I both telegraphed for your best rooms. Please show her to hers at once. She seems to be quite tired."

"I should think so, on a stuffy day like this," said the clerk, affably, "and coming south, too. I see you are from Atlanta. That is a higher altitude than ours."

"You bet it is." The voice was at Buckton's elbow; and turning, he saw Hambright, his fellow-passenger, smiling on him familiarly. "Well, I see you got through all right."

Though highly displeased by again meeting the man, Buckton nodded and forced a casual smile.

"It was pretty dusty and hot," he said.

"Won't you take a smoke before you turn in?" the drummer asked, extending a cigar.

"No, thanks; not to-night," Buckton declined.

"Take a drink? I've got the best samples on earth. My customers say I carry better samples than stock, but that's a joke. Name the brand and I'll lay it before you. I'm some drink-mixer, I am."

"Not to-night; thank you, all the same."

"Show the lady to suite seventy-five," the clerk called out to a bell-boy. "The gentleman goes to seventy-four. See to the ice-water for both parties."

"Dandy rooms you got," Hambright said, his eyes twinkling significantly. "I know this house like a book. I swear you Atlanta bloods are sports. You certainly keep the old fogies of the town wondering what prank you will play next."

Buckton thought rapidly. To a certain extent he was a judge of human nature, and he realized that no explanation to such a man was safer than the most adroit and elaborate one, so he elected to ignore the obvious innuendo. Chatting with him a few minutes longer, he turned away.

Half an hour later Buckton was in his little sitting-room, seated under a drop-light, with a newspaper spread out before him. Through the rather thin partition he heard Irene moving about the adjoining chamber. He sat for a moment longer; then, rising, he went to the connecting door. He caught his breath and held it as he rapped softly, very softly. The sound of movement on the part of Irene ceased. All was quiet for a moment; then he rapped again. He heard her coming. She unlocked the door, turned the bolt, and opened the door the width of her face. She had changed her dress. She now wore a pretty flowing kimono which she held over her white neck with her jeweled hand.

"What is it?" she asked.

He leaned against the door-jamb, and gazed into her eyes. "I must see you," he panted. "There is—is something I want to tell you."

She hesitated, holding the door. "I'm tired," she faltered. "Besides—Oh, Andy, I've been thinking that perhaps I ought to take the first morning train for the Hardys'! I could get there soon enough to—"

He leaned his flaming face closer to hers. He caught her hand and drew it down from her fluttering throat. "No, it is too late, sweetheart," he said. "We have burnt our bridges behind us. We can't go back now. We don't *want* to. We couldn't if we tried. We are human. You were cruel to me once; you can't be cruel enough to close this door to-night. *You know you can't, darling.*"

He saw her glance waver. Her hold on the door was less firm.

He pushed against it. She fell back, and he took her into his arms and pressed his lips to hers.

Will N. Harben

CHAPTER XIII

With Irene's farewell note in his pocket and ever present to his mind, Mostyn spent the remainder of the morning on which it was received mechanically instructing the elated Delbridge in his rival's new duties at the bank as its future president. At noon he tore himself away, plunging again into the streets, there even more fully to face himself and his coming humiliation. The hot, busy thoroughfares, steaming under the water sprayed upon them by trundling sprinkling-carts, were a veritable bedlam—canons of baked pavements and heartless walls of brick and mortar, plate glass and glaring gilt signs. Cries of newsboys—and cheerful, happy cries they were—fell on his ears in sounds so incongruous to his mood that they pierced his soul like hurled javelins of steel. The affairs of the world, once so fascinating, were moving on; a juggernaut of a thousand wheels was rumbling toward him. He drew near his club. On the wide veranda, in easy-chairs, smoking and reading newspapers, sat several of his friends. He started to turn in on the walk which bisected the beautiful greensward, but quailed under the ordeal. How could he exchange platitudes, discuss politics, market-reports, or listen to new jokes? He walked on, catching the eye of a friend and saluting with a wave of his cane. He decided that he would go to his sister's for lunch, but he was not sure that he would reveal his woe even to her.

He found Mrs. Moore in her cozy library, a handkerchief over her head, dusting the furniture.

"Got anything to eat?" he asked, seating himself on a divan and watching her movements with a bland stare.

"Will have in a few minutes." She turned on him, laying her duster on a book-case and removing her handkerchief. "I really believe there is something in thought-transference, Dick, for I felt that you were coming. But I don't know that this is a fair test, either, for it may have been because I knew Irene was away."

"How did you happen to know that?" he asked, in dumb, creeping surprise. "She left rather—suddenly." She smiled knowingly. "If you want me to be frank, I'll say that it is because your doddering father-in-law is getting to be worse than a gossipy old maid. He was around here an hour ago. He tried to be sly and throw me off, but I saw through him. He said Irene had left for Mrs. Hardy's house-party. There wasn't anything in that alone, you know, to make him bother to come around, for she certainly goes when and where she likes, but it was the way the silly old man went about what he was trying to discover. He asked me if I knew who had gone from here—the men in particular; and then I saw his hand. He wanted to find out if Andy Buckton went. He beat about the bush for a long time with a crazy, nervous stare in his eyes, and as soon as I told him I did not know he rose to leave. Irene is no doubt acting imprudently, as many of her set do, but if she doesn't look out her own father will start talk that never can be stopped."

Mostyn suddenly rose, walked to a window, and looked out.

"What time do you have luncheon?" He glanced at his watch. Mrs. Moore made no reply. She suddenly fixed a curious, groping stare on him and moved to his side.

"Dick, what has happened?" she demanded, touching his arm.

"Nothing," he answered. "I've been busy; I'm tired. I thought a cup of strong coffee might—"

Her fingers clutched his arm. "Out with it, Dick. Something has gone wrong at the bank. You are in trouble again. You've been plunging. I feel it. I see it in your eyes. I have never seen you look like this before. You haven't a bit of blood in your face." She grasped his hand, stroking his fingers. "Why, you are actually cold. What is the matter? What is the matter, brother? You can trust me."

He avoided her eyes, going back to the divan and sinking upon it. "You may as well know," he blurted out, in desperation. "Irene and Buckton have gone off together."

"No, no, no! Don't tell me that!" The woman paled; her lower lip fell and hung trembling. "You have heard gossip, as I have, and as every one has, and in your excited frame of mind—"

He told her of the note from Irene. He started to take it from his pocket, but changed his mind, recalling the allusion to Marie Winship, and not having energy enough to explain it.

"Lord have mercy!" she gasped. She sat down by him, her hand on his knee, her horrified eyes glued to his. "It is awful! I didn't think she would go that far—nobody did, because she refused him when she married you. I wish I could advise you, but there is nothing to be done now. Of course, she left the child."

"Yes, I'd have killed her if she had taken him. I would, by God! He's all I've got."

"And worse than motherless," Mrs. Moore sighed. "It is awful—awful! Irene is crazy for excitement and novelty. She has been getting worse and worse. She thinks she loves Andy Buckton, but she doesn't. She never loved any one but herself in her life. Mark my words, she will leave him. She will tire of him. She will never stand the disgrace of the thing, either. She has been petted all her life by society, and its cold shoulder will kill her. What a tragedy! But she brought it on herself."

"She didn't!" he said, grimly. "I had a hand in it. Her father had a hand in it. She was a straw in a mad stream. I can't blame her. I can't even be angry. I pity her. I'd save her if I could, but it is too late. The insane set that helped to wreck her life will chuckle and grin now."

A musical gong in the dining-room sounded softly.

"That's luncheon," Mrs. Moore said. "Let's go out. Do you want to run up and wash your hands?"

He shook his head dumbly, looking at his splayed fingers with the vacant stare of an invalid just recovering consciousness. "I want only the coffee; make it strong, please. I really am not hungry. The thought of food, somehow, is sickening. I've worked hard this morning."

Late that afternoon, still shrinking under his weighty secret, he went home. The slanting rays of the setting sun lay like kindling flames on the grass of the lawn. He saw little Dick and Hilda seated on the lowest step of the veranda; and, seeing him entering the gate, the child rose and slowly limped toward him.

"Dick got a stomach-ache," the boy said, a wry look on his rather sallow and pinched face.

Mostyn paused and bent down. "Where does it hurt you?" he asked, automatically, for the complaint seemed a slight thing compared to the tragedy lowering over them both.

"It's here, Daddy." Dick put his little tapering hand on his right side.

"He eats too many sweet things," the nurse said, coming up. "He's been complainin' of his stomach for the last week, but he will eat what he oughtn't to. I've got some good stomach medicine. I'm goin' to dose 'im well to-night an' make 'im stay out o' the kitchen. The cook lets him have everything he wants."

"Give him the medicine, and tell the cook she must stop feeding him." Mostyn took the boy in his arms and started on to the house. "You will stop eating trash, won't you, Dick?" The child nodded, worming his fingers through his father's hair. He took off Mostyn's hat, put it on his bonny head, and laughed faintly. Reaching the veranda, Mostyn turned him over to Hilda, who said she was going to give him a bath and put him to bed. When they had gone Mostyn went into the library. The great portrait-hung room in the shadows seemed a dreary, accusing place, and he was turning to leave when the rustling of a newspaper and a little nasal snort called his attention to a high-backed chair of the wing type in which his father-in-law reclined and was just waking from a nap.

"Oh, is that you?" Mitchell yawned and stretched his arms. "I was wondering when you'd get here. I've been to the gate several times."

"Anything you want?" Mostyn regretted the impulsive question the instant the words had been spoken.

The old man put his hands on the arms of the chair and stood up, feebly. "Yes, I want to know if your wife has written or telegraphed you since she got to Knoxville?"

"No," Mostyn thought rapidly, "but—but I hardly expected her to. She doesn't usually when she is away."

"It is the very Old Nick in you both!" Mitchell sniffed. "I don't expect you to know or care what she's up to; but I'm her own flesh and blood, and supposed to be interested more or less. Home is lonely enough when she is here in town, without her being off so much. Besides, I know some things—humph! Well, I'm no fool, if I *am* a back number. To-day I made it my business to inquire if a certain party—you know who I mean—was in town. I knew in reason that he wouldn't be, but I just asked to satisfy my mind. Do you get at my meaning, sir?"

"I think I do." Mostyn's own words seemed to him to come from the heavy folds of the portiere hiding the desolate drawing-room beyond.

"I thought you would." The retort was all but a snarl. "And, do you know, when I asked some of his friends about the club if they knew, I caught them looking at one another in an odd sort of way with twinkles in their eyes? Oh no, they didn't know where he was. But I found out, all the same. I met his mother down-town. She said he had gone on a hurried trip to Norfolk. You can see through that, can't you? I can, if you can't. Knoxville is on the way to Norfolk. The two are at that party together; and, not only that, I'll bet this whole town knows it. That ought to be stopped. I know my daughter, if you don't, sir. She is not acting right. She has plunged into pleasure and excitement till she doesn't know what she wants. A new string of diamonds wouldn't amuse her a minute. This giddy, fast life has actually cursed her. The other night I caught her taking morphine tablets to make her sleep—said she'd lie awake and think till morning if she didn't. She hasn't contracted the habit yet, but she can easy enough if she keeps it up. She takes a bottle of them wherever she goes. When I was young, a woman who was a mother of a child like hers loved it, nursed it, petted it, got natural joy out of it; but Irene seldom speaks to Dick, and he doesn't care for her any more than for a stranger, but he loves you—God only knows why, but he does. It is 'Daddy, Daddy, Daddy' with nearly every breath he draws."

Mostyn felt a force within him rising and expanding. A sob lodged in his tight throat and pained him. He was grateful for the deepening shadows, for the droning prattle from the old lips. He sank into a chair. The droning continued, sounding far off. A thousand incidents and faces (smiling and blending) sprang upon him out of the past—the happy, irresponsible past, the seductive, confident, ambitious past. Surely Fate was a mental entity, capable of crafty design against the heedless young. He remembered the vows of chastity and honor he had made during a revival in a country church under a blazing faith. He recalled how soon they were forgotten, how sure he was, later on, that Nature's physical laws were the highest known. Man was made to live, enjoy, and conquer all if he could. And he had succeeded. He had become rich and prosperous. Next he found his memory swimming through that black period of satiated desire and disgust of self.

"I wish folks would not mix *me* up with your private matters." The words rose sharply from the senile prattle and penetrated Mostyn's lethargy. "There's old Jeff Henderson—he had the cheek to come to me to-day to borrow money. Said his family was in rags and starving. Said you euchred him out of all he had and got your start on it. What in the name of common sense does he come to *me* for? I don't own you, and I knew nothing about that transaction, either. I reckon he's going crazy, but that doesn't keep him from bothering me."

Seeing the futility of explaining a thing he had many times explained, Mostyn rose. Before him the open doorway framed an oblong patch of calm gray sky, and toward it he moved, his mental hands impotently outstretched, a soundless cry welling up from the depths of himself.

CHAPTER XIV

On the first morning after his permanent removal to his plantation Jarvis Saunders waked with a boundless sense of freedom from care, which had not been his since his boyhood. Through all his short visits to the spot hitherto he had been haunted with the unpleasant thought of having to return to the city and the rigid demands of business. But it was different now. He lay in the wide, high-posted Colonial bed, stretched himself, looked at the sunlight on the small-paned windows, and sighed with complete content. From the outside came the chirping of birds, the crowing of roosters, the cackle of hens, the quacking of ducks, the scream of geese, the thwack of an ax at the wood-pile, the mellow song of the lank negro chopper, Uncle Zeke, one of the ex-slaves of his family.

Rising and standing at a window, and parting the pink and blue morning-glories which overhung it in dew-dipped freshness, Saunders looked down into the yard. He saw Aunt Maria, Zeke's portly wife, approach from the kitchen door and begin to fill her apron with the chips his ax had strewn upon the ground.

"You go on en ring dat fus' breakfus'-bell, Zeke," she said, peremptorily. "De fus' litter o' biscuits is raidy to slide in de stove, en de chicken en trout is fried brown. Everthing is got ter be des right dis fus' mawnin' dat Marse Jarvis is home ter stay. Fifteen minutes is long 'nough fer 'im ter dress."

"Ring de bell *yo'se'f*, 'ooman!" Zeke laughed, loudly. "Yo' gittin' so heavy en waddly yo' don' want ter turn yo' han's over. Look yer, 'ooman, Marse Jarvis ain't gwine ter let yo' cook fer 'im regular, nohow. He gwine ter fix de house up spank new, fum top ter bottom, en git de ol' 'fo'-de-wah style back ergin. He gwine ter sen' away off som'er's fer er spry up-date cook. Yo' know what, 'ooman? I'm gwine be his head house-servant, I is. My place'll be in de front hall ter mix mint-juleps fo' 'im en his frien's fum de city when dey skeet by in deir automobiles en stop over fer er smoke en er howdy-do. He gwine ter order me er long-tail, jimswingin' blue coat. He done say dat he'll look ter me ter keep you-all's j'ints oiled up so yo' won't walk in yo' sleep so much in de day-time."

"Go 'long, yo' fool nigger!" Maria sniffed, as she shook her chips down into her apron. "When Marse Jarvis stick er black scarecrow lak yo' in de front part de house he shore will be out his senses. He gwine ter mek yo' haul manure wid er dump-cart, dat what he is."

Saunders smiled as he stepped back and began to dress. "God bless their simple, loyal souls!" he said. "They shall never suffer as long as I live. My parents loved them, and so do I."

At the sound of the second bell he went downstairs. How cool, spacious, and inviting everything looked! The oblong drawing-room, into which he glanced in passing, with its white wain-scoting and beautiful oriel window at the end on the left of the entrance-hall, brought back many memories of his childhood and youth. He recalled the gay assemblages of summer visitors to his father and mother from Augusta and Charleston—the dances, the horseback rides, the hunting-parties, the music, the singing of hymns on Sundays.

"I must bring it all back," he mused. "That was normal living."

These memories followed him to the great dining-room in the rear of the house. As he took his usual seat at the head of the long table the delicious aroma of fine coffee, the smell of frying meats and hot biscuits came in from the adjoining kitchen.

The wide fireplace had been freshly whitewashed, and was filled with the resinous boughs of young pines. The several windows were open, and through them he had glimpses of his verdant lands and the mountains beyond. The portraits of his mother, father, and grandparents seemed to smile down from their massive frames on the white walls. The same silverware and cut glass which they had used were before him on the mahogany sideboard; the same china.

Aunt Maria had put the hot, tempting dishes before him and gone away. The pot of coffee was steaming at his side. Suddenly an impulse, half sentimental, came over him which he could not resist. He recalled how his father had always said grace; and, bowing his head, he whispered the long-silent words over his unturned plate and folded napkin. How odd! he thought: it was as if the short prayer had been laid upon his lips by the spirit of his father; the fervent "Amen" seemed to be echoed by his mother's voice from the opposite end of the board. Saunders's soul was suddenly filled with a transcendent ecstasy. His parents seemed to be actually present, invisible, and yet flooding his being with their spiritual essence.

"Surely," he said, the wonder of the thing bursting upon him like ineffable light, "there is 'a peace which passeth understanding.'"

After breakfast he went to the front veranda to smoke. He saw Tom Drake walking across a meadow to some drainage ditches which were being dug to destroy some objectionable marshes. The results of the man's work as manager had been more than satisfactory.

Presently Saunders descried a few hundred yards down the main road a woman on a horse. It was Dolly Drake; and, throbbing with delight, he hastened down to the gate, thinking that she might be coming to speak to her father, and would need assistance in alighting. But she had no intention of stopping, and with a merry bow was about to ride by when he stepped out and playfully held up his hands.

"Your money or your life!" he cried.

She reined the spirited young black horse in and sat jauntily on the side-saddle. Her color was high; she wore a pretty riding-hat, a close-fitting gray habit, and her eyes were sparkling from the exhilaration of the gallop along the level road.

"Take my life, but for Heaven's sake spare my money!" she retorted, with an ironical laugh.

"I think I have some news for you," he said, approaching and testing the girth of her saddle. "Sit still and let me draw it tighter."

"News," she said, with the eagerness of a child, as he pulled upward on the strap, "for me?"

"Yes, for you. I knew you would be interested in the bill before the House and Senate, and so I asked the Governor to write me if it went through."

"Oh, oh! and did you hear?" She leaned closer to him, her lips rigid with expectation. "I'm afraid there was a hitch after all. The taxpayers are so opposed to spending money."

"It went through like greased lightning," he smiled. "Your name and suggestions were mentioned in every speech that was made in both houses."

He saw her face fill with delight. She put the butt of her riding-whip to her lips, and her breast heaved high and sank, quivering.

"Oh, isn't it splendid—splendid?" she exclaimed.

"Thanks to you, Dolly—you, and no one else."

"No, no, it was growing all along. I only helped a little, perhaps. But it doesn't matter who did it; it is done. They will build the schools."

"And you and I will help with suggestions, won't we?" He looked at her, quite timidly. "I mean, of course, that we have learned some lessons in the house we are now building. We have made mistakes here and there that may be avoided in the future."

She said nothing, and he was sure that she purposely avoided his tentative stare. She bent over the horse's neck, ran the thick glossy mane through her fingers, and gently patted the animal's shoulder.

"Jarvis, you must tell me something about this horse," she said, firmly. "I'm going to know the truth, the whole truth, and nothing but the truth."

"You want to know his pedigree?" He was staring sheepishly. "Well—"

"No, I don't, and you know I don't. My father said that you wanted the horse kept in the stable at home in case—in case any one had to ride over here to communicate with him. But no one uses him but me, and he has to have exercise or he will be ruined. It is almost all that I can do to control him now. He breaks into a run the instant another horse passes him. Father said yesterday that he did not understand why you wanted us to keep him at our house."

The blood mantled the young planter's brow. "They say an honest confession is good for the soul," he stammered; "and, Dolly, the truth is that I sent the horse there simply for you to ride. You love riding and need the exercise. You are so peculiar about—well, about some things—that I was afraid you would be offended, but I hope you won't refuse this. I do love to see you on a horse. You ride as if you were born in the saddle."

She looked down on the farther side of her mount. "It is very, very sweet and kind of you," she said, falteringly. "I believe you mean it, still—" She broke off and failed to finish what she had started to say.

"You must not object," he went on, urgently. "It suits your father and me to keep a horse there, and if you are good enough to exercise him for us, well and good. If not, we'll send one of the negroes over to take him out once a day."

He saw her smile faintly. "Nobody could get around you," she answered. "Well, it really would break my heart to give him up now, and I shall ride him whenever I feel like it."

There was silence for a moment, which he broke.

"I am arranging a little surprise for your father." He nodded toward the grounds behind him. "Won't you get down and come in a moment?"

"What is it?" She was already kicking the stirrup from her eager foot.

"Come in and see." He held out his arms, as if she were a child willing to jump.

"You know my awful curiosity," she laughed, putting her hands on his shoulders and leaning downward. Her face sank close to his—so close that her breath fanned his cheek. He took her slight weight on himself as he helped her down. Throwing the rein over one of the palings, he opened the gate and stood aside for her to enter.

"What is it? Why are you so awfully mysterious?" she asked.

"Because my surprise may not come up to your expectations," he said. "Come with me."

He led her across the lawn to a small one-roomed brick house at the side of the main building, adjoining the white glass-roofed conservatory. Taking a key from his pocket, he unlocked the door and pushed it open and invited her to go in. She found herself in a well-lighted room comfortably furnished with easy-chairs, rugs, and a fine roll-top desk, supplied with new account-books and writing-material of all kinds.

"It is to be your father's private office," Saunders explained. "But he doesn't know it. It struck me that he would need a place like this to meet the hands in on pay-days and to do his writing. The furniture came yesterday. He superintended the unloading himself. He thinks the office is for me."

Involuntarily Dolly clasped her hands in sheer delight.

"Oh, how good you are!" she cried. "Nothing you could possibly do would please him more. You have given him his old pride back, Jarvis, and this will add to it. I have been wanting to speak to you about him, but I hardly knew how. He is absolutely a new man in every way, and it is all due to your confidence and encouragement."

He found himself without available response. She sat down in the revolving desk-chair and picked up a pen and pretended to write. "It is simply 'scrumptious!'" she laughed, merrily. "Oh, I should like—" she stopped abruptly, stood up, and looked at the door. "I must be going. Why, you've even given him a clock. And the maps on the walls will be very useful. That's our county, isn't it?"

As he nodded he followed her to the grass outside. "You started to say that you would like something," he ventured. "What was it, Dolly?"

"I should really like to be present when you show it to him and tell him that it is for him. Jarvis, I almost lost respect for him once. I almost ceased to love him, but it has all come back. I am proud of him again, and you are responsible for it. Why did you do so much for him?"

"Because he is *your* father!" He nipped the words as they were forming on his lips. Instead, he said aloud: "He is just the man I needed. We are working finely together. You must be present when I tell him about the office; he will be here this afternoon. I will detain him with some pretext or other till three o'clock. Couldn't you be here then?"

"Oh yes, and I'd like to bring my mother, Uncle John, and George."

"A good idea," Saunders said. "We'll have some fresh cider and cakes—the old-fashioned gingerbread sort."

When they had reached her horse, he held out his hand for her foot. She placed it in it, and he lightly lifted her to the saddle.

He stood at the gate and saw her vanish down the road. "Why didn't I say what I want to say? Why didn't I tell her how I feel and throw myself on her mercy? What is it that always checks me? Is it Mostyn? My God! does she still love him, and will he always stand between me and my happiness?"

CHAPTER XV

For Mostyn the week which ensued after his wife's secret elopement was a period of sheer mental torture. Every minute he expected the startling tidings to reach his friends and associates. Every morning at breakfast he studied the crafty and sullen face of old Mitchell and the swarthy visages of the servants to see if suspicions of the truth were dawning. At the bank he tried to overhear the conversations of the bookkeepers, sometimes fancying that a burst of low laughter or a whispered colloquy had him for their incentive. He was sure that it was little less than a miracle that the matter had not leaked out. With Delbridge getting into harness at his desk, he had considerable time on his hands, which he spent in long nervous walks, generally in the suburbs of the city. For that week he wholly neglected his child. There was something unbearable in the thought of the boy's future social status, left in the care, as he was, of an all but witless grandfather and a father upon whom the contempt of the public was so soon to fall. Infinitely horrible was the reflection that little Dick would inevitably grow into a comprehension of the family calamity and inquire as to its causes. It was Saturday night, eight days after the elopement. Mostyn had that day been irritated—that is, as much as a man in his plight could be irritated by any extraneous incident—by Delbridge's open criticism of the negligent condition of some of his accounts. The work of going over the books with his successor in rectifying really glaring mistakes detained him at the bank till late at night. It was twelve o'clock when he finally reached home, ascended to his room, and began to undress. He had thrown off his coat, when he heard voices and movements in the nursery adjoining his room. At once he was all attention. He had his usual overpowering yearning to see his child. It was as if the touch of the boy's little hand or a glance from his innocent young eyes might mildly soothe his lacerated spirits. It was the cry of kindred blood to kindred blood from the darkest deeps of despair—the incongruous cry of parent to offspring. He overheard the impatient tone of the drowsy nurse, and the fainter, rather rambling accents of the child.

"You go to sleep!" Hilda called out. "You'll disturb yo' pa. He just come home, an' he don't want no noise fum yo' this time o' night."

The gas was burning in the nursery, as was shown by the pencil of light beneath the door. Mostyn turned the bolt and looked into the room. A breath of warmer air told him that the servant had again neglected to open the windows sufficiently. He went to Dick's little bed, turning the overhead gas higher as he did so. The child looked up, recognized him, and with a cry of welcome held out his arms. Mostyn, bending down, felt the little hands clasp his neck. They were dry and hot. Dick's cheeks were flushed red.

"What ails him?" Mostyn cried, aghast, turning to Hilda, who had risen, thrown on a wrapper, and stood at the table, where a bottle and a spoon lay.

"I think he's got er little bit er fever, sir," she said. "It is his stomach gone wrong ergin. I'm givin' 'im his fever-mixture now."

"It hurts right here, Daddy." Dick made a wry face as he bravely pressed his hand on the lower part of his right side. "Dick couldn't play to-day."

"How long has he had fever?" Mostyn demanded, sharply.

"Jes' to-day, I think, sir. I never noticed it till dis evenin' about an hour by sun. He's been complainin' of his stomach fer mo'n a week, but dat is 'cause he eats—"

"It may be something serious." The words shrank back from utterance. "Why didn't you send for the doctor?"

"Huh!" the nurse sniffed, resentfully. "Yo' all expect me ter ten' ter everything. I *did* tell his grandpa, but he didn't even know what I was talkin' about, jabberin' all de time about Miss Irene stayin' off so long, en—en I don't know what all—*you* an' *yo* doin's 'long wid de rest."

The woman was approaching with the bottle and spoon. "Don't give him any more of that stuff." He waved it away. "I'll send for Dr. Loyd at once."

"Oh, Daddy, I don't want the doctor!" Dick began to whimper and cling more tightly round his father's neck.

"He won't hurt you; he is a good man," Mostyn said, tenderly. "He will give you something to make you cool off, so you can sleep."

Mostyn left the room and groped his way down to the telephone in the lower hall. A new fear had clutched him, a fear so compelling that all else was forgotten. A chill of grim, accusing horror was on him. His brain was in a whirl as he tried to recall the desired number. Did Providence, Fate, or whatever the ruling force was, intend this as his crowning punishment? Had the impalpable hand, reaching for him, descended on his offspring? He finally got the doctor's servant on the 'phone, then Dr. Loyd himself, who had just arrived in his automobile.

"Have you taken his temperature?" was the doctor's first question.

"No, we haven't a thermometer, and do not know how to use one, anyway."

"Well, I'll be out immediately," was the brusque answer. "I must see him to-night—don't exactly like the symptoms. I saw him in driving past your home the other day, and did not quite like his looks."

Mostyn dragged himself up the stairs. Passing Mitchell's room, he half paused at the door. Should he wake him and explain the situation? He decided against it. The child's condition would only loosen the man's pent-up wrath in the presence of the physician and perhaps delay the examination. He went back to the nursery, and, lifting Dick in his arms, he bore him into his own room, which was cooler. He dampened a towel in ice-water, folded it, and laid it on the flushed brow.

"That feels nice, Daddy," Dick smiled, grimly, "but it hurts here," putting his hand gingerly on his side.

A few minutes later the doctor's car was heard on the drive. Mostyn descended to meet him. They shook hands formally, and Mostyn led him up the stairs to the patient. The doctor was past middle age, iron-gray, full-whiskered, and stockily built. He took the child's temperature, and looked grave as he glanced at the thermometer under the drop-light, and washed it in a glass of water.

"One-hundred and five!" he said, crisply. "Big risks have been taken, Mostyn. I only hope my fears are groundless."

"Your fears?"

But the doctor seemed not to hear. He raised the child's thin night-shirt and passed his fingers gently over the abdomen.

"Tell me where that pain is, Dick," he said, softly. "Where does it hurt most when I press down?"

"There! there!" Dick cried out in sudden agony.

"I see. That will do. I sha'n't hurt you again." He drew the shirt down and moved back toward the lamp.

"I'm sure you will give him—something to reduce that fever."
Mostyn knew that the remark was a mere tentative foil against
the verdict stamped upon the bearded face. The doctor slowly
wiped the tiny tube and restored it to its case.

"I must be frank," he said, in a low tone. "My opinion is that
he must be operated on at once—without delay—early in the
morning at the very latest."

"Why—why—surely—" Mostyn began, but went no further.
The objects in the room seemed to swim about him. He and
the doctor were buoys floating face to face.

"It is appendicitis," Loyd said. "Of course, I'd call another
doctor in consultation before anything is done, but I am sure I
am not mistaken."

Mostyn's soul stared from a dead face with all but glazed eyes.
He nodded toward the door opening into the hall and led the
doctor from the room. In the hall he put his hand on Loyd's
shoulder.

"I am sure you know best," he gasped. "What do you
propose?"

"That I take him at once to my sanitarium in my car. In warm
weather like this you won't have to wrap him much. You'd
better get him ready now. I'll telephone the nurse to have a
room prepared."

"Very well." Mostyn was stalking back to the child when the
doctor detained him.

"And his mother—I don't see her about; is she at home?"

"No, she is out of town. Just now she is away."

Will N. Harben

"Well, you had better telegraph her."

"I—I don't exactly know where she is." Mostyn was vaguely thankful for the dimness of the hall light.

"You must find her—locate her at once."

"Is it really so—so serious as that?"

"I may as well be frank." The doctor cleared his throat. "It won't do any good to mislead you. The little fellow has a weak heart, as I explained the last time he was ill, and it seems worse now. Then—then, I am sorry to say that I detect strong symptoms of peritonitis. If I could have seen him a week ago—I presume the fact of your wife being away, and you being busy at the bank—"

Mostyn's head rocked like a stone balanced on a pivot. "Yes," he said. "I am afraid we were not attentive enough. Will you be ready soon?"

"Yes; tell Dick it is for a ride in my car. He won't mind it. He is a plucky little fellow. He has fought that pain for several days. We would have known it earlier but for that."

Five minutes later Mostyn sat on the rear seat of the automobile with his child in his arms. The doctor sat in front beside the colored chauffeur. Mostyn chatted with Dick about the ride, about the "nice, cool room" he was to have at the "good doctor's house"; but, to his growing horror, Dick had lost interest in all things. He lay passive and completely relaxed, a lack-luster gleam in his half-closed eyes.

"Am I speeding him to his execution?" Mostyn's very dregs whispered the query. "Is this my last word with him?" Seeing the faces of the doctor and the chauffeur directed ahead, and half ashamed of his tenderness, he bent down and kissed the child's forehead. In vague response Dick lifted his little hand to the overbrooding cheek, but immediately dropped it to his side.

"Go slowly over this rough place," the doctor ordered; and the speed lessened, to be renewed a little farther on, where the asphalt pavement began again.

Reaching the sanitarium, a spacious white building in pleasant, shaded grounds, they alighted. Mostyn, with his boy in his arms, stepped out. At the door a nurse took Dick into the house and bore him to a room on the floor above. She spoke to him in a motherly way. As she vanished up the stairs Mostyn saw Dick's small limp hand hanging down her side. Was it, he asked himself, a farewell salute?

"You may sit here in the waiting-room if you wish, or you may return home in my car," Loyd suggested. "I shall send it at once for the other doctors. You are really of no service here, and, of course, I can communicate with you by 'phone as to our decision."

"I'll be here, or close about on the outside," Mostyn answered. "I presume it will be some time before the consultation?"

"It must be within half an hour. I am not willing to wait longer."

Mostyn sat alone in the sitting-room. A clock on the wall ticked sharply. He heard the wheels of the automobile grind on the pavement as it sped away under the electric lights. He went out on the lawn. He felt in his pocket for a cigar, but, finding none, he forgot it. The dew of the grass penetrated to his feet. It seemed to him that he felt Dick's fever coursing through his own veins. He was still outside half an hour later, his eyes raised to the windows of the lighted room occupied by his child, when the automobile returned. Two doctors whom he knew got out and sauntered into the house. He heard them laughing over the mistake a so-called quack had made in the case of a credulous patient, Mostyn lurked back in the shadows—he would not detain them by a useless greeting. He followed them into the house. The nurse at the foot of the stairs was beckoning them to hasten. Mostyn was again alone in the sitting-room. Presently the nurse came in, evidently looking for something. Mostyn caught her eye, and she gave him a hurried but sympathetic look. He decided that he would sound her.

"Do you think an operation will be necessary?" he asked.

Her glance fell. "I have only Dr. Loyd's opinion. He thinks so, and I have never known him to be wrong in diagnosing a case."

"He thinks, also, I believe"—Mostyn's voice sounded as hollow as a phonograph—" that the child has hardly strength enough to resist the —the ordeal?"

She raised her eyes as if doubting her right to converse on the subject. "I think he *is* afraid of that," she admitted. "Your child is very, very sick."

"And you—you, *yourself?*" Mostyn now fairly implored. "According to *your* experience, do you think there is a chance of his living through it?"

"I really can't say—I *mustn't* say," she faltered. "I am only judging by Dr. Loyd's actions. He is very uneasy. Mr. Mostyn, I have no right to speak of it, but your wife ought to be here. The doctor says she is out of town. She ought to get here if possible; she will always regret it if she doesn't. I am a mother myself, and I know how she will feel."

Mostyn stifled a reply which rose to his lips. He heard, rather than saw, her leave the room, for a mist had fallen on his sight. In the patient's chamber above there was the grinding of feet on the floor. The chandelier overhead shook. The crystal prisms tinkled like little bells. Presently the nurse came to him.

"Dr. Loyd instructed me to say"—she was looking down on

his clasped hands—"that they have agreed that the operation must be performed at once. They all think it is the only chance."

An hour later the aiding doctors came down the stairs, glided softly past the sitting-room door, and passed out. He called to one of them.

"Is the operation over?" he asked.

The doctor nodded gravely. He had taken a cigar from his pocket, and was biting the tip from the end. "It was the worst appendix I ever saw, fairly rotten. Loyd will show it to you. It is a serious case, Mostyn. If Loyd pulls him through it will be a miracle. Peritonitis has already set in, and there is very little heart-action. He is sleeping now, of course, and every possible thing has been done and will be done. He is in the best of hands. We can do nothing but wait."

It was near dawn. Mostyn was pacing back and forth on the grass in front of the house. The dark eastern horizon was giving way to a lengthening flux of light. A cab drove up to the door, and a man and a woman got out. It was Mrs. Moore and old Mitchell. Mrs. Moore reached her brother first, and tenderly clasped his hands. As well as he could he explained the situation.

"Hilda telephoned me," Mrs. Moore went on, in a low, matter-of-fact tone. "She was almost in hysterics, and I could not understand her fully. I thought the operation was to be done there, and so I dressed and went in a cab. Then I found that Mr. Mitchell wanted to come, and so I brought him on."

The old man tottered forward. For once he had no comment to make. He passed them, slowly ascended the steps, went into the waiting-room and sat down, leaning forward on his stout cane, which he held upright between his knees.

"We'd have got here sooner, but he stopped at the

Will N. Harben

telegraph-office. Dick, he has sent a telegram to Irene in care of the Hardys. I saw by that that he didn't suspect the truth. I tried to think of some way to prevent it, but couldn't. I told him I was in a hurry, but he would stop. Now I suppose the truth will have to come out."

"It makes no difference," Mostyn answered. "It might as well come now as later."

They went in and took their seats against the wall in the waiting-room. Mitchell stared at them half drowsily, betraying the usual complacency of old age in regard to serious illness or death.

"Are they going to operate?" he asked.

Mrs. Moore told him that it had already been done.

"And Irene wasn't here," the old man sniffed, in rising ire. "It is a shame! I reckon she will have the decency to take the first train home now. This will be a lesson to her, I hope."

The nurse came down the stairs hurriedly. Her face was swept with well-controlled dismay. She paused in the doorway. Her eyes met those of the brother and sister.

"Dr. Loyd thinks you'd better come up."

"Is the boy—is—he worse?" Mrs. Moore asked.

"You had better hurry," the nurse answered. "There is only a minute—if that. He is dying."

A few minutes later Mostyn and his sister came down the stairs.

"Try to realize what the poor little darling has escaped," she said. "It may be the merciful hand of God, Dick. I know it is killing you, but that ought to be *some* comfort."

CHAPTER XVI

Irene and Buckton were still at the hotel in Charleston. On the second morning following the happenings of the foregoing chapter they were having breakfast served in Irene's little sitting-room. In the light from the window he was struck, as he had been struck before, by her listless mien and the thickening shadows of disillusionment in her eyes. He had to remind her that the coffee-urn was at her elbow, and that he would not take his coffee from any hand but hers before she filled his cup. Her eggs and bacon she had barely touched. He saw her hands quiver as she passed his cup. He tried to enliven her by his cheerful talk, telling her that she was getting weary of the town and that they must move on to Savannah to take the steamer.

"New York is the place for us," he said. "There we will have so much to do and see that you won't have time to get homesick. I really believe you *are* homesick, darling. You see, you are a belle at home, a favorite with every one, and here you have to be satisfied with just me. I know I am a poor substitute, but I adore you, while they—"

"Don't speak of home!" she suddenly burst out, almost at the point of tears. "One never knows what home is till one leaves it forever. Just think of it—why, it is forever—forever! When we left I did not consider that at all. I want to tell you something very strange. I almost feel—I hardly know how to put it—but I almost feel that a—a new spiritual nature is hovering about me, trying to force itself into my body. Why, I

Will N. Harben

feel so tenderly about my father that it seems to me that I'd rather see him at this moment and undo what I've done than to possess the world. Whenever I start to—to speak affectionately to you a cold hand seems to fall on my lips. That is why—why I locked the door last night. It was not the headache, as I claimed. I had been thinking of Dick—my husband. I believe he is trying to undo his past. I don't believe a man could love a child as he loves ours and be very bad at heart. Something tells me that I ought to have stayed by him at all costs. We were wrong in marrying, no doubt; but once it was done, once a helpless little child was in our care—"

"Ah, I see, Irene, it is the boy, after all. You don't mention him often, but little things you drop now and then show which way the wind blows. Your eyes are on every child we pass in the street. Without knowing it you are a motherly woman."

"Ah, if you only knew—if only I could tell you *something*—" She broke off, lowered her head to her hand, and he saw her breast rise on a billow of emotion.

"Something about your child?" Buckton queried, jealously.

She nodded faintly. He heard her sigh. She remained mute and still for a moment; then she said, falteringly:

"I have a strange conviction that there is truth in the belief of some psychologists I've read about who claim that in sleep our souls leave the body and see and experience things far away."

"I don't believe such rubbish," Buckton said, uneasily. "Do you know that people who harbor such ideas generally go insane?"

"I had a strange experience night before last." Irene quite ignored his protest. "It was something too vivid to be a mere dream. You know there is a difference between a dream and a real experience. I mean that one seems able to tell the two apart."

"Perhaps we had better say no more about it," Buckton suggested. "Don't you think a drive in the open air would do you good?"

But Irene failed to hear what he was saying, or was treating it as of little consequence.

"Listen," she persisted. "It was between midnight and dawn. I had been brooding morbidly, and sank deep, deep into sleep, so deep that the darkness seemed to close in and crush my spirit right out of my body. Then I was floating about, free to go where I liked. I felt awfully lonely and desolate. Presently I found myself on our lawn in front of the house, but unable to get in. I heard some one crying inside; it seemed to be Hilda. I couldn't tell what she was crying about, but I had the feeling that it was because something was happening to the boy. I went to the door and tried to ring, but had no hands—think of that, I had no hands! Suddenly I found myself in the hall, but unable to go up the stairs. Something seemed to clutch me and hold me back. I tried to cry out, but had no voice. I thought I heard my husband talking to the child, tenderly— oh, so tenderly! I was crying as I had never cried before. I wanted to see the boy. It was as if a new heart had been born in me or an old one resurrected. Then I heard the door of my husband's room open, and I shrank back afraid to meet him, for I thought of—of you and me being like this. Then I waked and found myself here in bed, my pillow drenched with tears. Oh, I wanted to die—I wanted to die then!"

"It was a nightmare," Buckton commented, uneasily. "It has all the earmarks of one. We are always, in such dreams, trying to get somewhere or away from something horrible."

"It haunted me all day yesterday," Irene sighed. "And last night I had to take one of my morphine tablets to get to sleep."

"I wish you'd give that up, darling," Buckton said, reproach-fully. "I saw them on your bureau yesterday and started to throw them out of the window. Doctors say it easily becomes a habit, and a bad one."

"I don't take it often, I really don't," Irene answered. "But I sometimes wonder if it would make any difference. I can sympathize with a hopeless drunkard, who, in a besotted condition, is able to forget trouble and sorrow."

"Finish your breakfast," Buckton cried, forcing a laugh. "We are going to take that drive. The fresh air will knock all those ideas out of your pretty head."

They spent the day driving about the country. They had supped at a quaint and picturesque cafe, and returned to the hotel. He was in her bedroom at ten o'clock, still active in his efforts to set her mind at ease, when a sharp rapping was heard on the door of his sitting-room adjoining.

"It is something for me," Buckton said. "Wait, and I'll see what it is."

Before he had finished speaking there was another and a louder rapping. Buckton hastened out, closing the connecting door cautiously. Irene stood up. She had a premonition that something disagreeable was about to happen. She heard Buckton unlock his door. Then she recognized the voice of the proprietor of the hotel.

"I want to see you privately, Mr. Buckton," the voice said.

"All right; won't you come in?" Buckton replied; and immediately the latch of the door clicked as it was closed.

There was a pause, during which Irene, holding her handkerchief to her lips, crept to the connecting door and stood with her ear close to the keyhole. She held her breath. The pounding of her heart seemed to fill the still room with obtrusive sound.

"You must pardon me, but it is my duty"—the proprietor's

voice rose with sudden sharpness—"to speak of your relations with the woman you brought here with you."

"My—my relations?" Buckton's voice had fallen low, and the tone was cautious. "Please don't talk so loud. She is not well and might overhear. What do you mean, sir—do you mean to insinuate—"

"You may call it anything you like," the proprietor retorted, in evident anger. "I've been in the hotel business for twenty-five years, and have never been charged with keeping an indecent house. When you arrived here I thought your companion was all right, but I now know who and what she is. I can rely on my information, so we won't argue about that."

Irene heard a scuffing of feet which drew the two men closer to the door at which she stood. The truth was that Buckton had drawn back to strike the man, who caught his hand and held it.

"Don't try that on me!" the proprietor said, calmly. "Your bluff is weak. Now, let me give you a piece of advice, young man. I've watched this thing with my own eyes and ears, and I know exactly what is going on. This is a strict, law-abiding, old-fashioned town. Decency has been reigning here for over two hundred years. The average citizen of Charleston has no sympathy for the sort of thing you are evidently trying to foist on us. You've got sense enough to know that all I have to do is to telephone the police to take charge of this matter and air it in open court. You might get it whitewashed in *your* town by some pull or other, but not here. I think, since you want to be insulting, that I'd better send for an officer."

Irene heard the proprietor moving to the outer door; his hand touched the latch, and it rattled.

"Wait!" It was her lover's voice, and it was contrite and imploring. "For God's Sake, don't give us trouble! We are leaving for Savannah in the morning. Surely you will not put us out to-night?"

"No, the train leaves at ten. See that you take it. I am not any more anxious to have this dirty thing get out than you are. Good night."

"Good night." The door closed. Receding steps sounded in the corridor outside. Irene reeled back to her chair and sat down. A moment later Buckton appeared. He was ghastly pale, trying to recover calmness and invent a plausible explanation as to why he had been called to the door. She gazed at him steadily.

"You needn't make up a story," she said. "I overheard."

He stood looking down on her helplessly. He swayed to and fro, resting his hand on the back of her chair.

"You say—you—heard?"

She nodded. "He told the truth about me. That's actually what I am," she said, grimly. "That is exactly the way the world will look at me when it knows all. It was lucky that I heard. As he was talking I kept saying, 'That's so—that's so,' and I wasn't a bit angry—not a bit. A bad woman—a bold, bad woman would have flared up, but I'm not that—God knows I am not. I have been tricked, blinded, led along by my imagination and ideals ever since I was a child. Now my head is on the block, and the Puritan world is swinging the ax. Oh, how I cringed just now! I, who have heard nothing but the compliments of men all my life, heard the truth at last. I've been vain, silly, mad. I could crawl in the dust and kiss the feet of an unsullied shop-girl. Well, well, what's to be done?"

"We leave for Savannah in the morning, and from there sail for New York," he answered. "I'm going to kill your despondency, dear. You must sleep now. Don't pack to-night. I'll wake you early in the morning, and will help you do it then."

"Well, well, leave me," she sighed. "I'll go to bed. I'll take a tablet. I want to forget. That voice—oh, God! that man's voice! He was a judge on the bench—all arguments in my defense had been set aside by a jury of truthful men. He pronounced my sentence. I'm to be swept out in the morning along with the dirt from men's boots. I—I—Irene Mostyn—no, no, not *Mostyn*—Irene *Nobody*, will not dare to look into the faces of black servants as I slink away in the morning with you—you, my choice, a man whom—before God I swear it—I no more actually love you than—"

"Don't—don't for God's sake; I can't bear it!" He was on the verge of tears. "I've been afraid of that. I thought you'd be happy with me, but so far you have been just the reverse. But I won't give up—I won't! You are my very life."

"Well, go, go!" she cried. "I must sleep. I rolled and tossed all night last night. I'll go mad if this keeps up. Get me a tablet from the bottle, and a glass of water—no, I'll take it later. Oh, oh, oh! I am sure now that my child is dead, and that his father is crazed with grief. That was what my strange dream meant. People say such things are prophetic, and I know it is so—I feel it through and through. The child of my breast died while I was here like this with *you*—with *you here in my bedroom.*"

"You really must try to be calm," Buckton urged. "Those are only morbid fancies. The world is before us, darling, just as it was when we left home. There is really no change except in your imagination."

A shrewd look settled on her face. She waved her hand toward the door. "Well, leave me alone then. Please do."

"All right, I'll go." He bent to kiss her, but with a sharp little scream that was half hysterical she raised her hands and pushed him back. "Don't do that!" she cried, almost in alarm. "Don't do it again!"

She glanced furtively about the room—at the closet door, under the bed, and, leaning to one side, peered behind the bureau, as if her mind was wandering. "Don't touch me. Little Dick will see you. He is here—I know it—I feel it. I can almost see him, like a misty cloud. He seems to come between you and me, as if wondering why you are here. He seems to be trying to comfort me. Lord, have mercy on my soul! Go, go! For God's sake, *go!*"

"All right, dear." Buckton moved away. His feet caught in a rug and he stumbled awkwardly. Passing out at the door, he softly closed it.

Finding herself alone, Irene rose and began to walk the floor. Back and forth she strode, wringing her hands, the flare of insanity in her eyes. She unfastened her hair, shook it down her back. Suddenly she fell on her knees by her bed, clasped her hands and tried to pray, but words failed to come. Rising, she went to the table and filled a glass with ice-water; then, going to the bureau, she took up the small bottle half full of morphine tablets and held them between her and the light.

"Ah!" she cried. "I see the way—the only way, but I must be quick, or I'll lose courage! Quick, quick, quick!"

She took a tablet into her mouth and drank some water. She took another, and another, then two, then three, and so on, till the bottle was empty. She walked to a window and threw the bottle away. She heard it crash on the pavement. She went to her bed, lowered the light, and lay down. Presently she felt drowsy; a delicious sense of restfulness stole over her.

Shortly afterward Buckton, who was up packing his trunk, heard her gleefully laughing. Wondering over the cause, and vaguely afraid, he opened the door and went to her. She was lying with her eyes open, smiling sweetly, and staring as if at some dream-object or person across the room.

"What is it, dear?" he asked, touching her forehead gently. He fancied that she was slightly delirious, and that it would soon pass away.

A sweet, girlish, rippling laugh escaped her lips. He had never seen her look so beautiful. A spiritual radiance had transformed her face, which was that of a young girl. Her eyes had lost their somber shadows. Ineffable lights danced in their depths.

"Little Dick and I were having so much fun. We were playing hide and seek in the clouds with thousands and thousands of angels like himself. He said that he felt no pain when he died and came straight to me because I needed him—think of that, I, a grown woman, needed a little boy like him, but that is because he is wise now, wise and old in the wisdom of Eternity."

She closed her eyes for a moment, only to open them again.

"Leave me quick! I want to sleep. Don't disturb me again to-night. Shut the door and don't open it. He is coming back, and—and he must not see you here. Oh, I love him—I love him! He is the only one I ever loved. We understand each other perfectly. He is the sweetest, dearest thing in the world. I had him in my arms just now, and he seemed to melt into me and become myself and yet remain himself. He is coming to take me away. Go, I am sleepy—so sleepy and—happy—oh, so happy! It is all peace and bliss out there, and endless light and—Love. Go, hurry! He is coming! I see my mother, too. She is holding him by the hand. They are beckoning to me."

She closed her eyes. Tints of dawn were in her cheeks. He bent to kiss her, but, fearing that he might wake her, he refrained, and softly tiptoed from the room.

CHAPTER XVII

Saunders was reading a letter one morning as he walked along the shaded road from the store to his house. It was from James Wright, the cashier of the bank, who was giving him some of the particulars in regard to the double tragedy in Mostyn's life.

"The whole city is shocked," the letter ran. "Nothing else is spoken of. Mostyn has the sympathy of all. He is bearing it like a man, but he is terribly changed. He seems more dead than alive. You'd hardly know him now. Of course, when Mitchell was unable to locate his daughter, to inform her of the death of her child, everybody began to suspect the truth, especially as Buckton's mother was almost prostrate, and made no secret of her fears.

"Mitchell happened to be at the bank when the telegram came from Buckton announcing the death of Mrs. Mostyn. Buckton called it heart-failure, but everybody knew from the wording that it was suicide. Mitchell did, I am sure. He read the telegram with scarcely a change of face. I happened to be close to him at the moment, and heard him mutter:

"'It is better so!'"

"He sat alone in Delbridge's office—seeming to shun Mostyn—without saying a word for half an hour; then he asked me to telephone the facts to Mrs. Buckton. I did so, and she drove down to the bank, so weak that she had to be helped from her carriage. She and the old man held a consultation.

They agreed to go together to Charleston, and thought for the present, at least, that it would be better to bury the poor woman there, so as to avoid further publicity here.

"Mitchell returned to-day. Nobody knows exactly what took place between him and the young man, but it is thought that out of consideration for Mrs. Buckton he kept his temper. It is rumored that she and her son have left for New York, and that they may not be back to Atlanta for a long time.

"Mitchell's trouble seems to have strengthened his mind rather than weakened it. He is not so flighty or talkative. He is offering his home for sale, and has ordered it to be closed at once. He says he is going to live with his nieces in Virginia, who will now, I presume, inherit all his property. He is not likely to leave a penny to Mostyn, who, to do him justice, does not want any of it, I'm sure.

"Mostyn is staying at his sister's. She is doing all she can to help him bear up. His condition is truly pitiful, and it is made more unbearable by old Henderson, who has made many bold efforts to see him. Henderson is openly gloating over Mostyn's misfortune. He goes about chuckling, telling everybody that the retribution for which he has prayed so long has come at last. I had to drive him away yesterday. He was peering through my window with a grin on his face, and started to shout in at Mostyn. Mostyn saw him, I think, but said nothing. The poor fellow is losing flesh; his eyes have a strange, far-off glare, and his hands and knees shake. I see now that we must persuade him to go away for a while. A man of iron could not stand up under such awful trouble."

Saunders folded the letter, and with a profound sigh walked on. A man on a wagon loaded with hay passed. It was Tobe Barnett, who looked well and prosperous. He was working on Saunders's plantation, and getting good wages under the friendly direction of Tom Drake.

Tobe tipped his hat, as he always did to Saunders.

"Awful about Mr. Mostyn, ain't it?" he said. "I read it in the paper yesterday."

Saunders nodded. "Very sad, Tobe. He is having hard lines."

"I never had nothin' agin the feller *myself*," Tobe remarked. "He always treated *me* right. Some folks said he was sorter wild in his ways, but I never blamed him much. He was young an' full o' blood. I've knowed fellers as wild as bucks to settle down in the end."

Tobe drove on. Saunders pursued his way along the shaded road. How peaceful the landscape looked in the mellow sunshine! How firm and eternal seemed the mountains, the highest peaks of which pierced the snowy clouds. Saunder's heart fairly ached under its load of sympathy. "What can be done? What can be done?" he thought. "I'd like to help him."

Presently down the road near his own house Saunders saw a trim form on a black horse. It was Dolly. She was coming toward him. She had not seen him, and he noted that she was constantly reining her restive mount in while she kept her eyes fixed on the ground as if in deep thought.

In a few minutes they met. She looked up, nodded, and bowed.

"I rode over to take a message to father," she announced. "He was in the wheat-field. I didn't want to bother to go around to the gate, so what do you think I did? I made my horse jump a fence eight rails high. Oh, it was fine! I rose like an arrow in the breeze and came down on the other side as light as a feather."

He caught her bridle-rein and held it to steady the impatient animal. "You really mustn't take such risks," he said, firmly." If the horse had caught his feet on the top rail he would have thrown you. Don't, don't do it any more. Don't, please don't!"

She avoided his burning upward glance. Suddenly a shadow swept over her face. "Of course, you've heard about Mr. Mostyn?" she said, softly. "Isn't it simply awful?"

He nodded, telling her about the letter he had just received. When he had concluded she sat in silence for a moment, then he heard her sigh. "I thought I'd had trouble myself, but, really, Jarvis, if I tried I could not imagine a more horrible situation. He is proud, and his humiliation and grief combined must be unbearable. Losing his son was the hardest blow. I think you told me he loved the boy very much."

"He adored the little chap," Saunders said. "And well he might, for the boy was wonderfully bright and beautiful. He doted on his father."

Dolly was silent. Saunders saw her white throat throbbing. "It is bound to produce a change in him," she said." It will either kill him or regenerate him. He has a queer nature. He is a two-sided man. All his life he has been tossed back and forth between good and bad impulses. How awful it must be for him to have to remain in Atlanta and be thrown with so many who know what has happened! His friends ought to beg him to go off somewhere."

"I am going to write him a letter to-day," Saunders said. "I shall assure him that my home is his, and beg him to come. Nature is the best balm for keen sorrow, and here in the mountains—"

"Oh, how good and sweet and noble of you!" Dolly broke in, tremulously. "You are always thinking of others. Yes, that would do him good. A city is no place for one in his trouble. I imagine that nothing will help him much, but you can do more for him here than any one can down there."

Saunders tried to meet her eyes, but they were steadily avoiding his.

Will N. Harben

"My God, does she still care for him?" the planter thought. "Does she still actually love him, and will not this trouble and his presence here unite them again? She has too great a heart to harbor resentment at such a time, and she may suspect that he still loves her. If that is so, I am simply joining their hands together—I who, if I lose her, will be as miserable as he. Oh, I can't give her up! I simply can't. She is my very life."

Dolly seemed to feel the force back of his agonized stare, for she kept her eyes averted.

"He will come, I'm sure," she said, musingly, and, as he thought, eagerly. "When will the letter reach him?"

"To-night," Saunders said. "I'll urge him to come at once. I'll make the invitation as strong as I can. Shall I—mention you— that is, would you like for me to express your—sympathies?"

"Oh no, I have already written him. I wrote as soon as I heard. I couldn't help it. I cried till the paper was damp. Oh, he will know how sorry I am."

"You have written!" Saunders formed the words in his brain, but they were not uttered. A storm of despair swept through him. He shook from head to foot. She and the horse floated in a swirling mist before him.

"He will appreciate your letter," he managed to say, finally. "He will value it above all else."

"Oh no, I don't think that." She gave him her eyes in what seemed to him to be a questioning stare. "In a deep, heartrending sorrow like his he will scarcely remember my words from one day to another. Do you know what I think, Jarvis? Down inside of him he has a deeply religious nature, and I predict that he will now simply have to turn to God. After all, God is the only resort for a man in his plight."

"You may be right," Saunders returned. "His whole spirit is

broken. But hope will revive. In fact, all this, sad as it is, in the long run may be good for him."

Dolly shook her rein gently. "I must go," she said, smiling sadly. "Good-by."

The horse galloped down the road. Like a fair, winged creature she floated away in the sunlight.

"Am I to lose her at last?" he groaned. "After all these years of patient watching and waiting is she going back to the man who could have had her but would not? God knows that is not fair. Surely I deserve better treatment—if—if I deserve anything. Can I urge him to come—will it be possible for me sincerely to pen the words which may seal my doom? Yes, I must—if I don't I would not be worthy of her respect, and that I must have, even if I lose her."

CHAPTER XVIII

The letter was written. It was full of manly sympathy and friendly assurances. It brought the afflicted banker three days later to the plantation. A delightful cool and airy room was assigned to him. The open sympathy of the mountaineers and the negroes about the place was vaguely soothing. Looking back upon the city, it seemed a jarring place of torture when contrasted to the eternal peace of this remote spot. Free to go when and whither he liked, Mostyn spent whole days rambling alone through the narrow roads and by-paths of the mountains, often reaching all but inaccessible nooks in canons and rocky crevices where dank plants and rare flowers budded and bloomed, where velvet mosses were spread like carpets, and ferns stood like miniature palms.

One morning Mostyn saw Saunders hoeing weeds out of the corn-rows in a field back of the house; and, taking another hoe, he joined him, working steadily by his friend's side till noon. And here he made a discovery. He found that the work furnished a sort of vent for the festering agony pent up within him. It seemed to ooze out with the sweat which dampened his clothing, to be absorbed in his heated blood, and after a cooling bath he slept more profoundly than he had slept for years. He now saw the reason for Saunders's partiality to country life. It was Nature's balm for all ills. In fact, he was sure now that he could not do without it. Nearly every morning after this he insisted on working in the fields. Sometimes it was with a plow, which he learned to use under the advice of Tobe Barnett, a scythe in the hay-field, or a woodman's ax in the depths of the forests. But still sorrow and shame brooded over him like a material pall that refused to be put aside. As he lay in his bed at night he would fancy that he heard little Dick calling to him from the nursery, and the thought that the voice and love of the child were forever dead to him was excruciating.

One evening after supper Saunders informed him that Dolly and some of her literary friends were to hold a club-meeting at the schoolhouse to discuss some topic of current interest, and asked him if he would care to go along with him. Mostyn was seated at the end of the veranda smoking. He hesitated, it seemed to Saunders, longer than was necessary before he answered:

"I hope you will excuse me, but you mustn't let me keep you away. I am very tired and shall go to bed early."

A little later Saunders left for the meeting. Mostyn saw him pass out at the gate under the starlight. The bell was ringing. Mostyn recalled the night he had gone with Dolly to a meeting of like nature, and the impression her speech had made on him.

"All that is past—gone like a wonderful dream," he mused. "In feeling I am an old man, bowed and broken under the blind errors of life. Saunders and I are near the same age. Look at him; look at me; he walks like a young Greek athlete. I have nothing to expect, nothing to hope for. My wife died despising me; my friends merely bear with me out of pity; my boy is dead; I have to die—all living creatures have to die. What does the whole thing mean? It really must have a meaning, for many great minds have seen nothing but beauty in it, not even excluding sorrow, pain, and death. There must be an unpardonable sin, and I have committed it. Some say that all wrongdoers may get right—I wonder if there is a chance for me, *a single chance?* No, no, I am sure there is none—none whatever. But, oh, if only I could see my boy alive again! I would be willing to suffer any torment for that, but better still—if only he might be immortal—if only he could live forever in happiness on some other plane, as good people believe, I'd ask nothing for my part—absolutely nothing! I brought him into the world. I am responsible for his marvelous being. I'd give my soul to save his—I would—I would—I would!"

He went to bed. He said no prayer. He accepted his lot without any idea that it might be otherwise. The night was profoundly still. He heard singing. It was at the meeting-house. Softened by distance, the music was most appealing. It seemed to float above the tree-tops, touch the clouds, and fall lightly to earth. His mind, weighted down by care, induced slumber. Dream-creatures flocked about him. He was a child romping in a meadow over new-mown hay. He had a playmate, but he could not see his face; it was ever eluding him. Suddenly he ran upon the child, and with open arms clasped him to his breast. The child laughed gleefully, as children do when caught in such games. It was little Dick. He held him tightly, fearing that he would get away. He spoke soothingly and yet anxiously. Endearing words rippled from his lips. Presently his arms were empty. Little Dick was gone, and standing near, a scowl of hate on his face, was old Henderson, who was shaking fierce fingers at the dreamer.

"Retribution!" he cried. "Retribution! Now it is your time—your time to suffer, and I am appointed to lay on the lash!"

Mostyn waked. The moonlight was shining in at the window. In the distance he heard voices. They were coming nearer. Standing at a window, Mostyn saw Saunders and Tobe Barnett as they were parting at the gate.

"As soon as Dolly stood up," Tobe said, with a satisfied laugh, "I knew she had it in for the whole dang bunch from the way she looked. An' when she swatted 'em like she did with them keen points o' hers I mighty nigh kicked the bench in front o' me to pieces. I throwed my hat agin the ceilin' an' yelled. She's a corker, Mr. Saunders."

Mostyn could not hear Saunders's reply. As he came on to the house he began to whistle softly. Mostyn saw him pause on the grass, light a cigar, and begin to smoke as he strolled to and fro.

"Happy man!" Mostyn said, as he went back to his bed. "He's never had anything to bother him. There must be a correct law of life, and he seems to understand and obey it. He used to try to get me to listen to his ideas, but I thought he was a fanatic. Lord, Lord, I thought he was a fool!"

CHAPTER XIX

The next morning, Saunders having left home on some business pertaining to the building of his new cotton-factory, Mostyn started out on one of his all-day rambles in the mountains. As he was passing the store Wartrace called out to him cordially.

"You ought to come around about one o'clock, Mr. Mostyn," he said. "A big crowd will be here to listen to John Leach, the tramp preacher. He's billed for my store, an' he never fails to be on time."

Mostyn passed on after exchanging a few labored platitudes with the storekeeper. He shrank from the thought of meeting a crowd even of simple mountain people. The high open spaces above silently beckoned to him. Never before had solitude in the breast of Nature had such appeal for him. He found growing interest in plants, flowers, insects, and birds. He wondered if they, too, suffered from grief and pain. At noon, when the day was warmest, he reclined on the mossy bank of a clear brook. He took off his shoes and bathed his feet in the cool, swift-running water, feeling the chill course through his veins. What was it that kept whispering within him that here and here alone was the balm for such wounds as his? Contrasting the mystic quiet of his surroundings with the snarling jangle of the life he had led in town, a faint hope of eventual peace began to spring up within him. Once he raised his hands to the infinite blue above him, and his thought, if not his words, was all but a prayer for mercy.

He was descending the mountain road near sunset. The valley into which he was going was already in shadow. Suddenly he heard a mellow masculine voice singing a hymn, and, turning a bend in the road, his body bent downward and swinging his hat in his hand, was Leach, the preacher.

"Well, well, well!" Leach exclaimed, gladly, when he was near enough to recognize him. "I heard you were in these diggings, and was sorry not to see you out at my meeting."

Leach took his hand, pressing his fingers in a tense and sincere clasp while he looked into his eyes tenderly. His strong face filled with emotion; his big lower lip actually shook.

"You needn't tell me about it, brother," he said, huskily. "I've heard it all, and I never was so sorry for a man in my life. You have been sorely stricken—you've had as much as you can stand up under and live. As soon as I heard it I said to myself: 'Here is a man that has to suffer as much as I went through.' Brother"—Leach still hung on to his hand—"you can't see it as I do now, and you will think I am crazy for saying it, I reckon, but if things work out right, you will see the time that you will thank God for giving you the load that's on you. Everything that happens under the Lord's sun is according to law, and is right—so right that average human beings can't see it. You've heard me tell about what I went through in prison, and I thank God for every minute of it. The backbone of my pride had to be broken, and it took that to do it. Are you in a big hurry?"

"No," Mostyn faltered. "I have plenty of time."

"Well, if you don't mind, let's sit here on the rocks," Leach suggested. "I want to see the sun set. I never miss a sunset on a mountain if I can help it. That's why I walked up here. A fellow asked me to spend the night with him on his farm in the valley, but I refused. The longer I live the more I want to get away from houses, tables, beds, and chairs. They are just babies' rag dolls and playing-blocks. I'll rake up a pile of pine-needles at the highest point I can reach on this mountain to-night and lie with my eyes on the stars-pin-hole windows to God's glory. Sometimes I can't sleep—I get so full of worship. I was reading the other day that it would take a fast train forty million years to get to the nearest fixed star. Isn't that awful? And think of it, when you got there, a billion times more would lie beyond—so much more that you wouldn't even then have touched the fringe of the wonderful scheme. It is too big for the mind of man to grasp, and so is the other, the realm of spirit, which is, after all, the main thing—in fact, the *only* thing."

They sat in silence for several minutes. The sun was now a great bleeding ball of crimson. Leach's big hands were locked over his knee. Now and then his lips moved as if in prayer. He smiled; he laughed; he chuckled. The sun sank lower and finally went out of sight. The sky along the horizon was an ocean of pink and purple, with shores of shimmering opal.

"Forgive me, brother." Leach turned his soft glance on his companion. "You don't want to talk, I reckon, but the Lord has given me the power to sort o' feel human trouble. I can see it in your face and feel it ooze out of your body like a sad, murky stream. I don't want to part with you to-night without helping you if I can. I wouldn't talk this way if I hadn't helped hundreds. I never have failed where they would open their hearts plumb wide. All I'd want to know would be what particular thing was standing in your way. Something must be in the way. You may think it strange, but I can almost feel it hanging over you, like a thing that ought to be jerked off."

Mostyn was tempted to reply, but he said nothing. Half an hour passed. It was growing cool, damp, and darker. He rose to go. The preacher stood up with him, and grasped his hand.

"I may never see you again, brother," he said, "and I'm sorry, for I feel drawn powerful close to you somehow. I'd like nothing better than to have you along with me. I'm going to leave this part of the country pretty soon. I want to see more of

God's beautiful world. I've always wanted to go to California, and I'm going to do it now."

"That will be fine," Mostyn remarked. "I am going somewhere soon myself. I don't know where, but somewhere."

"You'd better come along with me," the preacher said, eagerly. "We could pull together all right. I'd do my best to make you happy. I'd hammer at you till you saw the truth that has lifted me out o' the mire. God loves you, brother—He really does, and you will find it out some day. The worst sin in the world is simply not knowing God's goodness. It is as plentiful as rain and air. What do you say? Couldn't we go together?"

Mostyn was fairly thrilled by the idea. It was a strange suggestion, and appealed to him strongly. There was a soothing quality about the man that attracted him beyond any-thing else. "When do you leave?" he asked.

"In a couple of weeks. I wish you would go—by Jacks, I do! I know when I like a man, and I like you. I don't want to part from you like this. What do you say?"

"I'll think over it," Mostyn promised. "Shall you be in Atlanta again this summer?"

"I'll leave from there," Leach answered. "I have to go there to draw a little money that is coming to me."

"Well, look me up down there," Mostyn said. "I shall want to see you again, anyway."

They parted. Mostyn trudged down into the deeper shadows. He heard Leach singing along the rocky way as he ascended higher. How odd! But the going of the man left him more deeply depressed than ever. He felt like running back and calling on him to wait a moment. There was something he wanted to tell him. He wanted to tell him about a certain haunting circumstance and ask his advice. He wanted to reveal the whole story of Henderson's loss and his gain—of the old man's fall and his rise on the ruins of that wrecked life. But what was the use? He knew what Leach would say. He would say: "Make restitution, and make it quick, for God's eye is on you—God's wide ear is bending down from that sky up there to hear the words you speak."

Mostyn stood still in the lonely road. "Yes, he'd advise that," he muttered, "but I can't do it. It would take almost all I have left, and I must live. Leach can talk, but I am not in his shoes. I might be better off if I were. I know I ought to do it. I ought to have done it years ago. How can I refrain now when I have no one depending on me and Henderson has that helpless family of his? I robbed them—law or no law to back me, I robbed them. A higher law than man's holds me guilty. I wonder what—" He stumbled along through the thickening shadows beneath the trees, the boughs of which were locked and interlaced overhead. "I wonder what Dolly would say. I needn't wonder—I know. Many women would tell me not to bother, but she wouldn't. She would be like Leach—so would Saunders. Great God! I really *am* vile. I know what I ought to do, but can't. Then there is my child. If I have a hope left it is that he is safe with—God. Yes, that's it—*with* God. There must be a God—so many say so, and He must love my little boy, and both of them would want me to do my duty.

"Oh, Dick, Dick! my son, my son!" he cried aloud, "are you close to me now? Tell me, tell me what to do. Take my hand, little boy. Lead me. I need you. I am your father, and you are only a child, but you can take me out of this, for you are stronger than I am now."

The echo of his voice came back from the rocky heights. A cricket snarled in a tree. A nightingale's song came up from the valley. He heard sheep-bells, the mooing of a cow, the bleating of a calf, a farmer calling up his hogs. Groaning, and bowed closer to the earth, he continued his way.

CHAPTER XX

A fortnight later Mostyn returned to Atlanta. He spent the first day at his sister's home trying to pass the time reading in her library, but the whole procedure was a hollow makeshift. Had he been a condemned prisoner awaiting execution at dawn, he could not have suffered more mental agony.

Unable to sleep that night, he rose before sun-up on the following morning and walked through the quiet streets for two hours. What a mad, futile thing the waking city seemed! "What are these people living for—what, after all?" he asked. "But they may be happy in a way," he added. "The fault is in me. I am seeing them through self-stained glasses. It wasn't like this in my sight once—the town was a sort of heaven when I first entered it and began to attract attention. Yes, I am at fault. I have disobeyed a spiritual law, and am getting my dues. What is the use of holding out longer? I see now that I am beaten. I have got to do this thing, and be done with it."

After breakfast he went straight to the bank. Wright, Delbridge, and the clerks and stenographers seemed unreal creatures, with flaccid, vacuous faces, as he shook hands with them and answered their conventional queries about his vacation. "Vacation!" The word was not in his vocabulary. "Business! "That, too, was a corpse of a word floating on the still waters of past usage. "Money, stocks, bonds, market-reports!" They seemed like forgotten enemies rising to stop him. How could Delbridge smile in his smug way, as he chewed his cigar and boasted of a new club of which he was

Will N. Harben

the president? How could Wright put up with his moderate salary and stand all day at that prison window? What could the limp, pale-faced stenographers in their simple dresses hope for? Did they expect to marry, bear children, nurse them at their thin breasts—and bury them like close-clipped flowers of Heaven just opening to fragrance?

Seated at his desk, he asked a clerk to go to the vault and bring him his certificates of bank stock. Delbridge was passing, and, seeing them in his hands, he said, with his forced and commercial shrewdness:

"If you have any idea of selling out, Mostyn, I'm in a shape now to take that stock off your hands."

Mostyn's stare resolved itself into a glare of indecision. "What would be your price?" he asked, under his breath, and yet audibly—"that is, in case I—I found another use for the money?"

"The same price I gave Saunders," Delbridge answered. "You couldn't expect to make a better deal than that long-headed chap. If you really want to do this thing you'd better act at once. I have another plan on hand."

"You make it as an offer?" Mostyn asked.

"Yes."

"Then the stock is yours," Mostyn answered. "Figure it up and place the money to my credit. I may check it out to-day. I am thinking of leaving town."

Delbridge suppressed a glow of triumph in his eyes as he took the certificates into his hands. He spread the crisp sheets out on the desk. "Indorse them while the pen is handy," he suggested.

Mostyn dipped the pen and wrote steadily on the backs of

the certificates.

"That's O. K.," Delbridge mumbled, dropping his cigar into a cuspidor. "Now I'll credit your account with the money. Check on it when you like."

When Delbridge's back was turned Mostyn drew a blank check from a pigeonhole and began to fill it in. The amount was for one hundred thousand dollars. He made it payable to Jefferson Henderson. He was about to sign his name when a great weakness swept over him like a flood from an unexpected source. How could he do a thing as silly as that? A gift of one-tenth of the amount would delight the old man and take him out of want—perhaps win his gratitude for all time. Mostyn started to tear the check up, but paused. No, no, that wouldn't be in obedience to a higher idea of justice. If the old man had been allowed to hold on to his investment in that early enterprise his earnings would have come to fully as much as the written amount. Suddenly Mostyn saw the dead face of his child as it lay in the coffin surrounded with flowers, and a sob struggled up within him and burst.

"For your sake, Dick," he whispered. "I know you'd want me to do it. I know it—I know it."

Half an hour later he was out in the open air, walking with a strange new activity. His very body seemed imponderable. He crossed the railway near the Kimball House and went on to Decatur Street. Along this street he walked for a few blocks and then turned off. Before long he was in the most dilapidated, sordid part of the city. He knew where Henderson lived. He had seen the old man pottering about the narrow front yard of the grimy little cottage as he drove past it one morning with a friend.

As he drew near the house to-day its impoverished appearance was more noticeable than ever. It was out of repair. Shingles had fallen from the sagging roof. It had not been painted for years; the slats and hinges of the outside blinds were broken, and they hung awry across the cracked window-panes. There was a little fence around it from which many palings were missing, as was the gate. On the narrow front porch a ragged hemp hammock hung by knotted and tied ropes between two posts. There was a broken baby-carriage in the yard, a child's playhouse at the step, a little toy wagon, a headless doll, a piece of bread, and some chicken-bones.

Mostyn went to the open door and rang the jangling cast-iron bell. It brought a young woman from a room on the right of the bare little hall. She held a baby in her arms as she peered questioningly at the visitor. Mostyn knew who she was. She was Henderson's youngest daughter, who had married a shiftless carpenter and been deserted by him, leaving two children to be cared for by their grandfather. It was evident by her blank stare that she did not recognize the caller.

"I want to see your father," Mostyn said. "Is he at home?"

"He's in the back yard," she answered. "He hasn't been feeling at all well to-day, and he didn't go to town as usual. Who may I say it is?"

"Tell him it is Mr. Mostyn," was the answer. "I won't keep him but a moment."

"Mostyn—Dick Mostyn!" The woman's tired eyes flashed as she jerked out the name. "So you have come *here* to devil him, have you?" She shifted the infant from her left to her right hip and sneered. "I don't suppose he cares to see you. I'll tell you one thing—he's my father and I have a right to be plain—you and your treatment are driving him out of his senses. He can't think of anything else or talk of anything else. Sometimes he rages, and sometimes he breaks down and cries like a child. I never have fully understood what you did to him, but I know you ruined him. Come in. I'll tell him you are here. I hope to the Lord you won't hit him any harder than you have already. We are in trouble enough. Two days last week we went without anything to eat except what a neighbor sent in, and that nearly killed my father, for he is proud. One of my sisters is sick and lost her job at the factory. If I thought you was any sort of a man I'd ask you to have pity."

With her disengaged hand the woman shoved a door open and hastily retreated. He went into a little sitting-room and sat down. There were only a few pieces of furniture in the room. A worn straw mat lay on the floor; three or four chairs, all but bottomless, stood here and there; a small square table holding a lamp and a family photograph-album bound in red plush was in the center of the room. Oil-portraits of Henderson and his dead wife, in massive frames, hung on the walls. Henderson's wore the prosperous look of the time when his means and good will had been at Mostyn's service.

Holding his hat between his knees, the caller leaned forward tensely, wondering over the present spectacle of himself. He heard loud words in the rear. "I know what he wants." Old Henderson's voice rose and cracked. "It isn't the first time he has tried to browbeat me into holding my tongue. He's heard what I've said, and wants to threaten me with prosecution. But that won't stop me. I'll tell him what I think to his teeth—the low-lived, thieving dog! He *did* steal my money—he *did,* he *did!*"

Heavy footfalls rang on the bare floor of the hall; an outer door was slammed. The voice of Henderson's daughter, now full of fright, was heard admonishing her father to be calm. "You'll drop like the doctor said you would if you don't be careful!" she advised. "The man isn't worth it."

With dragging steps old Henderson advanced till he stood in the doorway. His long white hair was unkempt; he wore no collar or coat. His trousers were baggy, patched at the knees, and frayed at the bottom of the legs, where they scarcely reached the gaping tops of his stringless shoes. Mostyn had risen and now stood staring at his former patron, unable to formulate what he had come to say.

"My daughter says you want to see me," Henderson blurted out. "Well, you are welcome to the sight. You've dodged *me* often enough lately. Do you know what I tried to see you about the other day when I was there? It wasn't to get money, for I've given that up long, long ago. I wanted to tell you that I spend my days now thanking both God and the devil for the plight you are in at last. I believe prayers are answered—you bet I do—you bet, you bet! I've prayed to have you hit below the belt, and it has come in good measure. I see from the way you look that you feel it. Ah, ha! you know now, don't you, how it feels to squirm under public scorn and lose something you hold dear? They tell me old Mitchell sees through you and is leaving all he's got to Virginia kin. The dying of your child knocked all that into a cocked hat—your own child, think of that! I've laughed till I was sick over it. First one report come, then another, till your three staggering, knock-out blows was made public. I don't know how true it is"—Henderson wrung his talon-like hands together tightly—"but business men say there isn't much left of your private funds."

"Hardly anything now, Mr. Henderson," Mostyn answered. "Now that I have decided to—"

"Ah! *that* is true, then!" Henderson ran on, with a sly chuckle. "It is reported that Delbridge, the feller you started out to race against so big, has swiped the bank presidency right from under your nose, nabbed the cream of the business, and put it on a respectable footing."

"That is all true," Mostyn admitted. Thrusting his hand into his pocket, he drew out the check he had written. It fluttered in the air, for he held it unsteadily. "Here is something for you," he said. "It is late coming, Mr. Henderson, but it is yours. You will find it all right."

"Mine?" The old man's limp hands hung down his sides. He saw the extended check, but failed to understand. He gazed at the quivering slip, his rigid lips dripping, his eyes filled with groping suspicion.

"Yes, it is yours," Mostyn said. "I've been long getting to it, but I am now bent on making restitution as far as possible. I can never wipe out the trouble I've put you to during all these years, but this may help. If you had held your interest in that factory as I held mine it would have been worth one hundred thousand dollars to-day."

"I know it—I know it—what the hell—" Henderson stared first at the check and then at Mostyn. "What do you mean by coming to me at this late—"

"It is my check for a hundred thousand dollars, payable to you," Mostyn answered. "The money is yours. You may draw it any time you like."

Henderson's hand shot out. The long-nailed fingers grasped the slip of paper and bore it to his eyes. He stared; he blinked; he quivered. A light flared up in his face and died.

"You don't mean it; it is another one of your damned tricks," he gasped. "You can't mean that I am to have—"

"I mean nothing else, Mr. Henderson," Mostyn faltered. He moved forward and laid his hand on the old man's shoulder. A flood of new-born tenderness rose within him and surged outward. "I have wronged you through the best part of your life. This is your money, and I am glad to be able to return it."

"Mine? Oh, God! oh, God! oh, God!" Mostyn's hand fell from the sloping shoulder, for Henderson was leaving the room. "Wait, wait, wait!" he called back, imploringly. "I want my— my daughter to read it and see if—if it is like you say it is. I can't see without my glasses; the letters run together. I don't know what to believe or—or what to doubt. Wait, wait, wait!"

Mostyn heard him clattering along the hall, calling to his daughter in the plaintive voice of an excited child. "Hettie, Hettie, here! Come, daughter, come look—read this! Quick! Quick! What does it say?"

Mostyn stood at the little window. He heard the infant crying in the rear as if it had been suddenly neglected by its mother. He heard the young woman's voice reading the words written on the check.

"He's paying it back!" Henderson's voice rose almost to a scream. "It is twice as much as I put in, too. Oh, Het, we are rich! we are rich! He isn't so bad, after all! He's more than doing the right thing! Not one man in a million would do it; he's white to the bone! He's had sorrow—maybe that's it. They say trouble will turn a man about. Oh, Lord! oh, Lord!"

The next moment Henderson, his face wet with tears, stood in the narrow doorway. He held out his hand and grasped Mostyn's. He started to speak, but burst into violent sobbing. Mostyn was shaken to the lowest depths of himself. He put his arm about the old man's shoulders and drew him against his breast. A thrill of strange, hitherto inexperienced ecstasy passed through him. He thought of his dead child; he thought of his dead wife; he thought of the mystic preacher of the mountains; he thought of Dolly Drake. The whole world was whirling into new expression. It now had transcendent meaning. At last he understood. The heights could not be seen except from the depths. Joy could not be felt till after sorrow—till after total renunciation of self. What need had he now of money? None, that he could see. The world was full of glorious things, and the old man weeping in his arms was the most glorious of all.

CHAPTER XXI

The various rural Sunday-schools were holding an annual singing convention at Level Grove within a mile of Saunders's home. They were held once a year and were largely attended. Saunders had driven over with Mostyn, who had just returned for a short visit. A big arbor of tree-branches had been constructed, seated with crude benches made of undressed planks. At one end there was a platform, and on it a cottage organ and a speaker's stand holding a pitcher of water and a goblet.

Several years before Saunders had offered a beautiful banner as a prize to the winning Sunday-school, and year after year it was won and held for twelve months by the school offering the most successful singers. To-day it leaned against the organ, its beautiful needlework glistening in the sunlight. Wagons and vehicles of all sorts brought persons for miles in every direction. The weather was delightful, being neither warm nor cool. In the edge of the crowd were lemonade and cider stands, surrounded by thirsty customers. In the edge of the crowd a Confederate veteran with an empty sleeve had a phonograph on the end of a wagon, which, under his proud direction, was turning out selections of the most modern vocal and instrumental music. Another thing which was attracting attention was Saunders's new automobile, which had been driven up from Atlanta by the agent who had sold it. It stood in the roadway near the arbor, and was admired by all who passed it. Saunders himself had been busy all day helping place the seats and arrange the program. While he was thus engaged Dolly and her mother and Ann arrived. He saw them pause to look at his car, and then they came on to the arbor. Dolly was to play the organ, and she went on to the platform, some music-books under her arm. She had on a new hat and new dress, which he thought more becoming to her than any he had seen her wear. Happening to glance across the seated crowd, he saw Mostyn by himself on the outer edge of the arbor, his eyes— wistfully fixed on Dolly.

"He still loves her; he can't help it," Saunders groaned, inwardly. "I can see it in his eyes and face. Oh, God, am I really to lose her after all? She will pity him now in his loneliness and grief and turn to him. She can't help it. She won't harbor resentment, and is not a woman who could love more than once. She knows he is here, and—and that accounts for the glow on her face and tense look in her eyes. She knows he was weak, but she will hear of his repentance and atone-ment, and take him back. Well, well, I have no right to come between them, and yet—and yet—oh God, I can't give her to him—I can't—I can't! I have hoped and waited! It would kill me to lose her now."

He caught Dolly's glance. She smiled, and he went to her at the organ, where she stood opening her music.

"What do you think?" she laughed, impulsively. "They have asked me for a speech."

"Well, you must make it," he said, a catch of despair in his throat, for she had never seemed so unattainable as now.

"I've made up my mind," she said, firmly. "I sha'n't do it. I'm in no mood for it. They needn't insist. I shall play the organ, and that is enough for one day."

"She's thinking of Mostyn," Saunders reflected, bitterly. "She knows he is free now. She reads his regret in his face, and, woman that she is, she pities him—she loves him." To her he finally managed to say: "I saw you looking at my new car."

"Yes, it is beautiful," she answered. "And are you going to take me riding in it some day?"

"This afternoon, at the first chance you have to get away," he answered. "I had it brought over for that reason alone. I want you to be the first to ride in it."

"Oh, how sweet of you!" she smiled. "Then immediately after lunch we'll go, if you say so, Jarvis. I'm nervous about this dratted music. I've been practising it on the piano, and it is different to have to work the pedals of this thing and keep time with singers, half of whom want to go it alone because they have been practising in the woods with the hoot-owls."

He laughed with her, but his laugh died on his lips, for he saw her glance in Mostyn's direction, and thought he saw a shadow flit across her eyes. The fact that she did not mention Mostyn's return was in itself significant, he decided, and his agony became so intense that he was afraid she would read it in his face. He had never known before the full depth and strength of his love. All those years he had waited in vain. Fate was shaping things to fit another plan than his. Morally, he had no right to come between those two lovers. Mostyn had perhaps been unworthy, but God Himself forgave the repentant, and Mostyn showed repentance in the very droop of his body. Dolly would pity and forgive. She had already done so, and that was what had kindled the spiritual glow in her face. It was said that Mostyn had given away most of his fortune, and would have but a poor home now to offer a wife, but that would count for naught in Dolly Drake's eyes. She had loved Mostyn, and she could love but once.

Just then the director of the singing came up; and Saunders, after admonishing her not to forget the ride, left her.

"I must be a man," he whispered to himself. "I have had few trials, and this must be met bravely. If she is not for me, she is not, that is all; but oh, God, it is awful—it is unbearable! There was hope till a woman and a child died, and now there seems to be none. The angelic pity for another in Dolly's white soul means my undoing."

Passing out from under the arbor, he found himself alone outside among the tethered horses and mules. Looking back, he saw Mostyn, his eyes still fixed on Dolly as she now sat at the organ turning over the music with her pretty white hands.

"I must conquer myself; I simply must," Saunders said, in his throat. "My supreme trial has come, as it must come to all men sooner or later. If she still loves him, then even to be true to her, I must wish her happiness—I must wish them *both* happiness."

At this juncture he saw John Leach, the roving preacher, approaching, swinging his hat in his hand, his fine brow bared to the sunlight.

"How are you, brother?" He greeted the planter warmly. "I heard over the mountain that you all were holding this blow-out to-day, and I struck a lively lick to get here before the music commenced. Somebody told me that your friend Mostyn was here."

"Yes, he is staying with me," Saunders answered. "He is over there under the arbor."

"Well, I'll look 'im up," Leach answered. "Me 'n' him has struck up a sort of friendship. I tie to a fellow in trouble quicker than at any other time, and he has certainly had his share. He wants to make a change, he tells me—thinks of going off somewhere for a while. I've asked him to go to California with me, and he's thinking it over. Say, you know him pretty well; do you reckon he will go?"

"I hardly think so—*now*," Saunders replied. "He may have thought of it at one time, but he is likely to remain here."

"Well, I'll talk to him anyway," Leach said. "Ah, I see a fellow on the platform with a cornet. I reckon the fun is about to begin. Do you know, I enjoy outdoor singing more than anything else under the sun. It seems to be the way the Lord has of giving folks a chance to let themselves out."

He turned away, a rapt expression on his poetic face, and Saunders moved back among the horses. He caught sight of Dolly's profile against the boughs of the arbor beyond her. Taking a step to one side, he brought Mostyn's face into view. Mostyn was now all attention, sitting erect and peering between two heads in front of him, staring at Dolly, his tense lips parted.

The first contesting choir began singing, and the stragglers about the grounds drew to the edge of the arbor and stood listening attentively. When it was over there was applause. Then a young man, the superintendent of a Sunday-school beyond the mountains, made a brief address. After this there was more singing, and so the morning passed.

At noon it was announced from the platform that, as the singing contest was over and the award of the banner would not be made by the judges till the afternoon, lunch would now be served. Thereupon the audience rose to its feet and began to surge outward. There was much scrambling for baskets and hunts for suitable spots about the grounds for spreading table-cloths. Saunders, as had long been his custom, had prepared food for all who could be induced to accept his hospitality, and he now had his hands full directing his servants and inviting friends to join him.

While he was thus engaged he happened to see Mostyn alone in the edge of the bustling crowd, and he strode across to him.

"Don't forget you are to eat with me," he said. "They will have it ready in a few minutes."

He thought that Mostyn's eyes wavered. He was sure his lips quivered slightly when he answered.

"I have promised some one else." Saunders failed to see the call for such slow indirectness of response to an ordinary request. Indeed, a touch of color lay in Mostyn's cheeks. "John Webb came to me just now and said that Dolly—or perhaps it may have been her mother—in fact, I'm sure that it must have been Mrs. Drake—"

"Oh, I see, *they've* asked you!" Saunders broke in. "Well, I'll have to let you off. You may be sure you'll get something nice. They can beat my cook getting up a spread. Well, I'll meet you later. I see Leach over there by himself. I'll run over and get him on my list." Saunders tried to jest. "They say he lives on wild berries, and nuts, and anything else he can pick up. I guess he won't find fault with my lunch."

Saunders was the host of fifty or more men, women, and children. He was doing his best to see that all were provided for, and yet he had an eye for a certain group under a beech on a near-by hillside. His heart sank, for he saw Mostyn seated on the ground at Dolly's side. He saw something later that sent a cold shock hurtling through him. He saw the group after lunch rise from the cloth and gradually scatter, leaving Dolly and Mostyn standing at the foot of the hill. A moment later they were walking off, side by side, toward a spring in a shaded dell not far away. The drooping boughs of the willow trees shut them out of sight. Saunders, with a hopeless griping of the heart, went about directing his servants and helping some belated guests to get what they wished to eat. He heard himself joking, replying to jokes, and smiling with lips which felt stiff.

The remains of the food had been taken up and replaced in the big baskets when he saw Dolly and Mostyn strolling back from the spring. Mostyn held her sunshade over her, his arm touching hers. The distance was too great for Saunders to see their faces distinctly, but he would have sworn that both reflected joy and peace.

"Oh, God, is it actually to be?" he groaned, inwardly. "*Ought* it to be? Here am I, eager to gratify her every wish, while he can give her only the dry, crushed remains of his manhood, a bare scrap of his past affluence. He scorned the sweetest flower of womanhood that ever bloomed, and now crawls through his own mire to pluck it. It isn't right—it isn't right! God knows it isn't right to her; leaving me and my hopes out altogether—it isn't right to *her!*"

Cold from head to foot, Saunders retreated out of sight behind a clump of bushes. Figuratively, he raised his hands to the impotent sky and dumbly cried within himself:

"Oh, God, give me strength to bear it like a man! I was wrong in hoping. She is his; she loves him. She loves him. I am an outsider. I now know why I never dared tell her of my love— my adoration! It was the still, inner voice of warning telling me to keep in my proper place."

Presently he saw Dolly alone near the arbor, and, remembering his engagement with her, he went to her.

"I have come to see if you would care to go now," he began. "I believe there is only some irregular singing and speech-making to follow."

"I am free," she said. "My part of the work is over. I refuse to touch the stiff keys of that organ again to-day. My wrists are sore, and my ankles ache. But I've been thinking over that ride, Jarvis. I want to go, of course, but—Jarvis, I hope you are not oversensitive. In fact, I know you are not, and will understand when I say that somehow—don't you know?—somehow, I don't like to leave this particular afternoon, when there is so much to be done here. There are several boys and girls who are anxious to sing and be heard, and some of my young men friends are to speak. We might take our ride some other day."

"I understand, Dolly," he said, forcing a smile. He told himself that this last hint ended all. She and Mostyn were reconciled, and she wanted him to understand the situation. They were quite alone. No one was near enough to hear their voices. Suddenly an overpowering impulse possessed him. Why should he beat about the bush? All was lost, but she should at least receive the tribute of his love and despair. There could be no harm in telling her how he felt. His forced smile died on his lips. His eyes met hers.

"There was something I was going to tell you," he began, firmly. "All these years I've been holding it back, but I can't any longer. Dolly, you must have known that—"

"Stop, Jarvis!" she broke in, laying her hand on his arm. "I know what you are going to say, but don't! Some day I'll explain, but not now—not now!"

"Well, you know what I mean." he gulped, "and that is enough. You must have seen—must have understood all along."

"Don't—don't be angry with me," she pleaded. "You will understand it all fully some day. I may be an odd sort of girl, but I can't help it--I am simply what I am."

"I think I understand now," he said, "and I wish you all happiness in the world."

The singing under the arbor had begun, and with a helpless, even startled look in her eyes she moved automatically in that direction.

"I don't think you do, fully," she faltered. "I'm sure you don't. Men never quite understand women in such delicate matters."

She left him; and, finding himself alone, he crossed the sward and sat down in a group of farmers who were discussing crops and planting.

CHAPTER XXII

That evening after supper Saunders and Mostyn were on the veranda smoking together. The exchange of remarks was formal, even forced and awkward. Presently Saunders said: "I saw Leach looking for you at the arbor. Did you run across him?"

"Yes," Mostyn puffed, and Saunders heard him heave a sigh. "I had quite a talk with him. I can't fully account for it, but I like the man very much. It may be his optimism or wonderful faith. I know that he has a very soothing effect on me. The truth is, I have promised to go to California with him."

"Oh!" Saunders leaned against the balustrade, steadily scrutinizing the face of his guest. "He told me something about his proposition, but I thought that perhaps you would not be likely to go—not now, anyway."

"Oh yes, I shall go at once. I must go somewhere, and with him I'd have the benefit of a companion."

"But, of course," Saunders flung out, tentatively, "you will not remain away long?"

"I can't say for sure that I shall *ever* come back," Mostyn said, sadly. "Of course, I can't say positively as to that, but there is nothing—absolutely nothing to hold me here now."

The eyes of the two met in a steady stare.

Will N. Harben

"You can't mean *that*—I'm sure you can't!" Saunders faltered.

Mostyn seemed about to speak, but a tremor of rising emotion checked him. He smoked for a moment in silence; then, with a steadier voice, he began:

"I must be more frank with you, Jarvis," he said. "You have been a true friend to me, and I don't want to keep anything from you at all. Besides, this concerns you directly. To tell you this I may be betraying confidence, but even that, somehow, seems right. Saunders, to-day at that meeting as I sat there—" Mostyn's voice began to shake again, and he cleared his throat before going on. "As I sat there looking at—at the purest, sweetest face God ever made I began to *hope*. I confess it. I began to hope that God might intend to give me one other chance at earthly happiness. I even fancied that He might purposely have led me back here out of my awful darkness into light. I might not have dared to go so far, but she had her uncle invite me to lunch, and as I sat by her side the very benediction of Heaven seemed to fall on her and me and all the rest. It made me bold. I was out of my head. I was intoxicated by it all. Don't you see, I began to think, late as it is—shamed as I am before the world—I began to think that I might again take some sort of root among men and be worthy of—of the only woman I ever really loved? She and I walked off together. Her consenting to go gave me fresh courage. I determined to speak. I determined to throw my soiled soul at her spotless feet. I did."

"Don't say any more; I know the rest," Saunders said, under his breath. "I congratulate you. I congratulate you with all my heart." He held out his hand, but Mostyn warded it off, his cigar cutting red zigzag lines in the darkness.

"Congratulate me? My God, *you* congratulate *me*. Are you blind? Have you been blind all this time? She not only spurned my love, but in a blaze of righteous indignation she told me she loved you. She said she loved, adored, reverenced— *worshiped* you. She seemed to look on my hopes as some sort of insult to her womanhood. She didn't want *you* to know of her love, she said, but she wanted *me* to know it. She seems to feel—she seems to think that in all your kindness to her and nobleness you deserve a wife who has never fancied another, even in girlhood. She told me that her feeling for me was only the idle whim of a child, and that she pitied me as a weak and stumbling creature. She put it that way, with blazing eyes, and she put it right. I *am* weak—I've always been weak; and to-day, in trying to win her from you, I did the weakest act of my life. I confess it. You have the right to strike me in the face. I knew you loved her. I knew she had become your very life, and yet in my despair and damnable vanity I wanted to take her from you. I am trying to get right, but I fell before that dazzling temptation. In telling you of her love now I am tearing my soul from my body, but I want to atone—I want to atone—as far as possible."

Saunders turned his transformed face away. He said nothing, and the two stood in dead silence for a moment. Suddenly Saunders put out a throbbing hand and laid it on Mostyn's shoulder.

"I thank you; I thank you," he said, huskily. "You must excuse me this evening. I hope you can pass the time some way. I am going to her, Mostyn. I can't wait another minute. I must see her to-night!"

CHAPTER XXIII

CONCLUSION

Six years passed. It was autumn in the mountains. The air was balmy and crisp. The landscape was gloriously tinted by late wild flowers and the colors of dying leaves. A far-off peak, catching the rays of the afternoon sun, rose above the dun valley like a mound of delicate coral dropped from the cloud-mottled blue overhead.

A stranger, walking from the station at Ridgeville, was nearing the front gate of Saunders's home. He moved with a slow, thoughtful step. He was gray, even to the whiteness of snow. His skin was clear and pink, his eyes were bright and alert. As he opened the gate he became aware of the nearness of two children playing in a vine-clad summer-house on the right of the graveled walk. The older was a handsome boy of four years; his companion was a pretty little girl of two, whom the boy held by the hand quite with the air of manly guardianship.

"Now, see how you have soiled your dress," the boy said, brushing the child's lap with his little hand. "Mama wouldn't like that."

The clicking of the gate-latch attracted the glance of the children; and they stood staring curiously at the man who, with an introductory smile, was drawing near. He bent down and shook hands with them both, first with the little girl and lastly with the boy.

"I have come to see your papa and mama," he said. "Are they at home? I think they are expecting me."

"They are down in the meadow getting flowers," the boy answered. "They are coming right back. You can see them from here. Look, there by the spring!"

The stranger followed the direction indicated by the little hand, and his eyes took on a wistful stare as they fixed upon a couple strolling across the meadow, holding flowers and ferns in their hands. They walked quite close together, those two, and the distance seemed to enfold them with conscious tenderness.

"They are both well, I believe?" the man said to the boy, as the more timid little girl turned and toddled away.

"Yes, thank you," the boy answered, in words which sounded stilted in one so young. "They got your letter. I heard papa say so. You are Mr. Mostyn, a very old friend of theirs. They said I must love you and be good while you are here, because you have no little boy yourself."

"Yes, yes, that's true," Mostyn answered,, taking the child's hand in his. "Now you know my name, you must tell me yours."

"Richard," the child said. "I was named for your little boy that died and went up to God. Papa used to love him long, long ago in Atlanta."

Mostyn drew the child along by the hand. The delicate throbbing of the boy's pulse thrilled him through and through. Steps sounded in the hall of the house, and John Webb, not any older in appearance than when last seen, crossed the veranda and came slowly down the steps.

"Well, well, well!" he cried. "Here you are at last. It must be a powerful long trip from Californy. The folks didn't seem to think you'd git here till in the morning. They 'lowed you'd stop for a while in Atlanta."

"I finished my visit there sooner than I expected." Mostyn shook the thick damp hand warmly. "I've been living out in the open so much of late years that Atlanta seemed stuffy and crowded; besides, my sister has moved away, and I have no blood-kin there. I wanted to get into the country as soon as I could, and this seems like home in a way."

"That's what Dolly and Jarvis are goin' to try to make it for you," Webb went on. "Lord, they have been countin' on this for a long time! Seems like they don't talk of much else. I heard 'em say they was goin' to try to break you of your rovin' habit. They've got your room fixed up to a gnat's heel. It is the best one in the house—plenty of air and light. That's what they are out pickin' flowers and evergreens for now. They want it to look cheerful."

"It is very kind of them, I am sure," Mostyn answered, "but I wouldn't like to be in the way very long."

"You won't be in nobody's way here," Webb declared. "If this ain't an open house there never was one of the old-time sort before the war. Jarvis runs the place like his pa and grandpa did. You never saw the like o' visitors in summer-time. They pile in from all directions, close an' far off. Every friend that comes anywhere nigh has to put up here. Them two live happy, I tell you, if ever a pair did. They've got 'em a fine home in Atlanta, where they spend the winter, but they both love this best. Jarvis is writin' a book about mountain flowers, an' Dolly helps him. They travel about a lot; they take in New York nearly every year, but love to get back home where they say they can be comfortable."

"And the rest of the family?" Mostyn said. "Your sister and Drake, how are they?" "Fine, first rate. Tom still bosses the plantation. Jarvis tried to git 'im to quit when he married in the family—said he didn't want his daddy-in-law drawin' pay by the month—but Tom had got interested in the work and hung on. He's turned out to be an A1 manager, I tell you. He knows what's what in plantin', an' makes his men move like clockwork from sun-up to sun-down."

"And George and his wife?" Mostyn inquired. "Are they doing well?"

"Fine, fine. Got four likely children—three boys and a girl baby that gave 'er first yell just a month ago. That pair has struck a lively lick hatchin' 'em out, but it is exactly what they like—they say they want just as many crawlers under foot as they can step over without stumblin'."

"And you, yourself—" Mostyn hesitated. "Have you—"

"Oh, me?" Webb's freckled face reddened. "Not on your life. I'll stay like I am till I'm under ground. Not any of it for me. Other folks can do as they like, but not me—no siree! I reckon you hain't never"—Webb hesitated—"married a second time?"

"No," Mostyn answered. "I am still quite alone in the world."

Webb glanced toward the meadow. "I'll walk down there and let 'em know you are here," he said. "They would dilly-dally like that till after dark, an' then come home swingin' hands an' gigglin' an' sayin' fool things to each other. They make me sick sometimes. I believe in love, you understand—I think married folks ought to love each other, in the bounds o' reason, but this mushy business—well, it ain't in my line, that's all!"

He passed through the gate and started toward the meadow. Mostyn leaned on the fence. He saw the couple again. They were standing face to face arranging the flowers.

"I don't think I'd disturb them if I were you," he called after the bachelor. "There is no hurry."

"Oh, they would want to know you are here," Webb answered

over his shoulder, as he strode away. "They will come in a trot when they know about it."

Presently Mostyn felt a small hand creep into his. It was the little boy.

"Do you see them?" the child inquired. "I can't look over the fence."

"Yes, let me hold you up." Mostyn lifted the boy in his arms. "Now, now can you see?" he asked, the words sweeping from him in suddenly released tenderness.

"Yes, yes; and they are coming. Let's go to meet them. Will you?"

"Yes, and you must let me carry you. You know I used to love to carry my *own* little boy like this—just like this."

The child's arm, already on Mostyn's shoulder, slid closer to his neck till it quite encircled it. The soft, warm hand touched Mostyn's chin.

"Mama and papa said I must call you 'Uncle Dick,'" but you are not my really, *really* uncle, are you?"

"No, but I want to be. Will you—would you mind giving your old uncle a hug with—with *both* your arms?"

The boy complied.

"There, there!" Mostyn said. "Once more—tight—tight! Hug me tight!"

The child obeyed. "Oo-ooh!" he cried, as he relaxed his tense pressure.

"Thank you—thank you!" Mostyn kissed him; then he was silent.

With one hand on Mostyn's cheek the boy leaned forward and peered into his face curiously.

"Why—why," he faltered, his little lips puckered sympathetically, "what is the matter?"

Choose from Thousands of 1stWorldLibrary Classics By

A. M. Barnard
Ada Leverson
Adolphus William Ward
Aesop
Agatha Christie
Alexander Aaronsohn
Alexander Kielland
Alexandre Dumas
Alfred Gatty
Alfred Ollivant
Alice Duer Miller
Alice Turner Curtis
Alice Dunbar
Allen Chapman
Alleyne Ireland
Ambrose Bierce
Amelia E. Barr
Amory H. Bradford
Andrew Lang
Andrew McFarland Davis
Andy Adams
Angela Brazil
Anna Alice Chapin
Anna Sewell
Annie Besant
Annie Hamilton Donnell
Annie Payson Call
Annie Roe Carr
Annonaymous
Anton Chekhov
Archibald Lee Fletcher
Arnold Bennett
Arthur C. Benson
Arthur Conan Doyle
Arthur M. Winfield
Arthur Ransome
Arthur Schnitzler
Arthur Train
Atticus
B.H. Baden-Powell
B. M. Bower
B. C. Chatterjee
Baroness Emmuska Orczy
Baroness Orczy
Basil King
Bayard Taylor
Ben Macomber
Bertha Muzzy Bower
Bjornstjerne Bjornson

Booth Tarkington
Boyd Cable
Bram Stoker
C. Collodi
C. E. Orr
C. M. Ingleby
Carolyn Wells
Catherine Parr Traill
Charles A. Eastman
Charles Amory Beach
Charles Dickens
Charles Dudley Warner
Charles Farrar Browne
Charles Ives
Charles Kingsley
Charles Klein
Charles Hanson Towne
Charles Lathrop Pack
Charles Romyn Dake
Charles Whibley
Charles Willing Beale
Charlotte M. Braeme
Charlotte M. Yonge
Charlotte Perkins Stetson
Clair W. Hayes
Clarence Day Jr.
Clarence E. Mulford
Clemence Housman
Confucius
Coningsby Dawson
Cornelis DeWitt Wilcox
Cyril Burleigh
D. H. Lawrence
Daniel Defoe
David Garnett
Dinah Craik
Don Carlos Janes
Donald Keyhoe
Dorothy Kilner
Dougan Clark
Douglas Fairbanks
E. Nesbit
E. P. Roe
E. Phillips Oppenheim
E. S. Brooks
Earl Barnes
Edgar Rice Burroughs
Edith Van Dyne
Edith Wharton

Edward Everett Hale
Edward J. O'Biren
Edward S. Ellis
Edwin L. Arnold
Eleanor Atkins
Eleanor Hallowell Abbott
Eliot Gregory
Elizabeth Gaskell
Elizabeth McCracken
Elizabeth Von Arnim
Ellem Key
Emerson Hough
Emilie F. Carlen
Emily Bronte
Emily Dickinson
Enid Bagnold
Enilor Macartney Lane
Erasmus W. Jones
Ernie Howard Pie
Ethel May Dell
Ethel Turner
Ethel Watts Mumford
Eugene Sue
Eugenie Foa
Eugene Wood
Eustace Hale Ball
Evelyn Everett-green
Everard Cotes
F. H. Cheley
F. J. Cross
F. Marion Crawford
Fannie E. Newberry
Federick Austin Ogg
Ferdinand Ossendowski
Fergus Hume
Florence A. Kilpatrick
Fremont B. Deering
Francis Bacon
Francis Darwin
Frances Hodgson Burnett
Frances Parkinson Keyes
Frank Gee Patchin
Frank Harris
Frank Jewett Mather
Frank L. Packard
Frank V. Webster
Frederic Stewart Isham
Frederick Trevor Hill
Frederick Winslow Taylor

Friedrich Kerst
Friedrich Nietzsche
Fyodor Dostoyevsky
G.A. Henty
G.K. Chesterton
Gabrielle E. Jackson
Garrett P. Serviss
Gaston Leroux
George A. Warren
George Ade
Geroge Bernard Shaw
George Cary Eggleston
George Durston
George Ebers
George Eliot
George Gissing
George MacDonald
George Meredith
George Orwell
George Sylvester Viereck
George Tucker
George W. Cable
George Wharton James
Gertrude Atherton
Gordon Casserly
Grace E. King
Grace Gallatin
Grace Greenwood
Grant Allen
Guillermo A. Sherwell
Gulielma Zollinger
Gustav Flaubert
H. A. Cody
H. B. Irving
H.C. Bailey
H. G. Wells
H. H. Munro
H. Irving Hancock
H. R. Naylor
H. Rider Haggard
H. W. C. Davis
Haldeman Julius
Hall Caine
Hamilton Wright Mabie
Hans Christian Andersen
Harold Avery
Harold McGrath
Harriet Beecher Stowe
Harry Castlemon
Harry Coghill
Harry Houidini

Hayden Carruth
Helent Hunt Jackson
Helen Nicolay
Hendrik Conscience
Hendy David Thoreau
Henri Barbusse
Henrik Ibsen
Henry Adams
Henry Ford
Henry Frost
Henry James
Henry Jones Ford
Henry Seton Merriman
Henry W Longfellow
Herbert A. Giles
Herbert Carter
Herbert N. Casson
Herman Hesse
Hildegard G. Frey
Homer
Honore De Balzac
Horace B. Day
Horace Walpole
Horatio Alger Jr.
Howard Pyle
Howard R. Garis
Hugh Lofting
Hugh Walpole
Humphry Ward
Ian Maclaren
Inez Haynes Gillmore
Irving Bacheller
Isabel Cecilia Williams
Isabel Hornibrook
Israel Abrahams
Ivan Turgenev
J.G.Austin
J. Henri Fabre
J. M. Barrie
J. M. Walsh
J. Macdonald Oxley
J. R. Miller
J. S. Fletcher
J. S. Knowles
J. Storer Clouston
J. W. Duffield
Jack London
Jacob Abbott
James Allen
James Andrews
James Baldwin

James Branch Cabell
James DeMille
James Joyce
James Lane Allen
James Lane Allen
James Oliver Curwood
James Oppenheim
James Otis
James R. Driscoll
Jane Abbott
Jane Austen
Jane L. Stewart
Janet Aldridge
Jens Peter Jacobsen
Jerome K. Jerome
Jessie Graham Flower
John Buchan
John Burroughs
John Cournos
John F. Kennedy
John Gay
John Glasworthy
John Habberton
John Joy Bell
John Kendrick Bangs
John Milton
John Philip Sousa
John Taintor Foote
Jonas Lauritz Idemil Lie
Jonathan Swift
Joseph A. Altsheler
Joseph Carey
Joseph Conrad
Joseph E. Badger Jr
Joseph Hergesheimer
Joseph Jacobs
Jules Vernes
Julian Hawthrone
Julie A Lippmann
Justin Huntly McCarthy
Kakuzo Okakura
Karle Wilson Baker
Kate Chopin
Kenneth Grahame
Kenneth McGaffey
Kate Langley Bosher
Kate Langley Bosher
Katherine Cecil Thurston
Katherine Stokes
L. A. Abbot
L. T. Meade

L. Frank Baum
Latta Griswold
Laura Dent Crane
Laura Lee Hope
Laurence Housman
Lawrence Beasley
Leo Tolstoy
Leonid Andreyev
Lewis Carroll
Lewis Sperry Chafer
Lilian Bell
Lloyd Osbourne
Louis Hughes
Louis Joseph Vance
Louis Tracy
Louisa May Alcott
Lucy Fitch Perkins
Lucy Maud Montgomery
Luther Benson
Lydia Miller Middleton
Lyndon Orr
M. Corvus
M. H. Adams
Margaret E. Sangster
Margret Howth
Margaret Vandercook
Margaret W. Hungerford
Margret Penrose
Maria Edgeworth
Maria Thompson Daviess
Mariano Azuela
Marion Polk Angellotti
Mark Overton
Mark Twain
Mary Austin
Mary Catherine Crowley
Mary Cole
Mary Hastings Bradley
Mary Roberts Rinehart
Mary Rowlandson
M. Wollstonecraft Shelley
Maud Lindsay
Max Beerbohm
Myra Kelly
Nathaniel Hawthrone
Nicolo Machiavelli
O. F. Walton
Oscar Wilde

Owen Johnson
P.G. Wodehouse
Paul and Mabel Thorne
Paul G. Tomlinson
Paul Severing
Percy Brebner
Percy Keese Fitzhugh
Peter B. Kyne
Plato
Quincy Allen
R. Derby Holmes
R. L. Stevenson
R. S. Ball
Rabindranath Tagore
Rahul Alvares
Ralph Bonehill
Ralph Henry Barbour
Ralph Victor
Ralph Waldo Emmerson
Rene Descartes
Ray Cummings
Rex Beach
Rex E. Beach
Richard Harding Davis
Richard Jefferies
Richard Le Gallienne
Robert Barr
Robert Frost
Robert Gordon Anderson
Robert L. Drake
Robert Lansing
Robert Lynd
Robert Michael Ballantyne
Robert W. Chambers
Rosa Nouchette Carey
Rudyard Kipling
Saint Augustine
Samuel B. Allison
Samuel Hopkins Adams
Sarah Bernhardt
Sarah C. Hallowell
Selma Lagerlof
Sherwood Anderson
Sigmund Freud
Standish O'Grady
Stanley Weyman
Stella Benson
Stella M. Francis

Stephen Crane
Stewart Edward White
Stijn Streuvels
Swami Abhedananda
Swami Parmananda
T. S. Ackland
T. S. Arthur
The Princess Der Ling
Thomas A. Janvier
Thomas A Kempis
Thomas Anderton
Thomas Bailey Aldrich
Thomas Bulfinch
Thomas De Quincey
Thomas Dixon
Thomas H. Huxley
Thomas Hardy
Thomas More
Thornton W. Burgess
U. S. Grant
Upton Sinclair
Valentine Williams
Various Authors
Vaughan Kester
Victor Appleton
Victor G. Durham
Victoria Cross
Virginia Woolf
Wadsworth Camp
Walter Camp
Walter Scott
Washington Irving
Wilbur Lawton
Wilkie Collins
Willa Cather
Willard F. Baker
William Dean Howells
William le Queux
W. Makepeace Thackeray
William W. Walter
William Shakespeare
Winston Churchill
Yei Theodora Ozaki
Yogi Ramacharaka
Young E. Allison
Zane Grey